His Psychic Visions Began with an Accident. . . .

Halloran could not think. He could only collect impressions. The sponginess at the back of his skull must mean that he was bleeding on a cushion that someone had put there. But who? There was no one near him. The doors of the train were still closed. He could see faces through the glass. Hands and faces pressed against the tinted windows. Other dimmer faces behind them. Mouths moving. Fingers pointing.

"Wait. There's someone. A black guy. Wearing paint-stained overalls. . . . And who's that? A fat man in a bathrobe with wet hair. . . . " Halloran turned his head to look for other faces and the pain in his head sent spears of shock through his body. He felt a crunching sensation at the back of his skull. That was no cushion. That was his head that was all soft. Was there an accident? He must have fallen down. The fat guy would know. But Halloran couldn't speak. All he wanted to ask was what happened, but it wouldn't come out.

PLATFORMS

JOHN R. MAXIM

PUBLISHED BY POCKET BOOKS NEW YORK

POCKET BOOKS, a Simon & Schuster division of
GULF & WESTERN CORPORATION
1230 Avenue of the Americas, New York, N.Y. 10020

Published by arrangement with G. P. Putnam's Sons
Library of Congress Catalog Card Number: 80–15031

ISBN: 0–671–43421–7

First Pocket Books printing March, 1982

10 9 8 7 6 5 4 3 2 1

POCKET and colophon are trademarks of Simon & Schuster.

Printed in the U.S.A.

To Christine
". . . and all the tomorrows."

PLATFORMS

Railway Catastrophe at Amersham

BY JOHN D. POYNTER-SMYTHE

As many as fifty lives were reported lost this morning when a London-bound mail train smashed into a gathering of waiting passengers at the Amersham Depot. Reports are fragmentary as correspondents have been barred from the scene. However, information gleaned from area residents arriving by motor car suggests that the victims had been unaccountably standing upon the track bed and showed no awareness of their imminent peril as the engine approached the depot. The Home Ministry has placed the entire area under

CHICAGO COPS INVESTIGATE LAKE FOREST HORROR

By JEAN LISA

Detectives on loan from the Chicago Police Department are trying to piece together an eerie series of events that left five dead in and around the Lake Forest railway station. The most bizarre killings took place on the platform itself. A young woman was beaten and impaled and a male commuter's throat was literally torn out in the presence of at least sixty onlookers. Incredibly, none of these appeared to have any memory of what had occurred even though many were heavily sprayed with blood. Sixteen were hospitalized for shock.

The Lake Forest horror appeared to some to have been brewing in recent weeks. Local police had received reports of a disturb-

Continued on Page 16, Column 1

1

Halloran

Halloran had been seeing dead people since early spring.
Men and women he'd known, or at least had seen around town.
Familiar faces from the commuter platform, the hardware store,
the tennis courts. His head would start to hurt again and he'd see
them. And they were not ghosts. Not exactly. Not like any ghosts
he'd read about or seen in movies. These were solid and real and
alive. Acting just like always. Doing, if only for a few moments,
exactly what they would be doing if they were living. Until suddenly
. . . he couldn't quite get a handle on it. Until suddenly, they
seemed to realize they were dead. Like sleepwalkers waking up in
a place other than wherever they knew they ought to be. Now and
then they'd try to speak to the people passing nearby. Sometimes
they'd become frantic, jerking their heads in one direction and then
another. Sometimes shouting silently. Other times, most times, a
pall of sadness would come over them. And then they'd vanish.

Marty Kornhauser was the first. The first, anyway, that Halloran was sure about. He remembered every detail of the morning
it happened. He had replayed it in his mind so often, as if to
convince himself that the event was no more or less real than any
of the other events of that day. It was a Tuesday and it was April.
An ordinary Tuesday morning. Except for the headache. Other-

wise, it was shower and dress as usual while Barbara pretended to sleep, take a Percodan for the pain, walk to the station, buy his coffee and his stale glazed doughnut and his copy of the *New York Times*, and wait for the 7:33 to Grand Central.

On a plastic bench off to one side of the station door, he would pretend to read his newspaper, never going beyond the top right-hand corner of the first page. There were two reasons for this. First, his apparent concentration discouraged other men from joining him and chatting with him during the ride into the city. Halloran was tired of being asked how he was feeling. Second, Halloran liked to ration the *Times*. This was the Penn Central Railroad. Worse, it was the New Haven Line, vulnerable to total collapse every time a dog lifted its leg against a third rail in the Bronx. God only knew when it would arrive at the Riverside Station, let alone reach its final destination. If Halloran started reading too soon, he'd finish the news and sports and the crossword before even passing Fordham Station. Then he'd be reduced to reading editorials about energy, or working the bridge problem, or worst of all, having time to think. His thoughts would turn either to Barbara, or to his job, or to the Penn Central, all of which he despised. He knew, of course, that hating the Penn Central was a loss—like hating a buffalo herd for soiling the grass—but it was more fun than hating Barbara or an advertising agency. Besides, when the Penn Central got back at him, as it often did, he at least had lots of company.

From his bench, Halloran heard the station door swing open and closed several times. He had not lifted his eyes from an account of some hearing by the Senate Foreign Relations Committee. But it opened again and Halloran felt a cool wall of air. Not a breeze as in winter, but a presence that remained after the door had closed. Involuntarily, curiously, he glanced up. It was only Marty. Forgetting the chill, Halloran's eyes dropped once more to the *Times* item and he twisted another bite off his doughnut. The pain was coming back. And the Percodan wasn't helping and the train was already late and the doughnut tasted lousy and that was not Marty Kornhauser. He was dead, the bastard, and he shouldn't be because I cared about him and there aren't enough like him around and a month before he died I watched a rerun of *Rich Man, Poor Man* at his house and we talked about Wouldn't it be great if we beat it to Cannes with my kid and lived out our lives on a charter boat.

Halloran looked up slowly, trying not to move his head. It *was* Marty. And he was standing in front of the newspaper table fishing

2

for a coin in his pocket. But that couldn't be because Marty Kornhauser was dead three months short of his forty-third birthday of an inoperable sarcoma and twenty-eight Seconal capsules. "Kornhauser, Martin A., Riverside, Connecticut. Beloved husband of Catherine Bryant Kornhauser and devoted father of Steven L. and Laurie J. Kornhauser, died suddenly . . ."

Marty had picked his own time. He'd already lost thirty pounds and it was getting hard to breathe. So, on a single weekend in February, Marty played a round of golf on a frozen fairway, took Halloran to dinner and ate four lobsters, snorted half of Steven's cocaine stash, found a super M-80 firecracker which he used to blow up the mailbox of the jerk next door, spent most of Saturday night with a five-hundred-dollar call girl who came up from the City, learned to ride a motorcycle, smoked cigars in his bedroom at home, told his wife, when she objected, that she was a fat, boring and selfish tub of shit, spent Sunday night happily on the living room couch, hugged Steven and Laurie on Monday morning, and then drove to the station where he was found in his car on Monday night.

Now he was here. And he was picking up a copy of the *Times*. Or trying to. His hand looked like it was slipping off the stack of papers. He couldn't seem to get a grip on one. Marty Kornhauser. Halloran was looking right at him and Kornhauser was staring dumbly at his open hand. It wasn't passing through the paper, as if one or the other wasn't real. The hand would touch and the fingers would close but nothing would happen. Aside from that, and the fact that he was dead, everything else seemed absolutely normal. This was going to be the 7:33 and it was late and that was Marty Kornhauser and he was going to work. His jaw slack, Halloran could only stare, afraid that Marty would vanish if he moved or spoke. He watched stupidly as it appeared to dawn on Kornhauser that something was terribly wrong. It was as if he noticed for the first time where he was or at least that he was someplace where he did not belong. He looked dazedly around the room. Clearly confused now, he turned toward Victor, the news vendor who ran the coffee concession, and spoke to him calmly at first, and then with growing agitation. Victor was either ignoring him or could not hear him. The news vendor puffed a cigarette and pushed some change toward another commuter who'd picked up the *Wall Street Journal*. The commuter moved casually toward the platform door, oblivious to the man who was shouting after him. Now thoroughly upset, Kornhauser reached for the shoulder of a lawyer named Buckman and once again his touch had no effect. Or did it? Didn't the lawyer cock his head just a bit? Didn't he seem suddenly alert to a presence near him? The lawyer hesitated. Then he reached into his pocket for a dime which he slipped quietly into the change dish. The son of a bitch. He'd meant to beat Victor out of his profit on the paper until he saw that Kornhauser was watching him. But he couldn't have seen Kornhauser. Halloran's head felt like a hot sheet was tearing inside it.

Kornhauser was frantic. After one last desperate look around the small waiting room, he turned toward the door leading to the parking lot and then froze. He was staring at the closed door. No, it was the knob. How would he open the door? How did he get in? Somebody must have opened it for him.

"I'll get it, Marty," Halloran heard himself shout. Heads turned. His legs trembling, Halloran rose to his feet, knocking over his Styrofoam coffee cup and reached for the knob. God, his head hurt. It hadn't been this bad since . . . The abrupt motion dizzied him. A sparkly white mist clouded his eyes for an instant but he pushed through it, determined to help Marty Kornhauser through that door and back to wherever it was he ought to be. Halloran was too late. The door pushed open hard against the back of his hand and a small group of commuters came rushing through. One started to apologize but stopped upon seeing the look in Halloran's eyes. Halloran ignored them. With his other hand, he seized the door by its edge before it could close and turned to gesture toward Marty Kornhauser, knowing all the time that Marty would no longer be there because Marty was dead and his own head wasn't right yet. But Marty was there, his eyes locked squarely on Halloran's. Halloran saw recognition there, and joy and relief, but then that odd confusion again.

Kornhauser's lips were moving. There were words being spoken, or sounds, but they made no sense to Halloran. The sounds were faint but clear. However, the sounds, the vowels and consonants and even the inflections, were all scrambled, and they were coming not from Kornhauser but from the inside of Halloran's right ear. They were coming from the pain.

Halloran must have shut his eyes. Or blinked. Or glanced away for the smallest part of a second. Because Marty Kornhauser was gone. He didn't fade away. He was just not there. Halloran moved forward to the place where Kornhauser had been and stretched out his hand. There was nothing, not even a coolness. Halloran began

4

to sweat. Through a dim awareness that the room had emptied and the 7:33 was grinding slowly away from the station, he realized that the well of pain inside his skull had also gone away.

He wondered, not for the first time, whether he was going insane. Certainly something had changed since the accident—a bit of everything. He'd had it all until that other morning. A good job. Nice house. Attractive wife and a son he thought was neat. Friends. A boat. A few bucks in the bank. Now it all seemed terribly wrong. But why? How? Could his whole life have turned inside out because he was fifteen seconds late for the train one morning? One ordinary morning. A gulp of coffee and an Oh-my-God-I'm-late. A dash to the station and a vault up the platform steps as the doors of the 7:33 slid closed and the train began its quiet glide forward. Then a squeal of metal upon metal. It was stopping, he remembered thinking. They were going to let him get aboard. Then why was he lying on his back? Dully, he noticed the jointed rods that lay twisted and buckled beside his face. They were like the others that hung limp and broken from the top of the train. It's the pantograph. They busted the pantograph. Goddamned railroad. Gonna be late again.

Halloran could not think. He could only collect impressions. The sponginess at the back of his skull must mean that he was bleeding on a cushion that someone had put there. But who? There was no one near him. The doors of the train was still closed. He could see faces through the glass. Hands and faces pressed against the tinted windows. Other dimmer faces behind them. Mouths moving. Fingers pointing.

Wait. There's someone. A black guy. Wearing paint-stained overalls. Shaking his head and making a face like he's mad. And who's that? A fat man in a bathrobe with wet hair. He's mad at the black guy. Hold it. Something's changing. He's looking at me hard. Like I'm a freak. No, it's changing. That's delight on his face. The asshole is happy. Halloran turned his head to look for other faces and the pain in his head sent spears of shock through his body. He felt a crunching sensation at the back of his skull. That was no cushion. That was his head that was all soft. Was there an accident? He must have fallen down. The fat guy would know. But Halloran couldn't speak. All he wanted to ask was what happened, but it wouldn't come out.

In his mind, Halloran saw a plug that had been pulled out of a wall socket. If someone would pick it up and plug it back in, his mouth would work. Wait a minute. The fat guy is waving his arms at the painter. The painter looks like he can't believe what the guy in the bathrobe is saying. Do they know me? The painter's leaning close now, looking hard. I've never seen either of them. Never mind. The black one is talking. *Eesamooey.* That's what it sounds like. *Eesamooeyood.* Shit! My ears don't work either. Yes, they do. There're footsteps. People are coming. Look at the fat guy now. He looks pissed. The schmuck just stands there instead of helping and when people come to do something useful, he gets pissed.

That was all that Halloran remembered. He woke up six dreamless days later with a stainless steel plate replacing most of his occipital bone.

Is that Barbara? Yeah! Leaning over him, her face close to his, looking curiously into each of his eyes. Where is this? Pale blue walls with a television on a bracket mounted high in the center. Framed landscape prints on the walls. A spray of color on the window ledge, but it hurts to look over there. Barbara watching me like she'd watch a roast. Must be Greenwich Hospital.

With a satisfied nod, but an expression otherwise without pleasure, Barbara patted his hand twice and abruptly left the room. In what seemed like an instant, she was back. A doctor in tow. Except now she was as excited and bubbling as a schoolgirl on Christmas morning.

"He hasn't said anything yet, but I just know he recognized me," she trilled at the doctor, who was already moving his flashlight from one eye to the other.

"Peter?" asked the doctor, stepping back. "Do you know who I am?"

"Ji . . . Jim Wood."

"How well can you see me?"

"A little hazy."

"That should clear up quickly. Now I want you to squeeze my fingers with your left hand. Good. Now the right. Good. Wiggle your feet. No, you can't lean up. You're wearing a restraint to keep you from thrashing around."

"It all seems to work. How long have I been here?"

"About a week. Any pain?"

"No. A week? Jesus!"

"Do you know what happened to you?"

"Did a fat guy in a bathrobe push me into the train? Or a house painter?"

Doctor Wood smiled gently but showed no surprise at the

question. Another cranial trauma victim on the ward had fallen off a stepladder in his garage. What that man remembered was Lyndon Johnson hitting him with an ax.

"The train's pantograph shattered while you were on the platform. Part of it whipped down and whacked you over the back of the head. What you've got is a depressed skull fracture. There was considerable damage to the bone but that's been patched good as new with a prosthesis. Also some damage to the outer cortex of the cerebrum. We don't know yet whether there's functional damage but offhand, I don't see any impairment."

Peter didn't know what a cortex was and was too groggy to care. He became conscious of Barbara taking his hand and kissing it. Her eyes beaming, she gushed about how happy Jeff would be to hear that his dad was going to be fine and how we've all missed you and I've hardly left your side but don't worry about me and your boss says take all the time you need and he won't put anybody smart on your accounts, ha-ha, and the whole neighborhood has been calling day and night. Peter felt a pleasant warmth. He couldn't remember the last time Barbara had been so solicitous.

"Well," said the doctor, straightening, "I'm going to leave you two alone for a while. No more than fifteen minutes this time and no moving around or getting excited. I'll be back for a closer look this afternoon. I also want Doctor Zalman to stop in."

"Zalman? He's a shrink, isn't he?"

"Yep. Ever been to see him?"

"No. Doc, I'm not really big on shrinks. Is it necessary?"

"Zalman's okay." Halloran thought he was going to say, "for a psychiatrist," but he didn't. "Anyway, it's S.O.P. for serious trauma, particularly head injuries. Personality changes are not altogether uncommon. They're often subtle. Sometimes nothing more than an increased awareness of one's mortality. Nobody's especially looking for anything in your case, but if a change does arise, you'll be a whole lot happier understanding what's happening."

"I'll see that he behaves, Dr. Wood." Barbara took the surgeon's hand in hers. "And I'll never forget that you gave me back my husband." She was smiling through tears. Halloran was afraid she was going to kiss Wood's hand. The embarrassed doctor disengaged himself, made a thumbs-up sign at Peter, and eased himself out of the room. Barbara's smile—and her tears—vanished as if a switch had been thrown.

"Is your mind clear enough to understand what I'm saying to

7

you?" she demanded, in a voice that had suddenly dropped at least two octaves. Christmas morning was over. Barbara was looking at him like a roast again. Peter turned his face away so that she could not see the disappointment in his eyes. He'd allowed himself to hope, beyond any reason for hope, that some of her concern had been genuine.

"It's going to be something shitty, isn't it, Barbara?"

"No, as it happens," she answered quietly. "It's about an opportunity. A man from the railroad has called to offer his sympathy. He'll be coming by to visit you."

"That would be very nice." Peter, of course, knew what was coming.

"Don't be stupid. Nice has nothing to do with it. He'll be trying to ingratiate himself to you so that you'll accept a meager settlement. I want to get a half-million-dollar settlement out of this, Peter, and I don't want you to do, say, or sign anything that will muck it up."

"Go home, Barbara," he answered wearily. "I've been conscious for fifteen minutes and already you're depressing the hell out of me."

"I'll go because I have to," she said, stuffing her cigarettes into her purse and moving toward her fur. "I have a lot to catch up on after spending the better part of a week in this room. No doubt that hasn't occurred to you. But remember what I said. God in His wisdom has given us the chance to have some of the things you don't seem to be able to get us any other way. Don't let it slip away, Peter. Better yet, don't you even talk to that man."

Halloran kept his face turned to the wall as Barbara left the room. At least she hadn't patted him on the head on the way out. He felt a tear welling against his nose but felt too deeply tired to wipe it away. He kept his eyes closed until he slept. And when he slept, he dreamed of a thin and weathered black face whose eyes were fixed hard and questioningly on his—a face that asked, over and over, *Do you see me?*

It was a week before he left the hospital and another seven before he returned to his job. He was more than ready and, in fact, had been capable of at least a short work week for a month. But his job, of late, seemed so terribly unimportant. Less difficult in terms of intellectual effort than doing the Sunday *Times* crossword puzzle and not much more productive. Senior Vice President and Management Supervisor at an advertising agency. Parcel out the work load; pick over what comes back. Be a pal to the client; not too much advice; let him be the smart one. You get to make a few mortgage payments and pay the yacht club bill and maybe along the way a few thousand extra cases of dog food or toothpaste will get sold.

Could he really get half a million from the railroad? Wow! He'd quit his job in five minutes and open a bookstore. Barbara would shit, of course. With any kind of luck, she'd divorce him. Barbara would do anything to keep up appearances except endure the loss of those appearances. Giving up his title and his sixty-five grand a year in favor of a bookstore would do it. Definitely. Maybe a porno section just to drive her thoroughly up the fucking wall. Nah. There's Jeff to think about. The customers are good too. Tacky people don't come into bookstores. That's being a snob, Peter. You sound like Barbara. You know better but Barbara can't help it. It's in her genes. She's a Wentworth and three hundred years of that breeding would turn anybody into a pain in the ass. She also carried sense-of-humor genes and compassion genes but they'd been recessive since right after the honeymoon. Half consciously, he looked upon living with Barbara as the price to be paid for having a home, a few good friends, and a full-time son.

As long as he wasn't home too often. Barbara had made that clear in a hundred subtle ways. His presence after he came home from the hospital was an intrusion of her privacy, a violence to her daytime routine or her freedom from routine. His presence made obligatory, and therefore annoying, the courtesy of saying that she was going here or there whenever she had an errand to run. Having friends over for afternoon coffee or cocktails meant that she'd have to ask him to go to a movie or someplace. To forgo one or two of these ritual diversions, much less to ask Peter to join her, would not have occurred to Barbara.

It was this atmosphere that compelled Peter to return to work. This, and the depression that had been building after the sudden death of Marty Kornhauser. So terribly sudden. Only two days after they'd consumed an awesome dinner together, gotten thoroughly oiled on three bottles of white wine and two stingers each, and giggled like idiots as they pretended to be sober for the benefit of the policeman standing near the parking area. It was clear now why Marty had seemed so reluctant to let that evening come to an end. Such a good friend. Now he was dead.

On some days, Peter envied him. Marty had gone out smiling. He picked his own time and he cut the cord. Really not a bad way to . . . Ooops! If you're starting to think that way, Peter, it's time to get your ass in gear. We know that you're less than keen to start thinking dog food again and we know you're afraid of that station. . . . That's right. You can admit it. You are afraid of that station, aren't you? Zalman warned you. The shrink said not to be surprised if a few little funnies happen inside your head. You get kicked by a horse and you're going to be afraid of it, right? So, get on the goddamned train, before they find out that any one of a dozen people can do your job for half the salary. Just keep your head down.

Halloran saw Marty Kornhauser six round trips later. He was useless for the rest of that week but fought off the urge to call Zalman. Peter could not imagine what the psychiatrist might say that would leave him at peace with what happened. But he did stop hiding within the *Times*. Now he sought out familiar faces and forced himself to make small talk while looking around on the platform as little as possible. Then, after another ten round trips, as he climbed onto the railroad overpass one morning, he almost collided with Peggy Bregman, who was jogging across it in her wine-colored warm-up suit. The pain came again. Its surges seemed timed in a rhythm with her stride, building to the limen of unconsciousness as she passed him and then easing like a receding surf. Gripping the cyclone fence for support, Peter turned slowly and looked after her. Oh God, she was stopping. Slowing, anyway. Oh good Jesus, if she stops and turns don't let it be Peggy. Now she was picking up speed again. She's not going to stop. Then, with a violent shake of her head in a gesture of anguish, she spun to face him. The suddenness of her turn shocked Peter. Nobody can stop like that. But she did. And it was Peggy Bregman and she was looking right at him and she was real. Look at the shadow behind her. And then she was gone. Gone to wherever it was she went when a cerebral hemorrhage killed her on Thanksgiving morning.

2

Chicago

Jennifer pressed close to the window on the right side of the taxi as it headed north along Sheridan Road. The side streets that gave relief to the canyon of high-rises also allowed a fleeting view of Lake Michigan at each intersection. It reminded her of one of those old penny arcade movie machines where you turned a crank and a series of pictures flipped by, each slightly different than the last. Jennifer was concentrating at first on a tiny speck, far out over the water, that grew larger in each successive picture. By Devon Street, she could make out wings and a lumpy tail. Crossing Pratt Street, she could tell it was a 727 and two more specks had lined up behind it. By the time the taxi turned onto Touhy Avenue, the aircraft was roaring low overhead en route to its landing at O'Hare. She cast her eyes around the inside of the taxi, searching for another object on which she could lock her attention until the driver could find the address.

She tried counting her heartbeats. Seventy-four to the minute. A bit on the slow side. Soon they would get a lot slower. She closed her eyes and touched her fingertips lightly to her temples and, in her mind, watched the blood pumping through her brain, nourishing and cleansing. Higher up, the flow of blood cleared and became a crystal stream that coursed through her meadow and formed a lazily swirling eddy that lapped near the roots of her favorite tree.

"You alright, young lady?" The driver, an older man with a pleasant, laugh-lined face, was squinting at her through the rear-view mirror.

"Sure," she smiled, unembarrassed. She was not quite ready to come back but she didn't mind being tugged by this man. His aura was soft, blue and tranquil. "It's just an exercise. Helps keep the mind clear."

"What, you mean like yoga?"

"Something like that." She stretched and yawned as if she'd just awakened from a long nap. The driver glanced admiringly at the languid grace of her upper body and the wide good-humored mouth that smiled back at him.

"Myself, I don't need nothin' like that. My brain turns off the second I climb into this cab in the morning."

"Except when you dream about fishing in Wisconsin," she added.

"Hey, how'd you know that?"

"Just a guess."

"Well, that's one heck of a guess. That's exactly what I was thinkin' about. Here's your building, by the way."

Jennifer waited for her change and tipped the driver a little extra before sliding her long legs through the door, holding down the hem of her unaccustomed skirt.

"You have a good day, Miss. And listen. If you're comin' back after dark, you phone for a cab, okay? This neighborhood ain't too bad but I wouldn't want my daughter walkin' around it at night by herself."

"Thanks very much, Mr. Macowsky, but I think I'll have a ride."

She shouldn't have done that, she chided herself, as the taxi pulled away toward Western Avenue. Using his name was alright. He'd think she knew it from the hack license. But that stuff about fishing was just showing off, pure and simple. At least, though, it kept her mind off this address and that was the whole idea. It was better when the vibrations came in a rush, like right now, than in a vague trickle that started too soon. The early vibrations were often unreliable. Too much interference. Like tuning in a car radio too far from the station. Sometimes it would seem to have jumped to a different frequency. Other times you'd find it, but then you'd get an overlapping signal from other stations.

It was a brick three-story apartment house of fairly recent construction. Like a hundred others on the North Side. That was good. There wouldn't be too much interference here, either. Not like in those big old nineteenth-century town houses around it. Jennifer could feel the presence of a little girl. No, two little girls. One here. One someplace else but remembered here. And a lot of vodka. The fumes, not long evaporated, came from a third-floor window facing the street. That must be the apartment. She could feel faint smudges on the brick like stains made from rising smoke.

Alex was here. There was his yellow Volkswagen parked at the curb at a careless angle. Fine. He'll have everything ready. Jennifer took a breath and stepped into the mirrored lobby.

The door to apartment 4-H opened as Jennifer reached the landing. Alex Makepeace held up a hand while closing the door partway behind him and walked toward Jennifer at the stairwell. It was funny about Alex. He moved like a powerful cat when he wanted to or when he was working. A strong man. You'd never guess he was anything but straight unless you saw the softer, more pliant Alex when he was with his gay friends down in Old Town.

"She's all set, Jen," he said softly. "How much do you want to know?"

"I think I'm picking it up already. Suppose you just confirm but only with a yes or no, okay?"

"Shoot."

"Two small girls?"

"Yes."

"Both dead, but only one died here?"

"Yes."

"Mother an alcoholic?"

"Now she is, but . . . Sorry, Jen. Yes."

"We're going to try to reach the girls?"

"Yeah."

"Does she understand that I can't guarantee it? If the woman's emotional health is riding on the result of a séance, she's holding an awfully thin rope."

"Yes, I've been through that with her. Her doctor . . ."

"Go ahead. Just nothing about the children."

"The mother's been in and out of the rehabilitation center twice. Apparently drinking because she's loaded with guilt. She's now an outpatient but the betting is she'll be back in, or a suicide, unless she has something to hold on to. Her therapist is Mike Kessler. He doesn't admit to buying your act entirely so this is

13

strictly extracurricular and off the medical record. Fact is, Kessler accepts more than he's willing to let on but he has a foundation grant to worry about if he starts giving credence to the spook world. At the very least, though, he knows you're not a scam and he figures that by whatever mechanism she can get a line out, whether through you or in her own head, then maybe she won't drown."

"Well, okay," Jennifer said doubtfully. She didn't like being in this sort of position at all. There were always desperate people who wanted to believe that she was infallible in using gifts she didn't entirely understand herself. "Let's meet the lady."

She was standing just inside the door. A nervous woman of about thirty-eight but looking ten years older. The thin arms and legs and bloated abdomen of the advanced alcoholic. Her face was still slightly puffy but showed no sign of recent heavy drinking. Jennifer could see an aura quickly but blinked it away at once. It was a muddy brown and beginning to shrivel at the edges. This woman would not live very long.

"Please come right in. You're Jennifer Wilde. I've heard so much about you. And I read those stories in the *Sun-Times* from a couple of years ago. Dr. Kessler showed them to me yesterday."

"Hello." Jennifer smiled warmly and offered her hand. "I'm sorry, but I don't know your name."

"Oh, I'm . . ." She caught herself. "But Alex here said I shouldn't give you any information so nobody can think this is fake. But I won't think so. And I sort of expected that you'd know my name without being told. Dr. Kessler says he's seen you do that."

"He's seen me do it under controlled conditions. Sometimes I do it for fun. Not now, though. There are too many ways in which I could know your name. Alex might have told me in the hall."

"He didn't. I'm afraid I was listening."

"Then he could have told me before, or I could have looked at your mailbox. In any case, it wasn't fakery that Alex was concerned about. The point of withholding details is to lessen the chance that I'll mix what seems to be coming from the outside with what's already in my own subconscious mind. It's not always easy for me to know the difference. As for your name, what I'm picking up is 'Bug.'"

"Oh! Oh, my!" The woman looked like she was going to cry.

"'Bug,' and sometimes 'Ladybug,'" Jennifer grinned easily. "Who called you Ladybug?"

"You don't know?"

"Not a clue."

"My father. My God, I haven't heard that in must be twenty-five . . ."

"Okay, ladies." Alex clapped his hands together sharply. "Let's have done with the parlor games. I've got a dinner party to go to tonight." He gestured toward the kitchen. "That dinette table ought to do. The tape recorder's plugged in and there's a bottle of ginger ale in the fridge."

"Is it alright to ask questions?" asked Ladybug, somewhat more at ease than before but still clearly apprehensive.

"Only until she's ready to go under. If anyone comes through, that is, if anyone speaks through Jennifer to you, then you can answer. If that should happen, and it very well may not, I suggest you ask whoever it is for some information that only you and that person could have. But be careful otherwise not to interrupt when I'm talking to Jennifer or through Jennifer. As Kessler explained, I'm her control. I'm called that because Jennifer will have no knowledge or control of what goes on once she's under. She normally won't ever remember it."

"That's why there's a tape recorder?"

"Partly."

"What if something really private is on it?"

"Then you keep it. But I'd like Jennifer to hear it at least once."

"Don't we need a dark room for this?"

"Only in the movies. What we need is a restful room. No glaring sunlight. No extreme untidiness. In other words, a séance can be held anyplace where the normal person could relax."

Jennifer had seated herself while Alex was talking. She'd closed her eyes and her fingertips were at her temples again. Alex drew the Canada Dry bottle from the refrigerator and poured a glass which he placed directly in front of her.

"What's the ginger ale for?" the woman asked.

"She watches the bubbles. No more now. Jennifer's already started without us."

Alex watched carefully as Jennifer's eyes opened wide and she stared directly into the bottom of the glass. Her breathing slowed as she concentrated on the hundreds of carbonated bubbles that formed spontaneously and drifted slowly upward. Now it seemed that she was not breathing at all. Her mouth slackened and her eyes were beginning to glaze. The right eye started to drift off to one side as the oculomotor nerve in the midbrain relaxed in a sleep of its own. Jennifer was no longer there. She had gone to her meadow.

"Jennifer?"

No answer.

"I'm speaking to you, Jennifer. I'd like you to answer me, please."

—*Jennifer's not here.* The voice caused Ladybug to jump. It was, without question, a male voice.

"Are you Lictor?"

—*Lictor's not here.*

"Where is Lictor?"

—*Away.*

Well! This had never happened before. Lictor had been Jennifer's spirit contact for three years. Before that, it was Norman. Alex had heard spirits speak of moving on but never just away.

"Has Lictor moved on?"

—*No. Away.*

"Who are you?"

—*Andrew.*

"Are you going to be Jennifer's contact?"

—*No. Lictor. Never done this.*

"Then why did you come?"

—*Minding the store. Lictor.*

"Will you try to help us?"

—*Yes.*

"We want to reach Alice Connoly and Bettina Connoly."

—*Wait. I'll ask.* There was no sound or movement for several minutes. Alex took Ladybug's hand when he saw her growing pale.

—*Only Tom Connoly,* came Andrew's voice suddenly. Ladybug gasped and dug her nails painfully into Alex's hand. —*Wants to know is that Amy.*

"Yes. Amy's here." Alex turned to a terrified Amy Connoly. "Amy, was that your husband or your dad?"

"My husband," she whimpered. "He's . . . He died five years ago. I don't want to . . . He knows what a hash I've made of every . . ."

"Tom?"

—*No. Andrew.*

"Can we talk to Tom?"

16

—Don't know how. I'll ask.

"Are the children there with you?"

—Wait a minute. Silence for another few moments. Amy gripped the table with her free hand.

—Alice is here. Bettina's gone on. Tom says they are so beautiful. Tom says Alice so happy. Alice blows kisses at Mommy. Says teeth are straight. Says look at teeth.

Amy Connoly's body heaved upward in a convulsive sob. She clamped her free hand over her quivering mouth and a trickle of tears began to well along her fingers.

"Do you want to try to ask anything, Amy?"

She could only shake her head from side to side.

"Where is Bettina?" Alex asked.

—Gone on.

"Is Bettina happy?"

—Gone on. This last was said with a hint of impatience, as if happiness was clearly implicit in Andrew's answer. Amy released her grip on Alex's hand and raised it shakily as if asking permission. Alex nodded toward Jennifer.

"Is . . . Is Bettina mad at her mommy?"

—I'll ask Tom.

A longer silence this time.

—Bettina worried about Amy being alone. Not angry. Accident. Sorry about glass bird. Wants Mommy to come soon. Tom says all very happy. All very beautiful but don't come too soon. Fix first. Tub was accident. Don't be sad. Fix first. Tom will wait. Tom, Alice, Bettina all see you. All stay near you. Don't come too soon. Don't make time come. Fix first. Get new glass bird. Easier to find you.

Amy Connoly fainted. Alex snatched her arm to break her slide to the floor.

"Good-bye, Andrew. I'm bringing Jennifer back now."

—No. Lictor's coming.

"Lictor?"

—I'm Lictor. This new voice coming from Jennifer's body was a tone lower and had a ring of authority. *—You are Alex?*

"This is Alex." Lictor had never called him by name before. All kinds of surprises today.

—Tell Jennifer to see Bloomer. Amersham. Lake Forest. Same thing. It's happening again. Riverside. In Connecticut. See Bloomer.

"Where is Amersham?"

—Near London. Same as Lake Forest. Now Riverside. Work with Bloomer. Find Halloran.

"I know Lake Forest. I know Bloomer. Who is Halloran?"

—Halloran. Riverside. Halloran sees them.

Amy Connoly's sobs had become softer but her face was still hidden behind the damp towel that Alex had brought her. Jennifer was asleep on the living room sofa.

"Amy?"

"Y . . . Yes?" She flinched at his touch.

"Is there anything you'd like to ask me?"

"Where . . . Where's my Bettina?"

"What's your religion, Amy? Do you have one?"

"Catholic. Used to be. But lately . . ."

"Okay. You were taught what heaven was like. What it's really like. I mean, what my friends and I think it's like based on what we've learned from people who've gone over, is really not all that different. The one difference is that the spirit continues to grow, and as it grows it graduates to one of several higher levels. Do you understand that?"

"I think so."

"This life is only the first of several stages. All the rest get progressively better as the spirit grows. Bettina grew. For some reason, she grew faster than either Tom or Alice. She can visit down but they can't visit up."

"Tom said they were near me."

"They can see you. You have your very own cheering section."

"They don't hate me, do they?"

"Nobody hates you. You've had a rough time and they know it. I hadn't known about your husband."

"Tom was a fireman," said Amy, exhausted. "A stupid accident on the way to a false alarm. Bettina wasn't even a year old. Then four years later, I smacked up a car with Alice in it. I wasn't drinking. I just fell asleep driving. I didn't wake up until I was in the hospital and they kept saying I could see Alice later but all that time she was already dead. Then I'd drink and I'd hate myself and then I'd drink some more. A year ago, when I was good and loaded, Bettina cracked her skull in the bathroom and when I woke up she was dead and I wanted to be dead too."

"Amy," Alex took her hand, "you don't have to tell me anything at all."

"You already know, don't you?"

"I think I do," he whispered.

Amy looked away. Then, biting her lip, she faced Alex again.

"It really was an accident," she said slowly. "I was drinking and I got mad at something she did in the bathroom. I grabbed her and swung her too hard and her little head went right into that shower knob. And just like that, she was dead. Her eyes were wide open and she was dead. For two hours I just prayed and I tried to get sober. Then I took her to the hospital. Told them I found her like that."

"Amy, do me a favor. Tell Kessler. It'll help you get fixed up like Tom told you to."

"Will I really see them all again?"

"I believe that you will. I'm sure Jennifer believes it. But what about you? Do you believe that was Tom?"

"Of course I do. You and Jennifer didn't know about him."

"You only have my word for that. We could have known. And even assuming we didn't, it's also just possible that you were talking to somebody else. Some other consciousness. Even a living subconscious. It's happened before and we haven't always realized it. That's why I asked you to look for information no one else could know about. Amy, something very marvelous seems to have happened to you. I don't want you wondering later whether it really happened."

"But I did get proof. The glass bird. Only Bettina called it that."

"What is it?" Alex asked. "You mean like an ornament?"

"No. It's the top of a perfume bottle. L'Air du Temps. I always used to wear it. That's why I got mad at Bettina. She was playing with the bird and the whole bottle smashed in the sink. I've never used it since. But nobody in the world ever knew about that. Except them. Now they say I should start wearing it again. So they can find me easier. Oh, God. I'll buy buckets of it."

Jennifer was only beginning to shake off her torpor as Alex's Volks passed the marquee of the Drake Hotel and approached her apartment building on East Walton Street. She yawned aloud and patted Alex's knee to show that she was coming out of it.

"How'd we do?" she asked dreamily. "Did you get through to Lictor?"

"Not at first. It looks like he's training an assistant. Name's Andrew. Not very sharp."

"What about Ladybug?"

"Her name's Amy, by the way. We plugged right in. Got her husband. The girls are fine. I think she's going to get her head together."

"She won't have much time, Alex. She's diseased. Liver or kidneys, I think."

"How much shriveling did you see?"

"A lot. She won't be here for more than a year."

"Oh, good! That means . . ." Alex hesitated and then chuckled softly. "Sorry, Jennifer. I know you're not entirely comfortable with the way I look at dying. I said Oh, good and I meant Oh, good. I'd be doing her a favor if I . . ." He stopped when he felt Jennifer tighten.

"It's what I am, Jen," he said, as he backed crookedly into a parking space beneath a sign that said NO STANDING. "I'm a minor medium, a declared gay and I run a leather shop. I'm also the control for the most talented trance medium in the western hemisphere. I don't have to be or feel like other people. I'm not like other people. Certainly you're not either. You're not only a medium, you're an authentic mystic. You not only can communicate on another level of existence, you've actually been there. You could have a world at your feet and you choose to make a mediocre living illustrating children's books."

Jennifer squeezed his hand but said nothing. They'd had this discussion before. Alex's motives were basically decent. He admired her, she knew, and wanted only recognition for her. And Alex was kind. She could not persuade him, though, that kindness should never be forced; that death can never be a gift from the living. Jennifer shook the thought away before the memories of what Alex had done could start to come back.

"Alex." She squeezed his hand again. "Something's on your mind. Would you like to come up and have a glass of wine while we listen to the tape?"

"I left the tape with Amy. It got pretty personal toward the end." Alex lit a cigarette off the butt of another and inhaled deeply. "There was a message from Lictor. I'm afraid Lake Forest is happening again." He turned and looked directly at Jennifer. Her body seemed to sag.

"I don't believe that, Alex," she said after a long moment. "I was there last week. During the morning rush. I didn't pick up a thing."

"I meant it's like Lake Forest. It's happening now in Riverside.

In Connecticut. Lictor says it happened before even Lake Forest at a station called Amersham in London."

Jennifer grew cold.

"You knew about Amersham?" Alex asked. Jennifer did not answer.

"What does he want me to do?" she asked sullenly.

"He wants you to contact your horny parapsychologist friend, for openers."

"Mordicai Bloomer?"

"Yep. Also someone named Halloran."

"Who's Halloran?"

"I assumed you knew."

"Man or woman?"

"Lictor didn't say. But Halloran's got to be in Riverside. And probably a psychic."

"Why?"

"Because, according to Lictor, Halloran can do something not even the famous Jennifer Wilde or the concupiscent Mordicai Bloomer can do. Lictor says Halloran can see them."

3

Riverside

Barbara's Saturday was looking up. It certainly hadn't begun in a banner fashion. She'd had little sleep. What with Peter dreaming aloud or trembling half awake and then finally reaching for her. She'd had to spend half the night on the chaise until he was breathing sufficiently deeply for her to risk sliding back into bed. Then, with the sun not even up, he'd tried to use her. Pressing close and running his hand over her hip and asking stupidly if she was awake. Next claiming feebly that all he wanted to do was talk.

He left the house early, thank God. Muttering something insipid about sleeping with a block of ice and something else about never going near the train again. Fine. Let him drive to the City. He'll have to leave earlier and get home later and that will suit everyone very nicely. Even young Jeffrey. Lord knows why Jeffrey has been going out of his way to spend so much time with his father. Time that could be better spent becoming known by some of the more worthwhile families in town. And as for that block of ice remark, Peter might be surprised to learn that there have been two or three men who didn't share his warped perception. Men of accomplishment. Men of power. Men whose sexual drive was an instrument, not an indulgence.

But never mind that now. Leticia Browning called. *The* Leticia Browning. Asking Barbara *Wentworth* Halloran if she would care to join a small group for cocktails and dinner that very evening. Barbara couldn't believe her luck.

Leticia Browning. The grande dame of American historical novelists. The preeminent authority on the history of Greenwich and, for that matter, most of the Eastern seaboard. Anything south of Charleston, Miss Browning dismissed as a mercantile aberration that had no salutary role in the formation of the nation's character. Otherwise, she treated the early history of the nation with a respect that was scholarly and affectionate. The history of Greenwich, however, was more of a private passion. Four of her novels, including two national best sellers, were about the early years of Greenwich and the various incorporated villages the town contained. Leticia Browning made her home in Old Greenwich, now, like Riverside, just a town within a town but once the original settlement. From the garden of her sprawling white Colonial home near the shore of Long Island Sound, she could see the spot where the first group of settlers had stepped ashore. There was the huge flat basalt boulder, dropped randomly by the receding ice sheet whose southernmost edge had carved out the Sound. The very rock where, on a July day in the year 1640, Captain Daniel Patrick and the fiery Elizabeth Winthrop bargained with half-naked Siwanoy chiefs for the use of their land. The Indians, who had no more concept of the ownership of land than they had of air or water, gladly accepted twenty-five red coats from their odd-smelling but prettily dressed visitors and were, in short order, shot at for trespassing. The Siwanoys' grasp of the concept of trespass was equally imperfect.

Some attempts were made at converting the heathen and a few were successful. Conversion had practical value since it tended to persuade the converted that all subsequent disasters represented God's punishment for their sins. However, there was always the problem of backsliding. And no solution to that was found to be quite so effective as genocide. Accordingly, on one February night four years later, a Captain John Underhill marched his men through the moonlit snows of what is now Riverside, crossed the river that gave the place its name, and fell upon a large, peaceful, but sometimes inconvenient Indian village. Ringing the encampment which sat at the base of a bluff, Underhill's soldiers opened fire. The slaughter lasted through the night. By dawn, over a thousand Siwanoy Mohegans lay dead among burning huts in a misting rain that had begun to fall. Only eight survived. The greatest and most treacherous massacre in the history of the nation before or since had taken place. But the nation's written history had virtually ignored it.

The massacre led to an occasional burst of truculence by neighboring Indians, but it soon blew over. Greenwich grew on in the happy insularity that became its hallmark with the advent of modern times. As for Captain Underhill, he moved on to New Amsterdam, taking his fame as an Indian fighter to the cocktail party circuit of the day and inevitably found himself in public office. With equally inevitable proceeds from that office, Underhill took a wife of good Dutch family, sired two sons, and purchased a shipping company whose profits kept him in comfortable circumstances for the rest of his allotted span.

Underhill's two sons took over the business. Jakob went to sea as a Gold Coast slaver and eventually came to grief when a comely female Bantu, having been cleaned up and brought to his cabin for the night, bit off the offending organ while he slept. His younger brother, Japheth, managed to carry on the line after a fashion. Japheth impregnated one of his brother's nieces and was prevailed upon to do the decent thing only days before the arrival of his heir. Not long afterward, however, Japheth returned to what he'd thought were less troublesome sexual outlets and was arrested for performing an unnatural act with a sheep. The new English governor had him flogged and branded. His wife's older brother cut off his testicles with a quill knife. Japheth, once he could walk, hobbled off toward the Allegheny country and was not heard from again. The remaining young Underhill, named John for his grandfather, waited until he was twelve and headed north by east. He had two reasons for doing so. First, he correctly perceived that the Underhill name had lost much of its social luster in what was now New York. His mother had long since ceased to use the tainted name and, in fact, found it hard to feel any affection for the boy. Second, having absorbed all the stories of his grandfather's heroic forays against the murdering red savage, young John grew up on dreams of emulating those feats in the same Connecticut wilds.

After several months of wandering, and with winter coming on, he approached the cabin of an illiterate German trapper named Emil Wendenwirt and asked if he could work for his keep. Wendenwirt, who was in his early sixties and dreaded another winter of walking trap lines alone, agreed. So there, on Wendenwirt's homestead, young John Underhill grew to manhood. He learned trapping, skinning and dressing, and small-scale sustenance farming. Tending the trap lines, he traveled widely along the western edge of Connecticut and the southeastern portion of New York State, learning much about the local Indian tribes as he went.

When John was twenty, a census was taken by the English. Emil, who had no idea how his name was spelled and not the foggiest notion of the purpose of a census, left everything in John Underhill's hands. The result was twofold. John gave the census officer the approximate anglicization of Emil's name, which became Wentworth, and hedged his own bets by listing himself as John Wentworth, sole heir to any and all Wendenwirt property. Although he couldn't have known it at the time, this act would make him the founder of one of Greenwich's oldest families. It was the first of three important steps. Money and distinction were still to be acquired.

His opportunity came when the English, who had been paying a bounty for the hides of wolves and other predators, began offering a similar bounty for the hides of unruly Indians, particularly those who were allied with the French. John realized that he could pick up a few extra shillings by buying scalps from the Indians—as long as the hair was black—and turning them in for the bounty in White Plains. Only a trickle at first, because the Indians were not often willing to part with souvenirs of battle. Then John had a brainstorm. Since he knew the location of virtually every Indian burial ground in the territory, and since hair tends to decompose at a much slower rate than flesh, why waste perfectly good scalps by letting them rot under piles of rocks? Bounties quickly became the primary source of John's cash income and of his fame as well. Stories of the mysterious lone avenging woodsman named Wentworth circulated through the drawing rooms of New York. The awed and grateful British rewarded John with a land grant, comprising most of what is now northern Greenwich, for doing his part in protecting white settlers and their women from the rapacious lust of the savage. One of the women he protected, a pockmarked but otherwise healthy girl who claimed some dim relationship to the original Elizabeth Winthrop, pursued and wed the mysterious scout. The illustrious Wentworth family was born.

Leticia Browning, of course, knew all about the Wentworths from that period but had no idea that there were Underhills in the woodpile. Even so, she smelled a rat. Several of them, in fact. From pieces she'd assembled through years of historical detective work, Miss Browning developed a suspicion that, early in the Revolutionary War, a later generation of Wentworths had expanded its holdings by informing on more than a few local patriots. However, after the news of Yorktown reached Greenwich, they promptly began blowing the whistle on the local Tory families.

Leticia Browning was not fond of the current Wentworths either. During the wars of the recent century, no Wentworth had ever gone within an ocean of any shots being fired, or donated a pint of blood, or purchased any bond that was not a tax-free municipal. Moreover, Barbara Winthrop Wentworth Halloran was a relentless social climber who never quite understood that prominent and accomplished families welcomed and even sought out the company of interesting and talented nice people. Barbara was none of these. She was a fawning dullard in the presence of the sort she aspired to know and an imperious, contemptuous drip toward salesgirls, blacks, anyone with an accent that wasn't British, anyone with a trade, and her husband. That fellow Peter Halloran. A decent enough sort, she'd heard. Probably no gumption, though. Certainly no judge of women. But that was neither here nor there. Whatever else Barbara was, and no matter how transparent her motives, she was also a tireless student of her own family's history, and she might very well be able to fill in some gaps that plagued Leticia in researching her newest book. It was about the Mead Brothers, who were the Dalton Brothers of their day. Good stuff. Lots of hairs-breadth escapes and romantic dalliances. One such, an ungallant reference in one of Anson Mead's letters to "a toss with that grasping Wentworth lass again," was worth investigating. Which Wentworth lass? And was it possible that every generation of that family could have all the same unattractive characteristics one after the other? Then, in a later letter to Anson from his father, Jerad Mead, an injunction that the lad take care "lest the false old scalp hunter's ghost come to bedevil ye for triflin' with a Wentworth cow. There's Underhill's black heart within that clan." The false old scalp hunter could only be John Wentworth. Underhill might well be John Underhill. But what connection could there be? Leticia would have to be tactful in questioning Barbara. She'd also have to be pleasant and agreeable which, in this case, would require some effort.

Well, the presence of her other guests would help. Ira Zalman would be there. Another history buff, although psychiatrists seemed wont to take a different view of human events than the rest of us. And Mordicai Bloomer would be coming up from

Princeton. Perhaps he could be talked into conducting one of his séances. They were terrific fun. And often informative. Leticia didn't really believe that Mordicai was reaching spirits. Just his own subconscious, as Ira Zalman put it. Even so, Leticia often found fodder for her writing in the contacts Mordicai appeared to make. Details now and then that had sometimes proved astonishingly accurate. Others not so accurate, or at least contrary to existing records. Nevertheless, it would be fun to try again. Maybe he could reach Anson Mead. Or all the way to hell for old John Underhill.

Although Halloran was pleased that Jeff wanted to be with him, he'd just as soon have gone to the library by himself. He could do without Jeff's questions when his son saw the kind of books Halloran would be browsing through. But Jeff went straight for the boating section and promptly found a thin book on small-craft racing tactics. Halloran busied himself in front of a row of books about investing and estate planning until he was sure that Jeff had settled down for a while. Tucking a randomly selected business volume under his arm, Peter quietly ambled over two rows to the shelves marked PSYCHOLOGY/OCCULT.

Where to start? Aside from all the self-help and human behavior stuff, there were at least two dozen volumes dealing with some aspect of the supernatural. There was *Life after Life*. A best seller. Fascinating reading, actually, about the extraordinarily similar experiences of people, almost two hundred of them, who'd been clinically dead and then revived. Case histories assembled by a psychiatrist. But that wouldn't tell him anything about dead people walking around a railroad station. Even goddamn jogging! It gave him an idea, though. He'd ignore some of the more gothic titles and look for books written by authors who held some kind of advanced degree. He saw one. *Case Studies in Paranormal Phenomena*, by Leonard Gosser, Ph.D. Peter reached for the book but then quickly withdrew his hand at the sound of someone moving in the next aisle. He waited for the coast to clear, embarrassed at his own self-consciousness. He was a grown man, dammit, and could read whatever the hell he wanted.

To kill time while he recharged his nerve, Peter strolled a few paces to his left and found himself facing a cluster of books such as *Creative Divorce* and *The Second Time Around*. These started him on a whole new line of thought. Barbara. And the woman he might meet someday if there was no Barbara anymore. His mind composed a portrait of the two women side by side. One all too real. The other just a dream. First, there was Barbara, the way he usually thought of her now. Sour expression, curled lip in a superior sneer, looking as if she had the worst case of intestinal blockage in history. And then there was his dream girl. Clean and fresh looking, like one of those girls in the Ivory Soap ads. A serene face, high cheekbones, mouth a little too wide. She wasn't beautiful. But a good face. Certainly pretty. Very pretty when she smiled. Long straight ash-blond hair framing gray-green eyes that had just a touch of sadness in them. Maybe not sadness. Vulnerability. That was it. Like a fawn. Hey, he thought, this is really kind of strange. For a dream girl, she wasn't much like any girl Peter could remember dreaming about before. As a rule, he didn't even dream about blondes. Or girls with straight hair. Or dressed that way. His fantasy women usually wore bathing suits or peignoirs when they wore anything at all. Not blue jeans.

He was about to reach for *Creative Divorce* when his eye caught a tiny movement to his right. Peter turned and felt a hitch in his heartbeat. It was the book about paranormal phenomena and it was moving. Halloran stood frozen as he watched the book slide slowly from its bank of volumes, its center of gravity nearing the edge of the shelf. When at last it tilted and then crashed to the floor, Peter wanted to scream or run but could do neither. It was all he could do to control the panic bubbling within his chest as he stared stricken at the heavy book lying open on the tile floor. Something, some force, some unseen hand wanted him to read that page.

"No!" he whispered hoarsely. "I've had enough. Leave me alone. Goddammit."

"Huh?" came a sound from somewhere near the book.

"I said, leave me alone."

"Uh-oh! Sorry!"

"Wait a minute," Halloran rasped. "Who the hell is that?"

"It's Jeff," came the voice from behind the books.

"Did you see . . . Were you . . . Wait a minute. Did you push that book off, you little bastard?"

"That depends."

"On what?"

"On how mad you are."

"I'm not mad, goddammit."

"But you were scared shitless for a second there."

29

"I was not scared. I was merely startled. And watch your mouth."

"Sorry!" said Jeff as he rounded the aisle. "You looked like you were nervous. Like you were thinking about ripping off this book. What is it, dirty?" Jeff picked up the volume, glanced at the title, and then turned to the contents page.

Peter snatched it from his hand. He started to place it back on the shelf but could not resist a peek at the index. A quick scan showed that it seemed to cover everything. Telekinesis, automatic writing, clairvoyance, apparitions, necromancy—whatever the hell that was as long as it wasn't screwing dead bodies—spiritualists, mediums, stigmata and more. He snapped the book shut, abruptly angry with himself for taking that stuff seriously. But he could not bring himself to put it back.

Halloran hesitated on the library's front steps and gestured toward the park across the road.

"Jeff, I think I want to sit on the grass over there for a while," he said. "Want me to drive you home first?"

"No, that's okay. You mind if I stick around?"

"I'm going to be reading."

"Go ahead. Maybe I'll run a couple of laps around the park and then do some bird watching until you're done."

"You're into birds now?" Peter asked naively.

"Some. Pink Breasted Thrashers, for example."

Peter grinned. "Goodness! You are growing up. I think I even see your first zit."

Jeff poked him once in the belly and took off with a wave. Halloran watched him go, proudly and not a little enviously.

The book had several pages on the subject of Apparitions (see also Hauntings, Mediums, Spiritualists). Over eight thousand such reports had been collected by the Department of Parapsychology at Duke University. They were divided into apparitions while sleeping and while awake. In spite of the black face that kept appearing in his dreams, Peter passed over the sleeping category. Dreams were easier to deal with, whatever the explanation might be. The explanation he liked best was that he was dreaming and so what?

Within the waking category, several examples were given which were interesting but not particularly helpful in terms of his own experiences. Many cases in which dead people appeared before a relative, often at the very hour in which they died some distance away. The Duke researchers theorized that the purpose of the visit was to let the living relative know that the spirit of their loved one had survived physical death. The message was normally unspoken. The apparition itself was the message. But sometimes they spoke, or so it was claimed. Occasionally, warnings were expressed. Some relative is in trouble. Go help her. Or, don't go to such and such a place. In those cases, the person being warned usually didn't know that the person warning them was dead.

A subcategory was more interesting. Apparitions not involving relatives. The book recounted a whole cluster of reported apparitions in which the spooks would seem to be going about their normal daily business and seeming to have no interest in contacting anyone living. Maybe they don't know they're dead. That would partly account for Marty Kornhauser's behavior. Or Peggy Bregman's. Maybe Marty didn't know he was dead when he walked into the station, but after a couple of minutes he sure as hell knew it wasn't your normal weekday morning anymore. Nor was Marty putting in an appearance for Halloran's benefit. He never even saw Halloran until Halloran spoke to him. The black painter must be dead too. And the guy in the bathrobe. Could they all be hallucinations? No. Too hard to accept. He saw them as surely and as clearly as he sees this book. Or that willow tree. What if nobody else saw that tree? Would that mean he was hallucinating? No. He'd just walk over and kick it. But what good would that do? He'd still be seeing a tree that no one else could see. They'd all still think he was crazy. Maybe he was. Come to think of it, he only saw those people when his head was hurting. Or maybe his head hurt as a result of seeing them. Halloran wondered if mediums got headaches. And, for that matter, is there such a thing as a legitimate medium? Well, look it up, dummy.

Halloran's book was organized by subject in alphabetical order. Even so, through force of habit he folded over the corner of the page on which the discussion of apparitions began. In doing so, he covered the headline of the small preceding item, a paragraph headed "Amersham."

There were about twenty pages devoted to mediums. Mostly brief biographies of the more famous including a few confessed frauds. But among the supposedly legitimate mediums, those examined under controlled conditions, were some surprisingly eminent names. Arthur Conan Doyle, for instance. Interesting! It says here that the creator of Sherlock Holmes was also a doctor. And also one of the founders of England's Society for Psychical Research. The Society's membership read like a who's who of the Edwardian era. Arthur Balfour, who was Prime Minister of England shortly after the turn of the century, and Sir Oliver Lodge, Sir William Barrett, and F.W.H. Myers. All either mediums or researchers. Myers' story looked particularly interesting. A serious scientist bent at the outset on debunking the notion of contact with the dead, Myers ended up a convert. For every five charlatans he uncovered, there was always the one whom he was forced to conclude to be genuine. Finally, after publishing a book called *Human Personality and Its Survival of Bodily Death*, Myers himself promised that he'd try to contact the Society after his own death. The evidence that he did so, after a lapse of twenty years, is said to be overwhelming. He identified himself, as promised, by means of a quote from Robert Browning and did so through three different mediums in three different parts of the world. To further satisfy skeptics that collusion was unlikely, he not only spoke through mediums he was never known to have met, but he also misquoted the same line from a Browning poem. Myers' messages through various mediums, if true, painted the most complete yet tantalizing picture ever of the nature of life after death. He tended to avoid mental mediums except through the use of automatic writing and preferred to speak through trance mediums.

This was all very fascinating, Halloran thought. He'd have to read about Myers' accounts someday. For now, however, he's got his own problems. What's the difference between a mental medium and a trance medium anyway? Here it is. A trance medium normally goes into a deep, almost catatonic trance and the spirit takes over the use of his body. There's often a marked physiognomical change after which the medium both resembled and sounded like the deceased person. Sounds like a lot of bullshit. At least pretty easy to fake. On the other hand, though, some awfully responsible people have become convinced. Okay. What's a mental medium? A mental medium, it says here, is someone who is able to establish telepathic contact with the dead. The person talks to him and he tells everyone else what the dead person said. That also sounds like an easy way to make a buck. But once again, there were those controlled conditions resulting in information that would not have been explained any other way. Controlled conditions or not, mental mediums are only used when they're the only game in town. Too much danger of interference from the medium's own subconscious, his personality, his interpretations.

Halloran let the pages riffle through his fingers and slammed the book shut. He'd read it more carefully later. So far, however, he hadn't seen a word about a case similar to his. He rose stiffly to his feet, and turned toward the library parking lot where Jeff sat listening to the car radio. Jeff seemed surprised to see him.

"Hi! How'd you know I was here?"

"Where else would you be?" Peter shrugged. "And incidentally that runs down the battery." Jeff switched off the rock station. Halloran did not pursue the matter. But Jeff's idle question had a point. How did he know? Had he just forgotten about Jeff? Not at all. When Halloran got up from the grass with his book, he knew damned well that Jeff was sitting in a car he couldn't even see and that Jeff was listening to a Top Forty station.

"Dad?"

"Uh-huh?"

"Do you think you and Mom will get a divorce?" Jeff asked, turning in his seat to look at Peter.

"I have no such plan, if that's what you're asking. Why? You been worried about it?"

"Sometimes. But other times I wonder why you put up with so much shit from her."

"Because my choices, trashmouth, are to put up with it, work to make it better which I don't do anymore, get professional help which your mother won't do at all, or to divorce her. Divorcing her means divorcing you."

"I'm fourteen, Dad. I get to choose," he said soberly.

"You're saying you'd choose me?"

"On your worst day."

Halloran reached over and squeezed Jeff's shoulder. "It's not that simple. The law doesn't really say you get a choice. What it says is that the judge has to consider your wishes. He can still rule any damn way he pleases." Halloran could imagine the job Barbara would try to do on him in a divorce court.

"She says you're unstable," Jeff said, as if reading his mind.

"She said that to you?"

"Among other things. She said there's something wrong with a grown man who's afraid of a railroad station."

"She's a peach. Anyway, what do you think?"

"I think you've had some very heavy stuff on your mind ever since you were in the hospital and you're keeping it too private.

You can talk to me if you want. And as far as the railroad station is concerned, Dan Doscher's father won't go there anymore either. He uses the Old Greenwich Station now."

Halloran felt his mouth go dry. He had to bite his lip to keep from asking whether Carl Doscher had seen anything down there.

"Did he say why?" he asked instead.

"He just doesn't like the people at the Riverside Station."

"Yeah, but why not? They won't be any different from the commuters who get on at Old Greenwich. It's all the same town. If he doesn't like some of the regulars on one train, why wouldn't he just take a different train?"

"Who knows?" Jeff answered. "If you don't like the station, why can't other guys not like the station?"

Halloran ignored his son's question. "Jeff, this might be important to me." He paused, choosing his words. "Please tell me all you can remember about your conversation with Dan, including how the subject came up."

"There's not that much. We were going by on our bikes and Dan said that place gives his father the creeps. He said the people were acting funny and the last two times he was there, someone tried to pick a fight with him over some dumb little thing."

"How dumb?"

"Like standing in another guy's space on the platform."

"That's ridiculous."

"But that's what he said. So his father figures who needs that kind of heat because he only goes into New York a couple of times a week anyway and he changed to Old Greenwich."

"His dad's not a regular commuter?"

"No, he sells insurance. He works mostly from his house."

Halloran was relieved and troubled at the same time. He was relieved because he'd come to the welcome conclusion that Carl Doscher had probably seen nothing. That meant he needn't agonize over whether to approach him with a question that would have made him sound like a nut no matter how it was worded. Still, he was not able to dismiss the incident as an isolated case of either rudeness or oversensitivity. Not yet, anyway.

Halloran hesitated at the corner of his street, then switched off the turn signal and pointed the car toward the Riverside Station. Jeff glanced at him but said nothing as the car climbed the short hill to the overpass and proceeded to the parking lot on the station side of the tracks. The station was closed as on any weekend. Less than a dozen parked cars dotted the large lot. Why had he come here? On the chance that he'd see Marty Kornhauser again? Or that he'd see something, anything, that had somehow changed? There was nothing at all. Just an old red wooden station like twenty others on the line. Window boxes with flowers planted by a women's club. He'd half expected the flowers to be dead. Geraniums. Blooming and healthy.

Halloran stepped from his car, Jeff following, and climbed the raised platform. Still nothing. No headache. No vibrations. Just a dog sitting on the track bed chewing a piece of old meat. And a man watching him from the trestle. Hold it, Peter. How did you just know that? You haven't looked up. You haven't seen anybody. But you know a white-haired man in a blue shirt and tan ducks is watching you. Why don't you look up? If he's not there, then you'll know that whatever is happening is happening inside your head, won't you? Peter kept his eyes on the tracks. I'm not going to look up. If he's there, I won't like it and if he's not there, I won't like that either.

Anyway, what's that on the tracks? More meat? Yes, it is. Not quite dried out. And there's some more. Six, seven, eight pieces and a couple of bones spaced out along the track bed. What the hell is this? Somebody had to have put them there. To attract dogs? Is it possible that someone around here is so fucking weird that he's baiting the railroad tracks to get dogs cut in half?—*Yes, Peter, she's saying.* Who's saying? Is that Peggy? Peter spun around. Nothing. Just Jeffrey watching the dog. But there's the man on the trestle. White hair and blue shirt. You can't see his pants from here. Now, he's ducking back. Peter checked an urge to run up the trestle stairs after the man. He could hear the man's quick-paced footsteps moving away, now breaking into a jog. No, a run. That old guy is running away.

—*Let him go, Peter.* —*Peggy? Is that you?* —*Let him go, Peter. He's one of them. They don't want you here. Did you see what they wrote on the wall, Peter? Look behind you.* —*No. I'm not going to look. I know there's something written there. I must have seen it before. If I read it now, I'll think you told me and I don't think you're really there, Peggy.* —*What does it say, Peter?* —*I don't know and I'm not going to look.* —*Peter, it says* THIS IS OUR PLACE. *See for yourself.* —*No. I must have seen it before and forgot. I'm only going to look at the tracks until I get back to my car and get the hell out of here.* —*Peter, it's alright. Look at the tracks. Look at that beer can. The one bent in half. Do you see it? I can make it move. Mr. Hicks taught*

PLATFORMS

*me how. If I make the beer can move, will you turn around and
read what's on the wall, Peter?   —Yes. Wait. Can Jeff watch?*
—Yes, Peter. But hurry.   —Who's Mr. Hicks?   —Hurry, Peter.
"Jeff!"

"Yeah?" The boy strolled the few yards to where his father was
standing.

"Do you see that beer can?"

"The Budweiser? What about it?"

"Watch it and see if it moves."

"Why . . . ?"

"Just watch it."

"Hey! How'd you do that?"

The can lay on the ballast with both ends facing slightly up.
It was turning. Only a fraction at first. Then an inch, then a more
violent twist that spun it fully on its axis. The dog's ears lifted
and he slowly backed away.

—Peggy? He could feel her moving farther away.   *—Peggy?*
The pain was there again. He hadn't noticed. Except now it was
draining. Fading.   *—Peggy?   —They don't want you here,
Peter.* He could barely hear her now.   *—Who doesn't? You mean
dead people?   —No, Peter. Not us. Help us. But not here. They'll
kill you, Peter.*

From the shadows of a stand of junipers facing the eastbound
side of the tracks, Alex Makepeace could see two frightened men.
The one with the boy, moving dazedly along the station platform.
And the older man from the trestle who had just gone by. He
would follow the one who was running. The tormented and terrified
man who whimpered as he ran.

36

4

Tentacles

Leticia Browning gestured toward the hors d'oeuvre tray being offered by her housekeeper, who approached the small group in a new-looking white smock.

"Please, everybody, try some of Martha's chutney with cream cheese. She's the best cook in Greenwich. The best seafood cook in New England, by the way."

Mordicai Bloomer nodded appreciatively and spread a small amount on a Melba Round which he passed to Barbara Halloran. Ira Zalman took two for himself while Bloomer waited his turn. Martha made a face.

"Absolutely the best I've ever had," chirped Barbara after swallowing a tiny corner of the Melba Round. Martha turned back toward the kitchen, silently mimicking Barbara's remark as she went.

"I vault to the conclusion," said Zalman, still chewing, "that we are to be treated to one of Martha's seafood delights this very evening."

"We are to be treated, Doctor," Leticia smiled. "You are to be corrupted. We are to dine on the forbidden crustacean. Lobster. Steamed, not boiled. Right out here on the lawn under the eyes of God. To be proceeded by equally forbidden mounds of steamed clams dipped from their own broth into tubs of melted lemon butter. Or you can knock off the cream cheese chutney if you prefer."

"It sounds divine to me," said Barbara, who didn't mind lobster bisque or salad but considered the consumption of the entire creature to be barbarically indecorous. "Don't you enjoy lobster, Doctor?"

"Leticia was alluding to my religious proscriptions, Mrs. Halloran," he answered pleasantly. "However, she knows perfectly well that I'm an apostate in matters gustatorial." Barbara smiled at him blankly. "In short," he explained, "I'll eat the stuff."

"I'm glad," said Barbara vaguely. "Such a lovely setting for a shore dinner."

"Having a shore and all, you mean," observed Bloomer helpfully.

"Exactly. All it needs is a setting sun and a string quartet playing softly in the background. Something by Vivaldi. 'The Four Seasons,' perhaps. Especially the winter part. It has a cooling sound."

"I've got some Jethro Tull records in the house," Leticia replied dryly. "He's as cooling as we get around here. I can practically guarantee a setting sun, though."

Mordicai Bloomer looked appraisingly at Barbara. Nice body. No more than thirty-five. Blond hair, a bit overworked but probably natural. Yacht club tan. Eager to impress. Eager to please. Probably a pushover for simpatico cocks of good family. Well worth a shot. As long as he screwed her someplace where there was a television set or reading matter. Good tits but exquisitely boring. Bloomer never appraised himself. There was no need. That he was not a handsome man was irrelevant. His graying hair was tightly curled and seldom combed or brushed. His eyes deep and sad although there was no sadness behind them. His body of slightly more than medium height and powerfully built by nature. A tenured Professor of Anthropology for four years now. Well published. A Department Chair might be his in another five or less. But probably not. To Mordicai Bloomer, tenure meant the freedom and the security to pursue those avocations which drove him with greater force than did his academic concentration. One was his pursuit of women. Almost any women. Wives and daughters of his colleagues, students, women in airplanes, restaurants, laundromats or offices. Bloomer considered that he had an instinct, perhaps a gift, for spotting those women who searched without goals. For knowing the moment of their deepest vulnerability. To these women, he felt that he provided a wholesome service. For Bloomer undertook no affairs, no romantic involvements. There was rarely a second encounter and almost never a third. An uncomplicated and transient outlet for the yearnings of women. An adventure free from guilt or fear. Bloomer contented himself that he gave as good as he got. Much better than being in love. Women never seemed to want him when he loved them. Then they seemed to want to break his heart. One, anyway. Jennifer. He would never lose control like that again.

His second avocation, his passion really, involved another gift. Mordicai was a sensitive. A medium. He'd known it since he was twenty but suspected it long before. The teenage Bloomer would sit with pencil poised over paper and at odd times his hand would begin to write. His mind would drift and his arm would sleep and his hand would scribble furiously across the page. No punctuation. No capitalization. Just a stream of letters that were sometimes jibberish, sometimes coherent, occasionally in languages other than English. There were names, phrases, simple messages. But nothing especially dramatic or even actionable. *"george's boxes are with his aunt"* was an early message he remembered. He didn't know a George with missing boxes. There was never a related message. But there were dozens over time that were equally cryptic. Bloomer knew that he was intercepting psychic communications. He felt sure that they were not necessarily meant for him and by no means necessarily coming from any other world but his own. Nor did it occur to him that he might be able to send as well as receive.

One day during his junior year at Princeton, Bloomer's roommate entered their dormitory carrying a small stack of obscure and antique books which he'd borrowed from the university library. Another student opened the door and announced a phone call for the roommate who then placed his books on Bloomer's side of the study table and quickly walked out. All at once, Bloomer found himself to be inordinately distracted by the cracked old volumes. He tried without success to return his concentration to the anthropology text in front of him. He was becoming irritated. Why couldn't Keating keep his goddamned books on his own side? But after a moment's reflection, his own annoyance puzzled him. As a rule, he'd never had any territorial feelings about his side of the table. Not even about his side of the room, for that matter. And who was Nigel Soames? There it was. His right hand had just written the name across his notebook. Bloomer watched his hand move again.

"smallredbook"

He reached for the thin dyed leather volume and slid it out of the pile.

"thereisnosuch thingasdeath in naturenothingdiesfromeach-sadremnantofdecay someformsof lifearise"

Feeling flooded back into Mordicai's hand. Now what? What was I supposed to do with that? Bloomer turned to the index. Nothing. No mention of a Soames. On an impulse, he picked up his pencil and wrote, "So what?" He had barely dotted the question mark when his hand whipped like the carriage of a typewriter to the line below.

"pagethirtyfourrightcolumn"

Bloomer found the text. "There is no such thing as death," etc. . . . He picked up the pencil again.

"It says here Charles Mackay wrote that."

"theprigfilchedit"

Bloomer was both fascinated and amused. He was reasonably sure he'd never heard of Charles Mackay or the quotation before him. Certainly, he'd never heard of Nigel Soames. Maybe he was inventing him. For all those doubts, he was absolutely sure that he had never before laid eyes on the dark red book. How could he know that quatrain, let alone the page it was on?

"Bullshit!" Bloomer wrote.

"tobeexpectedfromvulgarcarnaltwit"

"Fuck you! Anyway, let me ask Mackay."

"cantnothere"

"Where's here?"

"secondlevelthird afteryourlevel"

"Are you dead?"

"nodeathjusttoldyou"

"I don't understand."

"cannotyetboytwit"

"Then why are you talking to me?"

"available"

"Does that mean I'm the only game in town?"

"uncouthphrasingaccurate hardlypreferredchoice"

"Why are you talking at all? To anyone."

"becauseican"

"Okay. What'll we talk about?"

"latergoingnow"

"Wait. Please don't go yet."

"busy"

Weeks went by before Bloomer talked to Nigel Soames again. His grades fell. Weeks in which he read and reread the scribblings in his notebook and struggled to convince himself that the exchange or contact had really happened. Gradually though, the contacts became more regular. Nigel began using Bloomer as a conduit for messages to the living from friends and relatives who had died. Some of these Bloomer chose not to pass on. He simply could not bring himself to risk the disbelief or suspicion or anger of the bereaved. Nigel, he learned, was fully capable of being rude, patronizing and deliberately insulting. So much for the concept of a saintly and tranquil spirit world. His questions on the nature of that world were routinely brushed off but over the years a picture emerged. It was a physical place of several different levels, something like the undergraduate and graduate sides of a university. One moved on according to spiritual growth. The lowest level, the one after physical death, and perhaps even the lowest three levels, were very much like earth. The spirits there had bodies, although of a substantially different density than the earthly bodies they resembled. They ate food if they chose to but there was no need. Mordicai didn't understand that, although Nigel once said that no eating was done for pleasure. They lived in houses if they chose but most did not. Their bodies could transport at will over great distances in an instant. There was, according to Nigel, earthly clothing and even sex "for those who needed them to make the transition easier." Nigel chided Bloomer brutally for asking such a *"cloddish but predictably prurient question."*

As Bloomer worked toward his doctorate, he applied himself with equal vigor to his study of the paranormal, concentrating on those disciplines which had to do with the survival of the human spirit. Cautiously, he began to make himself known throughout the semi-underground world of the spiritualist fraternity, a step that was professionally risky but otherwise immensely valuable to him in his avocation. An association with other reliable mediums meant that experiments in cross-correspondence were possible, the practice in which two or more mediums would receive the same message or separate parts of the same message. Subsequent checking of witnessed and verified notes would result in a message that was relatively untainted by the subconscious mind of the medium. Bloomer quickly rose to a position of eminence within the fraternity. He was, after all, an accomplished scholar who was well respected and had a fairly reliable spirit contact in Nigel. Moreover, his scholarship in both anthropology and parapsychology produced a symbiotic sort of relationship between the two. The study of man's development and the study of his spirit's development were entirely natural partners and mutually helpful in providing behavioral insights. In his world, he was known as Bloomer of Princeton, spoken with the same deference as Des Jardins of Rouen, or Lady Edith Pierce of Kensington or Hommada of Tokyo. These names, and his, yielded in luster only to Chicago, the name by which Jennifer Wilde chose to be known. For although each was more scholarly, more experienced, and although each could communicate consciously with one or more spirits while Jennifer could not consciously communicate with any without a control, Jennifer had a gift for which they would give all they owned or would possess. Jennifer could go there. For many minutes at a time, she could go there and rest there. She could draw her spirit from her body as one would draw a handkerchief from a jacket pocket and she could send it there.

But for Lake Forest, he would not have met her. It was Jennifer who found the key. Jennifer or the spirit who spoke through her. Many lives had been saved. Not all, but many. Many spirits had been freed. Not like Amersham. Not like the period of mounting madness that ended with a mass suicide of forty-one travelers ground into one long ragged mound of torn cloth and meat under the wheels of a train and cooking against the third rail for a quarter hour until the power could be shut off. Now, more than sixty years later, according to Lictor, fourteen of the precious spirits had still not been found. No spirit was lost at Lake Forest. Only lives. Thanks to Jennifer. Only one lost spirit, perhaps. A part of his. Lost to Jennifer. Oh, how he adored her.

Ira Zalman rejoined the group carrying a fresh drink and a slab of cheddar between two stoned-wheat thins.

"Mordicai, I understand we might attempt to explore the nether regions tonight. I hope so. I'm very eager to see how you operate."

"I'm afraid I don't do party tricks, Doctor," he said, a bit testily. "Or weddings or supermarket openings." Thinking about Jennifer had altered his cocktail party mood.

"I didn't mean it that way," said Zalman more soberly. "And I'll call you Dr. Bloomer if you'd like, but I'd like you to call me Ira."

"Mordicai's fine," he relented, "and no offense taken. I know

42

how Leticia likes to cast her social gatherings. I assumed you must be the guest skeptic."

"Not at all," Zalman protested. "What I am is a short Jewish psychiatrist. That's roughly the extent of what I know with any degree of certainty. I'm not even sure enough about anything to be an agnostic."

"An agnostic?" Barbara asked. "Isn't that someone who doesn't believe God can be understood?"

"Almost," Bloomer answered. "What I think Ira's saying is that he's not even sure enough to be sure he can't know something. Ergo, he's not an agnostic."

"If this party has been cast, by the way," asked Barbara, "what's my part?"

"The temptress, I'd guess," said Bloomer, turning to look deeply into her eyes. "The sex goddess. Lovely. Alluring. Untouchable."

Barbara felt her stomach leap.

"Who are your people, Mr. Bloomer?" she asked, her eyes beginning to shine.

"It's Mordicai," he replied. "And my people are the Bloomers of Boston." Which meant not a goddamned thing other than that his folks had lived in a Boston apartment when he was born but if she wants it she can have it.

"Oh yes. I believe I know of them."

"May I call you Barbara?"

"I'd like that."

"Speaking of God, Mordicai," Leticia asked, "what do your spirits have to say about Him. Or Her."

"Actually very little. I've never heard of a spirit contact, which I consider legitimate, in which a reference was made to a specific deity. Only a more general reference to a creative intelligence which, I suppose, can be any god you want it to be."

"How can you resist asking?"

"We do ask. They don't answer. I've had the feeling that they consider the subject so far above our grasp that they don't even bother trying to explain. I've also become convinced that the recently dead, say six months or so, don't understand any more about that than I do."

"A creative intelligence!" mused Zalman. "It sounds like the Schopenhauer view of God. A Chairman of the Board type who keeps order in the universe but takes no interest in the individual soul. If I'm inclined toward any view myself, it's that one."

"I suspect Schopenhauer has since changed his mind. The man was a grump. In the other world as I understand it, a human soul is a treasure, valued more highly than you'd value a newborn child."

"What about this reincarnation nonsense?" asked Barbara. "I imagine you rule it out."

"Not at all. From what I understand, some spirits are very definitely reincarnated."

"Really?" asked Zalman. "How do you reconcile that with the concept of the spiritual graduate school that you've described in some of your articles?"

"I'm flattered that you've read them."

"Don't be. As I've said, there's a lot I don't know about."

"In any case," Bloomer continued, "I don't see any inconsistency at all. Think of the earth as a borning place for the individual spirit, the individual personality. Think of the afterlife as a refinery or, if you wish, a grad school. But what of the spirits that cannot develop sufficient individuality on earth to be able to progress? Dead children. Mental defectives. Genetic accidents. Lifelong emotional disturbances including some criminals and congenital moral bankrupts. These are all accidents. And these are the reincarnated. Sent through the mill again and again until they develop satisfactorily."

"Absolutely fascinating," Barbara breathed.

"Absolutely heretical by most lights," said Zalman.

"What lights?" Bloomer asked. "You mean organized religion? Where's the conflict with any of the big three?"

"Well, for openers, you've denied the concept of eternal reward for faith and good works, not to mention suffering. That's sustained a lot of people for a lot of years. You're also saying that it doesn't matter how anyone behaves."

"On your last point, I'm not saying that at all. How you behave, or more accurately, how you grow, determines whether you're reincarnated or whether you enter at either of several levels. The lowest level is not an entirely blissful experience. Catholics would call it Purgatory. But the people at that level experience a far greater feeling of contentment and peace than is possible on the earth plane because they at least know where they're eventually going.

"On your first point, all I've done is clarified the nature of the afterlife by talking to people who live there. I know that's hard to accept but look at the overall picture in a purely rational way.

Assume for the moment that you knew nothing of religious dogma. I come and I paint two pictures for you. Picture number one. You live a good live with lots of prayer, self-denial and regular attendance at the right church. You die, you're judged, and if you pass you get to spend eternity being blissfully happy in the presence of some Michelangelo God all for a few lousy years of behaving yourself on earth. In effect, you're happily sitting on your can forever and it doesn't bother you one bit that a few people you love dearly on earth didn't pass muster. Those people, perhaps your father or your son, are spending a few billion years being tortured in hell. Again, for those few lousy years on earth. Even for a single unregretted act.

"Scenario number two. You're created, born, you grow and you do the best you can. You die and you are not judged. You are only made to understand your life as it was and as it will yet be. You are reunited with those you love at that point in time. Those with whom you have an existing spiritual affinity. They and others help you. They teach you. You feel enormous peace but you are also challenged. You have a reason for having existed and it is still ahead of you. You can and will grow and there will be no limit to your growth. The best you ever wanted to be multiplied a millionfold. Putting dogma aside, Ira, which would you choose?"

"The one where I can't lose."

Mordicai Bloomer regretted having preached. He'd come to know the signs. Subdued conversation. Forced gaiety. Thoughtful or self-conscious silences. But Martha's lobsters rescued him. No one can eat a lobster without talking about it. The merits of broiling versus boiling versus steaming. The effeteness of Lobster Thermidors and Lobster Newburgs. Atlantic lobsters versus the clawless Florida or California varieties. Did you know that a twenty pound lobster is a hundred years old? Really! Or that he takes six years to reach his one pound legal weight? Shocking prices! Bad enough here. Thirty dollars in many New York City restaurants. Once were so cheap that farmers used them for fertilizer. You can eat that green stuff. That's the liver. The red stuff means it's a female. That's the roe. Eat that too. They're both considered a delicacy. See how small that roe is? Lobsters are born the size of a mosquito. At least we know where lobsters go when they die. Ooops. Sorry, Mordicai. Do dogs get to go to . . . No, I'm not going to ask. You have to suck the meat out of the legs, Barbara. Here, let me help you with that.

When Martha finally began clearing the table for dessert, Leticia excused herself and escorted Barbara to the bathroom. Ira Zalman sat thoughtfully across from Mordicai, idly pushing his lemon slice around the finger bowl.

"Mind if I ask you something?" he asked finally.

"Shoot."

"What do you know about ghosts?"

"You mean like in haunted houses? Practically nothing. Not my area."

"How about apparitions? Hallucinatory or otherwise. Particularly the same apparition to two or more persons at different times."

"What've you got?"

"Probably nothing. In the past six months I've had two different patients. One a regular, the other a one-shot after he suffered a head injury. The head injury thought he saw two people who could not have been there when he got hurt. The other man has been troubled by dreams in which he says he saw two people. Both sets match. I don't think the two men know each other."

"Beats me," Bloomer shrugged. "How'd the guy get hurt?"

"A freak accident at the railroad station."

"That's where he saw ghosts?"

"Or whatever."

"The other guy saw them at the railroad station too?"

"No. In his house, I guess. He said they woke him up."

"Where's his house?"

"Right by the railroad station."

Mordicai Bloomer felt himself grow cold.

He barely touched Martha's cheesecake and strawberries. Or the brandy afterward. Better to keep the mind clear. Shouldn't have had those two drinks. Or the heavy food, for that matter. This was ridiculous. That's one of the problems with being a medium. You tend to think that every ordinary human fear is an intuition of some sort. Those guys at the railroad station just struck a nerve, that's all. No harm in two drinks. He came here for dinner, some historical or literary chitchat with Leticia, and his price of admission was to bullshit with skeptics like Zalman or birdbrains like the Halloran dame and maybe take a stab at making a contact if his mood was right and Nigel felt like answering the phone. Still, he was anxious to get on with it. He'd go through the motions of trying to find out about some dead Wentworths. Leticia would doubtless have prepared a list of questions for him to ask depending on whatever chapter she'd decided to write. If there's trouble, Nigel will brush off the questions and get down to cases. He might brush them off anyway. Nigel doesn't like parlor games either. You have to catch him in the right mood. Besides, we're going to try a séance first. Not really my kind of act but Leticia expects it. Séances are better show biz than automatic writing. More social. People get to sit around a table and hold hands and feel scary. Automatic writing contacts can be made sitting on the pot.

Bloomer excused himself from the table to go inside and set up the living room while Leticia arose to assist Martha in clearing away plates. Ira Zalman found himself sitting alone with Barbara, who was looking thoughtfully in the direction Mordicai had gone.

"Haven't had a chance to ask you, Barbara," he said, with a sip of his Benedictine. "How's Peter been doing?"

"Hmmm?" Barbara snapped out of her reverie. "Oh, Peter. About as well as I'd expect, I suppose."

"I gather he's having trouble getting back into his routine."

"An understatement, Ira. But then, Peter's always had trouble with routines. Or with responsibilities other men take for granted."

Zalman's eyebrow lifted. "That surprises me. Peter certainly struck me as a level-headed and responsible man. Quite an interesting man, too. A great many accomplishments. Athletic. Quite personable, at least before his accident."

"Responsible men are not afraid of railroad stations. Nor do they limit their social contacts to fourteen-year-old sons. As for Peter's accomplishments, I assume you're not referring to his mediocre and now tenuous career in advertising. Other men own advertising agencies by his age."

"I guess some do, yes."

"As for his past accomplishments, Peter should learn for his own good that he can't bask forever in the glory of being named to the All-East team as offensive left end. That was twenty years ago. They don't even have left ends anymore as he himself has ruefully noted. Now it's tight ends and wide receivers. That's the story of Peter's life. Brief flickers of glory. A trophy for this. A trophy for that. Pathetically unaware that no one but he would remember or care the following morning. His life has shown neither purpose nor dedication nor meaningful recognition. Like Mordicai's, for example. And your's too."

"I had a great deal of help from my parents. They were both doctors. Bloomer's father was a field archaeologist. I understand Peter's parents died when he was quite young. If that had happened in my case, it's doubtful that I'd be a psychiatrist. But, of course,

I also had an enormous amount of support from Natalie, that marvelous lady who married me."

I wonder, thought Zalman, whether I might possibly be getting through to her.

God, he's so Jewish, thought Barbara. What about Bloomer, come to think of it. No. That couldn't be Jewish. Not Beacon Hill Boston and a Princeton Professor.

"You know," he continued, "just last night we were going out to a formal affair and I was at the mirror fixing my black tie. Natalie looked over at me and said, 'You do that just like Cary Grant.' Now, I know I'm not Cary Grant. As I said earlier, what I am is a short Jewish psychiatrist. But it was very nice. It put a smile on my face that lasted the whole evening." There he goes again, thought Barbara.

Zalman saw her eyes flick behind him followed by the switching on of a soft smile. Who's approaching? he wondered. Mordicai or Leticia? It was Leticia.

"Mordicai's all set, people. Shall we go inside?"

"What are we supposed to do?"

"He'll explain. He enjoys explaining."

Bloomer was already seated at an oversize card table. At his right hand was a legal pad and pencil. In the center of the table was a small Swedish ivy. Ringing the table, perhaps eight feet back, were a series of burning candles. Directly in front of him sat an empty glass and a can of Fresca. Bloomer motioned the others toward their seats.

"Now," he began, "there will be absolutely nothing frightening about this. There's no reason for any nervousness. Most of us have prayed from time to time. We have prayed to something insubstantial. If a person answered you directly, you'd probably faint, even though you were, after all, looking for such a contact. That's essentially what we're going to do tonight. We're going to pray, and we're going to try to get an answer."

"Shall I assume," asked Zalman, "that the candles have a non-theatrical purpose?"

"Yes, you shall. The candles and this ivy plant as well. The candles are to help me locate any spirits that might join us. A spirit, remember, is not entirely insubstantial. It has weight and therefore density. As a doctor, you know that a human being will unaccountably lose several ounces of body weight at the instant of physical death. We believe this weight to be the soul, or spirit. It has sufficient physical density, or strength if you will, to cause a candle flame to flicker or to cause the leaves of this little plant to rise. Some have enough strength to move heavier articles, even pieces of furniture, or rap on tables, that sort of thing. But not all. Not even most. Lighter objects improve our chances, and their's, of making contact."

"Is it particularly thirsty work?"

"You mean the Fresca? No," he answered, pulling at the tab. "It's just a trick someone taught me as an aid in concentrating. I look deeply into the bubbles and try to lose myself in them. A crystal ball will do just as well, but they're expensive and such devices tend to put people off. It works. Try it sometime, Doctor, whenever you have cause to reflect deeply, or consider a problem in your practice or your daily life. You'll be surprised."

Bloomer poured the Fresca. *You're talking more than normal, my friend. And faster than normal. What's chewing at you? Settle down now.*

"One last thing and we'll start. Leticia wants to try to reach the first John Wentworth or, failing that, any of the Meads of the Revolutionary period. I can reach a spirit. I might even reach a spirit who says he's Wentworth or Mead. What I can't do is guarantee that the entity will actually be Wentworth or Mead, barring the revelation by them of some verifiable fact."

"The spirits lie?" Barbara asked.

"The spirits humor us, Barbara. You are to the spirits what somebody's three-year-old, not-particularly-lovable child is to you."

Bloomer ignored the face Barbara made. The bubbles were slowing now. Rising more gracefully through the clear liquid. He focused on the bottom of the glass where the tiny silver spheres came into being and quivered there, trying to burst their bonds. Wrenching themselves from the smooth glass and then swimming more languidly away and upward. Fooling Bloomer. One escaping while he watched another. He slid his left hand slowly into Zalman's right and Zalman in turn took Leticia's right hand and so on through Barbara until the circle was completed. Barbara's hand was dry and cold. He felt a blankness in her. Like a corpse. Unusual. Zalman's hand was warm and loving. Like a hug. He felt weight on Zalman. Weight easily borne and borne well. *So that's what a psychiatrist feels like. The weight must be the problems of his patients. One weight is greater than the others. Barbara. No, not Barbara. Him. Who is him? Him is someone close to Barbara. Him is afraid of railroad stations. Railroad stations again.*

What's going on? Jennifer would know. Easier for Jennifer. Jennifer can see auras. Jennifer. Spirits here. More than one. Several. Zalman pulling. He sees the candles. Flames swaying, not flickering. Bubbles let go in one great rush. Ivy leaves fly up with them. Same time. Who's here.

"There are several spirits. They seem confused. They can't . . . I don't think they chose to come here. Two women . . . many men. Can you move the leaves? If you can, move them upward. That's good . . . one of the women can move the leaves. Can you move just one side of the leaves? The side on my left? Good. The side on my right? Good. I will ask questions. If the answer is Yes, move the side on my left. If the answer is No, move the side on my right. Are there any Wentworths among you? No. Thank you. Are there any Meads among you? No. Thank you again. Did you know the Meads? No. Thank you. Do you know the Wentworths? Can you answer? Do you know the Wentworths? Yes. No. Yes and no? Does that mean some of you do and some of you don't? Yes. Do any of you know John Wentworth? No. Are any of you from the time of John Wentworth? No. Have any of you lived in the time of the Meads? Can't you answer that? No. Do you know who the Meads are? No. Yes. Wait. Do you know who the Meads were? Yes. Did you live before my lifetime? Sorry. Did you die before my lifetime? No. None of you? No. Are you troubled? Yes. Aren't the other spirits helping you? No. Are you with all the other spirits? No."

Bloomer was on the edge of panic. This had only happened once before. Or twice. He was now struggling to control himself. If only he were alone. What way is there to ask the question here? Finally, in anguish, he blurted it out.

"Did you die around the railroad station?"

All the leaves whipped up with a sudden shocking force. The candles blinked out. A phone rang. Bloomer looked furiously toward the kitchen where Martha rushed away from the open door.

"Can you answer that question?" Once more all the leaves shook violently. "Is someone else there? Yes. Is it Nigel? No. Do you know Nigel? Yes. Can I speak to Nigel? Yes."

Bloomer snatched up his pencil.

"Nigel?" he asked, as he moved the pencil to the legal pad. It began twisting in his hand even before the point touched paper.

"yesnigel"

"Who else is there?"

"lictor"

"Lictor?" he asked aloud. Why would Lictor talk to him? Why now?

"Has something happened to Jennifer?" he scrawled.

"*nojenniferwellictorangrysaysdontwastetimeonnonsense dontwastetimeonwentworthsnonehere alltherebackagainnotready-notwentworthseither underhills*"

"Who were all those spirits?"

"*dontknow*"

Bloomer stared at the reply for a moment. How the hell could he not know? He's right there. The hand moved again.

"*anticipate question iamhere lictorishere they-werenotherereachedyoufrom station stuckthere cannotseethem-therecannotreachthemthere*"

Oh, shit! The railroad station. It's Lake Forest again alright. But different.

"Don't understand. They were here. They reached here. Why can't they reach you?"

"*spiritsfollowedpath underhillpath lictorsaysthinkofstationas-octopus spreadstentacles fivesofar tentaclesarepaths thispathtoun-derhill otherpathstobornagainslikeunderhill spiritsfollowedthis-path underhillpath lictornigelcantgoinpath getstucklost gotojennifer jenniferknows hallorancanhelp hallorancan seethem going now*"

"Wait. Still don't understand."

"*halloranjennifer*"

No one spoke for several minutes. Leticia was the first to rise from her chair. She rounded the table and stood quietly at Mordicai's shoulder, her eyes straining to read the wild scrawl. Fantastic. First Mordicai's handwriting, then this new one. Completely different. Written in Spencerian script with little Victorian flourishes. The name Underhill leaped at her. There again. Underhill. Underhill. Underhill path. No such place. What did that say? Not Wentworths either. Underhills. My God! The Wentworths are the Underhills after all.

"Barbara," he croaked at last, "did you see anyone?"

"Who?" came her small voice.

"Anyone or anything."

"Only the leaves. And the candles."

"Who is Underhill? Do you know?"

"I don't believe so." It was true. She'd never heard the name. She knew only that the Wentworths were related somehow to the Van Damms of New Amsterdam and that they had sprung from the ancient Van Damm family of Amstelhuis. Leticia Browning said nothing. She had found a better subject for her next novel.

Martha stood transfixed in the kitchen doorway, terrified. The telephone call for Mordicai Bloomer had slipped from her mind entirely.

"Barbara?" he asked softly. "Do you have to be anyplace tonight?"

"Well . . . yes. Home . . . eventually."

He reached into his pocket and drew out a motel key. Bloomer placed it firmly in her hand.

"I want you to go to my room and wait for me. I'll be along very shortly."

"But I can't . . ." She began to protest but he shut her off with a squeeze of her hand.

"I need you, Barbara." Barbara looked up at Leticia, who smiled and nodded her approval. Anything to get them out so she can get to her files and her tape recorder. Barbara closed her hand over the key.

"Can't you come with me, Mordicai?"

"Soon, Barbara." He touched her cheek. "I have a call that I must make, and then I'd like to take a little walk with Dr. Zalman here."

5

Saturday Night

Jennifer sat cross-legged on her bed at the New Englander Motel, carefully scanning the two most recent issues of the Greenwich newspaper. She found nothing that struck a chord. No spate of violent behavior. No pattern, at least, of recent antisocial behavior such as developed in Lake Forest. An assault arrest in Greenwich proper and another in Cos Cob. Young people in both cases. Two arrests for criminal trespass. Five police radar citations, three minor collisions. Three stolen bikes and one stolen Moped. And one man arrested for tearing out his neighbor's tomato plants. Could Lictor possibly be wrong? Not likely. Could Alex have been mistaken? Still not likely, but possible. No, it isn't. Because, then, why would Mordicai be here? He must have gotten the same message through Nigel Soames. And, by the way, what was keeping Alex? It must be fifteen minutes since she felt him nearby. Oh. Here he comes.

The lock clicked and Alex pushed the door open with his foot. "Hi, beautiful," he grinned from the doorway, trying to balance a pizza that was sliding around inside a too large box and a liter bottle of wine in a paper bag.

"Oh, Alex!" she exclaimed delightedly. "How did you know? That's exactly what I've been craving for dinner."

"The spirits told me," he winked. "Not to mention Mario's neon sign. There's also a liquor store down the street that I reached just as they were locking the door."

"Here. Put it down on the newspaper." She spread out several thicknesses of *Greenwich Time* over the thin floral-patterned bed-spread.

"And incidentally, one does not dine on pizza. One goobers up on pizza. Pizza is not dinner. Any more than this horse piss is wine." He drew out the bottle and held it out from himself with two fingers. "Did you see what they've done to it? A screw-top bottle. No more cork. Not even the cheap crumbly thing that left a residue one could read like tea leaves. A screw-top bottle! The bastards aren't even pretending anymore. But it's cold."

"Alex, what happened to your eye?" she asked, pulling him forward into the lamplight. "Is that a bruise?"

"Stupid car door. Eat. Half pepperoni, half sausage."

Jennifer took a slice and ate it in silence. She then wiped her hands and face thoroughly before reaching for a second.

Alex watched in amusement. "Why don't you just shower between slices? Better yet, take the whole thing inside and eat it in the tub."

"You found something, didn't you?"

"A thing or two." Alex was no longer smiling. "Nothing peculiar in the papers?"

"No. What did you find? And how did you get that bruise?"

"The bruise is nothing. But it came from an aging fag named Ezra D. Cohen, who has a low threshold of pique and a sneak right-hand lead." Alex's face turned hard. "This town's in deep shit, Chicago."

He told her of his visit to the station and of the sign he saw. THIS IS OUR PLACE with OUR underlined three times. In Lake Forest it was YOU DON'T BELONG HERE. Close enough. He described the meat on the tracks. Two kinds. Possibly two different people with the same sick thought. That too had happened in Lake Forest, although it was dismissed at the time as an isolated symptom. He'd felt presences there. Many presences. He told her of the wide circle he'd made of the station, along streets and through yards and twice across the tracks, looking for paths leading from the station. He thought he'd crossed at least two but Jennifer would have to look tomorrow. Alex told of watching the two men who arrived as he completed his circle and of following the more frightened man to his house.

"I tried a bluff. I rang his bell and told him my name was Alex and I knew why he's frightened. I suggested that we sit and talk. Old Ezra went absolutely gray, shouted that I'm a goddamned liar, popped me in the eye and slammed the door."

"How do you know he was gay?"

"Because he wore a pink tutu and a ruby in his navel. Be serious, Jennifer."

"He lives near the station?"

"Within a hundred yards. Lives alone. Travels a lot. Has occasional roommates. I gave five dollars for that to a kid who was cutting grass. No real gossip, though."

"Did you get a chance to check the bookstores?"

"And the library. Same as Lake Forest. A sudden run on self-help books dealing with power and all forms of acquisition. All the me-first stuff. All how-to and sports books with the word 'winning' in the title. *Jonathan Livingston Seagull* is collecting dust and Thoreau can't be given away."

Jennifer had twisted her napkin into a dozen little folds as Alex spoke.

"Mordicai's here."

"Here in Riverside?"

"Uh-huh! I called Princeton and they gave me a number here. Leticia Browning, the historical novelist. I tried there and got the maid. She was very frightened, Alex. Something's happening over there. Halloran is with him."

"The maid told you that?"

"Before she hung up on me, yes. I asked if Mordicai was there. She said yes, but he can't talk now. On a hunch, I asked if there was a party named Halloran with him and she said yes, but they'll have to get back to me."

"Okay," he shrugged. "We'll wait for him to call."

"The maid didn't wait to take my number. I'm not sure she even got my name. But it may not matter. Mordicai's been here at the New Englander. I think he's coming back."

Alex studied Jennifer for a moment and picked up the phone.

"Mr. Bloomer's room, please. Mr. Mordicai Bloomer."

"No answer, sir."

He handed the phone to Jennifer.

"Ask for Bloomer's room number." Jennifer did so.

"I'm sorry ma'am. We can't give out room numbers."

"Thank you," said Jennifer, replacing the phone on its cradle.

"What room is he in?" Alex asked.

"Two-twelve," Jennifer answered, and closed the lid of the pizza box.

Peter Halloran had begun drinking at noon. Double bourbons without the usual water. There was no pretense that this was refreshment drinking or relaxing drinking. This was getting drunk drinking. If he dulled his brain, perhaps he would not go mad quite so quickly. He could slow things down. Take the edge off the fear. Think of something to do. Something. Anything. Burn down the fucking station.

The merit of that idea became increasingly evident as the afternoon wore on. He hated the place; it was made of wood; wood burned and he had gas cans in his garage. He would no longer have to drive blocks out of his way to avoid passing it. He would not have to look quickly away every time he saw a woman in a jogging suit or a businessman who looked like Marty. He'd seen Marty at least two more times that he was sure about. It was from a distance but Halloran was positive it was Kornhauser. Who else climbs out of parked cars that aren't there and strolls into the station leaving an empty parking place behind him? Halloran wasn't sure how many times he'd seen Peggy Bregman. He'd always looked away or turned around. Maybe that was why she decided to speak to him today. There was no mistaking the fat man in the bathrobe. Pointing at him in the parking lot, practically jumping up and down and pulling someone else by the arm. Maybe the black painter. Peter couldn't tell. All he saw was the arm not attached to anything. That was weeks ago. But he was there. Peter could feel them all.

There were three possibilities. He was crazy, or the place was haunted, or he was crazy *and* the place was haunted. If he was crazy, and he saw things he shouldn't see only around the station, perhaps he wouldn't see them anymore if there were no more station. If he wasn't crazy and the place was haunted, that might mean that dead people were trapped and he'd be doing them a favor by turning the station into a pile of charred boards. Trapped dead people or not, if he was crazy, it was only around the station. No station, no crazy. He couldn't lose. At least he didn't think so. Halloran would have another drink or two and try to think of a way he could lose.

By six o'clock, nothing had occurred to him. Halloran was also talking to himself. That was just as well, because he reminded himself that walking around with a red two-gallon gasoline can would be less than prudent. Soft-drink bottles would be much better. Molotov cocktails. Should be simple enough to make. A bottle, some gas and a piece of cloth for a wick. He found two bottles of Barbara's diet cola in the refrigerator. Less than one calorie per bottle. Good, she'll never miss it.

After dumping the contents into the sink and tearing up a pair of his shorts that he got from the laundry pile, Peter proceeded unsteadily to the garage. He filled the two bottles with gasoline, not bothering with the funnel that hung from a nail over the can, plugged each bottle with a strip of underwear, and placed them carefully inside a plastic garbage bag. By the time this process was completed, Peter had to change his shoes and trousers.

At nine o'clock, there was still no sign of Barbara. Jeff had long since retired to his room with a peanut butter sandwich and a bowl of popcorn and blocked out the world with the stereo headset he'd received on his last birthday. Barring a power failure, Peter did not expect that a short absence would be noticed. It would take him eight minutes to reach the station on foot. Perhaps ten, allowing for a little weaving. Better to leave the car at home in case his escape route turned out to be through somebody's azalea bushes.

Halloran began perspiring heavily from the moment he left his garage. What if someone sees him on the way down there? What if some damned dog starts barking? So what? He had every reason to be out for a walk near his own home. Yeah, but they might make a connection the next day when they find out the station was torched about the same time they saw him. The police might be around to question him. What if someone passed near enough to smell the gasoline? In that case, he'd give it up for this night and try again tomorrow. Okay, but what if someone smelled the gas on the way back? You can't have everything, Peter. Just get it done. Unless your head starts hurting. If that happens, it'll mean you're going to see them so you take off like your ass is on fire. Or maybe not. Maybe, if you can keep your nerve long enough, you ask them right out if they'd like you to burn the place down around them.

Sticking to the shadows wherever he could, and watching lighted windows for signs of movement, Halloran reached the station parking lot. He still had to cross the tracks to reach the station. The overpass was too risky. Too exposed. He remembered the older man with the blue shirt. He turned east and walked along the outlying bushes until he reached the end of the four-foot cyclone

PLATFORMS

fence that lined the track bed. It was darker there. Very little light
reached him from the low wattage platform lamps. A train was
coming. Shit! Holding the garbage bag in both hands to keep the
bottles from clinking, he hurried across the tracks before the powerful headlamp of the engine reached him. Breathing heavily, he
squatted beneath a sumac stand on the New York-bound side a
hundred yards above the station building. Passengers would be
getting off. He'd have to wait.

There were no more than a dozen. A lot, he thought, for a
Saturday night. One woman with a small child, both carrying
shopping bags. One kid with books under his arm. The rest all
men in business suits. Peter hoped they all had cars and that none
would have to call home and wait for a ride. The kid and the
woman with the little girl left the platform quickly. And two of
the men. A car started up. Then another. A third man approached
two others on the platform. Were they ignoring him? Peter couldn't
tell. The man stood there, looking embarrassed, confused, while
the other two ignored him. Abruptly, one of the two men turned
and shouted. ". . . out of here!" The single man hesitated, then
spun and stalked off, his head low and shaking from side to side.
Eight men, each wearing a dark suit and tie, now remained on the
platform. No two together now, they had put their briefcases down
randomly on the platform and were moving aimlessly about, each
in his own small area. What was that look on their faces? They
were almost smiling. Satisfaction! That's what it was. They were
basking! Some lifting their arms and stretching! Some with their
heads arched back. Like you'd do at an open window on a fresh
and sunny spring morning. My God, they were loving the place.
They didn't want to leave. Who was that on the end? Was that
Jack Gormley? It was getting hard to see. The lights were dimming.
Or was it Peter's eyes? No, it was the lights. A few moments ago,
he could read the Salem cigarette poster clearly. Now it was harder.
There must be a power surge when the train is near. The men on
the platform are stirring. They're breaking up. Oh-oh! Gormley
looks like he's going to cross the tracks. His car must be on this
side.

What was it about Gormley? Hadn't Polly Gormley complained
to him not long ago that Jack was becoming a workaholic? Sure
she did. Peter remembered wondering why. He had family money.
So did Polly, for that matter. Why was he suddenly breaking his
ass? He'd always struck Peter as a guy who enjoyed his home.
And especially his wife. And the town. That's right. Polly said

58

he dropped out of Boy Scouts and he stopped coaching the soccer instructional league and a few other activities that had always interested him in the past. Anyway, here he comes. Peter quietly made a knot in the plastic garbage bag and slid the package deeper into the brush, being careful to leave the bottle necks facing upward. He rose to his feet and turned toward the parking lot, hoping to look as if he'd left a car there. Gormley was less than fifty feet behind him.

The cold wall of air shocked Peter. The same that he'd felt the morning he'd first seen Marty Kornhauser. He threw up his hands as if to fend it off and braced for the searing pain that would soon be upon him. But no pain came. And his hands were warm. The cold wall was shallow. Perhaps only two feet deep. But it was wide. Stretching his arms to his sides, he could not feel the ends. It was moving. Flowing. Like an ocean current. It was not a wall. It was a stream. Halloran stepped through it and then turned to watch Jack Gormley's reaction.

Gormley felt nothing. If he did, he showed no sign of it. He was looking straight at Peter. And there was contempt in his expression.

"What are you doing here?" he asked roughly.

"Jack? It's Pete Halloran."

"You don't belong here. Get out of here." Gormley faced him, his hands balled into fists.

"Who the hell do you think you're talking to?" Peter flushed.

"I said get out of here." Jack Gormley placed his hand on Peter's chest and shoved. Peter fell backward, stunned and furious at the sudden violence. With great effort, he rolled sideways and tried to push himself to his feet. Too slow. Too much bourbon. What the hell was happening here? He felt a hand on his arm and another on the collar of his shirt. Pulling, half dragging him toward the service road that bordered the parking lot. He could not resist. It was all the struggle he could manage to keep his balance. Once there, Jack Gormley placed the flat of his hand against Peter's back and shoved him brutally onto the road. He fell heavily onto his hands and knees and then tumbled forward. Nearly helpless, Peter braced himself for the next assault. But none came. He twisted his body into a sitting position, and had to concentrate to focus his eyes. Gormley's back was to him now. Walking slowly, ambling, not to his car but back toward the westbound platform.

"You miserable bastard," thought Peter aloud, "you miserable sneaky bastard! I am going to come calling on you tomorrow and

I am going to tear your fucking head off for that. I'm going to be sober tomorrow and you are going to have a busted fucking jaw."

Gormley paid no further attention. He was absorbed now by something near the station. Halloran staggered to his feet and began stumbling up the service road toward the overpass, his face hot with shame and rage. He cursed his own cowardice for not at least taking the shorter route through the parking lot to the overpass stairs. He told himself that he was in no shape for a second encounter with Gormley. He would be tomorrow. By God, he would.

Another cold current. Moving. Wandering. Near the top of the service road. Peter stood for a moment within its flow, tempted briefly to follow it. That made no sense. He swam through it. The anger flooded back. Lurching forward, he crossed the overpass and stopped again on its southern end. More cold air. This is where he was when he saw Peggy Bregman. That first one! Wasn't that where he saw Marty getting out of his car? He wasn't sure. Again, he pushed on. A hundred yards up the hill toward his house, there was yet another. This was different. It felt the same but it felt different. It made him think of the old man in the blue shirt and the tan ducks. The hell with it. Gormley comes first. Oh God Almighty, was he going to clean his fucking clock. But for now, he would just follow his shadow home. Where the shadow was pointing him. In the lights of the car that was moving slowly behind him.

The car swung around as if to pass, then stopped a few yards ahead of Peter. He could see a dark figure reaching over to roll down the passenger-side window.

"Peter? Hi! Long time no see. Can I give you a ride home? Peter? Are you okay? Just a second. I'll give you a hand." The figure climbed from the car.

It was Jack Gormley.

Ira Zalman sipped his second cup of strong tea as he reread the words on Bloomer's legal pad. His flip manner was gone. He had seen and heard much that could not be explained, although he knew all too well how neatly he would have explained away the evening's events if he had not been there to witness them.

"Let's make sure I understand," he began, removing his glasses and turning his attention to Mordicai. "Nigel and Lictor are spirits who were once alive. Nigel is your spirit contact and Lictor is the regular contact of another medium named Jennifer or Chicago."

"She's much more than that, but yes."

"But at first you didn't reach them. You reached a group of other spirits, recently deceased or so they claim, who have somehow been overlooked. These spirits moved the candles and the plant. For the record, I do not suspect trickery. Then this writing began. Lictor, whose appearance to you evidently signals serious trouble, says there are no dead Wentworths. Is that correct?"

"In effect. Apparently, all the Wentworths of local history are the same handful of spirits who keep getting recycled until they get it right. None of them have made it beyond the second level on the other side."

"This," noted Zalman, "would be in accordance with the views you expressed earlier on reincarnation?"

"Yes."

"Then who are the Underhills?"

"No idea."

"But the overlooked spirits are stuck or lost around the station. And they got here by following some sort of path or tentacle called the Underhill path. There are five such paths leading to 'born-agains.' Wouldn't that suggest that our path led to Barbara Wentworth Halloran? Nigel seems to think that the name Wentworth was not honestly come by and that the Wentworths are actually Underhills."

"Where does it say that?" Mordicai turned the pad to face him.

"At the end of his first long sentence. 'All back there. Back again. Not ready. Not Wentworths either. Underhills.'"

"I suppose that's what it means. I'm not terribly interested in Barbara's roots. I'm interested in why they think she can help."

"Help what? To free the trapped spirits?"

"That's part of a much larger problem, but the answer is yes."

"I have reason to believe they might be talking about her husband. Ethically, I can't say any more."

"You mentioned two patients who hallucinated. I gather Barbara's husband is the head injury case."

"I'd suggest you confirm that through Barbara."

Mordicai Bloomer's fist slammed down hard, causing Zalman's teaspoon to leap off the saucer. "Goddammit, Doctor," he said, his face red, "either help me or say good night. You ask questions but you won't give answers unless presumably I ask for your professional or personal opinion. I don't need your opinion. I know what happened here. I know Lictor's existence to be a fact and I know there's big trouble. I don't care whether you believe it or not except to the extent that you can help. Your professional confidences are nothing compared to what can happen in this town. It's happened before and I was there to see it. I don't want to see it again."

Zalman watched Bloomer's outburst with clinical detachment and a profound curiosity. The man was entirely serious. Bloomer clearly believed what he was saying and was frightened by it. He seemed to be a man still awed by his gift and deferential in the extreme when this other consciousness chose to employ it. That there was another consciousness, Zalman did not doubt. But what sort of consciousness? A part of Bloomer's? An amalgamation of several living consciousnesses? An actual spirit that had a former physical existence? Some combination of the three? Zalman didn't know. He knew only that the consciousness existed, that it was a force capable of influencing human behavior and therefore of creating and altering events.

"I'll help you," he said finally. "Any way I can. What would you like me to do?"

"Several things. First, some detective work. I need to identify the other four paths. They're leading to a person. A born-again, as Nigel said. It's essential that we try to identify them and contain them to keep this from spreading. I want you to find out whether any of the area shrinks have been consulted about any emotional disturbance related to the Riverside railroad station. Get names and addresses. As much detail as you can."

"I'll still have an ethical problem. I'd have to assure the other psychiatrists that I'll keep the names confidential."

"You may change your mind if I can arrange a convincing enough demonstration. If I can't, we'll contrive some way for you to use the information. In the meantime, I'd also like you to send someone reliable down to the library. Perhaps a psychiatric intern. Have him look for unusual patterns developing over the past six months as reported in the local paper. Violence, divorce, so on. See if he can build any sort of cluster model around Riverside and around the station. Finally, I'd like a complete list of deceased Riverside residents over the past five years at least."

Zalman looked up from his notes. "Is that it?"

"For the moment."

"I'll get on the phone in a few minutes. First, however, you said you'd seen this before. Could it possibly have been in Lake Forest, Illinois?"

"It was," answered Bloomer, startled.

"My profession has penetrated the midwest, you know. We've examined that phenomenon, without conclusion, from the standpoint of hysteria. I'm eager, to say the least, to try a different tack toward understanding it."

"I'll tell you all I can if you'll make me a promise."

"If I . . . very well. What's the promise?"

"Stay away from the station. That station kills."

Feebly, Halloran returned Jack Gormley's wave as Gormley backed his BMW out of the driveway. He followed the headlights down to the corner. A flash of red brake lights and Gormley was gone. Exhausted, but feeling a curious calmness, Peter collapsed across the living room couch. Madness, he thought, staring into the blackness of the room. But if he was crazy, so was Gormley. If Gormley was crazy, maybe he wasn't. His own actions at least made some kind of sense. There was a sequence to them. They might have been the product of a troubled mind, even a disturbed mind, but at least one action was related to what went before it. Not like Gormley. He should have belted Jack. But why? What good would it do? Jack would honest to God have no idea why he was being punched. He'd tried asking Gormley about what had happened during the three minute ride up the hill. Gormley just looked at him. Even compassionately. Like he knew that Halloran had taken a few drinks too many and was confused. He was confused alright. But the bourbon had left him at the station. And here was Jack Gormley, who had just knocked him on his ass, now talking about having lunch together in the City someday soon. Lunch, for Christ's sake! And what about those other guys on the platform? The guys who were getting some kind of a charge just from being there. Were they just like Gormley? Halloran tried to remember who was there. He didn't know most of them. The one with the red strip of tape around his briefcase. That was probably Paul Weinberg. It must be Paul Weinberg. Would Weinberg have behaved the same way if he'd seen Peter? He would have. Just a feeling, but yes, he would have. God, if only he could talk to somebody. Barbara? Be serious. She's not upstairs anyway. Where was she, by the way? Bloom . . . Bloomingdale's? That's ridiculous. Bloomingdale's closes at nine. He could try talking to Jeff. Jeff's here. Just got in. Where's he been? Ask him in the morning. Zalman. He can talk to Zalman. Zalman wants to talk to him anyway. Good. Better if Zalman calls him than for him to have to call Zalman. Too tired to think about that now. Think of something pleasant. Restful. Think about the girl. The girl you thought about down at the library. The one who made you feel all cozy. Jennifer. Call her Jennifer. Nice name. Gentle name. Jen . . .

Polly Gormley was near tears when Jack dropped his briefcase by the door and leaned over to kiss her lightly on the forehead.

"You could at least have called," she said, more hurt than angry. "The Hendersons were here to play bridge. You knew that. I had dinner all set. It was embarrassing. They were nice about it but I felt like a dope. I would have been calling hospitals if you hadn't done this so many times lately. What's so important about your job that you can't even call? And on Saturday."

"I'm sorry, honey. Really. And maybe you're right. I don't know why I'm breaking my neck, either. Tell you what. Is Laurie asleep? Okay, how about going out for a late supper. Just the two of us. We'll forget about everything else and right now, tonight, we'll start spending more time with each other."

"Oh Jack, do you really mean it? That would be so nice. Do you think we can leave Laurie? What if she wakes up?"

"You're right," he said, "and I don't want you worrying about Laurie while I'm trying to seduce you over candlelight and wine. Got a better idea. Why don't we take a cold bottle of wine and a little cheese upstairs just like we used to. I'll light the upstairs fireplace, we'll pile up a great stack of pillows and I'll just lie there looking at your scrumptious body until I get enough nerve to touch."

She laughed delightedly. "You get the fire." She leered playfully. "I'll bring everything else we need."

Their lovemaking was unhurried, giving and exquisitely tender. A garment would be loosened and then they'd touch for a while until her fingers or his would drift across another clasp or button. More cloth would fall away. More flesh would dance in the lapping fire. That it had been so long, like this at least, made the loving more delicious. Polly slowed him each time he quickened the pace, each time his hands became more eager. She touched the nerves that made him shudder into a grinning helpless mass of love beloved. At last, when she could contain him no longer or control the thumping spasms inside herself, she brought him to her and ignited a groaning, flailing eruption of all the unspent passions of the months before.

Entangled in each other, they fell asleep. She on her back, snoring softly. The sound stirred him and he smiled lazily. Remembering. Their first time was much like this. She was so pretty then. So lovely now. He felt a draft. Just a breeze. Like a wave from an oscillating fan. Why does she have to snore like tha . . . The chill passed. Gently, he drew a sheet over her body lest it come again and rouse her or cause the tiny smile to fade from her lips. He felt it again. Across his feet. Now snaking up across his bare buttocks. Moving like a river that wanders over a plain. Now up across his back. How can anyone sleep when she snores like that? A briefcase full of work for Sunday and a killing appointment calendar for Monday and she lays there on her fat ass snoring and smiling. The breeze covered all of him now, and it followed him as he quietly drew himself astride her. She murmured contentedly at his touch, drifting slowly out of her dreams and in again. There was another dream. Not a nice one. She was afraid in it. Someone was after her. Someone had his hands about her throat and his thumbs were pressing hard upon her. Her face felt like it was stretching under her skin. Her eyelids parted. It was Jack. She was dreaming about Jack. And he was strangling her. The dream was scary. So hard to breathe . . .

Mordicai Bloomer had reached the door of his room at the New Englander and was fishing for his room key before he remembered about Barbara. At the time he'd slipped her his key at Leticia's house, sex was the farthest thing from his mind. She must be Halloran, he had decided. Who else could Lictor have meant? Even if she didn't know it, she must be psychic to some degree. Bloomer didn't want her to get too far away from him. But Zalman, after all, was probably right. Halloran had to be her husband. It all fit. Head injury. That was how Jennifer found her gift. Sort of. Hallucinations about vaguely insubstantial people around the railroad station. It was Barbara's husband, alright. Halloran. Peter Halloran sees them. But what to do about it? Maybe Jennifer has some ideas. Maybe she's called in. If she caught an early plane from Chicago, she could be here before noon. Just as well. That would give him time to learn what he could from Barbara and then get rid of her.

Bloomer returned to the front desk where the bored night clerk stepped away from his crossword puzzle and plucked a key from his room slot. There were no messages. With Jennifer very much on his mind, he proceeded once again to his room just off the second floor landing.

Outside the lobby entrance, the aging man in the tan ducks

moved back into the shadows of a privet hedge. His hands were shaking. He jammed them into his belt beneath the dark windbreaker he now wore, but the tremor surged quickly up through his shoulders and into his jaw. His right hand closed over the short billy club in his waistband and squeezed hard. What should he do? How long should he wait? The man who'd just left the lobby was not the man. Not the blond man he'd followed. It was only the same one who'd come in a few minutes before. Where was this man? Who was he? How did he know? He said his name was Alex. And what was it he knew? Did he know about his secret and did he also know about Charles? If he knew about Charles, Ezra Cohen thought, he'd have to make him promise not to tell. He'd have to make him. Even if that meant he'd have the two of them to dream about.

Bloomer, half hoping that Barbara would not be in his room, quietly opened the door and paused with his hand over the light switch.

"Don't turn on the light. Please!" came the voice from the queensize bed nearest the drawn window drapes. "Close the door and flip on the bathroom light if you like." In the dim illumination from the hallway, he could see her half sitting against the pillows, the coverlet drawn up beneath her naked shoulders. She was sipping wine from a plastic glass. The bottle and an ashtray sat on the nightstand between the beds. There were several cigarette butts in it and another smoldering between her fingers.

"I swiped a bottle from Leticia's," she giggled. "It's a domestic Chablis. Not very good, I'm afraid, but I didn't have time to study her list." Barbara chuckled again, clearly impressed by her own resourcefulness.

"Actually, it's a limited production private stock. Don't let the inelegant label fool you." Mordicai quietly closed the door. He reached for the night chain, then decided not to bother. It wouldn't be a long visit if he could help it. "Baron Rothschild himself called this Chablis a gentle kiss that soothes a weary palate." In fact, Bloomer had no idea what Barbara was drinking. But if she wanted to bullshit about wine, he'd bullshit about wine.

Barbara appeared to study the contents of her motel bathroom tumbler. "You know, I was sure it had a certain *je ne sais quoi*, but I assumed the wine would be muted by that dreadful lemon butter. Or by those revolting clams. It just goes to show. Quality in wine, as in people, will assert itself in its own time and in its own way."

Nervous chitchat, thought Bloomer. He was used to it. Not so pretentious as this, as a rule, but about what he'd expect from Barbara. Might as well get down to cases. "I wonder," he said softly, "what Baron Rothschild would have said about the way you look. If he'd seen you earlier in the evening, he'd have spoken of a woman of almost intimidating beauty and bearing. The end product of exquisite taste and breeding over generations. If he saw you now, again, he'd be compelled to change his mind. A Circe, he'd say. Irresistibly alluring. Unbearably sensual. Lying naked in the filtered moonlight. Your skin glowing like an alabaster Venus. Yet soft and firm like a young duchess in a Degas painting." He was now at her bedside. He sat gently on the edge, then leaned forward and lightly kissed her on the eyes. His thumbs across her eyelids, he brought his lips to hers and lingered there, barely touching. He felt a shock run through her body and a writhing at her hips. Her fingers fumbled at his necktie.

Afterward, she lay pressed against him, one arm stretched across his chest while he sipped her wine in the darkness. Actually, not bad, he thought. Her either. She certainly worked at it. But a touch awkward. Like it didn't come at all naturally. He could imagine what she must be like with her husband. For him, it would be like masturbating with somebody to talk to. Except that he probably couldn't talk to her. Not about anything real. Barbara was in a different world.

He kissed the top of her head softly. "Aren't you worried about your husband?"

"Hmmmm?"

"Your husband. Peter Halloran. Do you think he might be wondering where you are?"

"Killjoy! No, I'm not worried. And I don't care if he's worried."

"What kind of a man is he?"

"About a tenth of what you are. Let's not talk about him, Mordicai," she said sleepily. "Does everyone call you Mordicai?"

"A few call me Morty. But I discourage it. My students and some others call me Doc to my face and Spooks behind my back. At least, they do if they don't care what grade they get."

"I'll call you Mordicai. It suits you. It has dignity to it."

"I'm really interested in Peter for your sake," he said, giving

Barbara a reassuring squeeze. "Zalman said something about a head injury and some erratic behavior afterward. You're not in any danger, are you?"

"From Peter? I guess I could die of boredom. Or disgust. You're not Jewish, are you?"

"As it happens, no. Why do you ask?"

"Just wondered." Barbara raised herself on one arm, kissed his chest noisily, and then slid out of bed toward the bathroom. She moved slowly through the darkened room, taking care not to trip on the scattered articles of clothing. She felt the draft again. Very faintly. But still a draft. Goddamned drafts. Can't get away from them lately. Goddamned Mordicai Bloomer. Goddamned Morty. Goddamned Spooks. Why is he ruining everything by bringing Peter's na . . . She was out of it. In the bathroom. The warmth of Mordicai's touch still sending little waves through her. A marvelous man. So accomplished. A fantastic lover. Not the animal part so much as the words. The man himself.

She rose from the toilet and considered for a moment whether to flush it. Such a vulgar sound for him to hear. But better than having him find it as it is. She turned on both water taps to muffle the sound, then pressed the chrome lever on the tank.

Barbara studied herself in the huge mirror that covered one wall above the sink. Really not bad. Hardly a stretch mark. None at all when she's properly tanned. Not a freckle. Do something someday about those moles. Good body anyway. Anyone would be glad to have her as a wife. Mrs. Mordicai Bloomer. Professor and Mrs. Mordicai Bloomer. Dr. and Mrs. Mordicai Bloomer. She's one of the Greenwich Wentworths, you know. And he's one of the Beacon Hill Bloomers.

She switched off the light and opened the bathroom door. Better get going soon. Maybe a little longer. Ask him about his work. Ask him about all that crazy business at Leticia's house. Is that him breathing? Yes. He's fallen asleep. Such contentment. She did that for him. She can do that for him always. Draft again. Bitching draft. He doesn't care. He'll just take his little nap and to hell with anyone else. He'll care if someone digs her fingernails into his sleeping balls and twists them right off him. I'll show him something he'll never . . .

The wine bottle crashed upon the glass-topped end table. Bloomer stirred. Again it moved, hard against the heavy lamp. Bloomer bolted to his feet. He crouched naked. Arms forward in a combat stance. The bottle rocked on its side now, striking the lamp base, then clattering against the square glass ashtray. In the dim light he felt rather than saw the cold rage in Barbara's eyes. A heavy pounding behind her. Someone was at the door. Her husband? Barbara thought so. She'd kill him. She'd kill whoever it was. With a growl, she lunged for the doorknob and threw the door open wide. Bloomer couldn't see. He couldn't see the door. Just Barbara's naked back rushing into its light. A sharp slap. Then a duller sound of flesh striking flesh and Barbara flew backward into the room where she collapsed at the foot of the extra bed.

"Good evening, Mordicai," said Jennifer without looking at him. She flipped on the lights and bent over Barbara's body. "You've had more company tonight than you know."

6

Sunday Morning—
Halloran

Halloran eased himself through the door of Barbara's bedroom. That was the way he thought of it now. Since yesterday. Maybe longer than that.

Soundlessly, he crossed the deep-pile carpet to his section of the closet and bent to pick up his deck shoes. From the closet shelf, he took a fresh pair of jeans and a cable-stitch sweater, then turned toward the door again. Barbara hadn't stirred. He'd thought he heard her sobbing in the middle of the night. But perhaps not. The sound was gone by the time his head had cleared enough to listen through the darkness. He hadn't even heard her come in. Without glancing at her again, Peter turned to the door and closed it quietly behind him.

He felt curiously good. Well rested. No trace of hangover. Strong. Like the old Peter. It was odd, really. Yesterday, Saturday, was easily one of the most wrenching days of his life. At the very least, he'd have expected to wake up burning with humiliation over his encounter with Jack Gormley. Instead, he found himself feeling sorrow for Gormley. Wishing he could help him. Peter wasn't sure why and did not dwell on the thought. He felt a whisper

71

of sorrow for Barbara too. Also unusual. But better than the frustration and resentment that had twisted at his stomach every day for . . . how long has it been? Four or five years. Longer. Maybe for their entire marriage. It didn't matter. The marriage was over. All that remained was to end it legally. When did he make that decision? He didn't know. Only that it was made. Irrevocably. Amazing how calm you feel once you make up your mind about a dilemma that's been eating at you. Like when you quit a job that you hate. Even if you get fired from it. You feel relieved.

That's what he felt. Relief. About Barbara, about Gormley, and even . . . and especially, about Peggy Bregman. By God! That's what had him feeling so good. A large part of it anyway. Peggy Bregman had talked to him. She really had. It was her. He had definitely seen Peggy after she was dead and Peggy definitely moved that beer can. Peggy wasn't dead. Not the way he'd always thought of death. That meant Marty Kornhauser wasn't dead either. Or any of the others. Peter had seen them. Without question. So what if no one else could see them? That didn't make him crazy. It made them poorer for not being able to share his . . . ability. He felt a thrill run through his body. Part peace, part excitement. Whatever miracle had happened during the night, he had no inclination to question it. Some string had been cut. Some giant rubber band that had been stretching tighter and tighter, binding him to conventional thought as he struggled against it. Struggling to accept the idea that conventional thought no longer served. It was no longer real. It no longer applied. Reality was Peggy Bregman. Reality was recognizing that his marriage to Barbara was not a marriage at all. It was a sham. Jeffrey was reality. The preservation of the family unit was not. There was no family unit. It existed only in the eye of the census taker and in the casual perception of the community.

Jeff was already dressed. He sat at the kitchen counter spooning honey onto two toasted English muffins as he studied his small-craft racing tactics handbook.

"Want a muffin?" he asked, holding a dripping half out toward his father while keeping a finger on his place in the text. Peter downed it over the sink in three bites. "What do you want to work on today?" he asked.

"Practice roll-tacking and mark-rounding," Jeff answered through a mouthful of dough. "That's if you're sure you feel up to it. We don't have to if you're not in the mood."

"I feel fine," Peter answered. "Better than in months." In fact, he felt ten years younger and many pounds lighter.

"So? Let's move it." Jeff answered his father's grin with one of his own and crammed the last half-muffin into his mouth.

They heard the phone as they backed out of the driveway. Peter and Jeff swapped glances, then Peter accelerated the car in reverse. Let it ring or let her answer it. It was too beautiful a morning and too early in the day for either of them to face Barbara Halloran if they could help it. Once out of the driveway, Peter slammed the gear lever into first and peeled away from his front lawn. With both of them laughing, the car sped down the hill and past the railroad station before turning onto the lane that dead-ended at the marina.

If they'd left a minute later, Peter would have taken the call from Jack Gormley that would have begun, "I hate to bother you on a Sunday, Pete, but we were talking last night and I wonder if you could give me a hand with something. . . ."

Twenty minutes later, they might have passed the athletic youngish man who was Alex Makepeace striding purposefully up the hill toward his house and they might have seen whatzisname Cohen matching his pace a block or so behind. An hour earlier, at a few minutes after eight, they might have seen Paul Weinberg with his taped briefcase being dragged screaming from the station platform by the police.

Jeffrey skippered the small Flying Scot with growing confidence. Peter served as crew, smoothly bringing the genoa around on Jeff's tacks and jibes and trimming or easing to suit Jeff's point of sail. Jeff worked the tiller and the mainsheet with almost equal ease. For the first hour, the incoming tide was ripping and the wind was at a steady eight knots. They chose a red nun buoy to serve as a practice racing mark and rounded it repeatedly, first on a series of beats, then reaches, and finally jibing around on two or three downwind runs. Peter made an effort to give advice only when asked.

"You're ready to race this thing, my friend," he said finally. "Want to practice a few starts?"

"Did you bring the stopwatch?"

"Right here."

"Let's do it."

Farther out, beyond Greenwich Point, they found a black channel marker, a can, and a bright orange lobster trap float that lined up more or less perpendicularly to the wind coming in from the southwest. Using this as a dummy starting line, Jeff brought the boat head to wind until the luffing of the sails showed him the favored end of the line, the end closest to the breeze. Next, Jeff allowed the Flying Scot to fall off and began practicing a series of runs at the line as his father called off the remaining seconds of a five-minute preparatory run. Twice he managed to hit the line under full trim with three seconds or less remaining.

Halloran's mood continued to improve as the morning passed. Being on the water was just the thing. Sailing had always been a tonic for him. Clean and fresh, physically demanding and at once satisfying, requiring alertness and judgment whether during a race or on a recreational sail. Remote from the pressures of the shore. Better than remote. More a question of perspective. Nagging personal problems seemed to decrease in intensity and in complexity as the shoreline faded into a haze. They became simpler. More manageable. More definable.

Absolutely dumb, he thought, to have endured a miserable and destructive marriage this long. Maybe not. Maybe it really was better than being lonely. There wasn't anybody else. Still, he should have taken the chance. Except that up until now he would have been giving up a definite Jeff for a maybe woman who he might never meet. Now there was a woman. She wasn't real, his Jennifer, but thinking about her made him feel warm inside and that was real. Funny though, from the time he woke up, it was like he could feel her presence. He kept looking around on the way to the marina and on the way to the launch as if he'd more than half expected to see her. His Jennifer would like the water. She'd like sailing as much as he did.

"Hey, Dad?"

"Ummm!" Peter came back into the world. "Yeah, Jeff?"

"What's so funny?"

"I don't get you."

"You had a big shi . . . a big smile on your face."

"Just feeling good."

"You want to feel even better? Let's go in and get a cheeseburger."

"You're the skipper."

Jeff eased the boat off the wind and kicked the main out while his father snaked the jib sheets loose. The boat was running before the wind which now pushed from the port quarter off their stern.

"Dad, we can carry a chute," Jeff suggested hopefully. It was a short run home but what the heck, spinnakers are pretty. "If you'll fly it, I'll fold it."

Halloran saluted and dug the spinnaker gear out of the cuddy. "Let's see if you can get us in and rounded up to the mooring on just the spinnaker." He ran the sheet and guy outside the spreaders and around the headstay, then back through the aft blocks. When he was ready on the halyard, he waited for a nod from Jeff and then hauled away as Jeff pulled in the sheet. The spinnaker flapped for a moment before bursting into a graceful floating arc. Peter quickly dropped the genoa and the main and then settled back as the small boat surfed smoothly along with the grace and quiet of a tiny cloud.

"Dad?" Jeff asked with a hint of hesitation in his voice.

"Yeah, Jeff."

"It's good to see you nice and calm again."

"Thanks," his father answered after a pause. "I have an idea a lot of things are going to be different. Better." He wondered how long Jeff had been watching him. Certainly since the accident. Maybe much longer. Waiting to see how much he'd take. How far he'd go. What he'd do.

"Do you think . . . Don't get mad, but don't you think I'm entitled to ask you some questions?"

Halloran took a deep breath, tugged idly on the spinnaker sheet, and avoided Jeff's eyes for a few moments before turning to him.

"You're entitled," he said softly. "The problem is I haven't been sure of the answers. I still don't have all of them, but I've at least stopped ducking the questions. That's what's different about me this morning. It's not that anything is solved."

"The first question is you and Mom. What happens?"

"Divorce. With all possible speed."

"What happens with me?"

"I'll also go for custody. Unless you change your mind, there's a chance I'll get it."

"What if you don't?"

"Then I'll ask you at the time whether you want to disappear with me."

"Where would we go?"

"I'll start working that out. All I can guarantee now is that it'll be near water and that I'll be doing what I enjoy. We might not have such a nice house."

"I don't care about the house." He was grinning. But the smile faded and he struggled visibly to form the next question. At last he said, "I followed you last night."

"It's funny," Peter answered. "I had that feeling when I came in. What's your question?"

"What I want to ask is what's going on down at that railroad station and what it has to do with you. But first I'll tell you what I know. Okay?"

"Go ahead, Jeff."

"That station's been bugging you for months. Every time someone even mentions the place, your eyes go wide. Like yesterday, when I told you Dan Doscher's father doesn't like it either. I've been with you maybe a dozen times when we passed it in the car and each time you seem like you're looking for something down there or like you're afraid of something. But there's never anything there. Then yesterday, you get this book on ghosts and stuff and you get all uptight about even reading it. Next we go down to the platform and you show me a tin can that moves by itself and you're really scared. The same night, you go down there with bottles full of gasoline and I figure you mean to burn the place down. But you don't. You stash the gas and a couple of minutes later you're letting some guy push you around who you ought to be able to break in two. What's the guy's name again?"

"Gormley. Jack Gormley."

"Yeah, that's the one. Anyway, I really hated seeing that. I mean, you didn't even fight back or do anything at all to him. So I ran home. Then the next thing I know, the same guy drops you off at the house and he's acting like you're big buddies. This is like all within ten minutes. The next time I see you is this morning. You're in the best mood I've seen in I don't know how long and everything is terrific. Right after being humiliated by that Gormley guy. You've even made up your mind about Mom all of a sudden." Jeff paused, watching for his father's reaction.

"Do you have a particular question?"

"Yeah!" he exclaimed. "What's going on around here?"

It was still hard to answer. For a number of reasons. Not the least of which was the doubtful appropriateness of unburdening himself to a fourteen-year-old son. On the other hand, who had a better right to know?

But how much to tell him? How do you make him understand the parts you don't understand yourself? Don't start that, Peter. Don't start picking and choosing.

"You remember Mr. Kornhauser? Marty Kornhauser? . . ."

* * *

"Man!" exclaimed Jeff Halloran some twenty minutes later. "Is that ever hard to believe! How come you're the only one who can see these people?"

"I have no idea. And I may not be the only one." Peter shrugged. "A lot of people are acting very strangely."

"What are you going to do?" Jeff asked, his eyes wide.

"For openers, I'm going to stop running away from it. If they're there, I'm through trying to pretend that they're not. I'm going to try to talk to them and find out what I can do to help. If they're not there, if they're strictly in my head, then I'll assume that this head injury last spring might have crossed a couple of wires and I'll try to get help."

"You're not nuts," Jeff answered. "I saw that can move too."

"We could both have been hallucinating."

"That dog too? Remember, he backed away from the beer can."

"Then it might have been vibrations in the track bed or some other natural phenomenon like magnetism or whatever. Even going beyond the natural or normal, it's also possible that I made the can move myself. It's apparently been pretty well documented that certain people can cause objects to move just by the power of their minds."

"I know about that," said Jeff brightly. "There was this movie about it. That's called tele-something."

"Telekinesis."

"That's it. Have you made anything else move?"

"Not to my knowledge."

"Then I think it's you. I was going to say maybe it was and that you might have got this power to do that when you hurt your head. There's this guy on TV who bends nails by just rubbing them and he said he found out he could do it after he had this fever once. But I don't think that's it. I think Mrs. Bregman moved the can because she wanted to prove she was there. And I kind of think that your head injury has something to do with you being able to see her and to see other ghosts. I absolutely don't think it's your imagination. What was it she said about someone showing her how to move things?"

"She said Mr. Hicks showed her how."

"And you don't know any Mr. Hicks?"

"I don't think so."

"Then why should you imagine that? It's not important to you to know that someone showed her that or what his name is, is it?"

"No. As far as I know. But who can be sure? The human mind is barely understood. It's an enormously complex . . ."

"Will you stop complicating everything?" Jeff fairly shouted. "You were right the first time. You should keep it simple. If they're there, you should talk to them. If they're not, that's the time to worry about complications."

Peter wasn't listening. He was looking past Jeff's shoulder at the police launch that was closing on them rapidly, a uniformed officer with a loud hailer in his hand standing in the cockpit.

"Peter Halloran?" came the harsh metallic voice.

"Yes. I'm Halloran," he shouted back. "What's the trouble?"

"Would you drop your sail and heave to, sir?"

Peter quickly doused the spinnaker and sat dead in the water. The launch coasted to his port side.

"We're sorry to alarm you, Mr. Halloran," came the softer natural voice of the young officer. "There's been a violent death on shore. The investigating officers have reason to believe you have information that may assist them. They're waiting to interview you at the marina if I can give you a tow."

"Who's dead?" he asked, suddenly ashen. "It's not my wife . . . ?"

"No, sir. A Mrs. John Gormley. Her husband apparently strangled her during the night. He then took his own life this morning shortly after placing a call to your home."

Sgt. Turkus and a younger officer were waiting on the dock. He called a greeting to Peter and Jeff as soon as the Flying Scot was within voice range and kept up a rather boisterous friendly banter until the four reached the parking lot. Peter knew the sergeant fairly well but not that well. He assumed, correctly, that the show of good fellowship was for the benefit of the other sailors and bystanders.

"Thanks for the performance, Mike," he said, "particularly for Jeff's sake."

"My pleasure, Mr. Halloran."

"It's still Pete."

"Pete," he repeated. "Yeah. They'll be enough for tongues to wag about without giving them anything extra. Did the marine officer tell you what happened?"

"Only that Polly Gormley's dead and so's Jack. Do you have any idea why?"

"Some," Mike Turkus answered. He glanced at Jeff and back to

Peter. "Let's you and I take a walk. I have to ask you a couple of questions." Turkus gestured toward a shaded area at the edge of the parking lot. The two men strolled casually in that direction.

"Anything you want to tell me, Pete?" he asked, as they stopped near a row of blue jays resting on trailers.

"Such as what?"

"How about you and Polly Gormley?"

Peter snapped his eyes onto the sergeant's, looking for some sign that it was not a serious question. Turkus' face was hard.

"You're serious, aren't you?"

"I have to ask."

"The answer is there is no me and Polly Gormley. I'd damn near bet my life that there was nobody else and Polly Gormley either."

"When did you see her last?"

"Am I suspected of killing her?"

"Absolutely not. When did you see her last?"

"I dunno. Maybe a month ago at a party. For the record, I don't think I've even had a private conversation with her since I've known her. Also for the record, if you're looking for a boyfriend in her life, I think you're out of your skull."

"Maybe," he nodded. "Don't get sore, Pete. I'm just trying to make some sense out of it. When did you last see Jack Gormley?"

"He gave me a ride up the hill last night. Around nine o'clock."

"Did he seem alright to you?"

"Not entirely. I saw him shortly after he got off the train. I was cutting through the station parking lot. He saw me but he didn't seem to know me. In fact, he seemed annoyed that I was there. I just walked away." Peter decided that a slightly laundered version of events would not seriously impede the investigation. "Then, a few minutes later, he pulled up alongside and offered me a ride. Like nothing happened. I'd swear he didn't even remember seeing me."

"Did anyone else see you?"

"No. Well, maybe. I saw Paul Weinberg but I don't know if he saw me."

"Weinberg?" Turkus was genuinely startled. "Weinberg was on the same train?"

"Yeah. What about it?"

Turkus ignored the question. "How did Gormley seem when he left you?"

"Like I said, he was fine. A little small talk about seeing more of each other and he was gone."

"Did anyone see him drop you off? Not that it necessarily matters."

"Jeff saw him. He knew who it was before I came in the door."

"Mind if I ask him?"

"Not as long as you phrase it in such a way that he won't worry."

"I guess it'll keep. Why would Jack Gormley call your house this morning?"

"I don't know."

"How did you know he did call?"

"The water cop told me."

"That, I will have to check. If he did, he shouldn't have."

"Check whatever the hell you want, Mike. Now, I want to know what's going on."

"Just one more question. Why would Jack Gormley assume that you might be willing to help him dispose of his wife's body?"

Halloran's jaw went slack as he stared stupidly at Turkus.

"I don't believe that," he said, after a moment.

"That's what he asked." Turkus flipped his black leather notebook back several pages. "He called your home at approximately nine-fifteen this morning. Your wife answered. Her recollection is that Mr. Gormley, upon being informed that you were out, whereabouts unknown, left the following message. Quote, Tell him my wife is dead now and I wanted to know if he could spare an hour to help me haul her off someplace, Unquote. Your wife recalls that he made this statement in a calm and untroubled manner. Your wife took no action. However, at approximately eleven o'clock this morning, upon hearing from a neighbor that John Gormley was dead of a self-inflicted gunshot wound, she then notified us of her earlier conversation." Turkus snapped the book shut.

Peter kept his eyes on the ground for a long moment.

"I have an idea," he said finally. "But first I'd like a couple of answers myself."

"Such as?"

"What possible reason could you have to suspect an affair between me and Polly Gormley?"

"Not an affair, necessarily. I was looking for a connection. A reason why he'd pick you to call."

"Bullshit. That call could mean almost anything before it would suggest an affair."

Turkus glanced toward the young officer and leaned closer to Peter. "Okay. There was fresh semen in her. She was found on a pile of pillows in front of a fireplace. A bottle of wine. Two glasses. A very romantic setting. Possibly too romantic for a married couple. Possibly she had a lover up there and got caught." He held up his hand to hold off Peter's objection. "I know it sounds pretty cynical. But it makes at least as much sense as John Gormley making love to his wife in a setting like that and then choking the life out of her. You want to know what he did next? He went to sleep. The medical examiner thinks she was dead before midnight. You want to know what he did when he woke up? He went in to his twelve-year-old daughter's room, fucking twelve years old, and asked his own daughter if she could give him a hand hauling her mother's corpse down to the fucking station wagon. The daughter went screaming out into the street in her underwear. Gormley went after her. He got into the street and according to the neighbors he suddenly began crying and screaming like he just right then realized what he'd done. He's still yelling when he runs back into the house and locks the door. You ready for the weird part? All this, what I just told you, was before he called you and asked the same goddamned question. Just as calm and casual as before, he calls to ask you to help dump his wife. A little while after that, he sticks a shotgun in his mouth and pulls the trigger. His brains were still dripping off the bedroom ceiling when we got there."

Peter felt sick. His own torments seemed so small, so far away, compared to this. "What . . . what about fingerprints? There must have been fingerprints on the wine glass."

"There are. They're probably his. We'll know this afternoon."

"What's this got to do with Paul Weinberg?"

"Who says it does?"

"You did, dammit. You almost jumped when I told you I saw him on the same platform."

"I don't know that there's a connection, but Weinberg and his wife are both in the hospital. He's in the psycho ward. He got up this morning and got dressed to go to the office like always . . ."

"On Sunday?"

"His wife asked the same question and he broke her jaw. He stepped over her, kissed his kids good-bye, and walked down to the station. It's Sunday so his train didn't come. We received a call from some people with homes near the station who complained about a berserk man in a business suit screaming obscenities at a train that wasn't there. It took four cops to drag him away. Who else was on that platform last night?"

"Seven, maybe eight other guys. One woman. A couple of kids."

"Did you know any of them?"

"I didn't pay much attention. Why?"

"Because last night was the worst we've had in years in terms of domestic disturbance calls. One man threw a chair through his television set with no warning whatsoever. Another attempted to beat his wife after an argument over his job but was subdued by other family members. We had two calls alleging domestic violence that were canceled when the police arrived. In both cases, the husband claimed or seemed not to know what the officers responding were talking about. Both wives dropped the matter. I don't know what it means, but I'm going to find out how many of these men were on that platform with Gormley and Weinberg. There's something kinky going on at that station."

Halloran studied the sergeant's face. There had to be more to that last remark than the possible pure coincidence of Gormley and Weinberg being on the same train. "What else has happened that you know about?" he asked.

"Nothing I can talk about. It's a police matter. Anyway, it's nothing concrete. You said, by the way, you had an idea about Gormley's behavior."

"I'll make you a trade."

"No trades. Like I said, it's a police matter. You can be locked up, Mister Halloran, for withholding information."

"Do you want to trade or not?"

"You're going to force me to take you in for questioning."

"You do that and you'll get nothing. I can't afford to say anything because it'll make me sound as flipped out as Gormley. There are things I've seen that I'll never admit to seeing in front of witnesses. I'd feel the same way if I'd seen a UFO. The trade is I'll help you if you'll help me. I'll never repeat what you tell me but I'll never admit to telling you anything either. No one will believe the things I've seen."

"Don't bet on it. You're not the only one."

Peter's eyes widened. "Do we have a deal?"

"I'll tell you what I can if I have your word you won't repeat it. You have mine that I won't use your information without your permission."

"Good enough. You first."

Turkus sighed deeply and took a long look around.

"All I have are bits and pieces. There's an officer on my watch who swears he saw rocks and other objects lifting off the ground and flying several feet away in the station parking lot. He told me as a friend sometime after the event. That's unofficial. There's been no report. But he was very sure of what he saw. I personally stopped a man who was running from the station a few weeks ago. He was plainly frightened but would offer no explanation. I logged the time, checked the station area and found nothing unusual. By itself, I would have forgotten it. In the past two months, we've taken four complaints of threatening or simple assault from commuters against other commuters. Again, it may not sound like much but we've never had a similar complaint that I can find that was connected in any way with that station. A number of the area men are avoiding the station entirely. We see them on patrol in the morning. The same guys who've been walking to the Riverside Station for years are now walking in the other direction. Toward Old Greenwich. Last Wednesday night, a teenage couple was sitting in the parking lot smoking grass. A man in a business suit dragged the boy from his car and beat him severely. The man's been identified and charged. The man admits to being in the station at the time but denies any knowledge of the assault. I took his statement myself. I believe he doesn't remember. In the area at large, there's been a marked upswing in reported acts of violence. Not just domestic violence. Fights on tennis courts, fights over property lines, over parking spaces, fights in stores. One fight was a shoving match over who would get the top newspaper in a stack down at a stationery store. Not who would get the last paper. That would be ridiculous enough. This was over the goddamned top paper. There's been a clear pattern of increasing aggressive behavior, largely, and perhaps entirely, among the commuters who use the Riverside railroad station. That's about what I have, Pete. For what it's worth. It's also more than I have a right to discuss with you. I hope you have something for me."

"You won't believe it," Halloran warned.

"You'd be surprised."

"I'll start with the easy part."

Halloran began with a few more details of his encounter with Jack Gormley, the physical attack, Jack's night-and-day change in behavior, his apparent amnesia, but leaving out any mention of his plan to burn down the station. He gave Turkus Carl Doscher's name and the remarks attributed to him giving reasons for avoiding the Riverside Station. He described the curious behavior of the other men who stood on the platform the night before with Gormley and Weinberg. Grown men just standing there, loving the station, as Halloran chose to put it.

"The cop who saw things moving?" he said, after a pause to gauge the sergeant's reaction. "He's probably right. I saw something like it. The difference is, I know who made it move. She told me she was going to do it and she did. It was Peggy Bregman."

"Peggy Bregman? Isn't she . . . ?"

"Dead," he answered. "For almost a year. I've seen her several times since then. Yesterday, I heard her. She said she'd move a beer can to prove she was there and she did. Jeff saw it but he didn't hear her. She said a Mr. Hicks showed her how to move things. Maybe your cop saw her practicing."

"Who's Hicks?"

"I don't know. I have an idea that he's black and that he dresses like a house painter. Do you begin to see why I won't repeat any of this for the record?"

"Why would Peggy Bregman . . . If Peggy . . . Assuming that this woman or whatever spoke to you, why did she speak to you?"

"Two reasons. No, three. First, because I can see her from time to time and apparently no one else can. Second, to ask me to help them . . . help her. I don't know how or why. Third, to warn me to stay away from the station. She said they'll kill me. She didn't say who. I'm beginning to believe she means the commuters."

"Who's them?" Turkus asked. "You started to say she wanted you to help 'them.'"

"I think there are several dead people down there. I think Hicks is dead. I believe I've seen him. Also a fat guy wearing a bathrobe."

"Do you know his name?"

"If you don't ask me how I know because I can't tell you. But I feel that his name is Charles."

"First or last?"

"No idea."

"Why do I get the feeling you're saving the best part for the end?"

"You remember Marty Kornhauser?"

"Kornhauser? Yeah. Suicide last March or April. As a matter of fact it was at . . ."

"At the station," Peter nodded.

"You're saying he's down there too?"

"He was my first. Also one of my best friends. I've seen him several times, Mike. He's lost or stuck or something. We stood staring at each other as close as you are to me."

"What did he say?"

"Nothing. He saw me, and he seemed to get terribly confused and then he began . . . he almost cried."

"But he didn't try to communicate?"

"No. The black guy did. It was when I hurt my head. The fag in the bathrobe was with him. He said something to me but the sound was like it was going through a scrambler. Later on, I dreamt about the black guy and he was asking if I can see him. But that was just a dream. That might have been what he was asking me at the station but I don't know."

"How do you know he was a fag?"

"Who?"

"The fat guy. You said the fag in the bathrobe was with the house painter."

"I don't know how I know. However, now that you ask, I'm sure. The guy's a homosexual. And his name is Charles."

"Okay. Let's say every word of it is true. How do your dead people tie in with the Gormley murder-suicide or any of the other stuff that's going on around town?"

"I don't know, Mike. I'm sure there's a connection but I don't know what it is. I can only guess that whatever is affecting the behavior of the living is also causing the appearances of the dead. It's more than a guess, but still a feeling. Both of these have the same root cause."

"Would you be willing to take a lie detector test?"

"Of course not."

"What if I could guarantee privacy?"

"No."

"May I ask why not?"

"Because if I understand lie detectors, and hypnosis for that matter, all they'll prove is that I'm telling the truth as I believe it. They'll conclude that I'm a truthful screwball. No, thank you."

"They might also conclude that you're a psychic."

"I'm no psychic," Peter answered with a touch of annoyance, as if the word itself implied either fraud or impaired mental health.

"Use whatever word you want. But if everything you say is true, you see dead people no one else can see, you hear voices no one else can hear, you know the name of a dead man you never saw before and you even know his sexual preferences. What would you call that?"

"Feelings."

"Extrasensory perception."

"Feelings! Hunches! Intuitions!"

"What the hell's the difference?"

"One makes me a nut. The other doesn't."

Turkus raised his right hand and very deliberately brought it forward with his index finger against Halloran's chest. "Don't play word games with me, Pete," he said softly but with a hard edge to his voice. "People are fucking dying in this town. Weinberg's wife could have died. All the people who've gotten bloody noses so far could have died. People could be dying right now while you stand here defining your terms. I don't know whether you're a psychic or not, for Christ's sake. But I'll tell you this. If you're right, I don't give a shit what you are. You never heard of police departments using psychics to find missing persons or to solve other crimes? You ever wonder why? I'll tell you why. Because police departments deal in information. And if fucking Ronald McDonald danced into the station house and said the Pope was down the street dressed in a Batman costume and raping a teenager, we would check it out forthwith. Because the guy in the clown suit might be an actor coming from a supermarket opening and there really might be some psycho who looks like the Pope to a guy who's upset, and he might really be raping a teenager while we stand around laughing at the informant. If you have information, I want it. If you're able to help in any other way, I want that too."

"I've told you all I know, Mike," Halloran told him, gently moving the sergeant's hand to one side. "And that's the truth."

"I don't buy that."

"Why not?"

"Because you're too calm. No offense, Pete, but what you are is a heavily insulated commuter-businessman who has lost any street smarts and street tough he ever had. Your idea of a problem is a wet martini. Your idea of fear is when your boss's door is closed. Yet you're standing here talking about seeing ghosts like you'll talk about last week's Yankee game."

"I wasn't so calm. Up until this morning when I woke up, I wasn't calm at all."

"What happened this morning?"

"I don't know. Nothing. I guess I just decided to face it."

"Face what?"

"Kornhauser, for openers. I'm going to try to talk to him. If you want to go take off that uniform, you can come with me."

7

Sunday Morning—
Jennifer

The salesman pushed Bloomer's American Express card across the Formica table that served as a desk, then two application forms and a cheap ball-point pen that said ARROW MOTOR HOMES on the side.

"If you'll just sign the rental agreement, sir, you can be on your way. Right here at the bottom where I've checked, and then this next form for the plastic money people. You say you've driven a Winnebago Motor Home before, sir?"

"Ummmm? Excuse me?" Mordicai responded absently. He'd stopped listening ten minutes before. Somewhere between the pitch about reserving now for next year's trip to Disney World and the revelation of Arrow's co-op buying plan. No part of it was news to Bloomer, who'd rented several twenty-four-foot models in the past. One or two were even for recreational purposes. Nor was the salesman deterred by the fact that Bloomer's Princeton residence made him an unlikely sales prospect for a Connecticut dealer. Let him talk. Bloomer couldn't have concentrated on it if he wanted to.

"The Winnebagos, sir. You did say you've rented quite a few?

Always the same model? All the more reason to consider a purchase. The twenty-four is an excellent mid-range choice. Plenty of comfort for four adults or even a family of six."

"Yes . . . thank you," he muttered. "What did you say the full purchase price was?"

Bloomer, in fact, could not have cared less. He was stalling. It wasn't the Winnebago. Or the rental agreement. It was the pen. Bloomer was reluctant to pick up the pen. It might start writing. Right across Mr. Arrow's rental agreement in triplicate and he wouldn't be able to stop it. Much less explain it. He turned and glanced toward Jennifer as if for help, half expecting to see her lost in meditation. She wasn't meditating. Jennifer never seemed to do what he expected her to do. Or feel what he wanted her to feel. Look at her. I'm barely holding myself together and she's sitting there leafing through the Winnebago Guide to Eastern Ski Trails. Ski trails! Last night she walks into my room, finds me naked with an equally naked lady who is about to rip my balls off while a second lady, dead but presumably dressed, is trying to wake me up by bouncing a wine bottle all over the table. Jennifer cold-cocks Barbara, God knows how, and then gets right down to business while I'm wondering whether to get into some clothes or sit there like an ass with the bedspread up to my neck. She could at least have been bothered a little bit, finding me with a woman. She doesn't have to love me, whatever love is. But she could care at least that much about what I do. But no. She goes right on talking. Not unfriendly, but all business. Two or three times, Barbara would start to wake up and Jennifer would reach over and touch her neck and Barbara would be out for another fifteen minutes. When Jennifer finally went back to her room, Barbara woke up not remembering a damn thing except that she has this stiff neck. What happened? You tripped, Barbara, over a pile of clothing when you came out of the bathroom. You passed out a few minutes. Oh! I'm better now . . . my neck feels . . . I suppose I ought to get home. Call me tomorrow? Would you rather I call you? Fine, Barbara. By the way, you were marvelous. Then everyone went to get some sleep before the dying starts.

"Sign right here, sir."

We'll wake up and the dying and the madness will begin. We know it's just the first squall of a hurricane but we're supposed to stop it. Who says so? Lictor says so. Lictor tells his flunky Nigel what to do and Nigel tells his flunky Bloomer. Nobody tells Jennifer. They ask Jennifer. What the hell's so special about Jennifer? She wasn't even born with it. A fucking accident. A freak. And her fucking fairy godbrother. Alex. Another freak.

"Sir?"

Alex. A second-rate psychic and a third-rate medium. No better than ninety-nine point nine percent of all the mediums in the world who take months to get even a fragmented message from the other side and even then they get it wrong half the time. He's nothing without Jennifer. Nothing like the team Jennifer and I would make. We wouldn't even need Lictor. We'd go higher. All Alex is good for is . . . Sometimes he scares me more than Lictor. Can't get used to him. The things he does. The things he did in Lake Forest. Like it was nothing. Jennifer shouldn't be around someone like that.

"Have you changed your mind, sir?"

Jennifer looked up curiously.

"No . . . No," he answered, aware of her eyes on him. "Just thinking about your suggestion." He snatched up the pen and scrawled his name twice in three seconds and then shook it from his fingers.

Once outside with Jennifer, Bloomer began to feel a bit better. The day was bright and the air was cool with just a whiff of an early autumn. Jennifer had seen the tension in him and now she could see it beginning to drain off.

"Mordicai?" she said softly, taking his arm and folding it over hers.

"Yes, Jennifer."

"Would you like to talk?"

"About what?"

"About what's hurting you. It's more than the station, isn't it?"

"You know damn well it is."

"Why? Because I'm a psychic? Or because I'm a woman. You of all people should know the difference, Mordicai. I don't read minds."

"Then you give an awfully good imitation of someone who does."

"I know that you cared for me in Lake Forest, Mordicai, because you said so." She stopped and turned so that he had to look at her directly. "I know that you're feeling something for me now because of the way you're acting. Any woman would know it."

"You're a long way from being just any woman, Jennifer. Even before this happened to you, I don't think there was anything ordinary about you. By the way, what was that you did to Barbara Halloran?"

"It's called Shorin-ryu. An Okinawan style of self-defense."

"Like karate?"

"A little. With some Aikido thrown in."

"You hold, I presume, a black belt of the seventh dan."

"Nope," she laughed. "It's the first time I've tried it except at the school. I'm taking lessons from a man in Chicago in return for doing portraits of his family. It's good exercise and it's fun."

"It teaches you to put someone to sleep? Just like that?"

"No." The smile faded slightly. "That was something else." Jennifer dropped her eyes to his chest.

"I see."

"No, you don't see, Mordicai. You're being dumb now," she said, not unkindly. "Before this happened, as you put it, I was a twenty-two-year-old girl who was not as pretty, smart or talented as some, and more so than others. But I was more screwed up than most because I'd just lost a husband who I loved very dearly in the time we had together. You talk about 'this happening' like it was some sort of laying on of hands. What it was, Mordicai, was that I tried to kill myself. I didn't plan it, but I did let it happen. One night I drove into my garage and pushed the button that made the door come down behind me and I just sat there. Not wanting to go into the house and not wanting to shut off the engine either. So I sat. I sat there until my eyes closed and I couldn't feel the loneliness anymore." Jennifer stopped, not sure whether to go on. Bloomer knew all this. He knew everything that could be learned about her. But it needed to be said now.

"For sixteen days, I was in a coma, Mordicai. In that time, I saw wonderful things. Fantastically beautiful places. My father was with me. But not my husband. David had come and gone. Sixteen days. I didn't want to come back, but here I am. Parts of my brain had been cooked but I'm really not that different than I was before. Calmer perhaps, as you should be, because we both know what's going to happen when our lives are over. And yes, I can do things that other people aren't able to do. But not all day long, Mordicai. Not every day. What I am mostly is a thirty-year-old woman who laughs and cries and loves and needs just like anyone else. Just like you."

"Yes. Just like me, Jen."

"I don't love you, Mordicai."

"I know that."

"And I don't think you love me. You may want me, but then you want almost every woman. I might last longer than most because after I've been had, I'll still have value toward your work."

"Jennifer!" he flushed. "I won't have you cheapening . . ."

"Would you like me to stay with you tonight?" she asked softly.

"What?"

"I'll stay with you tonight if you like."

Bloomer felt his blood rush to his face. Disbelief. Anger. Shock. Desire. His most unlikely fantasy of the past three years being laid at his feet if she was serious. Or was she throwing him a bone?

"Just like that?"

She nodded. Her eyes were almost liquid and they were locked onto his.

"Why?" he whispered.

"Because."

"Jennifer, I don't understand."

"I told you I have needs. One of them is to be held when I'm frightened."

"You could have anyone."

"But I don't have anyone. Not anyone who would understand why I'll wake up shaking in the middle of the night. And I have some feelings to sort out."

"About me?"

"I don't think so."

"You could at least have said maybe. It's not Alex, is it?"

"Don't be silly. He'd be horrified."

"Do I know him?"

"No," she answered. Not yet, she meant. Nor do I. Not the way you mean, Mordicai. But I've gone to him. Once from the airplane as I was flying here. I found him in the public library. A boy was with him. His son. A good man. His son will be a good man, too. Unless . . . There was something . . . I couldn't tell. Too great a distance. But I went to the father again last night, when I realized it was the other Halloran, the empty one, that was with you. While you were with his wife, I was with him. I sent myself to him as my body slept. He was on his couch. It's green. Pale green with a muted floral print. There's an oriental rug in front of it and a commode that's used as a coffee table. There's a brass ashtray on it and a plant. A Wandering Jew. It should get more sunlight. He was asleep. Almost. And he was hurting terribly. I touched him and I drew the fear out upon myself. And much of the pain. I can deal with it better. I understand it. As he will deal with it when he understands. But he drew something from me too. I should have known. And he gave me more than I wanted to take. I think.

Yes, Mordicai Bloomer. I'll spend the night with you if you wish and we'll use each other because we need each other. But I'll be feeling his spirit while I'm feeling your body. Tonight it will be Halloran who comes to me. He wants to come. And he can come. The wound that scarred his brain has also crushed his chains. He will learn this. I'll try to teach him. And then perhaps I will find the gift that is so much greater than all the others. A gift, poor Mordicai, that you will never find because you spend your life looking past it.

"Jen?"

"Yes?"

"Let's just see what happens."

"Yes."

"In the meantime, it's going to be a long day. We'd better get this spookmobile back where we can use it. Zalman may have been trying to reach me too."

Alex Makepeace had been following the second current for two hours. It seemed at first that there was only one, a strong one, starting from the station. A steady stream, straight as a rod, that homed like an invisible laser beam on old Ezra Cohen's house. But then the stream began to undulate. Like the rising smoke from a cigarette held still except that it did not dissipate itself. The stream, to his annoyance, then passed the Cohen house. That, he thought, has to mean that the old boy is out. Maybe he scored last night. Good. That means, unless he's somewhere up ahead, that this is a new trail. Cohen's a definite. One down and four to go according to what Nigel told Bloomer. Have to keep an eye on our friend Mordicai. He acts like he's getting close to the edge. Terribly nervous this morning. Is it Jennifer's effect on him? Or more than that. Bloomer's acting rather like a man with a secret. An attractive man, though.

He proceeded up the hill on a slalomlike course, losing the stream here, picking it up again there. The Halloran house is up ahead. Knoll Street. Don't jump to conclusions, Alex. Slow and steady does it. The station was still at his back. Directly behind him. The current was pretty much sticking to the road. Convenient, but it wouldn't last. Shit! There it goes. Off into someone's rhododendrons. It's so much weaker. Wait a minute. The thing didn't turn. It divided. Part of it is turning. Alex followed the main stream for another block, satisfying himself that he could pick it up again later. He then doubled back to a side street just beyond the place of the fork. PALMER TERRACE, the sign said. Looks like a cul-de-sac. That means I'll be all the more conspicuous. Dummy! Should have brought a dog along. You can go anywhere with a dog. You can start and stop and sniff around without anyone looking twice at you. A leash would be almost as good. Alex unbuckled his belt and slipped it from his trousers. He folded the thin leather strap in two so that it formed a long loop and held it in his fist so that the buckle would dangle freely. He shook it. The buckle rewarded him with a plausible tinkle. The dog ought to have a name. How about Aramis? Excellent name for a dog. But not for this purpose. If, he thought, I have to pretend to call my pretend dog it ought to have a name that sounds like a dog. It will have to be Snoopy. Embarrassing as it might be for a grown man to be calling a dog named Snoopy, the name cannot possibly apply to anyone or anything but a dog. I'll say the kids named him and I am blameless.

Alex crossed the path less than halfway down the Palmer Terrace block. He'd guessed correctly. It was heading toward Knoll Street. He whistled for Snoopy and clapped his hands several times, then doubled back to the main road which would take him to the Halloran house.

Barbara's car was in the driveway, the same Ford wagon that she'd driven shakily from the New Englander parking lot several hours before. No sign of the husband's car. That might have been he who drove past on the station road. Man and boy both about the right ages. Very possibly the same man and boy who were on the platform yesterday. Didn't get a very good look. Come on, Snoopy. Let's check out the house.

Alex walked several houses farther down Knoll Street, and, having satisfied himself that the stream had not gone beyond, he turned back and walked quietly up the Halloran driveway. There it was. Through a garage on Palmer Terrace and then through the Halloran garage and right in through the kitchen door. Through the wall, actually. He crossed the backyard as casually as possible to the far side of the house and turned out once again to the street. He was sure now that the stream ended inside. Barbara Halloran. Two down, three to go. Alex wondered how Barbara enjoyed Mordicai and vice versa. Such a waste.

So far, so good. Two of the tentacles definitely identified.

Neither crossing through any innocent homes on any regular basis. No real danger of harm as long as Ezra and Barbara stay put. It's when they move around. God knows who the stream washes over when they're moving.

Alex returned to the main station road and picked up the other fork at once. He resumed his slalom as before but the road soon curved sharply off to the left. Damn. He would have to circle each block from here on. Spring Street was next. He found the stream near its end. It had passed directly through at least two homes. Getting weaker. The homes it touched, or the people in them, were tapping its energy. No, that's wrong. If anything's being tapped, it's the people. Maybe this one won't even end in the house of the man or woman who's causing it. Maybe it's someone visiting. Someone who, if we're lucky, lives closer to the station. Maybe it's Ezra.

Meadow Lane was next. A short street. Only four houses to a side. Can't feel the stream yet. But something else. A buzzing. Like bees. Frantic. It's like panic. Be still for a while, Alex. What was it? Try to tune in. Wish Jennifer was here. She'd pick it up in a flash. Is that screaming? Yelling? A fight someplace? No. Just one voice. A girl. Hysterical. There's a girl running. Is that her? My God, she's not wearing anything but panties and a filmy little top. And now a man. Her father? He's yelling after her. Crying. She's gone. Around the corner. Come on, Snoopy. Let's see what's happening. The worst he can do is tell us to get lost and mind our own business. But I'll lay you nice odds that our missing tentacle doesn't go any farther than that red house.

THE GORMLEYS, the mailbox said. 12 Meadow Road. And the door is wide open. Alex crossed the Gormley's front lawn, deciding that a frontal approach was best. A concerned passerby.

Alex paused at the door, his hand on the bell and his head leaning slightly past the threshold. A man's voice coming from upstairs. A calm voice. Friendly. What was that name he said? Barbara! Barbara Halloran! Peter! He just said Peter. He must be talking to Barbara Halloran on the phone. Alex closed the door behind him and crept silently up the flight of stairs. He heard a plastic click as he reached the top. The brief clatter of a telephone being replaced in its cradle. Another click. Different. And one more just like it. Alex recognized the sound. Spring locks on luggage or a briefcase. Then, the creaking of a bed followed shortly by the riffling of papers. Alex moved breathlessly toward the bedroom door that was ajar about a foot and a half. He could see the lower end of the man's feet, shoes and all, hanging over the edge of a four-poster bed. Then he saw her. Only an arm at first. He moved closer to the open door.

She was sprawled on pillows, totally nude and on her back. Her right hand was out of sight but the arm laid across an expanse of fire-brick. There was a sweet, porklike smell coming from the room. A fireplace. Her hand must be in the fireplace. That was the smell. Alex knew at a glance that the woman was dead. Her mature breasts hung off slightly to the sides and there was no motion from the chest beneath them. Her eyes were hooded but open and dull. Dried out and lifeless. He knocked firmly on the bedroom door.

"Who's that?" came the irritated voice. Alex pushed the door open.

"I'm a friend of the Hallorans. I wondered if I could be of any help."

Gormley's face brightened at the name. "Oh, sure. Where's Peter? Couldn't he make it?"

"He's out on some errands. Barbara asked me to look in. What can I do, Mr. Gormley?"

"The name's Jack," he answered, putting his papers aside and stepping out of the bed. "And look, I really appreciate this. I mean, being Sunday morning and all. I was afraid I wouldn't be able to get any work done."

"Did you want me to help you bury her?"

"I'm afraid that would take all day. If you can help me bundle her into two or three leaf bags, we can just haul her down to the dump. I was going to get my daughter to help but she . . ." Gormley's face clouded for an instant, as if he couldn't quite remember what it was about his daughter. "She . . . she had to go out. You know how it is with kids."

"Listen, Jack, I'm not going to feel like I'm helping if I pull you away from your papers. You sit right back down until we're ready to move her. Where are the leaf bags? Out in the garage?"

"Yeah. There's a box of Kordite bags all the way back on your left as you go in."

"Back in a second. By the way, Jack. Maybe you can do me a favor. Do you happen to have a pistol I can borrow?"

"Afraid not. All I have is a shotgun."

"That'd do nicely."

"In the hall closet right below where you're standing. Shells are on the shelf."

"Great. You promise you'll stick with your work now?"

"Appreciate it, ah . . . Hey, I don't know your name."

"It's Fred. I'm Barbara's cousin from Philadelphia. Be right back, Jack."

Alex knew he had to work quickly. Once downstairs, he glanced into the hall closet in search of a pair of gloves. Two pair of ski mittens hung from a hook in the rear. They wouldn't do. Use a kitchen towel. He found a dishcloth with a Colonial design and quickly wiped every surface he could recall touching. He then returned to the hall closet and withdrew the gun case. Holding the case in his right hand which was wrapped in the towel, Alex worked the zipper open, being careful to smudge any fragmentary prints he might have left on the tab. It was a Browning over-and-under shotgun. Breech loading. The box of shells was where Jack had said. Trap loads. They'll do well enough. Alex carefully loaded both barrels. It was clumsy work using the towel but he accomplished it in a very few seconds, then laid the gun against the stairs. The garage, set some thirty feet back from the house, was next. Alex forced himself to cover the distance slowly. It looked good. No neighbors' windows facing on Gormley's backyard. One neighbor to the rear, separated by a stone wall and a thick privet hedge. It was a low ranch with the garage on one end. He had an excellent chance of reaching the next street without being seen. Unless that neighbor had a dog. He approached the hedge and whistled loudly. No response. He picked up a rock and raked it against the stone wall. Still nothing. No dog. At least, none outside.

Inside the garage, he selected two large leaf bags and returned to the back kitchen door, tearing open one of the seams as he walked. He rolled his shirtsleeves up as tightly as possible and then slipped the torn bag over his head. With his fingertips, he pushed two armholes through the tan polyethylene. Running out of time. How long has it been? Ten minutes, maybe. Too long. Who's the daughter talking to right now? Is she able to talk? Are they believing her? What if they do? Do they call the police or do they come take a look first? Lock the front door. Push the button on the back door so it locks when it's shut. Alex picked up the gun and proceeded once more to the master bedroom.

Gormley was on his feet. He was staring at Polly. An expression on his face like there was something he was trying hard to remember. He turned his head toward Alex, reacting not at all to the plastic body shroud or the shotgun in Alex's hand. His eyes confused and his lips trying to form words, he pointed at Polly's swollen face. Alex felt the chill as the current swept over him. Then past him. It was searching for Gormley. Shit! He moved too fast. Gormley must have got out of bed too fast and jerked out of it. He was right on the edge of it.

"Don't move, Jack," he said gently but firmly. "Let it find you. The nice cool air. Spread your arms to help it find you. That's right. That's good, Jack. Okay. Back to work now. You just sit down and let me handle this."

Gormley nodded uncertainly, and fumbled for the pile of reports he'd been reading. Alex gestured toward Polly with his head. "They can sure be more trouble than they're worth, can't they, Jack?"

"Oh, she was alright, mostly." His voice was firm now. Decisive. In charge. "She just took so damned much time." Abruptly, he tapped a finger against the page he was reading. "Fred, you wouldn't believe this. So goddamned many incompetents around . . ."

Alex moved to the far side of the bed as if to read over Gormley's shoulder. Instead, bracing one knee on the bed, he seized the knot of Gormley's necktie and jerked him savagely across the room. Gormley gave a short angry shout that died on his lips. His muscles went limp and the confusion returned. For a brief moment he studied Alex's face, then turned his eyes again toward Polly.

"What . . . Hey . . . Did I . . . ?"

"I'm going to help you, Jack. I want you to open your mouth. That's it, Jack. Wider please. Good. Just hold this in your mouth for me a second." Alex pulled both triggers.

Ira Zalman was waiting in the lobby on a chair facing the entrance. He'd just purchased a copy of the Sunday *Times* at the desk and had pulled out the magazine section when Mordicai and Jennifer pushed through the doors.

"Where'd you come from?" he asked, rising to his feet. "Was that you in the camper?"

"It's not a camper," said Mordicai, extending his hand. "It's a Winnebago Motor Home. Hi Doc! Meet Jennifer Wilde. Jennifer Wilde, meet Ira Zalman."

"I was very excited about meeting you, Ms. Wilde. Now I'm more so. You're something more than I expected."

"Thank you, Doctor," she smiled shyly. "Mordicai speaks highly of you, too."

"Really? What did he say and why is he pretending he's not out to get me?"

"He said," she laughed, "that for a shrink, you have a decent sense of humor and an open mind. Shall we go upstairs?"

Mordicai replaced the phone after ordering coffee from room service. Zalman was making nervous small-talk with Jennifer. He was chatting and grinning amiably but his eyes and ears were probing, evaluating.

"What's the camp . . . excuse me, what's the Winnebago Motor Home for?"

"We just rented it. We'll be trying to make contact down at the station and we can't very well sit down in the middle of the parking lot. Not without the Winnebago. We'll also need the mobility to find certain hot spots both in the station area and elsewhere around town."

"Contact with whom?" he asked. "And you also said you'd be *trying*. I was given to understand that you have what amounts to a direct line to the spirit world."

"They have a direct line to me," she corrected. "They respond or talk through me when they choose."

"Is that often? From what I've read, a séance is very much a hit or miss proposition. How often do you get through? One out of ten, say?"

"Almost always."

"Could you do it right this minute?"

"Dr. Zalman, it's important that you remember something. That it's their nickel. I get through when the contact is important to them. The same can be said of Mordicai's contacts. Demonstrations are not important to them. Persuading a psychiatrist of their existence, however well-meaning he is, is not important to them either."

"May I ask why not?" but he held up his hand before she could answer. "Please overlook the apparent conceit beyond that question, Jennifer. Try to forget, for the moment, that I happen to be a psychiatrist. The question then becomes, Why do those in the spirit world not want me, Ira Zalman, to have proof that they exist?"

"What sort of proof?" Bloomer interjected. "Can you imagine any evidence that could not possibly be explained away?"

"I imagine I could think of something."

"Tell me then, do you believe that American astronauts landed on the moon in 1969?"

"Of course."

"Do you recall reading that there are still educated, or at least literate, people in the United States and in Europe who believe that the whole thing was a fake?"

"Your point, of course, is that no evidence would persuade them otherwise."

"Exactly. But this goes a few steps further. The spirits, our spirits, feel that they've given all the evidence of their existence, short of a guided tour, that's necessary for anyone with the will to consider that evidence. They feel that an acceptance of their existence requires far less in the way of blind faith than your belief, for example, in the events described in the Old Testament. The nature of their existence is something else again. They have no wish to have humanity at large to believe or know that the next plane of existence is nothing more complicated than the next evolutionary step after this one. It is, in fact, an altogether pleasant and exciting step. I know that. Alex Makepeace—he's Jennifer's control—he knows it. And of course, Jennifer knows it. We don't just believe it, Doctor, we know it. Jennifer has even been there for a couple of weeks and has been back for short periods many times since. Each of the three of us would be perfectly at ease if our lives ended tonight. But we can't go. We've been given a job to do even if it's only a messenger boy's job by their standards. However, if the population at large knew what we know, that there's really no such thing as heaven or hell or judgment after death as they've been brought up to understand it—that the lowest level of the next world is immensely preferable to the most exalted station of this world—I'm afraid that a few million people would decide not to hang around."

"You've actually been there, Jennifer?"

"Yes."

"Do I understand correctly that you went there immediately following a brain injury?"

"Of a sort, yes. But the brain injury was not a prerequisite. A great many people have had shorter but similar experiences."

"You're referring to those accident and illness victims who've recovered from the point of clinical death and reported out-of-body experiences?"

"Yes."

"In any case, whatever abilities you have date from your injury?"

"Yes. As far as I know."

"But do you have psychic powers?"

"We all do. Mine have been . . . unclogged."

"Jennifer, I'm holding an object in my fist. Would you be terribly offended if I asked you to tell me what it is?"

"What will that prove, Dr. Zalman?"

"That you have psychic powers."

"No, it won't. It will prove that I know what's in your fist. And not a thing more or less."

Zalman studied her for a long moment. "Of course, you're right. That was stupid of me."

"For what it's worth," she said, stretching her body backward across the bed, "What you're holding is a Kennedy half dollar."

There was a knock on the door. Zalman cast an irritated glance toward it and Mordicai rose to admit the room service waiter who entered carrying an aluminum tray over one shoulder. He made a fussy show of setting out the coffee decanter, cups, and assorted Danish pastries on the table desk near the window. Bloomer signed the check and had to say thank you three times before the waiter caught the hint and quietly left the room. Zalman sat rolling the coin in his fingers, deep in thought. Jennifer was right. It proved nothing. For here he was, he realized, wondering when she could have seen him remove it from his pocket.

"I know you'd like to get down to the business at hand," he said, "but I'll be more comfortable if you'll allow me just a few more questions."

"We'll tell you what we can, Ira," Mordicai smiled. Bloomer rather enjoyed watching his new friend struggle at the threshold of conversion.

"Shall I believe, Jennifer, that you can read my mind?"

"Not exactly, Doctor. I do get certain feelings. Not all the time."

"You are what is called a sensitive, is that correct?"

"Yes."

"Are you able to tell me how it works? What the thought process is?"

"It's not a sequential thought process. Nor can I read private thoughts except more or less to the extent that you can. Your training and experience, and, of course, your personal sensitivity, enable you to pick up emotions and various moods from your patients. I can do that too. I do it naturally and, I think, with more confidence because I'm not burdened with all the caveats that go with professional training. I don't pick up idle thoughts or even more serious thoughts if they have no direct relationship to whatever else is going on between us. For example, if you were thinking about cutting my throat right now, I probably wouldn't get it. You were, very naturally, thinking about testing me and that, I did pick up.

"The business with the half dollar is more difficult to explain. I knew that you were thinking in terms of a test. I had an impression that you were holding a Kennedy half dollar in your hand and wondered whether that would be the test. In effect, I created a small scenario in my mind and you acted it out. Now the question. Did I read your mind or were you sensitive to mine?"

"I might try to accept that if you'd simply seen a coin," he answered. "If I were going to take any object out of my pocket and conceal it in a closed fist, it would probably be a coin. But you named a very specific coin that might be found in my pocket four or five times a year."

"But you knew you had it. And you wanted very much to witness a demonstration of extrasensory perception. That you transmitted the information to me, Doctor, is just as easy to believe as that I took it."

"Telepathy?"

"Telepathy's a natural fact, Ira," Bloomer put in. "Well documented among virtually all life forms. Even plants. Certainly among ants and bees and homing pigeons. In spite of the documentation, there are still those who'll deny telepathic communication and call it instinct. Give it a reasonable label and you don't have to think about it anymore. It's as foolishly short-sighted as lumping geophysical phenomena such as earthquakes and meteorological phenomena such as hailstorms under the heading Acts of God."

"I read an occasional book, Mordicai," Zalman replied, somewhat miffed at Bloomer's presumption of ignorance or prejudice on his part. "As it happens, I'm aware of some of the federally-funded work being done toward the end of understanding and harnessing telepathy and thought projection. Would it surprise you to learn that experiments are being conducted even in the area of physical projection? The breaking down and reassembling of molecular structures? It's actually been done with the embryo of a salamander. Perhaps *Star Trek*'s transporter beam isn't so far away?"

Zalman poured a cup of coffee and offered it to Jennifer. When she declined, he kept it himself and took a large bite out of a prune Danish.

"But we're getting off the track," he continued. "Of the work being done concerning the power of the mind, the more interesting stuff postulates that these are indeed natural powers, perhaps chemically rooted, that can be physiologically explained and even learned. The studies concerning the function of the pineal gland bring us closer to home. Shall I assume that you're familiar with the pineal?"

"Probably from a different perspective, Ira."

"You refer, no doubt, to Descartes' contention that the pineal gland is the physical location of the soul, that the soul has mass, and that it's perfectly capable of independent existence without the body?"

"Descartes had lots of company," Bloomer answered. He knew that they were both showing off like college sophomores but what the hell! "More recently the gland has been shown to manufacture a hormone called melatonin that's chemically similar to LSD. Both are hallucinogens. The former is thought to be responsible for moods of elation and inspiration that are not experienced by the lower animals. Combine a living soul with a melatonin factory and you have a physical entity that's capable of seeing and understanding the physically imperceptible. Take a highly developed pineal gland, one that's larger than the average, and you have the pineal gland of every proven psychic or medium on whom an autopsy has been performed after death. Take a pineal gland that's been traumatized at some point and you have a Jennifer Wilde. Apparently, you also have a Peter Halloran."

"And you?"

"I'll have to wait for the autopsy."

Zalman smiled. *I'd love to be there*, he thought. *Especially at Jennifer's. Whatever she has, it's remarkable. And a hell of a lot more than she's willing to let on. To me at least.*

"Okay!" He clapped his hands together. "Let's talk about the station. What's happening and what are you going to do about it?"

"You were going to do some digging for us, Ira."

"And I have." He reached into his inside jacket pocket and withdrew a wad of notepapers. "I have an assistant still working on it. For now, here is a list of every deceased Riverside resident over the past five years. If this is to help you identify the, uh, spirits who appeared at Leticia's house, I'm afraid Mr. Kornhauser's death is the only one directly connectable with the station." He handed the sheet to Mordicai. "This next, for what it's worth, is a bar graph showing the incidence of various forms of antisocial behavior in Riverside over the past three years. That's extrapolated from police department records and you'll note that it's almost flat until about one year ago. Particularly note the shocking rate of increase over the past three months. This alone persuaded me that you might be on to something. I gather the same pattern emerged in Lake Forest?" Zalman passed the chart.

"Pretty much."

"Next, although it can't be charted quite so easily, my colleagues in psychiatry cite an approximately parallel increase in emotional disturbances that are consistent with police records. Not very many new male patients seeking therapy, but a good many wives expressing concern about apparent personality changes in their husbands. Almost all in Riverside."

Zalman started to hand his notes to Bloomer, who waved them off when the telephone rang.

"Hello? . . . Oh, yes Alex. She's right here." Jennifer rolled off the bed and took the receiver from Mordicai.

"Hi, Alex. What've you . . . ?" Alex had clearly brushed aside any pleasantries. Jennifer's face became a mask as she listened, stiffly, moving only when she gestured to Mordicai for a pad and pencil.

"That's three you're sure about? Who's the probable? Wait. How do you spell Weinberg?" Zalman's head snapped up at the name. "How about you, Alex? Are you sure you're all right? . . . No, Alex. Please, no. You stay away from there. . . . No, we haven't heard anything. Listen. Please don't do anything else except look around. We'll be down at the station by three this afternoon with the Winnebago. Meet us there. I think Peter Halloran will be there too. . . . Yes, I know, Alex. I'll try. Dr. Zalman seems to know him. Goodbye, Alex. Please don't . . . Please be careful." Jennifer replaced the phone but, for a few moments, seemed reluctant to take her hand from it.

"How bad?" Mordicai asked.

"It'll do." She tapped her notepad with a finger. "Alex has confirmed three paths. One is Barbara Halloran but we knew that last night. He's sure the second is a man named Ezra Cohen with whom he had an encounter yesterday. These two are fairly close to the station and should be no problem as long as they stay close to home. The third definite, . . ." she paused for a deep breath, ". . . is a man named Gormley, who killed his wife last night. The police are there now."

"Polly Gormley?" asked a shocked Ira Zalman. "What's his name? Jack? He killed Polly?"

"Where will the police take him?" asked Bloomer, ignoring Zalman. The psychiatrist looked at him. A curious question, thought Zalman.

"That won't be a problem," Jennifer replied, looking hard into Bloomer's eyes. "Alex says he shot himself before they could take him away."

Bloomer understood. An equally curious answer, thought Zalman.

"I thought I heard sirens when I pulled in here," Zalman recalled.

"Alex says the sirens haven't stopped for the past two hours. There's apparently trouble all over town. The first major trouble involved this Paul Weinberg who was enveloped . . . who lost control at the station this morning. I believe you know about him."

"Are you asking or telling, Jennifer?"

"No telepathy, Doctor. You reacted to the name."

"He's been a patient, although not lately. I have him under heavy sedation at Greenwich Hospital."

"I've got to see him today."

"You won't get anything out of him," Zalman shrugged. "As I said, he's sedated."

"He doesn't have to speak. If there's a path, it'll be all around him."

"What if there is?"

"Then you'll have to get him released. He can't be that far from the station."

Zalman almost dropped his cup. "That's out of the question," he sputtered. "The man is dangerous. He's already hospitalized his wife and one policeman."

"We'll take care of him, Ira," said Mordicai quietly. "Or Alex will. I think I can guarantee that Weinberg won't hurt anyone else." He glanced unpleasantly toward Jennifer.

Zalman rose to object but Jennifer quieted him with a hand on his arm.

"For now, just let me see him, Doctor. As for the rest, I think your decision will be far simpler by the end of the day."

"Jennifer, do you have any idea what you'd be asking of me?"

"We'll wait and see," she said quietly.

"Anyway," said Bloomer, "we still have to find the fifth path. That's if there are still only five. Ira, I asked you for a list of patients who are being treated for any disorder that's in any way connected with the railroad station."

"You did. And I have four names and addresses. But I can't give them to you."

Bloomer blinked. "Then what was the point in bringing the list?"

"I warned you at Leticia's that there'd be an ethical problem. Anyway, why do you need it? This Alex seems to be doing fine."

"It's a question of time. And Alex has a limited sensitivity. He won't be able to pick up a path if it goes too far from the source. Jennifer can pick them up anywhere."

"Then that solves my ethical problem. I'll simply drive Jennifer past each of these houses. If we find a path, she'll know where it's going and I'll identify the family member with the problem."

Bloomer looked questioningly at Jennifer, who nodded her agreement.

"What was that about Peter Halloran, by the way?" Zalman asked. "You've spoken to him?"

"No."

"Then how do you know he'll be there?"

"I just do. Ira, we'd better get down to the hospital."

"There's a lot more I'd like to know. We haven't even touched on the nature of the problem at the station."

"We can talk in your car. I just need a minute to freshen up, then let's meet in the lobby." She collected the small canvas duffel that served as a purse.

"I'll go with you," said Bloomer, slipping into his jacket. "I believe I left something in your room."

Neither Mordicai nor Jennifer spoke until the elevator doors closed on Ira Zalman. Jennifer knew why Bloomer had accompanied her and did not relish the discussion that would follow. She spoke first.

"What good are all those statistics, Mordicai? You knew what the pattern would be."

"They'll come in handy later if I want to publish a paper on the phenomenon. Zalman's involvement will serve to legitimatize the conclusions for the borderline credulous. Let's talk about Alex."

"I hope it'll be worth it," she said, ignoring his last few words. "You're taking a chance on a man who might not be able to deal with this, Mordicai."

"On the other hand, we can't touch Paul Weinberg without him. What about Alex?"

"What about him?"

"Don't fence, Jennifer. He killed that guy, didn't he?"

"He helped him over."

"Helped him over, shit!" Bloomer spat. "The man's a psychopath. He killed three people in Lake Forest including a woman and a sixteen-year-old kid. He damn near killed me when I tried to stop him and I don't even think the kid out there was infected."

"We've had this conversation before, Mordicai. You know he had no choice."

"Would you have done it?"

"I would have tried. For God's sake, Mordicai! What else could he do?" There was pain in the question.

"I don't know, dammit. Something. Anything. I don't believe Alex looks for choices."

"According to Alex, the man really loved his wife."

"That's nice. But so what?"

"What are they doing now, Mordicai? Right this second while you're standing here making us both miserable? You don't want to look at it that way, even though you know they're together and that they understand everything that's happened. Where would he be if Alex hadn't killed him? He'd be in a jail cell swinging back and forth between madness and sanity. The periods of sanity would be terrible. What's worse, wherever they put him, he'd still be tied to the station when we close it down. Anyone in his path is going to be lost. How many are still lost from Amersham after all these years? A dozen?"

"Fourteen."

"Fourteen!" she repeated. "Fourteen human personalities. Fourteen valuable people who are loved and missed and mourned from the other side. Fourteen active and aware consciousnesses floating for God knows how long through a world in which they can't participate in the slightest. Even Lictor has only been able to find one every ten years or so. We kept that from happening in Lake Forest and it's not going to happen here, either."

"Even if Alex has to wipe out half the town?"

"God damn you, stop it!"

Bloomer flinched at the vehemence of her outburst. He'd never seen Jennifer remotely this upset. She spun around with her back to him and pressed one hand over her mouth.

"How can you not understand?" she asked, struggling now to control herself. "Would it be easier for you if Alex were not homosexual? If his existence did not offend your concept of virility? Alex is a good and sensitive man. Whatever he does . . ."

Bloomer placed his hands on her shoulders and turned her gently around to face him.

"Look at me, Jennifer."

"Mordicai, let's drop it," she pleaded. "Please, can't we drop it?"

"Jennifer," he whispered, "you can think what you like about the way I choose to live. Or the way Alex lives. His homosexuality does make me a bit uncomfortable but that's not the problem here. And you're not this upset just because I don't feel right about Alex killing people. You knew that before. What is it? Alex about to kill someone else?"

"I don't know."

"What did you just start to say to me? You said, whatever he does . . . Does what?"

"I don't know that he's going to do anything."

"What feeling did you get?"

"It wasn't a feeling. He just said . . ."

"What did he say?"

"Oh, Mordicai . . ." Her shoulders shook with a single convulsive sob.

"What did he say, Jennifer?"

"He said it's wrong to keep that little girl here after . . ."

"What little girl? Did the man he killed have a little girl?"

"Yes."

Bloomer drew Jennifer to his chest and held her there for many moments without speaking.

"Can you stop him?" he asked finally.

"There's time. She'll have people all around her." Jennifer rummaged through her duffel bag for a tissue. "And he won't do anything before all the paths are found."

"Are you sure?"

"No."

"Is this like that kid in Lake Forest?"

"I think so."

"It can't happen, Jennifer. He has no right. Nigel Soames's worst fear of dealing with people on the earth plane is that they'll become totally amoral once they realize that they won't be handed a bill at the end. For all that Alex's heart is in the right place, he's crossed that line. Where does he stop? What if the man he killed has a mother in town? Or a sister? Does he do them the kindness of helping them over too?"

8

Sunday—Midday

Alex Makepeace was grinning to himself as he strolled down Summit Road, heading toward the fourth and last quadrant of his search area. It was Snoopy, his imaginary pet, that made him smile. Alex was getting used to Snoopy's company. He'd been thinking aloud and talking to the dog ever since slipping over the old stone wall that marked the rear of the Gormley property. Now, when a sudden rush of traffic appeared on Summit Road, he had to stop himself from calling Snoopy to safety. The silly impulse made him grin all the more and his smile was answered by some of the drivers of the passing cars.

Church traffic, he observed. Homeward bound. Families all combed and dressed. Some already picking through the Sunday paper and passing the comics into the back seat. The later cars will be carrying boxes of assorted Dunkin' Donuts and the children will be arguing over who gets what and how many. Don't open that box, he could almost hear the mother saying. You'll get sugar or jelly all over your good pants. Quite a few mothers were driving, now that he thought about it. Plenty of complete families, but several without fathers. Wonder if that's normal! Probably is. There'd always be a quota of golf and tennis widows going to church, or divorced women. Still, he'd give odds that church attendance was off lately.

Hello! There's a car not coming from church. That man and boy again. Him wearing a sweater and his son in a foul-weather jacket. I'd give even longer odds, Alex thought, that that's the talented Mr. Halloran. Go home, Mr. Halloran. See if you can get a nice Sunday brunch out of that termagant you married. A good last meal. With any sort of luck, you'll be a widower in a day or so.

Alex whistled for Snoopy as he picked up his pace. What's the matter, boy? What are you growling at? That house? Ah, yes. The gray one. That's old Ezra's house. But he's not in. Did you notice that he uses cold cream? No, of course you didn't. He does use it, though. You can smell it ten yards off. Probably bleaches out his liver spots too. A superannuated fag clinging desperately to the last fine wisp of youth. Which of God's creatures is so lonely? Looks like he's had at least one tuck, too. Must remember to look for scars behind his ears. Vain old faggot. Closet queen. Probably keeps *Playboy* on his coffee table and copies of *After Dark* under his bed. Bet he has a cat named Pyewacket or a parakeet named Obregon and the biggest collection of Judy Garland records in Riverside.

Hey! You know something? I have an idea. What do you suppose Ezra would do if I were to blacken both his eyes. I do owe him one, you know. The preening old fruit would stay indoors, that's what he'd do. He'd stay close to the station. What do you say, Snoopy? Why don't we see if he's got a nice comfortable patio out back with a chaise for me and a bit of shade for you until the old bird shows up?

If Alex had come back from the Gormley house the way he'd gone, he would have passed a path that should not have been there. He would have guessed it was Ezra moving about. He might even have seen him. But Ezra was behind him now, keeping his distance and perspiring heavily, ducking now and then behind a thick pin oak or into a driveway. Ezra's own path had wound around him now and enveloped him, leaving only the moving stream that connected him to the station. The stream followed Alex like a slow wave that matched its progress to his, or to Ezra's. Cohen, his eyes shining like those of a cat locked onto a bird, dried his sweating palm against his pants leg and felt for the billy still tucked inside his belt.

* * *

Barbara was on the kitchen phone when Peter and Jeff came through the back door. She did not look up to acknowledge their presence.

". . . and you were absolutely right about Martha. By far, the best shore dinner I've ever tasted. A magnificent lobster. And one of the more fascinating evenings I can recall. . . . Yes, Mordicai—Professor Bloomer—is a most refreshing man. Brilliant. We had the most marvelous chat over several cups of coffee. He seemed to think the Wentworths well deserve to be the subject of a book . . . You do? Leticia, I'm so pleased to hear you say . . . Oh, certainly. I can imagine how busy you are. The whole world is waiting for your next . . . No. I don't have his number but I imagine he'll be calling. Or you can simply call New Engl . . . Is anything wrong, Leticia? Oh, good. Well, let's not be strangers now that we . . . Yes, of course . . . Good-bye, Leticia."

Barbara made a little smirk at the phone as she hung it on the wall and then her face tightened into the severe visage reserved for the family.

"Jeffrey! You will please leave a note when you leave this house before I'm awake. And tell your father that a Sgt. Turkus of the police wants to speak to him but it can wait until he sits himself down at his desk and completes the insurance forms on his accident. I'm tired of explaining him to the claims agent."

"Dad's right here, Mom."

"Did you hear me, Jeffrey?"

"Yeah. So did my dad." Jeff headed for the stairs.

"Come back here, young man." Barbara kept her voice low and menacing.

"Look!" he said, turning in the doorway. "If you have anything to say to Dad, say it to Dad. He doesn't need an interpreter."

"Don't you dare talk to me in that tone," she hissed.

"Lay off him, Barbara," Peter said quietly. She ignored him. She snatched a long-handled spatula from its hook over the stove and hefted it in her hand like a club.

"Come over here, Jeffrey," she said, pointing to a spot on the rug in front of her. Jeff looked questioningly at his father who was leaning against the back door with his arms folded.

"Mother, I'm not going to walk over there and I'm not going to let you hit me with that."

Barbara struck the spatula sharply against her thigh like a riding crop. She snapped her head toward Peter and addressed him directly for the first time.

"Are you responsible for this insolence?"

"Nope," he replied calmly. "Jeff decided he'd rather not be hit with a spatula and he told you so. Sounds reasonable to me."

"That's all you have to say?"

"No. There'll be quite a lot. But for openers, Jeff and I are going to buy a golden retriever pup next week."

Barbara was momentarily stunned by this awesome non sequitur. She recovered quickly. Halloran winked at Jeff and saw his face brighten.

"There will be no dogs in this house."

"You're outvoted."

"By you and a child?" she laughed contemptuously. "That's the most pathetic thing I've ever heard."

"You're outvoted by me."

"Even more pathetic," she said, giving Peter her best I-smell-shit look. "Jeffrey, I gave you an order."

"You're not going to hit him."

"And who, may I ask, is going to stop me?"

"I am. I'm going to stop you from swinging that thing at Jeff. Your impulse then, is going to be to swing at me. When you do that, I'm going to knock you on your ass."

This time, Barbara said nothing. Her jaw dropped and she stared. First, with an expression of shock and fear but then, oddly, the beginnings of a cruel little smile that faded back into fear almost as soon as it appeared. Then a flash of anger lit her eyes and her lips curled as if poised to spew out vitriol, but nothing came. Just that half smile again and once more it slipped away. Peter felt a chill. *It's like there are two people in there,* he thought. *One as disagreeable as the other, but one much more dangerous.*

"Dad?"

What is it about her? What is it about that chill? It wasn't just a chill. It was cold. Then it floated away. Like last night at the station.

"Dad!"

Gormley was two different people. Now Barbara. Almost. She's somewhere on the edge. Do they give off cold air when they . . . or does the cold air cause it? Was Kornhauser two people? I don't think so. . . .

"Dad!"

"Yeah, Jeff."

"Let's get out of here."

* * *

The police sirens stopped shortly after noon. Too many calls to headquarters by unaffected citizens wondering what was happening. The police went about their work more quietly. A man named Fusco shot a neighbor's dog for lifting its leg against his azalea bush. He then announced he would shoot the neighbor if he made another sound. The neighbor said that Fusco, who had been his friend for over six years, did not seem to know him. On Lockwood Road, George Leonard backed his car over three bicycles that were blocking his driveway, knocking a child to the street, and drove off apparently oblivious to the mangled frame that his car dragged along. Ed McShane unplugged his color television set and threw it into the road outside his home. He explained to the police that his children were wasting too much time in front of it and seemed genuinely surprised that the police would bother to ask about it. A golfer knocked his playing partner of fourteen years unconscious with a putter after the partner called a penalty stroke on him. Activity at the emergency ward of Greenwich Hospital was at least three times its normal Sunday level. Many "accidental falls" by women and children. Six complaints of domestic violence answered by police. Unheard of on a Sunday morning, ordinarily considered the most stress-free and alcohol-free period of the entire week. Many more such calls, the police knew from their own statistics, went unmade.

Sgt. Mike Turkus was scheduled to go off duty at noon. At that hour, he returned to headquarters and then sequestered himself among the files on missing persons.

The clock on Ira Zalman's dashboard showed ten minutes to two. He put the Buick in gear and let it coast out of the hospital's sloping circular driveway. The visit to Weinberg's room had left him tense and troubled. Jennifer and Mordicai were visibly relieved.

"You're absolutely sure?" he asked Jennifer without moving his head.

"Yes."

"Beyond what I already know about his probable state of mind, how dangerous do you think he is?"

"He's terribly dangerous," she replied thoughtfully, "because he's thoroughly unpredictable, but mostly because he'll seem so rational. He might wake up and calmly ask for a sandwich and then just as calmly crush the skull of whoever hands it to him. Are you going to keep him doped up?"

"I've left instructions to that effect." Zalman signaled a left turn and swung onto the Post Road headed back toward Riverside. "Jennifer, I've been waiting for you to explain what's happening here."

"I know. And I've been trying to think how to put it into words."

"But you do know?"

"Yes, but . . ."

Mordicai leaned forward from the back seat and folded his arms between Zalman and Jennifer.

"Would you like me to give it a shot? I understand Jennifer's problem," he said. "No offense, Doc, but it comes down to how much you're capable of understanding, and then how much you ought to be told for your own good and ours. Before it's over, we'll have had to break a few laws."

"Don't worry about that, Mordicai," Zalman reassured. "I realize that you have no legal status here and that certain unsanctioned steps may be necessary. I would assume that such steps would fall well short of capital crimes."

"Don't assume that, Ira."

Zalman whipped the wheel to the right and braked to a sudden stop at the curb. "You can't be serious, Mordicai," he protested, turning almost fully in his seat.

"Do you begin to understand Jennifer's problem?"

"My God, Mordicai. Are you actually telling me that you would kill to save souls? Listen to yourself. You sound like Torquemada."

"And to save lives. Yes, Ira, that's what I'm telling you. We'll kill if we have to."

"Shall I assume that you would kill me if you felt the need? To keep me quiet, for instance?"

"To save ourselves, you mean? Absolutely not. We couldn't justify it. Whatever the personal cost."

"Jennifer? Do you feel this way?"

"Yes."

"You do realize that you sound like a pair of raving fanatics, don't you?"

"Hardly raving, Ira," Mordicai answered.

"Yes," Zalman was forced to agree. "Hardly raving. It makes you all the more frightening."

"Jennifer?" Mordicai looked questioningly at her when she turned.

"Dr. Zalman wants to help us," she said gently.

"Dammit, don't start that stuff with me," he snapped.

"I promise, Doctor," she said, putting her hand over his, "I promise you'll understand and that you'll be able to live with whatever happens. And I promise we'll try very hard not to hurt anyone. Mordicai was right. Our purpose is to save lives. A great many are in danger. If you saw a madman chasing your child with a knife, you might try to avoid causing his death. But you'd stop him, Doctor. You'd stop him any way you could."

Zalman turned his head away and for long seconds gazed idly out upon the passing traffic. When he finally spoke, it was to Bloomer.

"You said you could explain all this, Mordicai."

"I'm willing to try."

"Then you'd better start," he said, snapping off his seat belt and pushing the car door open. "Let's you and me take a little walk."

The two men strolled for half a block without speaking. Past the closed and darkened shops. The sidewalk was empty and shaded. Mordicai spoke first.

"Jennifer make you nervous?"

"Let's say I'm a chauvinist."

"Pig shit!"

"Then let's say I'd like to form my own opinions. I was damn near ready to flag down the nearest squad car until she touched my hand. Can she really do things like that?"

Bloomer nodded. "She's a gas, isn't she?"

"Yet I'm not afraid of her."

"What's to be afraid? You should have a daughter like Jennifer."

"Uh-huh!" Zalman grunted dubiously. "When do you start explaining?"

Bloomer took a breath.

"The whole thing might be easier to grasp from the psychiatric point of view," he began, "or more accurately, from an examination of collective mental processes in action."

"Psychodynamics?"

"Close enough. Let's look first at what Amersham, Lake Forest and Riverside have in common. Right off the top, they're all commuter stations. We know what a station is, but what's a commuter? He's more than someone who takes a train to work. The commuter tends to be a man or woman whose life goal is success as he or she understands success. Essentially, this type of success

PLATFORMS

involves material acquisition for its own sake and for the sake of
the power it brings. The property that's acquired, and the power
as well, are seen as a goal only until they've been obtained. What
happens then?

"At that point, many people pause to take stock of their lives
and conclude that what they've been working toward is not what
they want after all. Some drop out. Some change careers. Some
divorce their old spouses and get new ones who are more in tune
with their revised approach to living. Most, who succeed in identifying the root cause of their dissatisfaction, simply shift into a
lower gear and decide they're going to concentrate on enjoying
each day to the greatest extent possible. The happiest of all are
those who manage to find some new goal or dream that leans more
in the direction of the spiritual than the material. I'm not talking
about religion necessarily, or even the spiritual as you and I have
discussed it before. I refer simply to the deliberate development
of the self in terms of character, wisdom, purpose, and experience.
In short, getting to like oneself and getting a real charge out of
living. Finding a purpose in having lived.

"There are still other people who never do stop to examine
their goals. They keep pushing. The drive toward the acquisition
of property and power continues, but with a subtle shift in em-
phasis. After they pass their crisis point without any reevaluation,
they reach a stage where they no longer even delude themselves
that property is acquired for their ultimate enjoyment of it. It has
a new purpose. Actually several. It serves to help them persuade
themselves that their lives are being spent in a worthwhile manner.
It serves to demonstrate their success and therefore the correctness
of their choice to others. It, this property, also serves as a tool or
lever to be used in acquiring still more. A house is not a home
anymore. It's a place to show and a place in which to entertain.
The same can be said of club memberships in many cases or of
the purchase of unnecessarily expensive cars and boats."

Zalman stopped walking and raised a hand. "Mordicai, if I may
interrupt you. I feel that you are leading me by the hand through
some very familiar ground in order to prepare me for an unfamiliar
conclusion. It might save time if I assure you that I'm reasonably
conversant with the psychology of the career-oriented executive
and the phenomenon of the midlife crisis. You are about to offer
the hypothesis that those who reject a more spiritually fulfilling
approach to life, whether out of fear or selfishness or what, are
likely to suffer a spiritual and emotional bankruptcy. The conflict

118

you describe accounts for two-thirds of my practice. At least among the men. It also applies to virtually every affluent community in the industrialized world. What's different about Riverside?"

"Bear with me just a bit longer. I'll try to explain in broad strokes. This bankruptcy you describe is, of course, not an end result. It creates new conditions and those conditions create effects. Specifically, it creates a very powerful and very single-minded form of mental energy. A force. A tangible force. One that is measurable in brain wave activity. You are aware that brain waves, or thought waves, are fully capable of exerting their force whether it's in parapsychological areas such as telekinesis or in purely psychological areas such as suggestion or intimidation. The problem, Doctor, is not with Riverside. Or even intrinsically with the station. What the station is, is simply a gathering place where that force can concentrate into a sort of critical mass. It comes together. It builds there. Yet, ordinarily, it has no particular focus while it's at the station. It doesn't become a kind of groupthink or mass will. It's just energy. Essentially passive in itself. Like a storage battery. It sits there and it builds. Unlike a storage battery, it nourishes itself by feeding on itself and on the commuters passing through. Eventually it gets to a point where it's not so passive anymore. Keep in mind, now, the nature of this energy. It has its roots in the ethic of acquisition and the rejection of the spiritual. Eventually it begins to repel the spiritual like an opposite pole on a magnet. Right about here, the symptoms begin to show. Commuters who have retained a measure of spirituality begin to feel uncomfortable and then unwelcome at the station. Like begins to attract like. Alienation begins to occur in the homes of the infected. Yes, infected. It's the right word. Because this is no longer just a group of society's overachievers and workaholics. It's become a combined energy source that's beginning to control the individuals in the group. Are you with me so far?"

"Let's say it's conceivable," he answered cautiously. "Although I think I'd argue with your terms. The human brain is a masterpiece of electrical circuitry. Brain waves are electrical impulses and therefore energy. Electrical energy is composed of electrons which are matter. Two different densities or configurations of matter may well be incompatible. It's an interesting theory. But if the phenomenon you describe can actually happen, why should it zero in on relatively insignificant towns like Riverside, Connecticut, and Lake Forest, Illinois?"

"And Amersham," Bloomer added. "Who says it's only those three towns?"

"Is it or isn't it?"

"Actually, I don't know," he continued. "It may have happened on an immensely larger scale throughout history. Some nations are warlike and others are not. Some are warlike periodically for reasons usually analyzed in socioeconomic terms. Although the conditions leading to bellicosity tend to be of a one-shot variety, they fall well short of explaining overall historic patterns where the same results rise out of entirely different conditions. Many societies have become aggressively nationalistic to the point of mass insanity—mass hysteria, if you prefer—and have turned violently on those groups of citizens whose values and thought patterns were different. Nazi Germany comes to mind. Or Stalinist Russia. Or the China of today or the Mexico of tomorrow. On a smaller scale, the Salem witch trials didn't bag a single card-carrying witch but they got rid of a lot of that society's oddballs. If it all seems farfetched, bear in mind your own observation that brain waves are matter and therefore a physical force. As far as I'm concerned, this is an entirely natural phenomenon. Up to a point, it has nothing to do with the occult. And as you say, this subtle build-up of what I'll call a materialistic hysteria is probably going on in a thousand different places. What apparently makes Riverside different is another phenomenon involving an energy force. Another force, but this time its cause is technological.

"What Amersham, Lake Forest and Riverside have in common is that each are situated on electric railway lines at a location where the electrical amperage of that line reaches an abnormal peak. Amersham sits where the London Metro line junctures with the British Railway System. Two enormous power sources that collide where the systems meet. Lake Forest was found to be sitting in the middle of an electrical field caused by a blow-back from the Milwaukee and St. Paul line and also an arcing effect from the independently powered freight lines that virtually intersect it. Riverside is not only right on top of the power source for the whole New Haven line, but it also lies near a bridge that's regularly raised for boat traffic. The result in Riverside, as in the other two, is an almost constant power surge. That's two forms of electrical energy meeting in the same place and forming the critical mass that I mentioned earlier."

"What would an electrical engineer say about all this?"

"About the blow-back? He'd say it's there but it's harmless. By itself, it probably is."

"But you, and your spirits, don't agree."

"Obviously, Ira. People are dying who shouldn't die yet."

Zalman nodded slowly but said nothing. Thus far, he found himself able to accept Bloomer's hypothesis, if that's what it was, as possible. At least, not impossible. Certainly not provable. Small wonder that Mordicai and Jennifer felt compelled to act more or less on their own initiative. What action could they expect from the civil authorities? None at all. What, then, can Bloomer do? Destroy the station and its power source? Disperse all that energy? That's very likely his intention. Better not to ask. As for Bloomer himself, he was either of three things. First, a thorough lunatic. Albeit an articulate lunatic and one capable of assimilating a rational argument, but still a lunatic. Second, and equally aberrant, he might be a well-intentioned fanatic. A Torquemada who reasons like a Talleyrand and speaks like a Disraeli. Or third, the man might just be right.

"Mordicai," he said, putting a hand on Bloomer's shoulder, "you've explained why you're concerned. Are you able to tell me why you're frightened?"

"It shows?"

"It shows. Moreover, it's the single factor that makes me tend to believe you."

"Believe something else," he murmured. "I wish I'd never come here."

"The station frightens you?"

"Not the place so much, although I don't want to go anywhere near it. I guess I'm afraid that I'll lose my nerve when the time comes."

"Is Jennifer frightened?"

"More than you know."

"Of what? Of the spirits there?"

"No. The living."

"You said last night that the station kills. You warned me to stay away from it. I'm inclined to oblige. However, you also indicated that neither you nor Jennifer are in the least afraid of dying. If only the living can harm you, and the worst they can do is take your life, why are you afraid?"

Bloomer stopped walking and gestured back toward Zalman's car. The two men turned and began retracing their steps.

"It'll be hard for you to accept," he warned.

"Try me," Zalman said. Bloomer watched his reflection drifting by in the store windows as he pondered his answer. The reflection kept pace with him. He'd pass a door and the reflection would meet him again on the other side. What if that was really me in the window, he thought. What if I didn't show up in the next window?

"It's not the dying, Ira. I'm afraid of getting lost," he answered. "Stuck and lost. Stuck somewhere near the station or wherever I might drift afterward. Maybe for decades. Even centuries. Those spirits who came to Leticia's? They were stuck. It happened before. In England. A lot are still missing." Bloomer fell silent and walked on for several paces. "Ira," he said finally, "to get you to understand, I'd have to try to explain the physical nature of the spirit world. That might take hours. Even then you'd need a leap of faith to accept it."

"Care to try a digest version? I can save my questions for later." Mordicai stopped and turned to face the psychiatrist.

"There really is a spirit world, Doc. A real world. A physical plane. Hills, valleys, trees and even houses. Can you accept that?"

"Why not?" Zalman shrugged.

"Don't humor me, Ira," he said sourly.

"Who's humoring? I'm a Jew, remember? I believe in afterlife. What do you think I believe it looks like? A delicatessen? It has to be someplace."

"The someplace is right here. Around us. It exists concurrently with this one. Are you still with me?"

"Go on."

"It exists, but at a different density and at a different frequency than the world we know. We can't see it because it reflects light outside the range of what is detectable to the human eye. Your eyes can see only that part of the spectrum that lies between 400 billionths and 750 billionths of a meter in wavelength. That leaves a lot left over. Some nocturnal animals have a greater range and they're able to pick up infrared waves. Some humans, like Jennifer, can also see in a significantly wider range. She can see the heat aura that all life forms give off. So can an owl, by the way. In short, the spirit world exists but it exists outside our range of perception. There was a medium named Betty who died—you may have read about her—and then reported back what it was like. On the matter of perception, she said it was like looking through a fan. If the fan turns slowly, you're not able to see past it. If it speeds up, you can see through it. We can't see the spirit world because it's operating at a different pitch."

"Then why can't we touch it?"

"Same problem. Different frequency and different density." Bloomer drew a silver ball-point pen from his pocket and handed it to Zalman. "The pen, Ira, does it appear solid?"

"Of course."

"But of course it isn't. This pen is composed of molecules that seem densely packed but they're actually floating along with great relative distances between them. The similar density of your hand prevents it from pushing aside these molecules and passing through the pen. But what if your hand was of a substantially different density? Then you could pass through the pen or anything else. Material objects wouldn't slow you down a bit. The spirit world, like the spirit itself, vibrates at a much higher pitch than our own. Only a few people are able to see them."

"Jennifer again?"

"No. Halloran."

"Oh, yes. Lictor said so. You've concluded, no doubt, that Peter Halloran's injury has left him with a broader range of perception than the rest of us."

"So it seems."

"Speaking of Lictor, why can't he find any spirit that's lost?"

"Because spirits are not gods, Ira. Spirits are further-developed human beings. Even a spirit has to know where to start looking."

"I'd assume they're bright enough to start looking at the station."

Bloomer chose to overlook the wisecrack. "That's the other part of the problem. And why they need us. When Lictor first described Lake Forest to Jennifer, he spoke in terms of a mist covering the place. I think he was referring to an energy field that was incompatible with his matter and impenetrable by it. The spirits, even Lictor, are as afraid of getting stuck in it as I am. All of the spirit guides who were supposed to meet the various people who died at or near the station are afraid to come there. They believe they'll get lost. And the recently dead can't get out by themselves. My job, and Jennifer's, is to try to free them."

"I'm still not going to ask how. However, I would like to know how these 'paths' are such a cause for concern."

"That's simple," said Mordicai, "but also our biggest problem. You saw that Lictor, through Nigel, described these paths as the tentacles of an octopus. They're moving all the time. A good analogy. The spirits trapped at the station can get into and follow these paths but at least they're still contained by them. If we break the field at the station, the paths will dissolve. The spirits would then float away like balloons. They're apparently a bitch to find once that happens. For that reason, when we do get ready to break the field, we must be certain that all the people at the ends of these paths are accounted for and contained very close to the station area where they can be spotted and grabbed by the spirit guides. That's why Weinberg can't be in Greenwich Hospital when we make our move."

"Why Weinberg, incidentally?" Zalman asked. "Nigel's writing referred to these people as 'born-agains' or reincarnated spirits. Why do such people create paths?"

"I'm not sure I know. Except that they're defective spirits in some way. I suspect it has to do with the density of their spirits. Some aberration that makes them neither fish nor fowl. All of them seem to be spirits that have been recycled many times over without success."

"That's your theory?"

"For what it's worth."

"Why don't you just ask Lictor what the story is?"

"Jennifer's tried. Spirits tend to communicate very telegraphically. Sometimes they're maddeningly vague. Other times they repeat themselves. My own theory is that they're so used to communicating with each other telepathically that they have trouble using the less efficient spoken or written word with us. Whatever the reason, you may get a chance to ask Lictor yourself."

"Really?"

"This afternoon. When we get the Winnebago down to the station."

"Would he object, do you suppose, to answering two or three special questions?"

"Trick questions?"

"More like a request for credentials."

Bloomer shook his head dubiously. "Ira, I would urge you not to piss him off."

"What can he do? Hang up on me?"

Bloomer shrugged. No, he thought. Lictor won't hang up. Not today. Riverside's too important to him. And he knows we need you just like we might need Halloran. You have to deliver Weinberg. If you don't, and we can account for all the missing spirits before we pull the plug, then Alex must go to the hospital and help Weinberg over. Halloran has two jobs. He must try to reach the spirits no one else can reach, and he must enter the station when the commuters are there in force. He and Jennifer. They won't know any better and I'm not going to tell them. Halloran, at least, must be expendable. But yes, Ira. Go ahead and test Lictor. No one can say I didn't warn you. He's a tough old bastard who takes no shit from us messenger boys. Particularly this messenger boy who the great Lictor doesn't even deign to talk to unless he wants something. Fuck him. Go ahead, Ira. I'd like to see what happens.

"No, Ira, come to think of it. He probably can't do a damned thing."

9

Sunday Afternoon

The parking slot next to the Winnebago was empty. Zalman pulled in and, after removing the Greenwich street map from his glove compartment, locked the Buick. He waited with Jennifer while Bloomer opened the side door of the motor home. Mordicai then climbed into the driver's seat and the engine caught on the first turn. Backing out was less uneventful. He almost hit an airport limousine that was passing to his rear and managed to tick Zalman's bumper as he cut the wheels to the left. "Oops! Sorry about that Doc," he said.

"It's not your fault," Zalman smiled. "The Buick and the Winnebago must have the same molecular density."

"You're catching on," Mordicai answered, winking at Jennifer through the rearview mirror. "Incidentally, I wouldn't have guessed you'd drive a Buick. Particularly one that's basic blue."

"What would you rather have hit?" he asked.

"I'd figure you for a white Mercedes. Elegance with just a touch of dash."

"Not even close. What would you guess, Jennifer?"

"A one thousand c.c. Harley-Davidson with a German helmet?" The answer pleased Zalman. He had the feeling that Jennifer had just gone out of her way to avoid making a lucky guess. Even so, a Harley! Wouldn't that be a kick?

"Not even close, beautiful lady. You've lost your gift. Actually, given my druthers, I'd have two cars. I'd have a Porsche painted in international orange which would also mean I'd have to buy a tweed cap and a pair of those Italian driving gloves with the little holes in the back. And I'd worry myself sick about someone chipping the paint. My second vehicle would be a ten-year-old pickup which I'd use to get even and to generally bum around."

"What's holding you back?" Jennifer asked.

"I'm a psychiatrist, not a dentist. My kind of patients would be resentful of paying for the Porsche and mistrustful of the pickup. Individuality and conspicuous consumption are luxuries denied to shrinks, computer salesmen, and Mafia lieutenants. Yet most of my patients are those whose problems tend to be rooted in unproductive affluence."

"You do your utmost, I presume, to diminish the root of the problem," Bloomer grinned.

"Smart-ass!"

The banter continued through the streets and lanes of Riverside, first north of the Post Road through the areas of tract homes and commercial zoning, then southward toward Long Island Sound. When the light chatter showed signs of slackening, either Zalman or Bloomer would move to revive it. Bloomer, because it helped to keep his mind from dwelling on the confrontation that might now be only hours away. Zalman, to contain the tremendous excitement that he felt. Carl Jung or even Freud never got this close, let alone any suburban headshrinker like himself.

Zalman glanced back at Jennifer. Cool as ice, that one. Chatting along with us like it was a Sunday afternoon picnic. No, coolness isn't right. The girl gives off warmth like an autumn sun. It's peace. Inner calm. A dreamy quality. You expect her to be all tensed up and sniffing the air for that damned path like a nervous doe and the next thing you know she's laughing over some kid wrestling with a dog or getting all excited over someone's flower garden.

He was partly right about Jennifer. There had been tension but it was fading quickly. Tension over Alex. Tension from Alex. But not now. No longer. Wherever he was, she was picking up only quietude. There was tension as she sat in Zalman's car while the two men walked and talked. The tension of waiting. Of being far away and helpless. There was another stab of it back in the parking lot of the New Englander. Mordicai should have gone inside. What for? She didn't know. Probably nothing. Might as well enjoy the ride. Such a pretty town. Peter's town. Wonder how many times he's been on this very street. Maybe riding a bike. Or jogging with a dog. No. Peter doesn't own a dog. He should. Peter shouldn't live in that house of his, either. It's really very nice. A white Colonial with black shutters and a red door. Not for Peter, though. His house should have lots of wood. Natural wood. Perhaps even logs. With old oak furniture inside and leather chairs and quilts and a great huge fireplace. And bookshelves. Miles of them. Books. That's what Peter's life should be. Books, and a typewriter, and a basement full of tools, and a small sailboat, and a dog, and a boy, and maybe even . . .

"That house!" she shouted, pointing. Mordicai, startled, stomped reflexively on the Winnebago's brake pedal causing it to fishtail almost onto the nearest lawn. He recovered and returned his foot to the throttle. Tires crunched over bits of broken glass.

"I'd better circle the block," he said, realizing that a yellow motor home with squealing tires was a less than subtle vantage point.

"Ira? What do you say? Did she hit?"

"Right on the money," he answered. "Jennifer? What do you know about the people inside?"

"Their name's McShane. It was on the mailbox. What else am I supposed to know?" There was something else. Something about a television set. That glass. She couldn't place it.

"Which McShane is my . . . Which one came to see me?"

"No more bullshit, Doctor," she half pleaded. "The path leads to the man. He wouldn't have come to see you. His wife probably told you she was worried about him."

"Sorry, Jennifer. I guess I'm sold. Does that make five?"

"That's five. Let's get down to the station."

"How about laying in some groceries, Jen?" Mordicai suggested. "We may not be able to take a break later."

"The A & P's open," she nodded. "You two go ahead. I'm going to walk around for a while. Don't forget the ginger ale."

With a small wave, Jennifer hopped out at the next stop sign, bent down to scratch a Pekingese who'd come to investigate, and strolled off with the little dog trotting behind her. Bloomer looked at her in open admiration. Zalman, with mild bewilderment. Until a few minutes ago, Mordicai had seemed very much the captain of the team. Jennifer was a skilled associate who stayed in his shadow until her talents were needed. But not now. Jennifer was very clearly in charge. It wasn't so much anything she said. There was nothing particularly commanding about her manner. She was still very nice. Very gentle. But she was in charge.

Back behind the front desk of the New Englander Motel, in Mordicai Bloomer's slot, two folded messages waited to be claimed. The first was from Barbara. It informed Mordicai that she would await him in the cocktail lounge that evening at eight. The second message, taken shortly before noon, was left by Leticia Browning. It read: "Your damned Swedish ivy is flapping around my living room again."

Jeffrey Halloran sat on the walkway of the antique cast-iron bridge that spanned the western end of the station area. His chin was resting on his drawn-up knees and his attention was locked on his father in the parking lot below. His father was wandering about, apparently aimlessly, and with his hands held slightly in front as if he was feeling for a barrier. Jeff knew what it was. It was that cold air. Mr. Kornhauser was supposed to be inside it. And Mrs. Bregman. Hard to believe, he thought. But I saw the can. It moved. And I know my dad. What if he really gets to talk to whoever's there? Even one of them. Man! That would be so cool. Really ultimate. Except no one would believe it. Maybe he could get them to give proof. Like making a car float up in the air or making it snow or something. Where'd he go? Oh, there he is. He was behind the station so he could get up on the platform. Here he comes.

"Dad?"

Halloran looked up.

"Can I come down yet?"

His father shook his head firmly and indicated with the palms of his hands that Jeff should stay put. He turned and slowly retraced his path along the platform edge, pausing where the meat was seen on the day before and where the Budweiser can had moved. It did move, Jeff told himself again. Even that dog saw it move.

"Hi!"

Jeff jerked his head around. It was a girl. A woman. The sun was at her back and he hadn't seen her approach until she was standing almost beside him.

"Hello," he returned her greeting. "Am I in your way?"

"No. Don't get up." She smiled. "Did your dad lose something?"

"Well, he's trying to find something, yes. Do you know him?"

"Yes, I do. Sort of. Mind if I rest for a minute?"

"Sure. I mean, of course not."

The woman folded herself neatly into a comfortable version of the lotus position and leaned back against the truss frame of the bridge, her shoulder lightly touching Jeff's.

"My name's Jennifer, by the way."

"Mine's Jeff," he said, extending a hand. "Or did you know that?"

Jennifer nodded and then tilted her head down toward the platform. Halloran was at the far end heading down the metal steps. Near the spot where he'd encountered Jack Gormley. "He's a good man, isn't he, Jeff?" she said, more as a statement than a question.

"He's very okay." Jeff turned to study her face with interest. A fairly foxy lady, he thought. Wears tight jeans. Most of the women around here would look like a sausage in jeans. Good-looking for her age. A lot younger than Dad, though. Maybe not that much. "You're a friend of his?"

"Yes."

"Do you . . . Do you know what he's looking for down there?"

"Yes."

"Is he going to find it?"

"I have to be going now," she said. "Will you give him a message for me?"

"Sure."

"Do you remember my name?"

"Jennifer."

"Tell your father to sit in one place and to close his eyes and to try to think of bubbles floating up through water. Tell him to have only one name in his mind when he does this. That person will come. When that happens, he must speak to that person in his mind. Words will not work. Tell him this message is from Jennifer, and that I'll come to him soon."

"Where the hell did she go, Jeff?" Halloran was struggling not to raise his voice.

"I don't know," Jeff protested in the same emphatic whisper. "What do you want from me, Dad? I was just sitting there and she comes up and talks for a minute and she gives me this message for you."

"Well, why didn't you call me? Never mind. There was no reason why you should. What did this girl look like?"

"About my height. Maybe a little taller. Long dirty blond hair. Not dirty. Dirty blond. Fairly tasty."

"Wearing Levi's? About twenty-nine or thirty years old?"

"I'd say more like thirty-five."

Halloran nodded. That meant she was no more than thirty. To Jeff, any adult without gray hair was presumed to be thirty-five. Jesus Christ! It was her. Within a hundred yards of me if I only looked up. She's real. It's absolutely incredible but she's real. Wait a minute.

"Jeff! Are you sure this girl was real? I mean, looking back, does any part of it seem like a dream?"

"She touched me. Her shoulder did when she sat down. Then she put her hand on my knee when she got up."

"How about when she left? Did she walk or did she kind of float?"

"Dad . . ."

"I'm sorry. Damn. The thing is, I know Jennifer. But I only dreamed about her. It's hard for me to believe that there's a real person like that."

"It's hard to believe Mr. Kornhauser is still hanging around down here too. But you saw him, right?"

"I think I did."

"Are you going to try what she said?"

"What? The bubbles? How the hell am I supposed to think about bubbles? She said she'd come to me soon? Is that exactly what she said? Shit!" A car was turning into the parking lot. "I can't try it now. Here comes Sgt. Turkus."

Mike Turkus had changed out of his uniform. He unfolded out of his personal car wearing a torn blue sweater and a wrinkled pair of slacks that had probably been kept rolled up in his locker. He still looked like a cop. He squinted appraisingly at Peter before slamming the Pinto's door and walking toward the two Hallorans. He walked slowly, his hands tucked into his back pockets.

"Hello, Jeff," he winked. "Mind if I chat for a little while with your dad?"

Jeff looked up at his father. "Back to my post?"

"Yeah. Listen, yell if you . . ."

"I know, I know." Jeff trotted off toward the overpass. Halloran waited until he was well out of voice range.

"Mike, you look like you found something."

"Uh-huh." Turkus glanced after Jeff and then around to his rear. "Is this still strictly between us?"

"That was the deal. If we can help each other."

"This conversation never happened? I mean, it never happened, no matter who asks or when?"

"You have my promise. What've you got?"

"You're not nuts. In fact, I think you fingered a murderer. You described a fat man named Charles. You said he was a fag."

"Yeah. The one in the bathrobe with wet hair."

"I don't know about that part. Missing Persons has a file on a known homosexual who was reported missing by the Darien police four years ago last December third."

Halloran shook his head. "That seems too long ago. None of this was going on until last spring."

"As far as you know. Just listen. The guy's description says he's fifty-one years old, five feet ten inches tall and weighs two hundred and thirty-five pounds. You notice anything about his teeth?"

"The front two teeth protruded. Not the rest. Like a rabbit."

"That's the guy. That knowledge would ordinarily make you a suspect in his disappearance with possible foul play except that on the night of his being reported missing, Charles had told some people that he was meeting an alleged homosexual partner who happens to live right in the area here. The guy here was interviewed and claimed that Charles never showed up. The file says that he was extremely agitated during the interview but nothing ever came of it. For one thing, this Charles Arsvenure had packed a bag when he left his apartment where he was two months behind on his rent. It sounded like a skip-out. The Riverside man's nervousness was attributed to his fear of disclosure as a gay person."

"Who is he?" Halloran asked. "You mean he's a family man around here?"

"You don't have to know that. At the moment, I don't even know how I'm going to go about getting the case reopened. Anyway, there's more. Who was the guy you saw with him?"

"The black painter. I think his name is Hicks."

"Can you give me a description?"

"I guess so. He was shorter than the fat guy, even wearing a painter's cap. Call if five feet eight. Thin build. Age, anywhere between forty and fifty. Light complexion but definitely black. He had a patch of skin on the side of his neck that was, I don't know what it's called, it's like bleached out. Pinkish."

"Oscar Walker Hicks was an employee of the New York Central Railroad until February 28, 1956. He was assigned the job of painting the inside of the Riverside railroad station at the time of his disappearance. No connection with the other individuals as far as can be determined."

"No, of course not," Halloran said, "he just . . ." Hold it, Peter. Jesus! Hold it! You know where he is! You were about to casually tell this cop where Oscar Hicks is right now. How do you know? How the hell would you explain it to him?

Turkus' eyes narrowed. "Finish your thought, Pete."

"It was nothing."

"Bullshit! What do you know about this guy?"

"What could I know? I was in college when this man died."

"Come on, Pete. Right off the top, you know he's dead. I already believe you're a psychic and our deal still holds. Where is he?"

"What happens to me?" Halloran asked.

"What do you mean, what happens to you? Nothing happens to you. You get left out of it. You don't even get credit for helping to solve crimes and disappearances."

"Mike, if I tell you to look in an unlikely spot and you find some bones there, how are you going to explain why you looked there?"

"I'll lie, is how. Where the hell is Oscar Hicks?"

"Up in the attic."

"What attic?"

"The station." Halloran pointed. "Right up against the eaves on, what is it, the northeast corner. Like I know my own name, I know the guy sacked out up there and froze to death. When did you say it was? February? A cockroach couldn't live up there in February."

"Thanks, Pete."

"Well?"

"Well what?"

"Aren't you going to go up and look?"

"It's Sunday. The station's locked." Turkus reached over and tapped Halloran on the shoulder. "Listen, Pete," he said, "you accurately described a man that you couldn't possibly have known. If you say he's up there, he's up there. Give me some time to figure out how to handle it."

"You know, Mike, for a cop you don't seem too thrilled about solving two missing persons cases in one afternoon."

"I was hoping for more answers. A link with Gormley. A connection with all the other stuff that's going on. You heard?"

"I heard about McShane and some of the others. I don't get it, either. But I was about to try to ask when you drove in."

"Ask who?"

"I told you. Kornhauser. Or whoever answers."

"No shit? You can do that?"

"Let's give it a shot."

"Can you do it with me watching?"

"Mike, what do I know? I make advertising for dog food. All of a sudden I see dead people. I dream about dead people. I dream about fantasy people who turn out to be real and send me a correspondence course on spectral communication through me . . . Never mind. I'm going to sit down over there inside the cold air and try it."

"What cold air?"

"Don't ask."

For several minutes, Halloran cast about looking for a suitable spot on which to begin. None seemed at all appropriate. One doesn't sit down on a concrete slab platform on a green sunny day and evoke the dead. Not in any movie he ever saw. On the other hand, he never saw a movie with ghosts trying to buy the *New York Times* or jogging along in a wine-colored warm-up suit, either. He decided one spot was as good as another and sat down on the cement steps leading from the station to the center platform.

Turkus felt even more awkward. He settled on a molded plastic bench at what he hoped was a proper and respectful distance and fidgeted self-consciously, trying not to look directly at Halloran.

Bubbles, thought Halloran. Any particular kind of bubbles? How about a fish tank with an aerator? He visualized the tank he had when he was a kid and tried to concentrate on the steady stream that rose up from the air pump. No good. Fish kept nipping at them. He removed the guppies and mollies entirely and changed the brightly colored gravel to ordinary sand. Now the plastic sunken ship and the little diver distracted him. He took them out. Just bubbles now, and a few aquatic plants. How about bigger bubbles? Slower bubbles. Better. Now, larger and more fragile bubbles drifted like clouds through the clear water, winding back and forth and easing very gradually toward the surface. The green leaves of the plants turned gray and began to soften into the consistency of smoke. Columns of smoke. Spirits? Are you spirits? Hello? Anybody there? He covered his eyes with his hands to get a better look. Nothing. That doesn't work. Halloran dropped his hands but kept his eyes lightly closed. Drowsy. Going to fall asleep. Wait a minute. Who was that? Someone just pushed through the smoke and saw him watching and then took off like a thief. So fast. Come back. I just want to talk. Now someone's coming. It's him again. He's pulling someone else by the arm.

—Marty? It is! —Marty? —Pete? . . . Pete? . . . You're not here, are you? —Yeah, well, what do you mean? Am I dead? No. —Pete? Can you help us? Alex says you can help us. —Alex? Who's Alex? This guy, Pete. He saw you. Marty pointed to the blond youngish man who looked so upset. —Peter? Another voice. —Peter? —Who's that? Is that Peggy? — Peter, I told you. Get away from here, Peter. They'll kill you. —Peggy, it's okay. There's a cop here. —Peter, get back. Get back outside the mist. If you die in here, you can't get out. More voices. Everybody saying get out. —Well, how am I supposed to help? —Get out, Peter. Get back to the tree line. There's no mist there. —Will I be able to see you? —I'll try, Peter. Marty and I will try. —Peggy, is Oscar Hicks there and a man named Charles? —We're all here, Peter. Twelve of us. No. Now thirteen. Mr. Hicks is here longest. He'll try to help us through. Harder now. Get out now, Peter. Back to the tree line.

Reluctantly, Halloran opened his eyes fully. They were gone. He opened his mouth to summon Turkus but his throat caught and all that came out was a choking sound.

"Are you all right, Pete?" His face was pale and damp.

"Y . . . Yeah," he managed.

"You're crying. What happened just now?"

Peter felt the tears growing cold on his cheek and down along his throat. He raised a hand toward Turkus and gestured to a point on the outer edge of the parking lot, leaning his body in that direction. Peter didn't want to talk. Or move. Any more than was necessary. He was afraid that he would break the . . . emotion . . . that wasn't the word . . . the bridge that allowed him to . . .

"Peter?" Turkus had him by the arm now, leading him slowly into the parking lot. "Peter? Jesus! You look like you're in some kind of trance. What am I supposed to do?"

Trance, that was the word. Maybe. Not exactly. Concentration is better. Concentrate. Hold on to the string. "Don't talk, Mike. Wait. Let's see if they come out." Concentrate.

"Where?" the sergeant asked. "Right here?"

Peter nodded.

"You want to sit down? Here. Just sit down easy."

Peter shook his head and squeezed Turkus' arm. —*Come on . . . Marty? . . . Come on, Peggy.* Hot damn, there she is. *Peggy?* Oh, shit! What the hell is this?

Peggy Bregman appeared out of nowhere. Out of the mist that Peter couldn't see. Jogging! She's running again just like the first time. Like nothing ever happened. Here's Kornhauser right behind her. What's he doing? He's looking around. Damn. I know what he's doing. He's trying to remember where he parked his car.

"Marty!" Halloran shouted. Turkus jumped and tightened his grip on Peter's arm. Jeff came bounding down the steps at the far end of the station. Peggy sees him. She's stopping. She remembers. —*Good girl, Peggy. This way. Don't go back into it. Over here. Tell Marty. He still doesn't know what's happening.* She's stopping him. Pointing over here. Marty's smiling. He knows me.

"Peggy? Are you okay?" he asked. Peggy Bregman pointed to her lips and made a shrugging gesture with her hands. *"Beesacowoy,"* she said, and shrugged again. That's right, Peter thought. Words don't work. Sounds like a speeded up record played backward. —*Peggy? Marty? Can Mike Turkus see you?* —*No. Neither can your boy. Hello anyway, Jeff.* —*Can you wait a second until I tell them what's happening?* —*Not too long, Pete. We can't stay out here. What do you want to do, prove we're here?* —*Can you?* —*Yes. Save time. Tell the policeman to stand with his back to us.*

"Mike, they want you to stand over here, facing me."

"What for?"

"A demonstration. Just do it."

—*Peter, have him pull something out of his wallet and hold it where you can't see it.*

"Mike, take out your wallet and hold it behind your back. Take out a bill or a credit card or something and hold it so I can't see it."

Turkus fumbled for a moment. "Okay, I got it."

—*Peter, he's holding a Mobil card and a Red Cross Blood Donor card.*

"Mike, do you know what you're holding? Specifically?"

"Yes. One of my credit cards and another card. It feels like . . . am I supposed to tell you?"

"Peggy says it's a Mobil gas card and the other one is your Blood Donor card. You thought it was your beach card. You're an A-Positive, by the way."

137

—Very good, Peter. Do you realize you did that beach card and blood type business all by yourself? —Hey, that's right. Well, what good is that? Now Turkus and Jeff believe you're here but I'm not so damned sure. How do I know I'm not doing all of this?

"Holy shit!" whispered Mike Turkus.

—Relax, Peter. We're here. Sorry about the confusion when we came through. We get mixed up when that happens. It's like our memory picks up where it was when we were alive. Then we remember and we duck back in. It's too lonely staying out. Heartbreaking. Now it's dangerous. Alex says it is. He says if the power goes off, we'll float away. —Who's Alex? And where are you, anyway? —Alex is Jennifer's friend. And this place is really noplace at all. Between life and life. Alex says it moves at a different rhythm than either. This started as just a little ball but it's growing fast. When Mr. Hicks was lost it was just a little ball floating up near the roof. It's very big now. It reaches out all over the place. . . .

"Pete?" Turkus tugged at his sleeve. "Are you talking to them?"

"Wait a second, Mike." Peter shook off his hand. "What was that about Jenni . . ." *—What was that about Jennifer? —Peter, Jennifer will show you how to help. Alex says she's been waiting for you to understand. . . .*

"Pete?" The sergeant took his arm. "Who's there, dammit?"

"Marty Kornhauser and Peggy Bregman." Halloran started to point them out but realized that was silly and dropped his hand.

"What about Jack Gormley?"

"No. Just Marty and Peggy. Maybe he's inside . . ." *—Marty? Is Jack Gormley with you? —No. He went right on. Alex waited until he stepped out of the mist before he stopped his clock. —Does that mean Alex killed him? What for? I thought he killed himself and Polly. —Polly. Not himself. Long story. Don't tell the policeman. You'll confuse him.*

"Mike," Halloran answered, "Gormley's not here. He's gone wherever these people are supposed to have gone except they got caught in some kind of a mist."

"How many are caught?"

"Thirteen."

"Including Hicks and Arsvenure?" The sergeant was trembling.

"Yeah. They're both inside the mist."

"Listen, Pete," said Turkus, "I want you to ask who killed Arsvenure and where his body is."

*—We heard, Peter. We can hear him in your head. You know
Ezra Cohen? The old fart on Summit? He killed both of them.
Argument with Charles. Charles said he was going to tell. Charles
gets even. Charles and Mr. Hicks throw rocks at him when he
comes down here. Scares him shitless. Scared a cop one night too.
That wasn't Charles, though. That was Mr. Hicks teaching Peggy.
We can do things we couldn't do before but it takes time to
learn . . . Hold it, Peter. Someone's calling from inside . . .*

Marty Kornhauser gestured for Peter to wait and walked several
yards back toward the platform. Peggy followed close behind. He
held Peggy's hand as he leaned forward into the invisible mist.
Marty's body seemed to shimmer like hot waves rising from asphalt
except that the shimmer went in all directions.

"Did you ask them?" Turkus asked.

"Huh?" Peter's attention was fixed on whatever was happening
at the mist. "Oh, yeah. Wait a second. They're having a conference
on something else."

"Will you, for Christ's sake, tell me what they said?"

"Oh! Sorry! It was Ezra Cohen. The guy in that gray house
over there."

Turkus was too dumbfounded to speak. He could only fold his
arms across his chest and hug himself, totally forgetful of Jeffrey
Halloran's presence as this information was being passed.

"No shit!" Jeff exclaimed and whistled softly. Peter and Turkus
realized their mistake at once.

"Jeff? Not a word, do you understand? Not one word to
anyone."

"I'm cool. Dad? Can you ask a question for me?"

"What is it?"

"Ask if there are really UFOs."

"I don't think they'd know. And I don't care at the moment."

"How about if there's any buried treasure around here?"

"Jeff!"

"Well, how many people get to talk to ghosts? They ought to
know something besides how to move beer cans."

"Speaking of buried," Turkus interrupted, "did they say where
the body is?"

"No. I think that's what they're talking about. But to tell you
the truth, Mike, it's about the last thing I'm interested in."

Marty Kornhauser drew back from the mist and turned, pausing
for a moment to regain his bearing. He was solid again. Sort of.
He and Peggy looked almost normal but less . . . less dense. Peter

felt it more than he saw it. They both seemed younger and yet they seemed the same. Wrinkles! That was it. There weren't any except for the big natural creases of the cheeks. Even those were softer. It wasn't just the wrinkles. There was no detail. No pores or moles or warts. Marty had one. A wart. He used to. Right at the edge of his chin. It was . . . No, it's still there. But just a vague little mound. They even have shadows. Hold on a second. Their shadows are facing the wrong way. Now I remember what was nagging me after that first time I saw Peggy jogging. She was heading east toward the sun but her shadow was pointing south. Away from the station. Just like now. Anyway, here comes Marty with Peggy. Marty's grinning. It's nice that he's having a good time, for Christ's . . .

"What's going on . . ." —*Sorry. What's going on?* —*First, Peter, I have a message from Mr. Hicks. He says he's sorry you got hurt last spring but he wants, this is a quote, he wants the ofay fuzz to know it was him who's been busting up this fucking Toonerville Trolley cheap shit railroad what wouldn't give his wife a fucking nickel after his last week's pay. Hicks is a ticket. He's also our leader, you might say. Keeps us together and keeps us from being afraid. Wants you to try to reach him through Jennifer or Mordicai.* —*Who's Mordicai?* —*I don't know. I thought you knew. Anyway, give the message to Turkus. There's more. . . .*

Peter relayed the message to the sergeant verbatim. Turkus flashed a nervous grin. He was beginning to feel somewhat more comfortable. Jeff smiled broadly and threw a black power salute toward the mist.

"Ofay fuzz?" Turkus repeated. "Tell the old bastard he's out of touch. We're now honkey pigs and this honkey pig wishes he'd blown up the whole goddamned line a week ago. Ask him about the body."

—*We heard him, Pete. Don't turn your head, but there's a stand of sumac about sixty yards up the track on the right. Charles and his suitcase are under it. However, Mr. Hicks says don't tell Turkus just yet. He says you may need it to bargain with pretty soon.* —*What kind of a bargain?* —*You'll know when the time comes. Listen, Pete, it's all going to hit the fan very soon. If we don't talk again, will you do me a favor?* —*Anything, Marty.* —*I was a real shit the weekend before I took the pills. Toward Donna. Until I can tell her myself, will you just say that I'm okay and that I'm very sorry?* —*Me too, Peter. Will you talk to Tom and my kids? Maybe not the young ones. Maybe just*

Tracey, my oldest? —Well, yeah, I guess so. But won't they think I'm nuts? —Maybe, Pete. And maybe they'll want to believe you. Will you tell them? —Yes Marty, Peggy, I'll tell them. Do you have to go? —Yes. It's dangerous. And it really is depressing out here. So sad and lonely. We're okay inside. Don't let us get lost out here, Pete. You just don't know. Be careful, Pete. Careful of Barbara, too. Almost got Mordicai except Peggy was there. . . .

They were gone.

Peter Halloran sank slowly to the gravel and sorrowfully scanned the living world around him. Jeff sat at his side. Mike Turkus parted his lips to speak but thought better of it. Let him have a moment. The trees, Halloran noticed, were starting to turn. The dogwoods were showing small tongues of red. Another month and they'll be spinning to the ground. Until the spring. Then they'll come again. A little bigger. A little better. Wonder if dying is anything like that. Kornhauser must know. There must be a heaven. There's certainly a place that Kornhauser wants to get to, whatever it's called. A place where they all want to go. Where Polly and Jack Gormley are already. Should have asked. It doesn't really seem fair. Gormley there and them here. But who knows what's fair.

Now what? Why didn't they tell me what to do? All I know is I'm supposed to look up Jennifer and Mordicai. How? What do I do? Go home and wait for the phone to ring? Sit there listening to Barbara harp about the damned insurance company or what a disgrace I am to the asshole Wentworths until Miss Bluejeans knocks on the door and asks if Peter can come out now? We're going to liberate ghosts tonight. And what was that Marty said about Barbara. Be careful? She almost got Mordicai. Who the hell is Mordicai anyway. Sounds like a Charles Addams butler. Or an evil dwarf.

"Jeff?" Halloran put a hand on his son's leg. "I'm going to hang around here for a while. I'd like you to get on home."

"No way!" he protested. "I want to see what happens."

"You can't see anything anyway. Please, Jeff. I'd really like to have some time alone."

Jeff grumbled as he rose to his feet. "Will you call me if anything good happens?"

"Depends on how good. Go ahead, Jeff."

Jeff pushed to his feet, paused and then bent suddenly to kiss his father's cheek. He ran off toward the stairs before Peter could react.

"Not a bad kid," Turkus observed, looking after him.

Peter nodded. "He makes a few other things easier to take. What about Cohen, Mike? Is he the guy you had in mind?"

"Yep. You got a body for me?"

"You know what Marty said? He said Cohen killed both of them. Who's the other one? It's not Hicks. Hicks froze to death."

"I'll ask him when I dig up the fat man. Where's Charles Arsvenure?"

"Can't tell you, Mike. They said I should hold off in case I need a favor soon."

"You're admitting you know where he is?"

"Yeah. But you'll have to wait. Until tomorrow, I think."

"Pete, you're going to make me take you in."

"Come off it. What'll you put down on the blotter? That I wouldn't tell you what a ghost told me?"

"Then what's your favor? If, after all this, you still feel you have to bargain with me, go ahead and ask your goddamned favor."

"I don't know what it is yet. They do. I think they do. Mike, I'm afraid I'm just going to have to call you when I have a few things worked out."

Turkus reddened.

"You're telling me to get lost? Like you told your kid?" He stood over Peter, legs spread and hands on his hips. Peter ignored the belligerent posture. He held his hand out, inviting the sergeant to help pull him to his feet.

"Jeff left because I asked him to," he said quietly. "And because he trusts me. All I'm asking from you is to give me the time to find out what I'm supposed to do."

Turkus watched Peter's eyes for a long moment. "How long?" he asked finally.

"I don't know. Any time. Tonight, maybe."

Turkus drew a card from his shield case. "Two numbers," he said. "I'll be at one of them."

"Thank you, Mike."

Ira Zalman touched Bloomer's arm and pointed. "He's leaving, Mordicai. Halloran looks like he's going to stay. Still no sign of Jennifer."

"She'll be along. Let's get the Winnebago down there."

10

Lictor

The headache came. A light throbbing at the base of Peter's skull. Not much pain. An aspirin-and-lie-down-for-ten-minutes kind of a headache. What happened to the other kind? The tearing, popping kind that always came when he saw them. The baling hook that grabbed the soft tissue of his brain somewhere near the right eye and plowed slowly backward toward the plate in his head and heated it until it glowed white. What was happening? What was different? Was he healing? Or had he simply stopped fighting the messages his brain could now receive? That was close to what it felt like. Like he'd opened a heavy door that was being battered and pounded against from the outside. He could absorb the pressure. He could take it, accept it. That he had actually been talking to two real people who were no longer alive in the way he was alive seemed no more odd than talking to Mike Turkus. Less odd than his encounters with Jack Gormley back . . . My God, was it only last night? Less odd, in fact, and certainly less wrenching than his average conversation with Barbara.

How could he be so calm about what just happened? In the whole world, how many people could do what he just did? Yet he didn't feel special. Just . . . content. Did Galileo feel this way when the rest of the world thought the earth was the center of the universe? Did he feel superior? Probably not. Probably content. He knew. Well, don't get smug about it, Peter. Lots of people know, or think they know, and are actually very fucked up. Even Galileo isn't out of the woods yet. Didn't you read about a group in England called the Flat Earth Society? They believe the Apollo Program was a hoax and are offering a ten-thousand-dollar reward to anyone who can prove to their satisfaction that the world is round. Fat chance. Born-again Christians are much the same. Not fucked up especially. But they know. Or think they know. And they feel sorry for the rest of us. Wait a minute, Peter. Who says they're wrong? There's something to it, isn't there? What they're doing is accepting the existence of a superior spirit and looking for it to help and guide them.

You know something about that, Peter. What is it? That superior spirits exist? Hell, at the moment, even Peggy Bregman is a superior spirit and, considering that all she's doing is hanging around a railroad station in Connecticut, she's got to be right at the bottom of that ladder. There must be lots of fairly heavy spirits. Maybe the one you grew up hearing about is only one of them. Maybe He's a bunch of them. Maybe all of them. Whichever, Peter, you're getting out of your depth. Okay, but what is your depth? What can you do now that you couldn't do before besides talking to dead people? Can you move things like Peggy Bregman? Hey, wouldn't that be a hoot! There's a Yoo-Hoo bottle over near the weeds. Move it. Concentrate. Come on, bottle. Stand up and float. Too hard? Then how about just rolling over. Go, bottle. Just a little. Come on. I'm going to really concentrate now. Ready? Puuuuusshhhh. Shit!

Nothing. Scratch that one. Peggy can make a bottle dance all over a night table . . . Hey! Where'd that thought come from? But she did. It was in a dark place . . . a room . . . a bedroom. The bottle went off like an alarm clock next to this guy's bed. Peggy did that. Why? Who's the guy? Me. No, not me. There's somebody else there. Can't see. Jennifer knows. She was there. I think. Jennifer? You're here, aren't you? You're watching me. You're standing right behind me. Oh my gosh. I'm going to turn around and you're going to be there and I'm going to go right to pieces. That burning feeling means I'm going to wet my pants right in front of you. Oh God, don't let me do that.

"Jennifer?" he whispered. "Are you standing there?"
Nothing.
He turned slowly, letting his peripheral vision scan the shrub-

bery behind him as if he thought he'd be able to blink away any presence that came into his field of sight. But she wasn't there. No one was there. There's no one anywhere. It's like the whole town's taking a nap. No, there goes a car. And here comes a camper. Looks like it's going to park down there. And there's a girl sitting on the top step by the bridge . . .

He knew at once that it was Jennifer. Hair the color of straw. Long slender legs encased in denim. A catlike grace and softness that he could see even at this range of a hundred yards or more. Her head and shoulder leaned against the railing. One leg folded across her lap. She was asleep. Or, she'd been asleep. She was starting to uncoil now. He could almost hear a purring yawn as she laced her fingers together and stretched with her palms toward him. So lovely, he thought, but beyond that he could only stare. He fought an urge to run to her. He wanted to go bounding in slow motion across the gravel surface toward her as she rushed in a sylphlike float into his arms, like a hundred perfume commercials he'd seen. But he was afraid. Afraid she'd just sit there wondering who the nut was running across the parking lot. Afraid she'd vanish as he neared her. Afraid to even talk to her. Afraid to hear her voice. Fearful that it might not match the vision he carried of her. That she might not know him. That she might not especially care. That she might be chewing gum. That she might say, "Hi. Your name's Halloran, right? Glad ta meetcha." He'd rather have the dream.

She was on her feet. Moving down the steps. Looking up toward him. Was that a smile? Careful, Jennifer. Hold onto the railing. That's right. She's looking at that camper. Was she waiting for it? Oh, damn. Maybe it isn't Jennifer. Just some girl waiting to be met by a . . . No. She's looking at me again. And that is a smile. Big and wide, but lips almost closed. A shy smile. The same full, sensuous mouth and big sad eyes like a wounded doe. She's coming. What do I do? Stand here like a dummy? What do I say to her? Nice to see you again? Been looking forward to making your acquaintance? I bet you're a Pisces? Met any interesting dead people lately? My name's Pete, married, one child, and I'm deeply in love with you?

She was walking more slowly now. More hesitant. As if she was considering moving no closer. Peter forced his legs to move a few steps, then a few more. Jennifer waited. He drew within twice an arm's reach of her and stopped, still not altogether certain that the girl was real. Not yet able to speak, he searched her eyes for the thought behind them. They were moist and bright and they were vulnerable. They were eyes without defenses. A small scar high on the cheek next to one of them. A long-ago tomboy accident. A blemish. That's what he was looking for. She was not like Kornhauser and Peggy Bregman. She was . . .

"Hello," she said, in a tiny voice.

"Hello, Jennifer," he answered, and she smiled, with teeth this time, at hearing him say her name. At hearing him know her name.

Peter could think of nothing else to say. Nothing that needed saying. There were many questions but they could wait. The most important of these were answered. She was real and she was special. And she had come to him. Twice before this. And he was special to her. God only knew why, why him, of all the men who would give all they had to be looked at the way she was looking at him. Slowly, she raised one hand and held it toward him, palm downward, as if inviting him to touch. For a long moment, he absorbed the meaning of the tanned slender fingers reaching for him. Then he took her hand and shuddered, grinning foolishly at the thrill that ran through his body.

Zalman watched with interest as Bloomer's face darkened. "Looks like Jennifer's introduced herself," Mordicai had just remarked. Zalman heard more than a little petulance in his tone. Bloomer turned his attention back to the legal pad that sat on the small Formica dining table before him. "Nigel?" he wrote again and then rested his pen point against the lined yellow paper. Nothing came, as nothing had come after the dozen or more calls that ran down the margin above it.

"They're coming this way," Zalman said, turning from the curtained window. "Not terribly urgently, I'd say. They look like they're out for an afternoon stroll on the beach."

"Jennifer could do with a bit more growing up," Bloomer said sourly. "This is hardly a time for high school handholding with a married suburban schizoid."

"Who says he's a skitz?" Zalman asked, one eyebrow up.

"Okay, a married suburban ad man, then."

"What's wrong with being in advertising?"

"Nothing at all. Unless you're a grown man. Unless Show and Tell has never lost it's fascination for you."

"Mordicai, I vault to the conclusion that you have an emotional interest in Jennifer which you now feel to be threatened."

"What's that supposed to mean?"

"That you're stuck on her and he's in the way."

"I know what it means. Anyway, it's not that. It's just that she deserves better than . . ."

"Better than Peter? Personally, I'd start from the other end. Peter deserves better than your good friend, Barbara. In fact, if Adolph Eichmann had a Barbara, I'd feel less put out by your contention that there's no such place as hell."

Bloomer didn't answer. If you want to see hell, he thought, stick around for another day or so. In the meantime, don't worry, Ira. I'll be civility itself as long as we need the unique talents of Mister Hot-Shot Halloran. If we need them at all.

Zalman opened the Winnebago's side door before Jennifer could knock. "Hello, Jennifer. Good afternoon and welcome, Peter." Bloomer's crack about high school behavior might have some merit, he reflected. Peter Halloran looked absolutely moonstruck. And not much more so than Jennifer. On top of that, Peter seemed genuinely astonished to find his erstwhile psychiatrist sipping beer in a Winnebago. Zalman cleared his throat.

"Peter Halloran, I want you to meet Professor Mordicai Bloomer, who is a Ph.D. in anthropology associated with Princeton University, and who is a colleague of Miss Wilde in the equally fascinating discipline of parapsychology. I, Peter, am a neutral observer concerning the matter. Mordicai, this is Peter Halloran."

Bloomer affected a pleasantly sincere expression and extended a hand to Peter. "Glad to have you with us, Pete."

"Thank you," Halloran answered, "although I'm not sure what . . ." Barbara? What was it about this man and Barbara? "I believe you know my wife." Why did he say that? How could Barbara know . . . ?

"Yes, I do. We met last night at Leticia Browning's house. In fact, I thought at first that she was the gifted Halloran we were told to find."

"Told to find? By whom?" Peter asked.

"I haven't explained that," Jennifer said. "Peter, there's a lot you must try to absorb in a very short time. Facts that you'd never have accepted up until the past hour. Otherwise, one of us would have contacted you sooner."

"Would an act of faith save time?" he asked. Halloran would have believed almost anything coming from Jennifer. However, little was required in the way of suspending disbelief.

"Yes, it would," Bloomer answered for Jennifer. "You can ask questions as we proceed. I suppose I needn't remind you that anything said and done here must remain absolutely confidential."

"Has anyone here seen Alex?" Jennifer asked. Her question was meant as much to blunt Mordicai's officious manner as to determine where Alex might be and what he might be doing.

"He's late," said Bloomer, looking thoughtfully at Jennifer.

"Alex?" Halloran asked. "What's he look like?"

"Blond and nice looking. About thirty," she replied.

"I think I saw him."

"You probably did. He's been gadding about Riverside all morning."

"No. I mean here. He's one of the people who was with Marty Kornhauser and Peggy Bregman." Peter turned to Zalman. "And Doc, do you remember I told you I saw the other two? The black painter and the fat . . ."

A strangled sound came from Jennifer's throat. She looked like she would have fallen had her hand not gripped the lever on the side door of the Winnebago. Even Bloomer had dropped his superior manner and stared stupidly at Halloran while groping to support his stricken partner. Zalman reached her first with an arm about her waist. Just when she seemed about to faint, she pushed herself upright and snapped her head toward Bloomer. The expression startled Halloran. An accusing look. A probing look that pierced beyond the denial on his face.

"I swear, Jennifer," he said, his powerful voice now choked and weak, "Ira and I have been together . . ." She was no longer listening.

"Lictor?" she called, staring past Bloomer. Bloomer stopped and listened. Even Zalman looked around and at the ceiling. What the hell is this, thought Halloran.

"Lictor?" she called, this time a tearful shout.

"Jennifer!" Bloomer put a hand on her arm but she shook it off. "Jennifer, I don't think you can get him here. I couldn't get Nigel. We must be inside."

"Inside what?" Halloran asked. "You mean the mist? We are inside it. You have to go over to . . ."

Jennifer burst out the door and fell heavily to the gravel surface. She sprang to her feet and ran toward the station platform with Halloran close behind. Zalman tried to follow but Bloomer restrained him. Then Bloomer slid into the driver's seat and turned the key. The Winnebago was roaring in reverse toward the service road before Zalman could struggle into the dining bench. Jennifer was on the platform now. Halloran close by and bewildered. Hanging back. She was calling his name. Alex's name. She was calling

it in her head. She was screaming his name. Oh-oh. That one
wasn't in her head. Somebody's going to call the cops if she keeps
that up. Wait a second. Jennifer? There he is. I hear him. Don't
you? No, I guess you don't. Jennifer was sinking to her knees
now. Sobbing. Come on, Jennifer. Just go over there near the
grass. Where I was before. She doesn't hear me either. Well, use
words, stupid.

"Jennifer?" he touched his hands to her shuddering shoulders.
She seized his right hand with both of hers and squeezed until he
thought she'd crush the bones.

"Peter?" she sobbed. "Please help me?"

"I'll help you, sweetheart," he whispered, his lips close against
her hair. "Come with me. Just a little way. I'll help you."   —
Hey Alex! Stick around!

She was very weak. He held her against his side, supporting
her as they walked. First to the end of the station platform, then
down the iron steps and back toward the weeds. Jennifer went
limp, explosively, like a burst balloon. He swung his left hand
under her legs and lifted her, shocked at her lightness, to the grassy
shade of a hemlock on the edge of the parking lot. There was
Alex. Half out of the mist. What was that around his body? Arms?
Arms. They were holding on to him. His feet were still inside.

—Alex? I think she wants to know what happened to you.
*—Peter! You're a good man. Nice man. You're just as talented
as Bloomer and not nearly the prurient shit he is. Stay with Jennifer. No one like her in this whole country. Tell her I said to do
this one right. Tell her I'm fine for now but please do this one
right . . .*

"Get back inside, Alex," came the firm stentorian voice that
bellowed near Peter's right ear. He flinched and turned, covering
Jennifer with his arms. There was no one.

"What the hell was . . ."   *—Alex? What was that?*   —
Please, Lictor? Just let me talk to Jennifer. To let her know . . .
—Alex, who the hell are you talking to?   *—Peter, it's Lictor.
He's the . . .*

"Inside, Alex, if you please." Holy Good Christ, thought Peter.
That voice is coming from Jennifer. It sounds like John Carradine
doing horror movies and it's coming from her. What is this? One
of those multiple personality crazies? The three faces of Jennifer?

*—No, Peter. Lictor's her spirit contact. He talks through her.
She's a trance medium, Peter. There's only one Jen . . .*

"Alex!" Alex Makepeace backed into the mist. Peter squirmed

149

around so that he could look directly into Jennifer's face. She was asleep. Totally limp. Her features soft and at peace. He felt an urge to lay her down beside him and hold and cradle her until she slept away whatever pain she felt for Alex. Who was he? A lover? It didn't seem so. But someone very close to her.

"You are Halloran." Her face changed. The muscles did something. They rearranged themselves. Then they relaxed again.

"Yes, I'm Halloran. Who are you?"

"Carry Jennifer to that conveyance."

"I asked you a question."

"At once!" The voice was firmer. If that were possible.

"You can go fuck yourself, Lictor."

Jennifer's body stiffened as if in spasm. Her head jerked twice and then she was soft and limp again. Barely breathing. Halloran held her closer.

Inside the Winnebago, Bloomer's pen twisted in his hand. He brought it down upon the yellow pad, hard enough to puncture several sheets.

"lictorangry wait"

"Nigel?" he wrote. "What's happening?"

"wait"

Bloomer rolled down his window and tapped his horn. "Halloran?" he called. "Get her in here."

"There's something wrong with her," he shouted. "She's hardly breathing."

"I know," Bloomer answered, motioning with his hand for Peter to keep his voice down. "She's just sleeping. Get her in here." Peter hesitated for a moment, then swept her into his arms and stood erect, moving toward the side door of the camper.

"What happened?" Bloomer asked, as Peter kicked the door aside and eased Jennifer onto the cushions of the dining bench. Zalman leaned past Peter and peered into one eye while feeling for a pulse with his other hand.

"You know who Lictor is?" Halloran asked. Bloomer gave a sharp nod. "After Jennifer fainted, he told me to carry her in here and get lost. I told him to go fuck himself."

Bloomer gave a low moan which Peter ignored. Halloran was anxiously watching Zalman.

"She's asleep all right," the psychiatrist said finally. "Pretty deeply, but she's asleep. She'll be out for a while unless it's important to wake her."

"What's going on, Doc?" Peter asked.

Zalman glanced at Bloomer and then at Halloran. "In as few words as possible, this town, and particularly the station, is in the grip of a kind of hysteria that is a negative symbiosis between the mental energies of certain residents and the energy generated at this station. A freak occurrence, really, but it's happened before. It's capable of not only altering behavior but apparently it can create a kind of third world that sits between life and death. I realize this is terribly difficult for you to grasp. I'm not even sure I . . ."

"Does Jennifer believe all that?"

"Jennifer knows all that. This is her second time around."

"That's good enough. What has to be done?"

"Cut the power, I'd assume. But it's not that simple. Freeing the people who are trapped here presents other very grave problems. And this is much further along than last time. More like the first time. Years ago in England. Cutting the power might not be enough to disperse . . ."

"Here's Nigel again," Bloomer called.

"What did he write?" asked Zalman.

"Lictor very angry. Halloran show respect or leave," Bloomer read.

Peter flushed. "Who is this Lictor? A spirit? Someone who was alive once?"

"Peter, please . . ."

"Answer me."

"He's a very highly developed spirit. Very . . . powerful."

"Does that mean like God?"

"No. Nothing like that. He hasn't even passed the corporeal stage . . . Never mind. That's too complicated for now. Think of him as a senator or a governor."

"But he's not so highly developed that his pride can't get in the way of saving thirteen people. Tell him I said that. Then tell him I said to help us or get lost."

"Tell him you said it?" There was a glint in Bloomer's eye.

"Tell him."

Mordicai scribbled across the page filling four lines. Halloran sensed that he was adding a few digs of his own. The pen dropped to the next blank line and waited.

"reckoningwillcomehalloranbloomer"

Bloomer stiffened. Halloran leaned over his shoulder to read the response which he shrugged off as meaningless. He lifted his eyes to the writing in Bloomer's hand above it. Halloran smiled. Bloomer had quoted Halloran as calling Lictor an arrogant stuffed shirt with all the spiritual development of a slug. Judging by the sweat breaking out on Bloomer's forehead, Lictor had correctly perceived that Halloran was an unlikely author of such a remark.

"Tell him I'll be here. Or there. Or whatever. Then repeat: Help us or get lost."

Bloomer repeated the message, this time verbatim. He had to hold the pen in both hands when he finished. There was a long pause before it moved again.

"natureof help" the pen wrote at last.

"Ask what happened to Alex," Halloran said. Bloomer scribbled.

"crossedover stuck"

"I know he's stuck. How did he die?"

The pen moved immediately, without waiting for Bloomer to write the question.

"dontknow wasinpath cantseein askbloomerjenniferabout- paths"

"Paths? How many are there?"

"fivenow fiveemptyspirits mostdangerous tomorrowmore many- more"

"I . . . I can save time," Blooomer stammered. He told Peter about the octopuslike mist that enveloped the station and the tentacles that spread through the town attached like umbilical cords to living people who, through genetic defect or circumstance, were too weak to resist the energy force that was sucking whatever humanity their spirits held. "They become amoral to an almost inconceivable extent. That's once they're enveloped. Until then, the path is like a long tongue of cool flame licking at them. In between licks they're pretty normal. Once the path has enough strength to envelop them, the horror starts. It's not ax murders or anything like that. In its way, though, it's more frightening. Imagine that such a man wants to use your lawnmower. He'll simply go to your garage and take it. If you challenge him, if you in any way interfere with his goal, even if his goal is to cut a goddamned lawn, he'll crack your skull and then roll you off the lawn which he'll finish mowing without giving you another thought. He'll even put your mower back where he found it."

Halloran studied Bloomer. There was no question but that the man believed what he was saying. So did Halloran. Jennifer was right. An hour ago he would have dismissed Bloomer and even Zalman as lunatics. But now . . .

"Do you know who the five are?"

"Yes."

"Lictor or Nigel told you?"

"No. They can't see them. Can't get near them. It would be like you trying to live on a gas ball like Pluto. Alex and Jennifer can feel the mist. Apparently, so can you. They found them."

"Gormley was one?"

"Yes."

"You know Alex killed him?"

Bloomer nodded.

"Who killed Alex?"

"Probably one of the other four."

"Who are they?" Peter asked. "Besides Barbara. My wife."

Bloomer told him.

"Ezra Cohen's the way to bet," Peter told him, not bothering to review his conversation with Marty and Peggy. "Anyway, Weinberg was in the psycho ward. McShane's apparently been home since he posted bail, and Barbara's more of a shit than a killer."

Bloomer declined comment.

"Just these four?" Halloran asked. "Only these four are dangerous?"

"For now," replied Bloomer. "But not tomorrow. Almost everyone at the station will be enveloped. Even if only for a short time. That's when they're deadly to anyone not like them. That's when our own heads are going to be on the block if we're here."

Zalman laid Jennifer's hand across her waist. "Pulse is stronger," he said. "Mordicai, you told Peter they'd be enveloped for a short time. Why not simply let them catch their trains and go?"

"That's impossible. Nigel said there'd be many paths tomorrow. That has to mean they'll be fanning all over New York City. We'd never be able to contain the spirits that are here right now, let alone God knows how many more who'd fall into all those paths. Lictor can't let that happen. It's his job to stop it."

"And he's forcing you to help him?" Peter asked. "If it's his problem, why don't you let him fix it?"

"We . . . Jennifer and I, we want to help."

"Are you saying Lictor can't do anything without help from people like us?"

"He can't do anything physical."

"Like knocking down a power line?" Peter asked.

"Yes. Like that."

"I don't believe that. Christ! If old Oscar Hicks, he's the lifter among the people in the mist, if Hicks can throw rocks at cops and smash pantographs and twist brakeshoes off trains, Lictor can sure as hell drop a crowbar into a generator."

"He just can't." Bloomer was sweating more heavily than before.

"Mordicai," said Zalman, who'd been watching him with interest, "you implied earlier that spirits like Lictor can't go near a power source or any electromagnetic field. Was that a true statement?"

"It was true."

"However, I have the strongest feeling that Lictor has an alternative. An alternative that you find unacceptable. Is that a fair statement?"

"How do I know what Lictor can do?" Bloomer's face was beginning to flush. Zalman could almost hear his pulse rate climbing. The man was not simply lying; he was trying to bury a frightening truth. Zalman caught a motion on Peter's face and turned to look at him. There was a quizzical expression there and his lips were moving.

"Amersham?" Peter asked. "What did Lictor do in Amersham?"

Zalman fought to control his astonishment. "Peter," he asked, "what do you know . . . what have you known about Amersham?"

"Never heard of it. He's thinking about it."

"Doesn't that astound you that you can . . . Never mind. We must have a long talk later. Mordicai! Am I correct that forty-one people died in a mass suicide at Amersham in 1912?"

"Yes."

"Why did they destroy themselves?"

"There are a couple of theories," he answered vaguely. "Mass hysteria, according to the shrinks of the day."

"What's your theory?"

"Parapsychologists generally believe that the station developed an almost rapturous importance to the commuters. The suicide was their way of never leaving it."

"Do you believe that?"

"It's as good as mass hysteria."

"Mordicai," Zalman said patiently, "I'm asking what you believe."

"That's it."

"Peter?"

"He thinks Lictor . . ."

"Hold it." Bloomer angrily faced Halloran. "Who the hell are you to look inside my head? You're a baby at this."

Zalman was enthralled. He'd seen more of the capacity of the human mind in the past eighteen hours than he had in thirty years of study and practice. Peter could actually, literally, read Bloomer's mind and Bloomer knew it. It deflated him terribly and it frightened him. Zalman imagined how he must be struggling to avoid a mental image of Barbara's heaving body. He saw Halloran squinting, mouthing words again, blithely indifferent to Bloomer's expression of anger.

"Hockey?" Halloran asked. "Are you thinking about a hockey game? Now you're switching to football. The Eagles. Joe Kuharich's 1967 Eagles. Norman Snead. Irv Cross. Chuck Bednarik. Oops. There go the Eagles."

Jennifer was conscious. She rose slowly from the Styrofoam settee into a half sitting position. Her face was pale beneath the tan. A rivulet of dried tear bleached her cheek but her eyes were dry now.

"Tell him, Mordicai," she said very softly but with authority.

Bloomer turned. A half dozen expressions seemed to flash across his face. First relief, then confusion, then anger, then fear and all shadings of emotion in between. He settled back on relief.

"We were concerned about you, Jen." He affected a gratified smile as if she'd had nothing more than a case of the vapors. "How do you feel? How about if you and I get some air until your head clears?"

Halloran recognized the stall. He chose to say nothing. It was Jennifer's show.

"Tell him, Mordicai," she said again.

"Tell him what?" he hissed. "What we think we know? What if we're wrong, Jennifer? And right or wrong, what if they break off contact because you and I shot off our mouths?"

"We may not want to know, but we do." Jennifer rose to her feet and stepped close to Bloomer, her body almost touching his. Her eyes locked upon his. Bloomer began to sweat. "Mordicai, they have a right. I want you to explain. You're better at explaining." Bloomer looked away.

"The forty-one people?" Halloran whispered, staring hard at Bloomer. "Lictor killed the forty-one people?"

"Mordicai?" Jennifer touched his cheek.

"I . . . I think perhaps . . ."

"Mordicai!" she repeated more firmly.

"I more than think so," he said finally. "You know." He turned toward Halloran and Zalman. "She does know. It's true. Lictor killed them. Lictor made them step in front of the train. Most of them, anyway."

"Most of them?" Zalman asked.

"He was selective. Somewhat. He spared a few younger ones. He only took the regular commuters who were . . . developed. Well-developed personalities. Mature personalities. And only those who were infected by the mist."

"Lictor can do that?" Peter asked. "This thing, whoever he is, can actually throw a crowd of people in front of a train? You said he couldn't do anything physical."

"He can't," Bloomer sighed. "He can only get into their minds. And only then if their spirits are . . . empty . . . or almost . . . well, it's very much like death. Spiritual death. Leaving only a living animal. That's the only death Lictor cares about. The other death doesn't bother him any more than watching your son fall asleep at night would bother you."

"Mordicai," Zalman raised a hand, "are you saying that these people had become zombies? That Lictor can influence their actions by an act of will? If that's so, why couldn't he have simply dispersed them? Out of harm's way? To the South Pole if necessary."

"I've already explained that, Doc." He glanced from Zalman to Halloran and shrugged toward Jennifer as if to confirm his belief that Lictor's capabilities were beyond their understanding. Jennifer nodded her encouragement.

"Beyond a certain point," he continued, "these men and women are very much out of control. Definitely out of Lictor's control. He cannot, in any case, contravene their free will. My impression is that it's against whatever rules he has to follow. Nigel says the rules are quite strict on at least two points. First, there can be no definitive proof of the afterlife for reasons you already know. Second, there can be no altering of human conduct through interference with the human personality. Nothing beyond comfort and inspiration. In most cases, this last point is moot because I don't think he can do it anyway."

"What does out of control mean?" Halloran asked. "You mean going quietly berserk like Jack Gormley?"

"No. That behavior is more in the nature of a symptom. You have to go back a step. Once these commuters fall into a sort of spiritual limbo, they become goal oriented to an extraordinary degree. The changes are shocking. They become incapable of simple pleasures. Pleasure for its own sake becomes irrelevant. A distraction. Certainly pleasure for someone else's sake. They lose almost all ordinary human perspective. Almost all discretion. If their goal, for example, is to get to the other side of a street, they'll take the shortest route regardless of traffic. If they get hit by a truck, they'll keep crawling. If they safely reach the other side, their minds will become momentarily blank until either they remember why they crossed the street or until the next stimulus hits them."

"What sort of stimulus?" Zalman asked.

"Anything at all. It might be external. Like a travel poster. They might not go to the South Pole but they'll go looking to buy a ticket to Bermuda unless they get a stronger urge in the meantime. The stimulus might also be internal. An old grudge. They might go looking for some slob who humiliated them in high school. Even if the high school is a thousand miles away. They might also decide to humiliate someone nearby in the same way."

Bloomer paused once more and looked to Jennifer for support. But her eyes were soft and sad and they were fixed on Peter Halloran. Halloran's eyes were dreamy. Almost happy. Christ! They were talking to each other. Bloomer wondered why he was wasting his time using language. Then he remembered Zalman.

"They are also, Doctor, extremely susceptible to suggestion." He emphasized Zalman's title as if to chide Halloran for his inattention. Halloran ignored Bloomer's petulance but reluctantly broke off his union with Jennifer.

"For example," Mordicai went on, choosing his words more carefully now, "if a group of commuters should think that a train is already in the station with its door open, they will step into it whether it's there or not. If they step into the suggested train while the real train is coasting into the station . . ."

"Amersham!" Zalman whistled. He'd known what was coming but was no less stunned. "I'm still not sure I understand," he said, shaking his head slowly as he spoke. "You've been saying that Lictor either cannot do such things or is forbidden to do them. Yet, you're saying that he did in fact do them. That he broke the rules."

"Let's say he found a loophole."

"A loophole!" Zalman repeated.

"Advanced spirits find loopholes?" Halloran was amused in spite of himself.

"It's not funny, actually," said Bloomer curtly.

"Mass murder isn't funny. Insanity isn't funny. But there's something fundamentally ridiculous about that pompous prig circumventing an ethical code that we're supposed to be aspiring toward. If you want to take direction from him, be my guest. Personally, I'm more comfortable with my own values."

Bloomer cringed inwardly at what he considered an insanely reckless declaration of defiance. Whatever happens to Halloran, he thought, he certainly has it coming.

"You must try to remember, Mr. Halloran, that there had been no precedent to Amersham. In Lictor's judgment, therefore, no rule applied. Nigel says it was a spontaneous decision. On the morning it happened, Lictor realized that all but a couple of the infected Amersham citizens were right there at the station. Moreover, there was only one morning train at the time. He apparently reasoned that a major accident would require a power shutdown. He saw a chance not only to free the infected spirits of the living, but also the trapped spirits of the physically dead. He presumed that they would all be at the station in one tight cluster. Lictor organized a small army of his own spirits to be on hand to help them over. Mostly deceased relatives and friends of the Amersham people.

"If Lictor's cold-bloodedness seems incredible to you, you must keep in mind that this . . . entity . . . takes the long view where death and suffering are concerned. He had a problem to solve. And he envisioned not a mass murder as you put it, but an act of mercy and an altogether happy family reunion.

"Be that as it may, there were over seventy people on the platform that morning. Forty-one of the doomed and over thirty witnesses. Imagine what the witnesses saw. There they were, idly watching the oncoming train, perhaps folding their newspapers or picking up their briefcases. Suddenly, as if on signal, people on either side of them calmly walked onto the tracks and sat down in imaginary seats while a very real train was screaming and grinding down on top of them. Records of eyewitness accounts say that none of them ever flinched or ducked or even looked up. The train was moving very slowly but it couldn't stop. The further it rolled, the more the tracks were greased by the ground up meat and fat it had already passed over, spitting out chunks of human bodies as it went.

"Every single witness went into shock. So did the first two policemen who arrived on the scene. One later arrival reported that each of these appeared to have either vomited or fouled themselves. The platform was slick with regurgitated breakfasts, human waste, and sprays of blood and tissue and other fluids. Many fainted. Many simply fell to the platform and thrashed about in that revolting mess, screaming as their hands or eyes fell upon some new horror. Then to complete this scene from hell, a thick and black oily smoke began to roll from under the carriages as the hot third rail cooked and charred the two tons of butchered flesh that the train had troweled against it. It began to choke those still inside the train. Some of the passengers smashed windows or clawed their way to the doors only to be trampled back by those nearest doors who had seen the charnel house outside and could not force themselves to step into it. Three of the witnesses died within those first minutes. Two on the platform and one on the train. Probable strokes or heart attacks. They're not even counted among the forty-one beneath the train. They became asterisks. Three human existences reduced to parentheses. Uncounted even to that degree were two more who died within the week. Untreated shock. But why stop there? Several more, perhaps many more, were eventually institutionalized. Opium sedatives and gin killed the engineer within the year. Who knows how many others drank themselves to death or were scarred so badly that they could not hope to live a normal life? What was the cost in human spirits that were so shattered that even death did not release them? How many had to come back again?" Bloomer smiled cruelly at the expression of disgust and horror on Peter's face. "Tell me, Mr. Halloran. Do you still want to fuck around with Lictor?"

"How do you know all this?" Halloran asked.

"I've read every word that's been written about Amersham. I've personally spoken to living relatives of those who were there."

"I mean about Lictor."

"Bits and pieces from Nigel. More in the nature of a friendly warning. I've also heard Lictor speak through Jennifer. On top of that, Jennifer's spoken to people in a position to know, even though Lictor tries to prevent that. Whether you believe it or not, Jennifer's been where Lictor is."

Halloran looked at Jennifer and knew at once that it was true. But there was more. He squinted again. Concentrating. What was it? What was Bloomer holding back? What had gone wrong? For all the rationalization of Lictor's motives and values that ought to be perverse by any standard, what it came down to was that Lictor had failed. Totally. Disastrously.

"It's the paths," he said slowly, very softly. "The paths. Lictor didn't know about them, did he? He killed for nothing, didn't he?"

"He lost nineteen. Fourteen are still lost."

"Nineteen out of how many?"

"We don't know. But it's true. He didn't know about the paths. Jennifer found them in Lake Forest. He must have known she would. Or could."

"Could what?" Zalman asked. "See them? Feel them?"

"Lictor can see them too. He sees that they're there. He just can't see inside them. Jennifer can. So could Alex, up to a point. And now, of course, Mr. Halloran here. But only Mr. Halloran can communicate with the dead inside the paths and also inside the mist. Only Mr. Halloran, among the living, can actually see the spirits when they step out of the mist."

The pain came. Like a drum roll. Bad. Blinding. Halloran could not focus. He couldn't think. There was something. He almost had it. It wasn't coming from Bloomer. Or from Jennifer. Why did the pain come now? Jennifer? Can you take some of it? Just a minute. Somebody's trying to block me with the pain.

"There's something wrong here," said Zalman.

Jennifer ignored him. She stepped forward, reaching. Her hands touched lightly against Halloran's temples.

Better, Jennifer. Thank you. I almost . . . No. It's bad again. They're trying to block you to . . .

"Move this camper," Zalman snapped. "Mordicai! Get this thing close to the platform."

"What for?" Bloomer asked. He turned to Peter. "You look ill, Mr. Halloran. Perhaps if you lie down for a . . ."

"Move it, Mordicai."

"It's where I want it, Doctor. Please remember that you're a guest in . . ."

Ira Zalman brushed Bloomer aside and climbed behind the wheel. The engine turned at once. Now his own head was . . . funny. He slid the gear shift lever into drive. Through the windshield, he could see the station moving closer. Then it stopped. Two feet from the front bumper. No. Wait. He hadn't moved. His foot was still on the brake. How could the station be . . . ? Zalman eased his foot onto the gas pedal and touched it lightly. The camper was moving now. Through the platform. His head began to clear. There was another platform now fifteen feet away. Very clear now. The real platform. Zalman let the camper bump hard against a parking lot stanchion before he threw it into park and shut off the ignition. He'd done it. Something tried to stop him but he'd done it. He wasn't even sure he knew why.

Ira Zalman rose from the driver's seat and turned to face Bloomer. Bloomer was sweating. Halloran was shaking his head as if to assure himself that the pain had gone. Jennifer, still touching Halloran, studied Zalman's face for a moment and then turned her eyes piercingly upon Mordicai Bloomer. Bloomer seemed to be choosing his words.

"You people don't know what you're doing," he said with effort.

"Peter?" Zalman asked.

"Yes?"

"Are we inside the mist?"

"Yes," Jennifer answered for him.

"This Lictor, Jennifer," Zalman asked. "Is he trustworthy in your opinion?"

"I don't really know him. He speaks through me. He's certainly arrogant. And condescending. Not especially admired, even by his own kind. But does he lie? I don't think so."

"Is he capable of being disingenuous, then? Of dissembling?"

"Jennifer and I know what you're asking," Peter volunteered. "You're asking if the man might be covering his ass. What's bothering you?"

"I had an intuition. It came while Mordicai was explaining Amersham. I refuse to call it a psychic perception. In any case, I almost had it. Peter almost had it. Then his head . . . something was happening to him. You, Jennifer, were distracted by Peter's pain. You, Mordicai, were trying to distract all of us. Particularly when I felt a powerful urge to move the camper. Lictor can't see us here, can he?"

"You knew that," Bloomer answered. "I explained it to you."

"He tried to stop me. He tried to make the station seem closer just like he put a train in front of those commuters at Amersham. One of my intuitions is that Lictor doesn't want us inside the mist. We're out of his control here, aren't we?"

"What control?" Bloomer almost shouted. "He simply can't help us to help him while we're in here. Why are you trying to make something sinister out of it?"

"But it is sinister. Interference with my free will is sinister. You said he's not able or not permitted to do that. But he tried. You also said that he suggested a train to the people at Amersham while they were on the station. He couldn't have. If there was a mist at Amersham, he couldn't have done that."

"Obviously, he found a way," Bloomer answered, almost absently. His mind was elsewhere. It was, Zalman suspected, trying very hard to be elsewhere.

"Peter?"

"The Philadelphia Eagles again."

"Why are you trying to block us, Mordicai?"

"I'm not. I . . ."

"Peter?"

"Alright, goddammit. Lictor's on their shit list. He's desperate. He wants to move on but he can't. He's been frozen in grade, even demoted, ever since he made a hash of Amersham. Except for Lake Forest and this mess here, all he's been doing is looking for the missing Amersham souls. He needs a clean win. In terms you can understand, he wants out of his job."

"What actually happened at Amersham?"

"It was as I told you. Except that he got to those people before they reached the station. He tried to make it look like a spontaneous decision. A forgivable error under extraordinary circumstances. He knew what he was doing, though. Or thought he knew. But he didn't do it cleanly. He missed a couple who had paths leading to them. The spirits were in the paths."

"I'll ask you again how many he got, aside from the nineteen he lost."

"None. It was a total disaster."

"Wasn't there some way he could have drawn them out of the mist? At least then he could have seen where they were."

"He can't see them. In or out."

"Sure he can," Peter said. "He saw Alex. He even told him to get back inside."

"That was through Jennifer's eyes. He can't do it by himself."

Zalman studied Bloomer. Not sure what he was searching for. There was more. More than Bloomer's glib addenda to what he had told before. Why had he held it back in the first place? It wasn't a particularly damning revelation to have it come out that Lictor had exceeded his authority. That Lictor must function under certain constraints. That Lictor's abilities have their limits. Even that Lictor is capable of dishonesty. So why is Bloomer frightened?

Why is Ira Zalman frightened? Why is Ira Zalman even trying to puzzle this out when a certified psychic like Jennifer is available? In some ways, her capabilities are greater than Lictor's. And there's Halloran. In other ways, even more talented than Jen . . . Halloran and Jennifer. They were watching him now. They were trying to follow his train of thought but they couldn't. He could feel them slipping alongside and flying wing to wing for a short distance until a string would be yanked and they'd be pulled away. What was he just thinking about? He'd almost just had it. More talented. That was it. They don't need Lictor. Together, they . . . They only need each other. Bloomer knows that. Bloomer doesn't want that to happen. Bloomer. Lictor. Lictor and Bloomer. Here comes Halloran off my wing again. Jennifer's still out there by herself. What was it she said this morning? About the half dollar? She said the other person's thoughts have to be relevant. Or logical. Not complex. But Halloran's starting to get it. Here he comes. My God! How do I know this! Bloomer and Lictor. But what about them? Am I psychic? Or am I reasoning differently because I'm accepting information I'd never have accepted before? Peter! Peter's doing more than that. Peter knows.

"You son of a bitch!" Halloran took a step toward Bloomer.

"Wait just a goddamn . . ."

"You set her up," he snarled. "You sold out Jennifer. You made a deal with that turkey, didn't you?"

"That's ridiculous." Bloomer paled. He backed away from Halloran.

"You made a deal. You'd get Lictor off the hook and you'd have Lictor all to yourself. You get to be able to do everything Jennifer can do. Lictor will teach you. But what's the price, you bastard? Jennifer's supposed to die tomorrow, isn't she?"

"You can't . . . You don't know what you're talking about. Ira? Tell him. I didn't know a damned thing about Riverside until last night. You were there when I found out."

"That wasn't his question, Mordicai. Riverside must have been inevitable. You knew that. You also knew about these paths. But you acted as if their existence was news to you. Whatever your motives, the question is this. What did Lictor promise you?"

"Nothing. Not a damn . . ."

"Peter?"

"Recognition. A verifiable spirit contact. Publication. World acclaim. No more second fiddle to Jennifer. Chicago gone, whatever that means. Only Bloomer of Princeton."

"And no more Alex?" Jennifer's voice was small and soft.

"No!" Bloomer screamed. "That wasn't part of it. You didn't need that fucking fag anyway. You needed me. I'm smarter than you are. I've spent my life at this. I'm not a goddamned accident like you are and like this man is. I'm a scientist."

Halloran balled his fists and moved toward Bloomer. Jennifer's hand stopped him. There were new tears welling in her eyes.

"You knew he'd take Alex, didn't you?"

"No."

"Mordicai?"

"I knew he'd . . . rearrange things."

"And what happens to Alex now, Mordicai? Will there be an oversight tomorrow? Will Alex somehow be lost?"

"No. No, Jennifer, I swear that's not . . . Lictor can't afford to lose anyone else. Not even Alex."

"And me, Mordicai? Is Peter right? Was I to cross over tomorrow?"

"Oh, Good God!" Bloomer blanched. "You can't Jennifer, I loved you."

This declaration shook Halloran. He had not wanted to hear that. He hadn't wanted to think of anyone loving Jennifer. Far less, of Jennifer loving another man. Any other man. But he knew, of course, that there must have been others.

"Loved, Mordicai?" she asked, not unkindly. "Past tense?"

"Don't do this to me, Jennifer."

"What else, Mordicai? What else would Lictor arrange?"

"How would I . . . Be reasonable, Jennifer. Why would he tell me? He knew I'd be near you. You'd know. He might just as well write it on my forehead."

"Then guess, Mordicai. Concentrate and guess." Her voice was stronger now. Calmer. Very calm. She turned her head slightly to one side of Bloomer's face. Her pupils, Halloran saw, seemed glazed over in an instant. She was not looking at Bloomer although it was clear from her manner that she was watching him intensely. But not with her pupils. It was more the sides of her eyes. She was pinioning Bloomer. Probing him, through the gray-green halo that was her iris.

Whatever she was doing, Bloomer knew it. Appearing suddenly stricken, he raised both his arms as if to ward off a blow. No. He's more like hiding something. He's folding his arms across the top of his shaking head. What the hell is this, Halloran asked. Is she hurting him?

"Jennifer? Please?" Bloomer's voice was almost a whine. Like a little boy. Damn! He was begging. My God, what was she doing to him?

"Tell me, Mordicai," she insisted quietly. "What would have happened?" Her eyes were still fixed upon a point off Bloomer's left shoulder.

"It . . . It would have worked out . . . for the best. You could see . . . David again. Be with him . . ."

Halloran felt another stab. David. A husband? A lover? Then another thought. Whoever David was, how could he have lived with this? What happened to him? What happens to people who cross Jennifer Wilde's path?

Bloomer dropped his arms viciously, his fists crashing to the table. The fear, if that's what it was, had given way to anger. Defiance. Jennifer, Halloran saw, was looking directly into his face again. Whatever it was, whatever she saw, no longer mattered to Bloomer.

"Damn you, Jennifer," he half croaked. "Damn you for a fool. It didn't have to be this way. You could have had everything. You and I. First everything here and someday everything there. But you! You spent years just pissing it away. Drawing pictures. Children's books, for God's sake. That's like a brain surgeon running a taco stand."

He paused for breath. His head down, one finger raised and wagging at her as if she were an exasperating child.

"Don't you still, even now, know what you are? You're more than the President of the United States, Jennifer. It's true. Think of it. What does a President worry about? Oil cartels? Inflation? Getting reelected? His place in history? Jennifer, these things are nothing. These are for children. Like finger painting. Because, Jennifer, Presidents don't know that history doesn't matter. Presidents don't know how much more there is. But we know. You and I know. For God's sake, Jennifer! Don't you see what that makes us?"

The sadness in Jennifer was more profound than before. "How can you believe that, Mordicai?" she asked, her voice almost a sigh. "How can you believe we're that important?"

"You need me, Jennifer," he warned. "Now more than ever."

"Please go back to the motel, Mordicai. Bring your pad. Lictor will want to speak to you, I think."

"What can you do without me? You don't even have Alex."

"I have Peter."

She looked at Peter as if for confirmation. As if to hear him say, "Yes, Jennifer. Through whatever comes. For as long as it takes. Through any risk and any pain. At any cost. For tonight. For tomorrow. For all the tomorrows."

But not now. Peter looked away. Toward Zalman. Zalman read the look and shrugged. The shrug said, "I know, Pete. She makes me nervous, too. One minute you want to take her in your arms and the next you want to run like hell." The eyes said, "You're stuck on her, you poor bastard. You can't run. You can't run at all."

"The hell I can't," Halloran said aloud.

Jennifer seemed to shudder deep inside. Then there was silence. No one spoke. Peter? Can you hear me? You can't, can you. I can't hear you, either. I can only feel you. In this way, Peter, we're just like everyone else. I can hear your heart beating and you can hear mine. You can if you listen. If you stop being frightened by my mind. I can't help what I am, Peter. I can only help what I do with it. Who I share it with.

She reached for Bloomer's pad that still lay on the tiny dining table. In silence, she wrote four lines. She tore away the page and placed it, folded twice, in the pocket of Bloomer's jacket. He would know to read it later. Away from the Winnebago. Beyond where Peter could reach into his mind. The message said:

> I'll come to you tonight, Mordicai.
> For all this morning's reasons.
> And for another.
> If you still want me.

"Goodnight, Mordicai," she said, and watched him go.

11

Paths

It was more than a tummy ache now. Leticia was hurting. Still, she was reluctant to stop. Four chapters outlined since breakfast. Amazing. The Underhill/Wentworth book was writing itself. It was as if her mind and memory were the data bank of a computer whose keyboard had a button she'd never thought to push before. That was it. One button. One little switch made the difference between a browsing library and an on-line computer. Old random circuits became linked. Forgotten storage disks were tapped. Extraneous information ignored. Bits and pieces of now-related fact came flowing forward. There were names and dates and odd oblique references, heretofore incongruous. Inconsistencies heretofore dismissed. They were not part of a whole. John Underhill the Second and John Wentworth were the same man. No question. It was no longer simply belief in the legitimacy of Mordicai's séance. Whether by supernatural agency or by chance, the séance had provided the key. The button. Wentworth. The false old scalp hunter referred to so cryptically in Jerad Mead's letter to his son. Underhill. He'd come back to claim the land that his ensanguined grandfather left littered with a thousand Siwanoy ghosts. A land purchased at a dreadful price and then abandoned. At least by the butcher himself. The thought was obscene. A thousand lives ended because a minor soldier was between wars and bored. If only there had been some provocation. Some motive. However mean it might be. And then the grandson. Not forty years later buying the same land again with Siwanoy dead. Perhaps some of the same dead. Is that possible? Could very many of the thousand scalps have survived intact for that length of time? Quite possible, knowing John Underhill/Wentworth. Not at all hard to imagine him picking through the moldy bones and gathering hair. Sorting it. Oiling it with bear grease to give it luster. Gluing the hair to patches of skin from a freshly killed pig and then identifying one of the more squeamish of the young bounty officers who would avert his eyes and hold a perfumed kerchief to his nose while paying out the two pounds six. Not hard to imagine at all. No wonder Barbara Halloran developed as she did. A genetic trash heap surrounded by a desert.

Steady, Leticia. Don't allow yourself to be derailed. There have been enough interruptions without you creating your own. Mostly Martha. Behaving so strangely today. Refusing to answer the door because she was polishing silver. Quite icy when I insisted. Then her lunch of oyster stew. Insisting that I eat. She should know better by now. I don't need food when I'm writing. Oyster stew at that. Particularly after last night's shore dinner. This story is all the nourishment I want. But Martha insisted. It wasn't even very good. Certainly not up to her standards. Gritty. Still feel it in my teeth. Then that stupid plant dancing around every time I took a mouthful. What was I to make of that? That the plant was hungry? A seafood loving plant? A Catholic plant, perhaps. Not likely. Not a Swedish ivy. Lutheran, if anything. Let Mordicai figure it out. If he ever returns that call.

Leticia plucked the sheet from her typewriter and leaned back in her thickly-cushioned leather chair. She pressed both hands lightly against her abdomen. It was hard. Hard and more than a little tender. Gas. Nothing but gas. Next time she'll tell Martha what to do with her oyster stew.

Forget that now. So much to do. She turned her head to the bookcase that covered an entire wall of the tiny paneled study. All historical works except the *Britannica* on the middle shelf. Many were historical fiction. No less instructive in their way than the indexed and footnoted volumes. The fiction, most of it anyway, dealt more with people than with places and dates. Less of what happened and why, but more of how it affected lives. She smiled, satisfied. It was all up there. In pieces, perhaps, and still to be ferreted out and assembled, but her next book was there. There and in her card files and in her heart.

Across the room, atop the carved wood mantle with the inlaid blue delft tile, were her own books. Eleven now. Between bookends made of small brass cannons and centered under a Gilbert Stuart. Eleven. Plenty of room for an even dozen. God, she loved this room. Dark and warm. Womblike. Her desk. Her books. Her fireplace. Her typewriter. There were times when she almost wished she were an invalid so that she wouldn't have to leave it. Except to lecture occasionally. Except to go to the head. Like she'd better do now. She felt a burning in her bowel. Damned oyster stew. Wish the bathroom was closer. The one with the bidet. She'd need it. Funny taste in her mouth, too. Metallic. A tickling in her throat. Oh, well! A good purge won't do any harm. Leticia felt a bubble rising high in her chest. She placed the back of her hand against her lips and coughed softly to clear it. Oh, my! Wow! That didn't feel good at all. She dropped her hand to her lap and then reached with it for a fresh sheet of paper. A splash of color against white Eaton bond had caught her eye. Was that blood? On her hand? It is blood! Leticia picked up the sheet and blotted its clean back surface against her mouth. The paper came away pink. What on earth caused that? It must be from her throat. She knew that much. Abdominal blood would be darker. Almost black. A spasm hit her. Folding her almost in two. Her hands slamming against the keys of her typewriter barely stopped her cheek from dashing against the carriage. A short and ragged line of upper case characters smudged the underside of her chin.

"Martha!" she rasped.

No answer. She must have heard. She could hear Martha clearly in the kitchen. Not twenty feet away.

"Martha?" she shouted, and another spasm hit. "Martha? Will you come, damn you? I'm sick."

"I'm baking, Mizz Browning," came Martha's untroubled voice from the pantry area. The calm dismissal startled Leticia into momentary silence.

"Martha!" Her voice was choked as she struggled to keep it even. "Please will you help me this second? I'm spitting up blood!"

"When I'm finished, Mizz Browning." There was annoyance in Martha's tone. But the announcement was firm. Almost ominous. It seemed to say, Do not bother me again, Mizz Browning. Whether you're having a stroke, or whether you've lost your mittens or whether an intruder is slitting your throat, do not bother me while I'm baking.

Leticia took a breath with which to scream her rage but caught herself. The scream would hurt. God knows what damage it would do. A buzzing began in her ears. Or was it . . . ? No. It was Martha. Martha's Mixmaster. I'm dying and she's out there making dinner rolls.

Slowly, carefully, she pushed herself to her feet. Not slow enough. Her whole torso, crotch to throat, exploded in a white flash of pain. Half blinded by tears, she groped and staggered to the door of her study. She could see the kitchen. And Martha. Humming monotonously in time with the Mixmaster. Her forearms dusted with flour. Leticia retched again and bile surged into her mouth. More than bile. There was that grittiness again. Like over-size grains of sand, they crunched between her teeth or settled to the sides of her tongue. Involuntarily, she wiped her mouth again and when she did she felt a pricking at her lips. Again the hand came away bloodied. Darker blood this time. And something else. What were those bits? Pieces of shell? They're shinier than that. And clear. Like glass. Oh, good Jesus! Oh, sweet Jesus Christ! It *is* glass. In the oyster stew? How? . . . Martha? . . .

"Martha?" she whispered, her cheek pressed against the open pantry door, bloody spittle smearing across the white enamel surface. Martha glanced at her, then turned back to the mixer, nodding her head as if timing the beats. She raised her left hand with its index finger poised as if to tell Mizz Browning she'd be with her in a minute. Then she nodded once more and snapped off the switch.

"Croissants," she said, with a small satisfied smile.

"Wha . . . What?" was all Leticia managed.

"Croissants," Martha repeated. "You can have fresh croissants for breakfast. The rest we can freeze." Leticia blinked.

"Martha!" she struggled for control. "Martha, I think I'm dying."

"These will make you feel better," Martha answered confidently. "With orange blossom honey. Maybe some of the English marmalade you get from Fortnum's."

"Oh God!"

"Or with whipped butter if you like. But try the honey first." Martha moved to the top oven and set the dial.

"Martha, for the love of God . . . Did you feed me ground up glass?"

Martha looked at her quizzically. She seemed to be considering the question. Her expression thoughtful, she opened a can of shortening and began spooning measured amounts into a bowl. Leticia might as well have asked if she'd paid the plumber's bill last month.

"Lunchtime," she answered finally as if it were a distant memory. "That was lunchtime. You were keeping me from . . . Yes, Mizz Browning. That was lunchtime."

"Please . . ." Leticia's eyes were wide with horror. "Can you please . . . Whatever you . . . Can you please get me to the hospital?"

"I guess . . ." Martha pondered. "After the date-nut bread. I'll have to come right back, though."

The novelist's legs were weakening. Trembling. But she knew that if she sank to the linoleum she might never get to her feet again. The car keys. They were on a hook by the kitchen wall phone. Near the door leading to the garage. If only she could . . . She'd have to. She'd have to make it. There was Martha humming again. Like there wasn't a thing in the world wrong. Oh God, it's so insane. It just can't be happening.

Leticia braced herself against the yellow Formica counter and edged her way across the kitchen. Martha's back was to her. Frightened, weeping, trying to stifle the sobs that made new tears inside of her. Martha! Martha was trying to kill her. She only had to wait. She was going to let her die. Never make it. Martha will never let her reach the car. Have to try anyway. Just a little farther.

Leticia lunged the last few feet clawing for the key ring with both hands. Her momentum hurled her into the wall phone, knocking it half off its mounting and sending the receiver crashing to the floor. Martha jumped at the loud plastic clatter, turned toward Leticia, then fairly leaped the three yards to the glass oven door.

Something changed in Martha. For only a second or two, she hesitated at the oven window, staring blankly at the bread that had not fallen after all and then more confusedly at Leticia's reflected image in the glass. She spun as if she'd been stricken.

"Oh Lord in heaven!" she cried, "Mizz Browning, what ha . . ." And then it was gone. Her features relaxed and her outstretched hands fell back to her sides. A veil had fallen away and now it was back. Martha strolled easily back to her mixing bowl. She made no move toward Leticia, who stood staring dumbly at her fingers. The keys were there. She could get to the car. To the hospital.

"Mizz Browning?"

"Huh? . . ."

"You know what's good with date-nut bread?"

Leticia's bowels let go.

On the fourth floor at Greenwich Hospital, Paul Weinberg's feet dangled from the edge of his bed, his fingertips rubbing his temples as an aid to concentration. It was hard to remember. That nurse . . . lying on the floor . . . what was her name? Laurie something. She was just washing his face a minute ago . . . talking to him. Did she faint? It was something like that. He could remember lowering her slowly to the floor . . . holding to keep her from . . . from what? Falling? No, that wasn't it. He was holding her by . . . by the throat. But why? There must have been a reason. A perfectly sound reason.

The briefcase. That was it. He asked for his briefcase and all she'd do is smile and say he wouldn't need it because he's got his medication coming and the last thing he's going to want to do is read a lot of boring old business junk. Junk! She spends her time pouring piss out of the bedpans and she calls what I do junk. Where is my briefcase, anyway? That closet? Better be there. Tomorrow's Monday. Isn't that what the police said? They said I couldn't get my train this morning because it was Sunday. Liars! There would have been a train. There's always a train.

The briefcase was on the closet floor next to his shoes. No socks. Just shoes. What else did they take? Weinberg felt his jacket pocket. His daily reminder was there and his appointment calendar. Bet there wasn't a single day until Christmas without at least one meeting scheduled. The compartment behind the calendar bulged fat with business cards. Other men's cards. Even some women. Women who produce. Not like nurses and stewardesses. And wives. Once the children are in school, at least. All those cards. All people who wanted to see him. To spend time with him. That was junk? Three new breakfast cereals readied for test market in less than a year. By his efforts. Was that junk? They wouldn't even have existed without him. Not quite the same, anyway.

His wallet was gone. They took it. His watch and car keys too. And his necktie? Why would they take the necktie? Who steals my purse, steals trash. What do they steal when they steal a necktie? Never mind. The briefcase and the daily reminder are all that matter. But that's wrong. The tie does matter. And the socks. The way I dress says who I am. To be successful, one must look successful. Not like some bum. Open collars are for slobs and Israeli politicians.

Weinberg slipped into his suit trousers and the custom tailored pale blue shirt and, with his briefcase, settled into the vinyl lounge chair near the window. The cushions hissed out air as he sank in. At a touch, the briefcase sprang open under the press of its contents. A calculator clattered to the tile floor. He studied it for a moment and decided to leave it there. Too much effort. Tired. Must be those shots. They can pick it up when they come to collect that nurse and bring back his tie and socks. If he didn't waste any more time, he could finish the paired comparison test analysis on Super Swissberries before they bothered him again.

But it was no use. He couldn't concentrate. The necktie. You can wear yard clothes or you can dress for business. There's no in-between. A man in yard clothes is a man who's taking the relaxation he's earned and using it to recharge the old batteries. A man in a business suit without a tie or socks is a man who's let the fire flicker out. A man to be knocked off by the kids moving up. That'll be the day.

Weinberg spotted the nursing station call button on the wall at the head of his bed. Why don't I just buzz, he thought, and tell them to have my property here in five minutes? My belt, too. Maybe not. Maybe that's no good. They'll want to talk about Laurie there and by the time I've explained I could probably knit a new goddamned tie. Priorities! How do you get people to understand priorities? To learn to focus. On the other hand, maybe it's a quality that can't be learned. You either have it or you don't. A talent. A gift. Hey! There's a thought. Isn't there a gift shop down in the lobby? They sell ties. Also socks and belts along with fake plants and stuffed animals and all that other crap. Nuts! They have my wallet. No problem. They can put it on the room tab.

Weinberg finished dressing. First his vest, then his suit coat. He winced in disgust as he pried his bare feet into his shoes but felt better after tugging his trousers low upon his hips so that no skin would show at the ankles. The briefcase was next. He considered leaving it. Better not. Not the way things disappear around here. And who knows who might be in the next room. Could be a competitor. Getting his lungs cleaned out from eating my dust. Not very likely, to be sure, but why take an unnecessary risk? Besides, this room makes an inefficient office. No desk. No place to spread papers out. Too many people wandering by in the halls.

Who are they, anyway? Visitors. Time-wasters. Loiterers. On a mission to bore the sick and helpless.

He forced the briefcase shut with some effort before remembering the calculator on the floor. The hell with it. Leave it on the night table with a business card. Weinberg withdrew a card from his daily reminder and scrawled "property of" with an arrow pointing to his name and title. Then in bolder letters, "DO NOT REMOVE." There! One of the nurse's shoes, kicked loose in the short struggle, lay on its side toward the door. He picked it up as a tidiness reflex and stood for a moment as if searching for an appropriate place to put it. No place occurred to him. Weinberg left the room with the shoe in his hand. He passed the night nurse's station where he paused to place it on a gray metal desk whose occupant, her back to him, was busy at a file cabinet.

"Here you are," he said, and turned toward the elevator.

"Thank you, Doctor," she answered absently.

The Super Swissberries analysis took two hours at a table in the staff cafeteria. Not bad, considering all the distractions. First a lot of babbling about a man scaring the life out of poor Louise in the gift shop when she tried to explain that this wasn't a hotel and he couldn't charge gifts to his room but he took them anyway when she ran to get help and isn't that awful? As if she doesn't have enough trouble raising two kids after that bastard took off on her and wouldn't you think a hospital was the one place where you wouldn't be bothered by all the nuts and thieves running around these days? Next, a tearful Candy-Striper bursting in with news about them finding Laurie Beals dead and they think that same guy who might be a shoe fetishist according to Harriet Lehman and Louise is lucky to be alive if it was him. They're searching the whole hospital for him but he's probably gone. It seemed to Weinberg that he knew something about all this but it would have to wait. Priorities!

Then later, a more subdued buzzing about Leticia Browning, yes, *that* Leticia Browning, showing up all bloody and half dead in a car she damn near drove through the Emergency Room door. Deep shock. Surgery. Internal bleeding. May not make it. No one knows what happened. What a day this is turning out to be.

The police were the last straw. Six of them. Sitting two tables away with a floor plan of the hospital and a street map of some kind. They tried talking to him. At least, he heard them say his name a few times. Weinberg paid no attention. It looked like Super Swissberries could hit a four percent share nationally by the end of its introductory year and deliver a pre-tax of a million four in year two. The police broke like a football huddle and rushed out. They'd be back. They left the floor plan. The hell with this. Get more done at home. Even if I have to walk.

Sarah McShane moaned softly as she eased the phone back into its cradle. The tears welled again. Damn you, Zalman! Where are you? She's already left two messages with the indifferent voice that was Zalman's answering service. No point in a third.

She wiped the wetness from her cheek and then dried her fingers against her bare forearm. Goosebumps. Her fingertips moved up her arm to her left shoulder as they had several times since she fell hard against the piano bench. The thickened tissue was softening now. Still, there'd be an ugly bruise. The skin was already beginning to discolor. A sick-looking yellow inside a purple curl. For perhaps the fifth time, Sarah considered calling the police. They'd see the bruise. They'd know it didn't happen by itself. But what would she tell them? That her husband threw her out of his den when she tried to wheedle him into taking a break from his work? That he swept the drink she'd offered him to the floor? That he might have killed her then? That she'd swear he would have killed her without ever changing his expression if the clock hadn't chimed just then. Six-thirty. *Wall Street Week* was on TV. He stepped over her like he would a sleeping dog and crossed the house to the family room. To the small black and white Sony that filled the cavernous space where the color set had been.

Oh, Eddie! What's happened to you? What could have happened so quickly? You were never much on stopping to smell the flowers. But at least you used to know they were there. And at least you never hurt me like this before. Never frightened me like this.

The ping of the oven timer startled Sarah. Only meatloaf. But what if it sets him off again? What will he do if I call him for dinner? Or if I don't call him? Hit me? Scream at me? Or worse, much worse, just stare at me with those empty dead eyes.

Exhaustion! Maybe that's what it is. No relaxation. No fun. Nothing but charts and market letters and multiples and the damned Dow Industrials. Not much sleep. If only he'd take something. One good night's sleep. He won't, though. Probably taking Dexamils to stay awake and work. What do they call them these days? Uppers. Uppers and downers. What if . . . ? There's still some

Seconal upstairs, isn't there? What if I sprinkled a couple on his meatloaf? One good night's sleep.

Sarah had to hurry. *Wall Street Week* had ten minutes to run. Ed would be up and back in his den, dinner forgotten. Now, dammit. Do it. Before something happens.

Stupid damned safety caps! Oh, God! The capsules burst from the neck of the brown plastic bottle and danced over the kitchen counter. She snatched up two like they were jacks. Maybe more than two. Maybe ten. Oh, Christ, maybe all of them. Enough so a couple of bites will do it. I'll stop him after he takes a couple of bites. Somehow, I'll stop him.

Quietly, nervously, Sarah set a place mat on the coffee table nearest Ed's chair. He did not look up from the screen. The plate came next. Two thick slabs of meatloaf, green peas and pearl onions, au gratin potatoes. Almost his favorite meal, not counting corned beef roasted in the oven. I'd kill for your meatloaf, Sarah, he used to say. Sarah, he'd say, if I ever miss one of your meals, start digging up the ransom because I've . . . because I've . . . The tears came back. He wasn't touching it. Sarah covered her face and ran to her bedroom.

The old man grunted to his knees and felt behind the storm windows that had leaned against the garage wall since spring. He whistled softly in the darkness. Nothing there. It should be here, he thought. Near his master. Dogs always stay near the master. Especially when the master's dead. Then they sit by his body and they howl. All except this damned dog.

Ezra Cohen groped his way to the side wall until his foot touched the canvas covered pile. He prodded along its length with his toe. Hello, Alex! Getting a bit stiffer now, aren't you? A little less cocksure, right? Cocksure! That's a joke, Alex. Don't you think that's funny? No, I don't suppose you do. You thought you knew so much. You thought you knew all about me, didn't you? All about me and Charles. Poor Charles. He just wouldn't understand that there was a time and place for him and other times and places that were not for him. Well, the two of you can talk it over. You'll have plenty of time for each other. I'm going to plant you right next to him tonight. Maybe on top of him. Would you like that? By the way, how do you like it, Alex? Rude of me! I never thought to ask. Are you a pitcher or a catcher? Not that I care anymore. Might have once. Another place. Another time. Because you're really quite beautiful. Not so much now, of course.

But you were beautiful. On top of him will do nicely. Keep him out of mischief. Perhaps he won't have so much time on his hands for petty little pranks. Like throwing rocks at me. Oh, yes, I know it's him. Right now, though, I'm afraid I don't have much time for you either. I'm more interested in where your little dog got to. Can't have him hanging around here whining and sniffing, can I? Can't have him digging.

Cohen was almost beginning to wonder whether there ever was a dog after all. He never did actually see him. But he heard him. He certainly heard Alex talking to him. Calling him. Damned right there was a dog. Name of Snoopy. Must have run off after a squirrel or some damned thing just before he got there. Good thing, too. Else he wouldn't have know where Alex was waiting. Wouldn't have found him stretched out comfy as you please back on the patio. Wouldn't have been able to slip around the house in back of him. And afterward, the patio was so much easier to clean off than the rug would have been. Just a couple of minutes with the hose and old Alex's brains are feeding the marigolds. Better keep looking. Better check the front again.

Ezra picked up a fallen twig and began prodding the hedge that lined the frontage of his yard. He moved slowly, checking each deep shadow, and making those mouth sounds which he imagined would attract a dog. He froze. There was a movement outside the hedge. On the road.

"Snoopy?" he whispered.

The figure moved again. Not a dog. It was a man. A small man sitting at the curb.

"Who the hell is that?" Ezra demanded nastily.

"You talking to me?" came the voice from the darkness. It wasn't a man. The voice and shape belonged to a boy.

"Who's that? What are you doing out there?"

"Waiting for my dad." The boy's head turned back toward the station.

"Well, get on out of here. Get away from my house." Cohen moved closer along the hedge.

"It's a public street, mister," the boy answered calmly.

"I told you to get. Did you hear me?" Only the hedge separated them.

"And I told you it's a public street. Would you mind not bothering me, Mr. Cohen?"

Ezra Cohen's hand slid to his belt. The billy. It wasn't there. It was drying back on the patio where he hosed it off. The belt might do as well. A couple of bites of a belt buckle will show a smart kid where he belongs and where he doesn't. Jeff turned as he heard Cohen pass through his gate. He saw the buckle flash in the light of the street lamp.

"I said move, sonny. Move or I'll make you move."

Jeff was more annoyed than alarmed. He knew this old bird was supposed to have killed someone. But if he did, he must have done it while the other guy was sleeping. Cohen couldn't run fifty yards to save his life.

"If you touch me with that, Mr. Cohen, my dad is going to come down here and wrap it around your neck."

Cohen stopped. His eyes seemed to cloud over in thought. A curious calm reflection where there should have been anger. It gave Jeff a chill.

Ezra was not troubled by the threat. No consequence that was indirect bothered him in the slightest. No abstraction. His thought process, like that of the others, was perfectly linear. He knew that the father might come. But that was not a threat. It was an interruption. This boy was an interruption. Find Snoopy. Boy. Strangle Snoopy. Boy. Bury Alex. Bury Snoopy. Boy. Too much boy. Boy loitering. Bothering. Get away. Take away. Police. He'd decided.

"I'll call the police now," he said, in an oddly vague way, as if he were thinking aloud.

Jeff grunted in disgust and rose easily to his feet.

"Go ahead, you old faggot. But when they come, they're going to come with shovels." He turned away and began climbing the hill toward his house. Cohen stared after him, a new equation forming in his mind.

Barbara Halloran's dining room table fairly groaned under the weight of the residue of Wentworth generations. Stacks of albums were heaped upon one end. Gilded leather albums now dried and cracking, a few less ancient binders of cloth and heavy board, two vinyl books of photographs. Two old Bibles lay open to their family record pages, a framed mail-order family crest between them. Genealogical miscellany littered the other end. Headstone rubbings, letters from county registrars and church sextons, diaries, journals, yellowed newspaper clippings encased in plastic, birth and death certificates, nuptial documents.

Her three-ring binder notebook was open before her. She worked slowly, carefully, an entry here, a deletion there. An occasional adjustment wherever a birth date followed too closely on the heels of a wedding. At least two female forebears whom she considered particularly interesting saw their given names changed to Barbara at a stroke of Barbara's pen.

Leticia will be fascinated. And grateful. Perhaps grateful enough to suggest a dedication page. To Barbara Wentworth Halloran. No. To Barbara Wentworth, without whose tireless . . .

"Anything for dinner, Mom?" Jeff asked from the kitchen door.

"It's Mother," she said, without looking up.

Jeffrey shrugged. "Anything to eat, Mother?"

"You should spend some time at this table when I'm finished, Jeffrey," she said, while scribbling a new notation. "It will make you very proud. It's time you knew what it means to be a Wentworth."

"How about if I make a peanut butter sandwich?"

"And you are a Wentworth. Not even your father can thin blood like that."

"Right."

"Actually, I'm glad to see you spending so much time with him. I really am. It disturbed me at first. But blood will tell. The more time you spend with him, the more you'll be able to see what a Wentworth is. And when Leticia Browning's next book comes out, everyone else will be able to see, too."

"That will be grand, Mother," Jeff deadpanned.

"Of course, we won't be here then. We'll be in Princeton. Perhaps even Oxford." She smiled expectantly at Jeffrey, anticipating his delight at the news.

"That'd be truly neat, Mom. Mother. Being a Wentworth and being in Oxford, too. It really sounds super keen. What about the peanut butter sandwich?"

"There's Beef Bourguignon in the fridge." Barbara pronounced it "Bihrf" along with an instantly acquired British accent. "Afraid you'll have to heat it up yourself. So much to do. So much to plan."

"Okay. Then I'm going to bed early." He turned back into the kitchen.

"Oh, Jeffrey?"

"Yeah, Mom."

"Just one thing more," she said, not unpleasantly. "If you bring a dog into this house, I'm going to poison it immediately."

Jeff made his sandwich and took it upstairs.

12

Jennifer

Bloomer was gone. Long enough for the sun to begin spreading out behind the trees. Long enough for the chill of dusk to fall in long shadows across the camper. Long enough for Jennifer to feel alone.

Halloran might as well be gone. He'd hardly spoken. At least not to her and not to Zalman. He was deep within himself. At times, he seemed to be listening to sounds, perhaps voices, that she could not hear. A part of her began accusing Peter, calling him cruel for the way he turned from her. But she forced those feelings down. He couldn't help it. It was all so much for him.

Jennifer herself had spoken very little, except to ask about dinner. Halloran only shrugged in reply. We need to eat something, she'd insisted quietly. There's some canned salmon in the grocery drawer, and noodles and onions. She could make a nice skillet casserole and a salad. And there's a bottle of wine.

Peter answered with a fleeting nod and looked away at once. Zalman glared at him. He pretended not to notice.

"Thank you, Jennifer," Zalman said pointedly. "That's very thoughtful of you, indeed."

Jennifer acknowledged with a smile that rested for a moment on the back of Halloran's head and then fell away. She winked it once more, reassuringly, toward Zalman, then kicked off her shoes and stepped into the compact galley. Zalman watched her. He watched her with interest and no small amount of pleasure. Slowly, almost daintily, she gathered the utensils she would need and laid the ingredients before her on the counter top. He studied each move. Each expression. A tiny frown when the stove failed to light and a little satisfied smile when the gas flame caught. A furrowing on her forehead when she examined the head of lettuce that Bloomer had bought. She would not have chosen it.

Zalman watched her with a growing sense of wonder. There was so much to this young woman. An inner peace of almost impossible dimension. The girl had every right to be a basket case by now. An emotionally devastating day. The loss of Alex. The treachery, if that's what it was, of Mordicai Bloomer. All on top of God knows what else. But for all of that, her every motion, each tilting of her head, remained exquisitely feminine. Serene. She was not a small woman, yet she managed to seem petite. Because she was barefoot? Perhaps, although the shoes she stepped out of were only deck shoes. Was it because she was so slender? But she wasn't really, was she? Certainly not thin. All the curves and symmetry were there. A sleek body yet an ample one. No, it was more her manner. A quiet grace. A gentleness. That inner peace again. The Jennifer that she chooses to show almost makes one forget the Jennifer inside. The strength inside. A strength, it seems, that Jennifer tries very hard to keep inside. To keep hidden. Lest men like Peter, for example, see that strength and not trouble to look for the human being in there with it. Did I say serene? A very unhappy human being.

And what of you, Peter? You great ass. It takes a special kind of man to deal with Jennifer. To accept all that she is. To see that strength in a woman in no way diminishes a man unless he allows it to diminish him. You gravely disappoint me, Peter. You are first drawn to a woman you have idealized and then you are repelled when you discover that the woman has substance. What were you hoping to find? A squaw? A pliable creature who would chew your moccasins to make them soft and lower her eyes when you spoke? A thirty-year-old geisha in blue jeans?

Zalman could see Halloran's reflection now in the darkened window. An open hand covered the lower part of his face but the eyes seemed to be shining. The flesh below them pressed upward. Is that a grin underneath the hand? What about any of this is a goddamned bit funny?

Peter let the hand slide from his face and turned deliberately to face Zalman. There was indeed a glint of humor in his eyes. Zalman saw, in fact, that he was struggling not to grin, a struggle that took all the more effort when Peter saw the annoyance on Zalman's face.

"How about taking a short walk with me?" Peter asked and pressed the hand across his mouth again. Zalman looked questioningly at Jennifer, who held up five fingers as she continued stirring. She met his eyes for the briefest moment longer than was necessary. He thought he saw a plea in her expression.

The station lights were on. They gave off little light against the still gray sky but enough to deepen the shadows that were beyond their range. Zalman followed Peter. He hesitated at the foot of the platform stairs as if he considered climbing them. Instead he turned and walked alongside the rank of parking meters that lined the platform railing. Zalman saw him cock his head as if to listen, and then resume his progress with his face curled into an almost blushing smile.

"You're hurting her, you know." It was Zalman who broke the silence.

"I know that," Peter said, but still the smile.

"Then may I ask what's so damned funny?"

Peter barely stifled a laugh. Zalman stopped and glared at him. He would have turned back toward the camper had Peter not reached a hand to his shoulder.

"I'm sorry, Ira," he said, tightening his jaw to force away the grin, "I guess we both have a lot to get used to."

"What, beyond the obvious, does that mean?"

"For openers, we could both hear every word you were saying in there."

"I hardly said anything."

"Except what a jerk I am. A great ass, more specifically. There was also a very reasoned analysis of Jennifer's charm and a less generous assessment of my delicate male ego. There was something else I didn't catch about chewing moccasins. I didn't catch it because I was getting the same kind of heat from Peggy Bregman."

Zalman sputtered as Peter knew he would and could not help but enjoy the moment. Psychiatrists, he knew, were rarely at an intrapersonal disadvantage. My God, thought Zalman. He tried to remember what he'd said . . . thought . . . about Jennifer. He tried to match his thoughts to her smiles and frowns. He threw up his hands, abandoning the effort.

"You could have stopped me." Ira Zalman was profoundly embarrassed.

"It was too interesting. It was also pretty much correct. Besides, you can't dump on me for repressing my feelings and then get all strung out when I find out about yours."

"Still," Zalman pouted, "there's room in any relationship for a private thought or two. I begin to understand your discomfort with Jennifer."

"Wrong, Doctor," he said, "I don't have that problem. She can't hear me any more than I can tune in to her. I don't know why, but she really can't hear Peggy or any of the rest of them, either. So far, I'm the only one who can."

"And that revelation, I gather, is the source of your improved attitude toward the lady in the camper?"

Halloran's smile faded. "Improved is a good enough word, I suppose. To be honest, I still won't be comfortable with her until I'm sure she can't do to me what she did to Bloomer. Call it a flaw in my male ego if you want. Call me a disappointment. But when I saw that, Ira, I really wanted to walk."

"Saw what, exactly?"

"Jennifer got inside his head. You saw Bloomer waving his arms trying to block her out. It was either mind control or something very close to it."

"Nonsense," he sniffed. "Jennifer has neither the ability nor the will to do anything of the sort."

"We both saw it, Ira."

"Yes, but I'd seen it before. I'd even discussed it with Mordicai. If you in your ignorance were put off by an occurrence that was new to you, you might have had the goodness to ask what was happening rather than leap to the conclusion that you were witnessing sorcery."

"It didn't seem like the right time to ask for a commentary," Peter remarked dryly.

"What you saw was Jennifer reading Bloomer's aura."

"Bloomer's what!"

"His aura. It's a sort of halo whose color and configuration can show the emotional state of the person giving it off."

"And Jennifer saw this thing and read Bloomer's emotions?"

"That's more or less correct." Zalman nodded.

"And that's your idea of an everyday occurrence?"

"More so than you realize," Zalman replied, sensing that he'd moved a bit too quickly. "Let's back up. Every energy source, Peter, particularly every heat source, gives off a halo just like those station lights. The human body happens to be a heat source. The halo it gives off has come to be called an aura. The human aura, or halo, if you're more comfortable with the term, changes according to the energy level of the individual. That energy level is obviously affected by stress, by illness, by fear, by tranquillity and so on. Many animals can see auras in other animals because of the type of eye they have. They can even recognize or sense the meaning of the aura's various permutations. Similarly, some humans are able to detect an aura and Jennifer is one of them. It's not an acquired ability. One has to be born with it because it's a purely physiological phenomenon much as there are people with superior night vision and others who can eat French fries by the bucket and not get fat. There's nothing remotely supernatural about what you saw."

"You're saying that an aura is like a lie detector?"

"It can be," Zalman agreed. "In this case, Jennifer could read a lie in the shadings of Mordicai's aura or else Mordicai thought she could. The result would be the same in either case. When Mordicai raised his arms in a gesture that you took to be a warding off or some intrusion into his psyche, it was merely an instinctive, if futile, attempt to block Jennifer's vision of his aura. Much like you'd cover an open zipper with your hands."

Halloran remained doubtful. Jennifer had done more than just watch Bloomer to check his color scheme. She turned something on. She did something by twisting her head to one side. "She never looked at him, Ira. All that time she was looking to one side."

"Once again, there's a simple explanation. Do you want to hear it or would you prefer to believe that the nice lady who's in there fixing your dinner is a witch?"

"I want to hear it," Peter answered. I want to hear it very badly.

"It's all in how the human eye perceives an aura. If you check with any ophthalmologist who's been in practice for a few years, he'll surely tell you that he's seen several patients who've complained about seeing colored halos around people. They think it's something wrong with their vision. It isn't. The human eye is composed of many hundreds of little light receptors. Those in the center of the eye are cone shaped. Those at the sides are rod shaped. The cone shaped receptors pick up color. The rod shaped receptors do not pick up color but they pick up a wider frequency range of light waves. All of an animal's receptors are rod shaped. Hence, they don't see color but they do see auras by looking directly at them. A human whose rods are particularly sensitive can see the aura and see it in color if he or she looks at the aura through the rods. In other words, peripherally. Jennifer was not getting into Mordicai's psyche, as you put it. She was simply looking off to one side so she could see what sort of colors Bloomer was flashing."

Zalman's explanation, and his apparent conviction that it was both true and reasonable, relieved Halloran. Not entirely, but any measure of relief was welcome.

"I perceive a lingering concern." Zalman raised an eyebrow.

"How would you feel . . . ?"

"How would I feel what?"

"If a woman could read you like that?"

"One can. My wife. Natalie Zalman."

"Natalie can see auras?"

"Natalie can see when I'm hurting. Or when I'm frightened. Or run down. Or frustrated. She can see when I need her and she can see when I need to be alone. I'm sure she can see when I'm lying. I solve that problem by not lying to her. Most of the time, I can see these things in her, too. And neither of us has seen an aura in our entire goddamned lives. You ask how I'd feel if a woman could read my soul? My answer, you putz, is that I wouldn't have it any other way. Not if the woman was my woman."

—Peter? —I hear you, Peggy. —You really are a dope about women but I'll have to explain the facts of life to you later. Things are happening. I'm not sure what. I'm afraid recess is over, though. You and Jennifer better get this show on the road. —Okay, Peg. I have a couple of ideas. In the meantime, you and the others stay close to the station. —Can't, Peter. We're going to take a look around. We'll try not to go far . . .

"Ira?"

"Yes?"

"You'd make a good psychiatrist."

"Go on inside, Peter. I'm going to finish my cigarette."

"What cigarette?"

Zalman shook his head in despair. Peter flushed and grinned, then turned the latch and stepped inside the Winnebago.

She was waiting for him. She stood at the galley, facing the door that he entered, a pot holder twisting in her hands. Her eyes were wide and defenseless, probing his. They each murmured a sound as if on cue and each stopped and waited for the other. Peter nodded, and gestured for her to speak.

"I . . . I know it's hard," she said.

"It's . . . confusing," Peter said gently. "I wouldn't have thought so. I would have thought that nothing could be easier or more beautiful than to . . ." He fell silent. He knew he would have stammered if he went on.

"Dinner's ready," she whispered.

"If . . . If you could just give me a little time to . . . I mean, I don't know why you should especially, but if I could have just a little time . . ."

"I found some hot biscuit mix too," she smiled

Even the first few sips of wine with dinner caused Halloran's brain to float. He realized with a shock that he'd eaten nothing since a bite of Jeffrey's muffin that seemed like a month ago. He kept from inhaling the aroma of Jennifer's skillet casserole only by pausing to trowel butter across a series of steaming biscuits, staying neck and neck with Zalman, and using the last of them to wipe his plate clean. The two men argued happily over whether they'd never in their lives been hungrier or whether they'd simply never eaten a better tasting meal, and agreeing gallantly at the end that it must have been Jennifer's artistry that turned packaged food into an epicurean miracle. Wizardry, Zalman almost said, but bit his tongue.

The wine's effect was tamer now. For that reason, among others, the conversation which had flowed so easily throughout the meal showed signs of being forced. Pauses appeared and grew longer as each of them sought, perhaps undeliberately, to forestall the topic of the station. At least for a little while. To pretend it was an ordinary night in an ordinary place. An evening of friends and lovers. Jennifer was the first to withdraw into herself for she knew that the first questions would be asked of her. She knew that unless Peter and Ira had expanded their perceptions of the possible and had developed, in so short a time, a broader view of life and death, certain of her answers would be terrible for them to hear. Especially Peter. Zalman could separate what was callous and what was necessary. What was cruel and what was Jennifer. Zalman could be clinical. Peter enjoyed no such detachment.

"I guess it's time to ask," Peter said, pouring out the last sips of wine among the three small glasses. "Jennifer, is there anything we can learn from what worked for you out in Lake Forest? How much of it will apply here?"

Jennifer's face showed her disappointment. She had hoped, beyond any reason, that Peter would have a plan. She knew, of course, that it would have been a poor or dangerous plan if no questions had been asked. But it would have been his plan. Anyone's plan. As long as it wasn't hers.

"Not very much," she replied uneasily. "Lake Forest was simpler in many ways."

"I seem to recall," Zalman offered, "reading about a suspicious accident that stopped the trains out there. Shall I assume that the accident was part of an organized effort?"

"That's one of the differences," she nodded. "There was time to organize. And Lake Forest was not as far . . . gone . . . as Riverside. Please don't be offended by this, but the major difference is that Alex was there. I don't think either of you are capable of . . ." She left it there.

Halloran laid his hand across Jennifer's arm. Zalman saw her free hand begin to move toward Peter's and then draw back. Peter touched her cheek and turned her face toward his.

"I'm not Alex, Jennifer," he said softly. "I can't be what Alex was. Whatever he was. But I'm going to help you. If you need to hear a reason why, I'll try to give it to you. But I'm going to do it. I promise."

"You could be very badly hurt."

"I guess I know that."

"I don't want you hurt."

Peter dropped his eyes to Jennifer's hand. Absently, he fingered a silver Navaho band she wore. "What are you saying, Jennifer? Are you asking me to back off?"

"No, that's not what . . ." Now Jennifer looked away. "I suppose I do need to hear a reason."

"I'd do this for you. If there were no other reasons, Jennifer, I'd do this for you. Whether you asked or didn't ask. Because I . . ." Halloran stumbled and paused, cursing himself at once for his lifelong clumsiness with women whom he cared about. "There are other reasons," he went on, surrendering again. "Peggy and Marty among them. But the biggest is that in my whole life I've never done anything very worthwhile. Nothing, except for raising a son, that really made much of a difference. Neither have most of the people I know. But then they've never had this chance. I'm going to do it, Jennifer."

Her free hand stirred again and again it lay quiet. Zalman took it in his own.

"I'm not Alex, either," he said. "I'm not even sure I'm the old Ira Zalman anymore. The old Ira Zalman would stay far away from anything that might get him thrown in the pokey. But two things I am. I am Doctor Zalman and there's no way that Doctor Zalman can walk away from this. I am also a friend. And Ira the friend won't walk away either. Still, I'd like to know exactly what happened in Lake Forest. There was a person, I recall reading, who stalled a car on the tracks and then . . ."

"It was a trailer for carrying boats. One of Alex's friends stole it from the marina in Belmont Park. The Chicago tracks aren't like here where you have overpasses. The streets run directly across the tracks and each crossing has one of those cantilevered traffic gates that drop across the right side of the road when the train is coming. Alex's friend simply ducked around the gate and crossed in front of the train. It was pretty well timed. It was done at a point just above the southbound station and the train was the first commuter express of the morning. It hit the boat trailer and tore it off the car's hitch. The bumper came off too but the car and driver were okay. Alex was . . . We were hoping that it would be enough to derail the train. It was moving slowly. No one would have been hurt. But it did at least stop the train and it did some damage to the train's undercarriage. We were lucky, as it turned out. We found out later that a derailment would have meant that they'd shut off the power at once. It would have been too soon."

"There was the same kind of mist around that station?"

"Yes."

"With people inside? Dead people?"

"Yes. About as many as here. We learned that later, too. At the time, we had no one who could see or hear them unless they happened to step out of the mist. But we didn't know that, either. We didn't even know that could happen. All we could do was make sure Lictor's people were all around the station waiting for the mist to lift."

"What about these paths? Were there paths in Lake Forest?"

"There were four. Two of them, a man and a woman, were already at the station. That's where I was. Once I tracked down the paths, my job was to stay on the platform and . . . keep an eye on the ones who were already there. Alex was responsible for the other two and for cutting the power. He went to the house where the first one lived. The farthest. About a half mile from the station. It was a man and he was alone. His wife had moved out with the children a couple of days before. Alex had to move quickly. He knocked the man unconscious and bundled him into the trunk of the man's car. Then he drove it down to the station and left it there."

"Inside the mist, I gather?" Zalman asked.

"Inside the mist." Jennifer took a deep sighing breath before continuing. "The second house was very near the station. Like the Cohen house is here. Alex found the man ready to leave to catch his train but his wife was dead. He'd murdered her during the night. Why doesn't matter. It doesn't take much of a motive. There was a boy there, too. A teenager. And he was in shock. Alex told me about it later. He said that the man knew his wife was dead but just didn't understand that there'd be consequences to her murder. He didn't even seem to understand that she'd still be dead when he came home that evening for his dinner. The man was going to work and that was that. Alex . . . could have just let him go. The man would have gone to the station and the mist would have been lifted before he could board a train. But . . . when that happened . . . the man would know. He'd know what he did. He'd go to prison. More likely, to a mental hospital."

"Alex killed him?" Peter asked.

"Alex killed both of them."

"Both of whom?" Peter's eyes widened. "The boy too?"

"He felt it was an act of compassion."

"And you actually believe that?"

"Yes, Peter," she said evenly. "I know that."

"Could you have done that yourself?"

"I don't know. I don't think so. Not unless . . ." her voice trailed off.

Zalman tapped the table. "We can argue philosophy and all the what ifs sometime next week. Right now, I'd like to know what happened next."

"Killing that man eliminated the last remaining path. It flowed back into the station. Alex followed it to make sure. He said it was like water flowing downhill. I felt it too. I could feel the force at the station building. Thickening. There were people on the platform who were normal or nearly so. Many of them felt it. Not the way Alex and I did. They seemed to feel an oppressiveness. A sense of being unwelcome. Many of them left. A few even ran. It was a relief that they were leaving as long as the right people stayed. The biggest relief was knowing that the paths did flow back into the station. We were afraid until that time that they'd simply dissolve. But they don't. As long as the power remains on, the paths can be drawn in. Once the power is off . . ."

". . . any deceased citizens, presumably including the three in this family, might be lost," Zalman completed her thought. "Drift away, was the expression Mordicai used."

"Yes," she nodded, "if Lictor's messengers failed to spot them."

"What was Alex's plan for cutting the power?"

"Not much of a plan, really. There's a power relay station several hundred yards south of the Lake Forest platform. The blow-back came from there. Did Mordicai explain? The power surge creates an electromagnetic field that . . ." She stopped when Zalman waved off the technical explanation. "Alex blew it to bits with four sticks of dynamite."

"That was it?" Halloran asked.

"It broke up the mist, if that's what you're asking. The relay station was destroyed and it was never rebuilt. It really wasn't ever needed, as it turned out. The railway generators had more than enough amperage to bypass it. That was one of the tragedies of Lake Forest."

"One of the tragedies? I'd say it was the least of them. You had three people dead. And two of the three wouldn't have died if Alex hadn't killed them."

Zalman could see the disappointment on Jennifer's face. And a deep weariness that wasn't there before. He could almost see her thinking, Poor Peter. You just don't know. It's just been too fast for you. What good can you do if you can't even see that a death is not a sorrow except to the living.

"Peter," she said, "we all have to be careful not to lose our perspective. Lake Forest could have been an enormous tragedy. As it was, there were more than three who died. Five, as I recall. It seems to me there was a woman . . . Yes. It was the woman who drove that car.

"She was Alex's friend," Jennifer confirmed. "The girl who stalled the train. She was a dancer named Angela Marcos. Angela was supposed to do her part and quietly disappear. But instead she walked down to the station. I don't know why. Perhaps out of curiosity. Perhaps to help me. Whatever her reason, Angela climbed out of her car and calmly walked along the tracks to the station platform. They watched her coming. The commuters. They saw what she'd done. Of course, they didn't know why she did it. I'm not sure they would have cared whether it was a legitimate accident or not. They knew only that she'd stopped them. That she interfered with them."

Peter's lips parted but Zalman silenced him with a touch before he could speak.

"At first, I thought she'd be alright," Jennifer continued, clearly anguished by the scene she was replaying in her mind. "They let her pass. Staring at her with those dead eyes and then staring at the train and then back at her. They reminded me of wooden soldiers. Angela saw me and she waved. She felt so cocky about stopping a train. Then she gave a little dancer's kick and headed toward me. I think the kick is what set them off. There was a man behind her. Not one of the paths. Just a man with a briefcase, walking, no expression on his face at all. No anger. No hurry. Then I saw the briefcase swinging high over his head like an ax and there was Angela sprawling across the cement platform. I screamed to her. I could see blood all over her knees and on the side of her head. One of her shoes came off. Angela probably didn't even know where she was by that time, let alone what was happening to her. She tried to crawl to get the shoe back. The man, the one who hit her, he just watched. Still no expression. Nothing.

"Another woman, this one happened to be one of the paths, an older woman, picked up the shoe. I thought for a second that she was going to help. She didn't, though. She took the shoe in both hands and she tore off the heel. God knows why. She was pulling at Angela's other shoe when I got there. And another man was reaching for the beads she wore around her neck. And then someone else was pulling at her top. Trying to rip it but he couldn't because it was buckskin. I kicked him. As hard as I could, I kicked him square in the stomach. It must have lifted him a foot in the air but he never even looked up at me. He kept tearing at Angela's top. Angela's head must have cleared a little by then. She tried to get up. The man with the briefcase hit her again and this time the briefcase broke open. Papers flew everywhere. That man sat down and began gathering them up. Really slowly. One paper at a time. Sorting them. Putting them in order. All this time his expression never changed.

"More people moved in and were tearing at Angela's clothing. They were all around this man and he just sat there quietly sorting papers. Angela started screaming. I think I must have been screaming already. But do you know what was the most horrible of all of it? No one else was making a sound. It wasn't like a crazy mob. These people weren't even especially aware of each other. No noise. No yelling. Just hard breathing from some of them. Just the tearing and ripping and that man's goddamned papers being shuffled. I'd pull one of them off of her and another one would move in. There was one moment . . . I remember it like slow motion . . . when all I could see were her legs. Almost straight up in the air. Kicking feebly. Her hose was hanging off all torn and bloody . . . it looked like flaps of skin. Her legs . . . they must have excited one of the men because he got down between them and . . ." Jennifer's tears reached her chin and hesitated there before curling down her throat. Peter squeezed her hand.

"No!" she choked, snatching it from him. "You wanted to know. You wanted to believe that Alex was the worst part of what happened there."

"That's not what I said, Jennifer," he answered earnestly, his own voice near the edge of control.

"Well, I'm coming to the worst part. You're going to hear it. Because the next time you think about Lake Forest I want you to have something else to think about besides Alex the killer."

"I don't have to hear it. You're going to tell us that Angela was raped and then murdered. You don't have to go through that again. And I don't need any more proof that Riverside Station will be just as dangerous or that Alex did what he thought was right."

Halloran gestured with his hand, offering it again to her. She looked away. She crossed her arms and hugged them tightly against her sides. You know so little, Peter, she thought. You make it sound like an old news report. Raped and murdered. Such a small and simple phrase to wrap up what happened there and put it in a small and simple box. Angela was never raped. The other path saw to that. The man with the umbrella saw to that. The man with the red and black golf umbrella with the long spike on its tip. The spike that pinned Angela like a bug to the station platform. The spike he leaned on with his body and drove deep into her ear until it popped through the other side of her skull like it was a melon. The naked bloody legs that convulsed and trembled for the longest time and then went rigid in a scream that made no noise. The dull blank eyes on the man with the umbrella. The kind of eyes you'd expect on a man who was pulling weeds or picking lint or half napping while getting a haircut. Eyes that showed no light at all until I grabbed away his red and black umbrella with both my hands and sucked it out of Angela's head and rammed it through his goddamned throat.

"There was another man who died," Zalman recalled. "Arthur Simpson, as I recall the name. Dead of a stab wound. Was he one of yours?"

The question startled Jennifer, coming so quickly upon her train of thought. But she saw no accusation on Zalman's face or in his mind. Only a mild bewilderment at the look in her own eyes.

"No," she answered. "He was just a commuter."

"Was anyone ever prosecuted for any of the deaths?" Peter asked.

"There were no witnesses."

"No witnesses? Out of how many people on that platform?"

"No one remembered, Peter. This wasn't like Amersham. For better or for worse, Lictor ended the Amersham nightmare quickly. For the living at least. Lake Forest took a while longer. Long enough for the untouched to be frightened away. None of the others remembered a thing. Only that a dead girl with torn clothing and a dead businessman with an umbrella were somehow at their feet. Only that a woman was holding the dead girl's hand and crying, trying to wipe off her face and close her eyes. Only that a man came running off the tracks and that he was crying, too. Only that he snatched pieces of cloth and clumps of hair out of their hands that they didn't even know they were holding. And that he crawled through the dead girl's blood and held her close to him until the other woman pulled them apart and took him away."

"Alex!" Peter nodded.

"Yes, Alex. The man you thought was so callous."

"Jennifer, I never said that . . ." Halloran stopped himself, unwilling to continue an argument that had no purpose and could have no end. "Please, Jennifer. Why don't we let that go for now?"

"Alex was a good man."

"Okay. Let's agree that Alex is a good man."

"Not is, Peter. Was. I'd like to hear you say that."

"Jennifer," Zalman whispered, placing a hand on her shoulder, "Peter's right. Why don't we leave that alone for a while?"

"He still can't see, can he, Doctor?"

"Neither can I, Jennifer. Not the way you do. But we're not seeing through your heart."

Jennifer stiffened. She turned her head toward Ira Zalman.

"A psychopath?" she asked. Her look was cold.

"Yes," he said gently, no longer surprised that she could hear beyond his words. "That's what I'm thinking. You might as well hear it spoken. I'm sure that Alex was a good and decent person in almost every way that mattered. Alex happened to regard death as an event that should be celebrated. That much is fine. He also regarded death as a gift. That's not so fine. Not when he saw the gift as being his to give. You've offered us a picture of a man who does not mourn the dead unless they happen to be his own dead. That, Jennifer, is a dangerous man. In my judgment, that's a psychopath."

"You sound like Mordicai."

"And you sound like a normal woman with all a normal woman's emotions. One of them is loyalty. Coming to grips with the idea that Alex's reasoning process might have been impaired ought not to diminish your regard for him."

"There was nothing wrong with Alex," she said stubbornly.

"No, Jennifer," Peter said. "It's something else and I can't quite put it together. Why Angela?" he asked. "Why did they go after Angela and ignore you?"

"That," Zalman added, "was to be my next question."

"I told you. They knew she stopped the train. She interfered with them."

"But you said you were trying to stop them from hurting Angela," Peter reminded her.

"Of course I was."

"Then you were interfering. Why didn't they attack you?"

The point of Peter's questioning dawned on Jennifer. It was indeed odd. Odder still that she'd never wondered about it before. "I really just don't know," she said, shaking her head.

"Did it have anything to do with any ability that you have?" Zalman asked. "Is it conceivable that you were able to will them away in some manner?"

"No. Nothing like that. I can't do anything like that." This last part was spoken to Peter.

"You have no idea why Angela and not you?" he repeated.

"None at all. Are you sure it matters?"

"It matters," Peter answered. "I just don't know why."

"Perhaps we'd better move along," Zalman suggested. "I believe we have some decisions to reach." Peter and Jennifer returned from their private worlds as if awakening from a nap. "Can I assume," he continued, "that whatever plans we make will rule out the taking of lives?"

"I would think so," Halloran answered. Jennifer did not respond to the question.

"Do you agree, Jennifer?" Zalman asked.

Halloran didn't wait for her answer. "This is a different ball game, Ira," he said. "As long as I'm able to reach Peggy and the others, all we have to do is ask them to sit tight and stick together at the station. Then we pick the best way to shut off the power, do it, and go home."

"Jennifer," Zalman repeated, "can it be that simple?"

"Why not?" Peter again answered for her. "The power lines here are overhead. We can sabotage them in a dozen ways from any overpass. One bullet from a .22 would shatter those white ceramic things or I could drop a length of chain over the hot wire. For that matter, Hicks can probably tear up the wires all by himself. It was Hicks who knocked off the pantograph that hit me. Either way, as long as we can keep everybody together, we don't even have to worry about where the other paths are. They'll be empty and, according to you people, they'll just disintegrate when the juice is off."

"The danger," said Jennifer wearily, "is that someone else will die within the paths."

"Who?"

"Anyone."

"You mean a random death? Someone who coincidentally happens to die on this particular night within one of those little streams?"

"It could happen."

"Sweetheart," he responded patiently, "the odds on that have to be at least a million to one." Jennifer's face softened at Peter's use of an endearment but her head shook firmly.

"It still could happen. Especially in Riverside. Especially tomorrow."

Peter hesitated, repressing an impulse to brush aside that scant probability. Jennifer, he realized, was too fragile at the moment. "Okay. Suppose we ask Peggy and the others to patrol the paths until we're ready to cut the power. Call it six-thirty tomorrow morning. At six o'clock, they come back here and wait."

"Spirits have wristwatches?" Zalman asked.

"Now that you ask, yes. Marty was wearing one."

"They don't work," Jennifer said. "There's no such thing as time there. Not the way you . . . It doesn't matter. It's too risky. Someone could still die."

"In half an hour?"

"Peter, it could happen."

"Then we'll have to chance it."

"We'll chance it?" She looked up. "Us? Peter, we're the ones with the least to lose."

Peter leaned back and threw up his hands in frustration. "Look," he said slowly, "Ira and I said we wanted to help. We'd both also like to stay out of jail if possible. The way to do both is to hit fast and get the hell out of here before anyone gets hurt."

"Perhaps," Zalman interjected, "Jennifer could tell us exactly what her concerns are. If they're legitimate, we can try to plan around them."

"They're legitimate," she answered. "But I don't know if you can . . ."

"Try us, Jennifer," Zalman said softly.

"There's one problem that has two parts," she began. "First, until the paths are pulled in, Lictor's people can't get close to the station. They'll stay outside the farthest reaches of the paths. Someone could be missed when the power goes off. They're more likely to miss anyone who happened to die within the paths because the paths are always moving. Even there, Peter, I know that the likelihood isn't very great. But the penalty is terrible. Think of all the Amersham spirits who are still missing. I'll tell you about one of them, a man who was found in 1964. The man's name was Roger Perkely. Would you like to know where he was found? It was in Osaka, Japan. Hommada just happened to be in Osaka and he just happened to be conducting a séance . . ."

"Hommada?" Zalman asked.

"A Japanese psychic. One of the three or four best in the world. Hommada just happened to pick up Roger Perkely while Perkely was drifting by. It was the purest chance. Even then, many psychics would ignore any interfering spirit in order to concentrate on their primary contact. But Hommada was surprised to find an Englishman there and he asked, simply out of curiosity, who Perkely was and where he was from. Perkely said he was from London and Hommada almost let it go at that except that the man seemed confused. On the wildest hunch, he asked if Perkely was from Amersham. When he said he was, Hommada broke off his séance and followed Perkely, who was still drifting, on foot while telling an assistant to call Lady Edith Pierce in London, who then contacted Lictor, who then went and picked up Roger Perkely personally. This was after fifty-two years. Would you like to know how he spent that time? Perkely drifted slowly, very slowly, toward the southeast from Amersham. Slowly enough to catch an occasional glimpse of his children growing up, of his wife with her new husband who turned out to be a rotter who beat her. He eventually drifted into London proper where he stayed until the second war. Occasionally, he'd see someone he knew and he'd watch them grow old and die and then be gone. The war dislodged him. He thought it had to do with the bombings. Perkely drifted southeast again, all the way across the African continent until he was stuck again in the horse latitudes of the Indian Ocean. He was there for almost twenty years. The only other human beings he caught sight of were on passing ships. He wanted desperately to kill himself except, of course, that he was already dead but he wasn't even sure of that. He knew he had substance of some kind. Not enough to perform any physical function but enough to be affected by wind or concussion or other forms of energy. Finally, around 1962, there was a prolonged climatic shift, the same one that caused all that drought in Africa. It pushed him northeast and eventually to Osaka. That accident ended fifty-two years of a dreadful isolation. Perkely didn't even have a house to haunt. Except for the accident, it could have been a hundred years. Or five hundred." She placed her hand on Halloran's. "Peter, Roger Perkely is just a name to you. But what if it happened to someone you loved? What if it happened to . . . ," she caught herself, ". . . to your son?" she said instead.

"Let's get down to some decisions," Halloran said, squeezing her hand. "We're going to go for a clean sweep." The light returned to Jennifer's eyes and she grinned broadly for the first time in days.

—*Peggy? Are you there? Peggy?* "Peggy doesn't seem to be around. I'll try Marty. Hell, I might as well try Hicks." — *Mr. Hicks? . . . Oscar Hicks? Are you around anywhere?*

"Damn!" Peter returned to his fish tank, concentrating, trying to remember the earlier sequence of taking away the fish, and then the gravel, or was it the sunken ship that . . .

—*No need for that, man. You got an open line.* —*Mr. Hicks?* —*The same. You got me on the first ring. We just been busy.* "I've got Hicks." —*Listen, Mr. Hicks. First about the power lines. Can you knock them down or shut the power off in any way?* —*In the negative, Mr. Halloran. Would have done that a long time ago.* —*Well, what about that pantograph you bounced off my head? Isn't that just as hard?* —*My apologies for that, by*

*the by, but it worked out pretty good so far, didn't it? Anyhow,
I can't do that in no reliable way. The things I done have got to
be half busted to start with which of course ain't that hard to find
on the Toonerville here. I just sort of pushed them over the edge.
You want rocks slung at somebody though, I'm your definite
man.* —Okay, Mr. Hicks. Hold on for a second. *—Ain't goin'
nowhere . . .*

"Hicks can't cut the power. It's okay though. I know a way
to do it."

*—Listen, Mr. Hicks. Marty says you're the leader in here.
—That's mighty white of him. Sorry. Couldn't help that. But, yeah,
I got seniority.* —Okay. Are you able to make sure everyone is
at the station tomorrow morning at about six-thirty? That's when
I'm going to cut the power. *—Yeah, but don't do it by time. Do
it by train. I know when the trains are better'n I know what time
it is. The train you want to stop is the 6:52 to Grand Central.
We'll be here but you better not be. Lots of people in this town
ain't playin' with a full deck right about now.* —We'll be careful. You just have all thirteen bunched together. *—Population's
growin'. We got fourteen now and one more maybe comin'. Mizz
Bregman, she's out takin' a look.* —Who's the fourteenth?
*—Another white lady. A nurse. Come all the way up from Green-
wich Hospital.* —Hold on, Mr. Hicks. *—I'm holdin' .*

"Ira, there's a nurse from Greenwich Hospital in there. Wait
a second."

*—Mr. Hicks? How did she die? —Dude strangled her. Name
of Paul somethin'. He's got one of them paths hooked onto him
that Alex was talkin' about . . .*

"Weinberg killed the nurse," Peter told Zalman. "Shit! That
means he'll be under heavy guard."

*—Ain't so, Mr. Halloran. That dude's a walkin' dude now.
Mr. Kornhauser's out there doggin' 'im 'cept it ain't gonna do no
good. The man's gonna go back home like nothin' happened . . .*

"Weinberg escaped from the hospital. Hicks says he's walking
home. Ira, do you want to take a shot at finding him before the
police get him?"

"I'll need a car," Zalman answered, rising to his feet.

Halloran fished out his keys and, as an afterthought, drew a
business card from his shirt pocket. "You'll have to walk up the
hill and take my car. It's in the driveway. But first go to the pay
phone on the platform and call Mike Turkus at either of these
numbers. He's a police sergeant. Tell Mike I'm cashing in my

favor. He or you, or both of you, have to find Weinberg before the other cops get him, and bring him . . . bring him here. Maybe we can lock him in my trunk like Alex did last time."

"You'll both be alright?"

"Yeah, Doctor. But keep checking in. Marty Kornhauser's out following him now. If Kornhauser comes back, we'll know about where he is."

Zalman hesitated, reluctant to break off the experience of an unquestionable spirit contact, then made a disgusted sound and took off at a run. Peter could hear his footsteps crunching toward the platform stairs.

—Mr. Hicks? —Hangin' on, Mr. Halloran. —You said it was almost fifteen. Who's dying? —Another one of them path people. Mizz Bregman thinks his wife done him but didn't mean to. Alex says she done us all a favor. —His wife? That has to be Ed McShane. —That's the dude. A stock market fella. —And he's still alive? —Yep. He's sleepin' pretty good. Any gooder and he ain't wakin' up. —Mr. Hicks? —Gotcha. —Give me just a few seconds.

Peter blinked away the glaze through which he'd been envisioning Oscar Hicks as they talked. Jennifer was watching him wide eyed, expectantly. He returned her gaze but his mind was not on her nor on Oscar Hicks. It was on Peter Halloran. And Alex Makepeace. A man was dying. A telephone sat a few yards away, probably still warm from Ira Zalman's hand. What would Zalman have done? Peter knew the answer. Zalman would have called an ambulance and then rushed to Ed McShane's house where he would have tried to purge whatever it was that was killing Ed McShane. What would Alex have done? Peter knew that answer, too. Alex would have let the telephone grow cold. Alex would have let him die. He would even have stopped Ira Zalman. Any way he could. He would have done it to solve a problem and because of a conviction that Ed McShane would be better off dead than living. Peter shared no such conviction. But Peter had a problem. He also understood Alex Makepeace as neither he nor Mordicai Bloomer had understood him before. The platform telephone grew cold.

—Mr. Halloran? —Yes, Mr. Hicks? —I know what's eatin' at you. —It's gone now, Mr. Hicks. —Mr. Halloran? —Yes? —I'm scared too. I'm talkin' like I ain't, but I am. I'm scared to stay here and I'm scared to leave. Alex says it's a good place we'd go to and that I'd get to see my kin and such, but I'm

still scared 'til I see for myself. And I'm scaredest of all of what's in between if somethin' goes wrong. I'm lonely scared. Because I can't show it to these folks here. They look to me, you know?
—*I know, Mr. Hicks.*   —*Listen, Alex here wants to say some-thin'. First off, though, thank you. You and that lady. I do thank you, Mr. Halloran. You do it right. Do it good. We'll take care of this side . . .*

"Jennifer, it's Alex." Her head jerked erect and her nails dug into Peter's palm.

"Oh God, Alex? Can he hear me Peter?"

—*Alex?*   —*I'm here, Mr. Hallo . . . I can call you Peter?*
—*Peter's fine.*   —*Yes, I can hear her. Through you, I can hear anything she says out loud.*

"He hears you, Jennifer."

"Alex? I love you, Alex." She beamed at Peter.

—*That's like a brother, in case you're wondering, Peter. Our relationship had certain limitations.*   —*I know. I heard.*   —*From Mordicai, no doubt. Macho Man. I'd wish him a plague of herpes except it's wrong to speak ill of the living. Tell Jennifer I love her too, very deeply, and that I always will.*

Peter repeated the message.

—*Now tell her that you love her too.*   —*What?*   —*Tell her. She needs to hear it.*   —*Soon maybe, Alex. Not just now . . . If there is a later.*   —*Don't let her go, Peter. You're a terrible fool if you do.*   —*We'll see, Alex. Listen, shouldn't we be talking about tomorrow morning?*   —*No need. I know what to do here. You just stop the train. I'm going to look over these paths one more time. There's something odd about one of . . .*
—*Alex? You still there? Aha! Your moral dilemma has been solved for you. Here comes Peggy Bregman leading the Wall Streeter by the hand. Hmmph! Looks more like a bartender than a capitalist.*   —*Yeah, that sounds like McShane. Alex?*   —*Present.*   —*Thank you.*   —*Don't mention it. You can return the favor, though. Two favors actually. First, make sure that you nail Cohen's ass. Miserable old faggot. What he did to my hair will make you sick. Second, tell Jennifer when she gets back home to grab my Beatles collection before the vulture I rent from lays his grubby hands on them. Particularly my White Album. It's a first pressing and the jacket's autographed by John Lennon. I want Jennifer to have it.*   —*Anything else?*   —*Mr. Hicks wants a final word. Peter, you have a marvelous gift. You can't know how marvelous. While it lasts, look for ways to use it well. Ask Jennifer*

to teach you. The hardest will be knowing when not to use it. Ask Jennifer . . .   —Mr. Halloran?   —Yes, Mr. Hicks.   —Don't ride that train no more. Even after this is done. Ridin' them trains ain't no way . . .

Halloran wasn't sure what he'd expected in the way of a reaction from Jennifer. More tears, if anything. But there were none. She absorbed his account of the chat with Alex as if Halloran were reading a letter from a dear old friend who'd moved out of the country. One who's not really gone. Just away for a while. It was still hard to get used to but getting easier. Certainly, his own attitudes were changing. Here he was, bantering pleasantly with a murder victim whose body was probably not yet cold and discussing strategy with a Penn Central worker whose skeletal remains lay scattered by rats not fifty feet from where he sat. A week ago he would have . . . A week ago? Good God! It had been so much less. Who would have believed it?

"Peter?"

"Huh? . . . I'm sorry, Jennifer. Did you say something?"

"I said I'm going to have to get back to the New Englander."

"Oh!" he said, aware that for all his waffling, the disappointment was probably plain on his face. "I was going to stay right here tonight. I thought you might . . ."

"I have to reach Lictor," she said when he faltered. "He won't know what we're planning."

"Why can't you reach him here? Can't we just back the camper out of the mist?"

"I need Mordicai. I can't do it by myself."

"You have me. I can talk to Lictor through you just like Alex did. In fact, I just did that this afternoon. You certainly don't need a man who tried to sandbag you like Mordicai did." Peter felt a deep uneasiness that he did not fully understand.

"I need him, Peter. I need to reach Lictor through him, or through Nigel, because I can't risk a trance. Lictor's not very happy with any of us right now. He's also probably desperate. If he takes over my body, I might not get it back for a while."

"He can do that?"

"He's not supposed to, but he can."

"What happens to you?"

"There's a place I go. I call it my meadow."

"An imaginary place?" Peter asked idly.

"No," she answered. Then, "At least, not to me," when she

saw his brow wrinkle. Not imaginary at all, Peter. And if I stay there too long, I won't want to come back. Not even to you.

"Can I come with you? To the New Englander, I mean?"

"I'll be safe. I'd like very much for you to stay here. To sleep here. Zalman will be back. Alex might want to reach you. But you should also try to sleep."

"I'll try, but I doubt if I'll . . ."

"Will you promise me something?"

"Sure."

"Will you be in bed with the lights out by eleven?"

"That won't give me much time. I have some hardware to pick up that I'm going to use to stop that train. Then it has to be put in place. Then, like you said, Zalman might be back."

"Peter," she touched her fingers to his chest, "will you promise me?"

"I promise," he smiled. Peter felt a bit silly for even having raised an objection. He saw clearly now that, except for getting the hardware and rigging it, being in bed at eleven was the most important and sensible thing he could do. He knew that when she touched him.

13

Bloomer

Bloomer was near the edge of control. He sweated heavily in spite of the chill that flowed toward the setting sun like an incoming tide. It did not draw off the heat of humiliation that he felt on his cheeks or the fear that seemed to suck the warmth from his body. He wanted to run. He wanted to go someplace where it was warm and light and where no one looked at him the way Jennifer and Zalman did.

For the second time, he stopped under a streetlight and read the note that he carried in his palm. It made no more sense to him than before. *I'll come to you tonight,* she'd written. What the hell was he to make of that? Bloomer knew what the words meant. But what did Jennifer think they meant? Did they mean that she understood? That she forgave him? Understanding is alright but she can stuff her forgiveness. There was nothing to forgive. He picked a horse to bet on and that was all he did. A political decision. When you vote for a President it doesn't mean you endorse every damn thing he does. It's only good sense to try to go with a winner. If Lictor came out on top, so would he. If Lictor lost . . . then he'd see what he could salvage. Lictor sure as hell wouldn't give up easily. Nor would Mordicai Bloomer.

Bloomer, walking fast with his head low, was past the New

Englander entrance before he realized it. He was almost past the parking area and well beyond the dim yellow light that shone through the lobby doors. He started toward them but hesitated. What was he going to do in there? Sit at the bar and get gassed? Go to his room and wait obediently for Jennifer to show up? Pass the time chatting with Nigel, who, goddammit, should have known what Halloran could do and should have warned him? Like hell he would. He fished out his car keys and tossed them thoughtfully in his hand. Get out of Riverside. Get the hell away from all of it at least for a while. Maybe more than a while. Get on the turnpike and maybe keep going all the way back to Princeton and read about Riverside in tomorrow night's New York *Post*.

Bloomer drove for an hour, aimlessly, before the Yale University signs reminded him that he had turned north instead of south. It made no difference. He wasn't going anywhere. There was no place far enough. EXIT HERE FOR THE YALE BOWL, the sign read. He swung onto the ramp and stopped at a light at its base. The Yale Bowl. Princeton versus Yale for the Ivy League crown. Fat chance.

The car behind his gave an impatient blast of the horn. Bloomer took his foot off the brake and eased his Datsun to the left and under the expressway. With a sigh, he climbed onto a southbound lane.

Princeton and Yale. Tomorrow would come and tomorrow would go and Princeton and Yale would play football. Lictor would rise or fall and Halloran would live or die and Princeton and Yale would play football. It's possible to look at life that way, he supposed. That nothing really changes. But it does, of course. It will for half the good citizens of Riverside. And for Jennifer. And for Halloran. Oh, yes, Mr. Halloran. You too. I have news for you. I have good news and bad news. The good news is that you're better than Jennifer. Really! You see, Jennifer can't quite pick up other people's thoughts the way you can. Not unless it's the mental equivalent of talking aloud to oneself. That's why she can be blocked if one knows how to do it. You, Mr. Halloran, are much harder to block. There! Isn't that good news?

And now, the bad news. What, allow me to ask, are you going to do with your new toy? Assuming, that is, that it's going to last for a while. It often doesn't, you know. Will you go back to playing advertising and use it to find out what your insipid client is really thinking while you drink lunch with him? Will you start showing off with it? You probably will. And then they'll have you, Mr. Halloran. They will. The sinister They. And they'll never let you go. Your own government, if you're lucky. Some other government if you're not. You'll find out how free you are. Even if you only have it for weeks or even days, they'll never let you go. Like the Irishman a few years ago. Duffy. The salvage diver. He came up too fast one day and simmered his brain in his own carbonated blood. Not too much. Just enough to close one tiny circuit in his brain that's not supposed to close. Just enough that he could hear doctors talking without moving their lips. He could hear them. Right through the thick caisson walls of his decompression chamber. What fun that was. The switch opened again in a week but what fun while it lasted! And then Duffy was gone. But where? The British swear they don't have him. The Americans never heard of him. Has anyone here seen Duffy? Duffy? Who's Duffy? Sorry, but we don't seem to have any record of an Irish salvage diver, you say?

Want to hear more? How about the young Frau Speerman, late of Hagen, Germany, who did no more than sneeze one day. A violent sneeze but a sneeze nonetheless. It left her blind. There are circuits and there are circuits. It also left her with a third eye, rather like Jennifer's, that could detach itself and go see what her sister in Bremerhaven was doing at the same moment. It also got her kidnapped. Frau Speerman, you say? Sorry. Or Matsushi Hommada, who can't even take a bath without a bodyguard or Lady Edith Pierce, who had to blackmail a Prime Minister to be left alone and protected. Or Jennifer, avoiding the curse by trying to pretend that the blessing does not exist. Avoiding the risk by throwing away the reward. There's always an in-between. I could have shown her what it was. Halloran, Halloran, you bastard. I love her.

He realized he was screaming.

The new layer of perspiration had almost dried by the time Bloomer cut his motor in the space next to Zalman's Buick. He sat there for several minutes staring blankly at a wall. No emotion had the strength to rise within him. At last, wearily, he let the Datsun's door fall open against Zalman's car and lifted an old man's legs to the parking lot surface. Bloomer lurched through the lobby doors waving off the desk man who drew two pink slips from his message slot as he entered and held them aloft. Oh hell, he thought, pressing the elevator button. Better to take them now so he could shower and wind down in peace without getting calls

PLATFORMS

from the desk. He turned toward the clerk who had already concluded that Bloomer was drunk.

Bloomer fanned the two messages between his fingers. Leticia
and . . . Oh, shit! Barbara. Ms. Wentworth will be in the bar at
eight o'clock. What time is it now? Shit! Shit! It's already almost
eight. Too late to call her at home and tell her to stay there. She's
probably inside right now. Bloomer was sure that a cocktail chat
with Barbara would leave him asleep on his bar stool within fifteen
minutes. Taking her upstairs would be worse. Aside from whatever
small satisfaction he might get from fucking Halloran's wife again
and then sending her packing, she might not be so easy to send.
The woman was dangerous. He'd already seen how dangerous,
although it remained hard to believe. How anyone could be so
profoundly boring and yet potentially lethal would rank among the
enduring mysteries of the path phenomenon. She can wait twenty
minutes, he decided. Long enough for a decent shower. Bloomer
shoved both notes into his jacket pocket and climbed the stairs one
at a time.

"You always look so clean and fresh," she observed as he
reached her red upholstered booth in the New Englander Lounge.
Her arm extended toward him, wrist limp, and her cheek was
turned to receive a kiss. Even in that sentence he could see that
she had changed. A curious wooden quality had come over her.
There was a certain tonelessness beneath the compliment and the
smile was more a widening of the mouth. Bloomer took the outstretched hand and kissed it. What the hell, he thought.

"I hope you haven't been waiting long, Barbara," he said,
sliding in next to her. "On the other hand, your presence here is
an act of charity. You embellish this bistro like a fine painting."

The compliment, whatever it meant, pleased her. She nodded
and smiled approvingly although her reaction was not the schoolgirl
squirm he'd come to expect. The smile narrowed. "I'm sure you
won't make a habit of being late," she said evenly.

Barbara lifted her stemmed glass and took a sip of what appeared to be Chablis. Bloomer turned and signaled the cocktail
waitress. It crossed his mind to order a shot and a beer just to put
Barbara off but he really wasn't in the mood for such games at
the moment. Nor would he have done it anyway.

"A Scotch on the rocks, please. Ambassador Twelve if you
have it. And a Perrier on the side." Barbara again nodded her
satisfaction.

"We have a great deal to discuss, Mordicai." Her look was softer and she purred the words as if anticipating the pleasure that she was about to bring him. "First, some wonderful news. Leticia has agreed to write a definitive history of the Wentworth family. Isn't that marvelous?" There was joy in her words but not in her manner. Again, that deadness.

"I'm overwhelmed," he said.

"Of course, it's long overdue."

"Criminally overdue. Well worth the wait, however."

"You'll find it quite an asset socially. And if there should be another child," she said, dropping her voice and squeezing his hand, "it would open a great many doors. The right doors."

"A child, Barbara?" his eyes widened.

"A daughter would be lovely. Daughters can be so much more manageable. But one can't have too many sons if one's purpose is to perpetuate a line or to begin a new branch."

"Naturally." Holy smoke, he thought. Now he wished he'd returned Leticia's call. She was probably buzzing him to warn him of the turn this asshole's mind had taken. He pulled the message slip from his pocket and unfolded it, straining to read the message in the dim light. "Your damned Swedish ivy," it read, "is flapping around my living room again."

"Unless you feel I'm past my best age," Barbara added.

Bloomer was staring through Leticia's message, dimly hearing an alarm bell somewhere. If that plant was moving, it was being moved by one of the people trapped at the station. Most likely, the same woman who moved it during Leticia's séance. They moved along a path to get there. Barbara's path. But how . . . ? Of course! That was it. Barbara was out there again today pestering Leticia about her idiotic book. The alarm faded to a hum. But it didn't go away entirely.

"Mordicai, I was speaking to you."

"Hmmm?" He shook off the thought. "Oh, excuse me, Barbara. I was considering your remark about your age."

"And?"

"It's utter nonsense, of course. You are one of those outrageously fortunate women who grow more handsome with each passing spring. Although the choice must rest with you whether, having already fulfilled that part of your destiny, to subject that magnificent body to the discomforts of childbearing, you may well conclude that a Wentworth carries a greater obligation to procreate than others." In other words, do whatever the hell you want.

"I'll concede that it's tempting, Mordicai. You and I could produce a most remarkable child. A genetic masterpiece."

Holy Christ, he thought. She actually said it. His hand returned the squeeze. "Barbara," he whispered, "I have a notion that even Leticia may agree with you. Have you talked to her today?"

"You've felt that too?" she asked. "Interesting! She's been quite the matchmaker where we're concerned, hasn't she?"

"Barbara, have you seen Leticia today?"

"Today? Why, no. Not since last evening. I did speak to her on the telephone though. I thanked her for last night and for bringing you into my life and we discussed . . ."

"What time was that, Barbara?"

"At about noon, I suppose. Mordicai, this is not what I wish to discuss."

Bloomer glanced once more at the message slip. The call had been taken at twenty to one. The alarm was getting louder. If the plant was moving, someone was trying to get Leticia's attention. Urgently, from the sound of the message. That someone had to be inside a path which meant someone else had to have brought the path to Leticia's house. Five paths. Rule out Barbara and that's four. Which leaves Cohen, McShane, Gormley and Wein . . . Wait a minute. Gormley's dead. That leaves a total of four, but Nigel said there were five. Damn! Bloomer wished he'd kept that note pad when he left the Winnebago. Never mind. He didn't need it. Nigel damned well said there were five. There's a new path just since last night and it's been to Leticia's house. It's even later than Jennifer thinks. Who was the new path? It certainly isn't Leticia. But it's a little too close to her for comfort. Martha? Is that possible?

"Barbara, will you excuse me for a moment? I have to call Leticia before it gets any later."

"We were talking about our children." The grip hardened.

He looked down at her hand, studying it curiously. It was indeed a grip and in fact it had been right along. Even Barbara's handholding had a new grotesque mechanical quality to it. He drew her hand to his lips and kissed the back of her wrist, his lips lingering there until the grip relaxed. Then he pushed to his feet and backed a step from the table. "We'll have a lifetime for that," he said, and turned toward the lobby telephone.

Barbara's face was a mask when he returned. The stem of her wine glass had snapped and the tulip-shaped upper part lay on its side. He thought he saw a smear of blood between her fingers.

Bloomer had more on his mind. Martha. There was something very queer about her. No, Mr. Bloomer. She went to the hospital. . . . Why is she in the hospital, Martha? . . . So I can bake. Thank you for calling, Mr. Bloomer . . . Goddamn! It did get Martha.

"We'll finish now," Barbara said glacially.

"What?" His attention snapped back to her. "Finish what, Barbara?"

"We have much to discuss. Finding the proper house in Princeton for the three of us, the announcements, the guest list. You'll want to prepare a list of your best people from Boston and review it with me."

"It'll have to wait." He saw the fist tighten and a rivulet of blood squeeze through her fingers. "Barbara, there's something wrong at Leticia's house. I've got to run out there."

"We'll finish now," she said, heavily accenting the last word.

Easy, Mordicai, he thought. She's very near the flash point. He forced himself to smile.

"No one could want that more than I do, my darling. But if Leticia is in trouble, she may not be able to write the book. How could anything be more important than that?"

Barbara's face showed signs of softening. Bloomer decided to trowel it on. "Without the book, Barbara, our wedding will still be one of the major social events of the last several years. Perhaps even the decade. A union of the Wentworths of Greenwich and the Bloomers of Boston." Yeah, he thought, right up there with a supermarket opening. "But with the book, Barbara, with a book that may also be the literary event of the decade, my God, it'll practically be a marriage of state." Steady, Bloomer. You're pushing it.

But Barbara was buying it. At least reflecting on it. Or was she? Barbara had drifted off someplace. Her shoulders were drawing up as if she was taking a deep breath, except she wasn't and her head was cocking gradually to one side. Like something was pulling at her. Then suddenly she was released.

"And then we'll make love," she said. It was like a hand had reached into her brain and switched stations.

"Wha . . . ? We'll make love when, Barbara?"

"Afterward."

"After what? After the wedding?"

"No. After you see Leticia. You'll want me after you see Leticia."

How the hell am I supposed to react to that, he thought? That

211

a few minutes spent with Leticia Browning, absorbing the enormity of the Wentworth project, and impressed to the roots of his soul by the magnitude of the treasure being offered him, would doubtless return him enflamed with passion?

"I want you now, my dearest love," he ventured. "But of course you're right. It will be so much better, so much more meaningful, when I know."

"Yes."

"Then you think I should go to her?"

"Certainly."

"You'll be alright here? Will you have another glass of wine?"

"Perhaps. Until you return. Perhaps I'll go home for a while. There's Peter."

"Peter?"

"He'll interfere."

"Yes, I suppose he will," Bloomer pressed.

"We can't have that."

Lictor, he thought, you tricky bastard. You're in there someplace, aren't you. I have no part in this. Remember, I don't want to know this.

Bloomer rose to his feet. She made no move to stop him. No gesture of protest. Not even a farewell. She was like a wind-up doll that stopped in the attitude it was in when the spring ran out. He patted his car keys and headed toward the lobby just as the elevator doors closed in front of Jennifer Wilde.

She'd said little during the ride to the New Englander, not even questioning Peter on the details of his plan. Perhaps she didn't want to know, he thought. Or maybe she simply trusted him. He only knew that he wanted to finish what he had to do so he could be in bed by eleven o'clock. She was right about him needing his sleep. And she'd be back early. Five in the morning, she'd said, before even the first dim light appeared in the sky. At that hour, they would ride one more time through the streets of Riverside. One more wide circling of the station. One more sniffing out of the paths that were there and those that might have grown in the night. What if there were more? She had never said, now that he thought about it. If more appeared, they'd have to take care of them somehow. Don't worry about it, Peter. That's her department. You just do your part and get to bed by eleven. Nothing else seemed quite so important.

Halloran parked the camper on a small side road just before

the bend that led into the marina parking lot. He picked a spot that was on the property line between two houses so that the owner of each might assume that the camper belonged to the other. In case they noticed. A car would have been better, less conspicuous. He switched off the headlights. In the darkness, Halloran felt his way to the highway emergency kit that lay under the rearmost bunk and removed the tire iron that was clamped to its lid. He stood erect and hooked the iron over his belt so that it ran down the inside of his pants leg. Next, he reached into the cabinet above the galley stove and drew out a handful of wooden matches which he dropped into his jacket pocket.

Halloran stepped quietly from the camper and moved at once to the shadows at the side of the road. Then he thought better of it. Better to seem like an evening stroller than to look like a man with something to hide. Alex would have brought a dog. Funny thought. It was not even a good idea because dogs have a way of barking when you most want them to be quiet. Alex would have brought a pretend dog. A leash. That's what Alex would have done. He would have carried a leash. Peter shrugged away the thought, attaching no significance to it.

The moonlight glinted on a single car at the far end of the lot near the main clubhouse. That would belong to the night watchman. A little reconnaissance might not be a bad idea. He slipped past the small frame building used by the junior sailing club and onto the beach area. The sand made quieter walking. The next building, just short of the swimming pool and its complex of lockers, was a maintenance shed where mooring equipment was kept. A row of mushroom anchors lined the steps to its single door. Halloran tried the door and ran his fingers down over a small brass padlock, then pressed a thumbnail into the wood beneath it. It was weathered and soft. The lock would come off easily.

Locating the watchman was the next order of business. He wasn't sure what good that would do since the man would certainly be patrolling the grounds at intervals. But there was comfort in knowing where he'd be at least at a given time. Halloran stayed near the water. He was less likely to be noticed there and more apt to be believed if he had to explain his presence in terms of an urge to take an evening stroll along the shore and look out over the black waters of the Sound. Particularly if the old guy had any sailing blood in him, which seemed probable.

The shoreline curved back into the pool area and then almost to the corner of the main clubhouse. The watchman's car was only a few feet away. Halloran approached it and stopped to listen. Where are you, my friend? Are you grabbing a little nap upstairs or are you watching me from behind a bush? He let his hand fall against the car's rear fender and at the instant that it touched, he saw the watchman. The man was near the launching area at the far side of the clubhouse and he was urinating off the dock. A building sat squarely between them but Halloran could see the old man clearly nonetheless. A short man in his sixties wearing a red and black checked mackinaw. There was a stub of cigar in his mouth which he managed to spit past as he shook himself off and turned down toward the tennis courts.

Halloran was fascinated. He closed his eyes and the man was still there. Next, Peter covered both eyes with his hands, believing that doing so would put the watchman into even sharper focus, but now the image vanished. What did that, he wondered? Was he out of range? No, not that. He let go of the car is what it was. Halloran pressed his palm once more against the car's trunk and the watchman came back. Weaker than before, but he was there. At the tennis building. Passing the water fountain near the reservations board. He could barely see him. It was more like feeling him now. Apparently distance mattered. And touching something that belonged to the watchman also mattered. Halloran crossed to the driver's side and reached for the door handle but stopped himself just in time. The inside light would flash on like a beacon if the door were opened. He withdrew the hand but this time the watchman did not vanish. There was a dimming but the man was still there, his swing taking him toward the junior clubhouse. It must be the handle, Halloran thought. He could pick up more of the man through a thing that he touched often. Perhaps his skin oils were left on the chrome or perhaps his scent. He rubbed his fingertips over and around the door handle, then rubbed both hands together in a washing motion and finished by wiping them across his cheeks. The watchman was clearest of all now and he was coming closer. He was past the maintenance shed and into the pool area, very nearly matching the path Halloran had taken minutes earlier. Halloran ducked low behind the hedge that lined the pool and moved toward the shed in a line that ran parallel and opposite to that of the watchman.

The lock pried loose with an easy levering of the tire iron. He entered noiselessly, closing the door behind him. Not yet daring to light a match, he felt for a towel or cloth with which to cover the small window facing the parking lot. His hand ran over a section of tarpaulin. Using two screwdrivers which he found among a selection of tools arrayed on the workbench, he pinned the tarp across the window. Satisfied, he fished for a match and struck it on his thumbnail. The grappling hooks were where he knew they'd be. He'd seen them used many times for snagging moorings that had to be hauled up for replacement or repair. There were four of them. Several lengths of chain lay coiled on the floor behind them. The watchman was at the kitchen freezer now, pushing a spoon into a five-gallon container of coffee ice cream. The spoon bent. Halloran decided he could risk lighting one of the storm lanterns that hung on hooks across the back wall.

In the dim light, he found a box of shackles and selected four that appeared to be stainless steel. With these, he fastened a length of chain to the rings at the ends of two grappling hooks, then repeated the procedure with the other end of the chain. The watchman yawned and ambled to the reading room where he picked up a copy of *Sports Illustrated* and shuffled off with it toward the kitchen again. He was dimming once more. Must be the range, thought Halloran. No. The watchman stopped but he's still dimming. Halloran touched his cheek. There was a film of perspiration on it. And on his palms. Damn! It washes off, whatever it is. No matter. He was finished. Halloran slung the chains over one shoulder with the grappling hooks dangling behind. He blew out the lantern and pulled loose the tarpaulin before sliding the tire iron back into his pants with his free hand and stepped out onto the sand. Sorry about the door, he thought to himself on the way back to the Winnebago. You can pick up the other stuff sometime tomorrow. If Halloran felt guilty at all, it was because it was all so easy.

Bloomer was certain that Martha could hear the doorbell. He could see her through the kitchen door. She sat at the kitchen counter polishing a silver tea service. She would stir at the sound of the chime but would not look up. The wall phone hung at an odd angle near her head. He tried the knob and the door swung open.

"Good evening, Martha," he said pleasantly.

"Evenin', Mr. Bloomer," she nodded.

"That's a very lovely tea set. Of course, it doesn't matter how lovely unless it's polished properly."

Martha glanced blankly at him while continuing to rub. Apparently, thought Bloomer, rapport won't come that easily.

"Is anything wrong with the phone?" he asked. He straightened the receiver as one would straighten a picture and a mist of plaster dust drifted to the floor.

"Don't make more mess. Have to call the man about that."

Bloomer gestured toward the silver flatware that was waiting its turn. "Anything I can do to help?"

"Job's mine to do. Thanks just the same." She finished the creamer and put it aside, inspecting it as she set it down. "Mr. Bloomer," she said, "Mizz Browning isn't here and I don't have time to visit with you tonight."

"You said she's in the hospital?"

"It's where she said she's goin'."

"What's wrong with her?"

"Spittin' blood. Made a mess of my kitchen."

"May I use this phone to call the hospital?" he asked. Martha glanced dubiously at the plaster dust but didn't bother to answer. Bloomer lifted the receiver and pressed several buttons. "Hello, I'm calling to inquire about Leticia Browning. Yes, I'm a relative. This is her brother. Morton Browning." The hospital operator asked him to hold. Martha frowned at the lie but said nothing. ". . . Yes, this is Mr. Browning," he said to the new male voice that came on the phone. There was a long pause and his eyes widened. "Ground glass? No, Doctor, I can't imagine where she'd . . . What sort of danger is she in?" His eyes burned into Martha but she did not appear to notice. He had an impression that she was trying to remember something. "Yes, Doctor . . . The police? Yes, I suppose that might be a good idea. No, I'll be right here at my sister's house. Please call if . . . Thank you, Doctor." He placed the receiver on the hook and more white powder fell. Martha saw it and shook her head in annoyance.

"Martha," he asked softly, "do you understand that Mrs. Browning might be dying?"

"No such thing," she replied casually. "A good night's sleep and she'll be like new."

"How did she get the ground glass?"

"Mr. Bloomer, I told you I don't have time to visit."

"I'd like an answer, please."

Martha sighed. She folded her polishing rag and laid it on the newspaper. Then she slid from the stool and crossed to the sink where she began washing her hands. "Sit down, Mr. Bloomer. We got some nice salad from dinner. Mizz Browning wasn't here to eat it."

Bloomer took a breath in an effort to keep his voice soft and calm. Martha shut off the tap and took a sponge to wipe the sink dry. He thought he could hear the abrasive scrape of broken glass against its surface.

"I guess Mrs. Browning must have interfered with you in some way. Is that right, Martha?"

Martha didn't answer. She wrung her hands dry in her apron as she crossed to the refrigerator and opened the door. Bloomer watched as she withdrew a small teak bowl that was covered with foil and a mason jar filled with what he took to be salad dressing. With these, she returned to the sink and placed them on the counter. Bloomer's eye jerked to the Wandering Jew that hung in a macramé web near her head. It had moved. Something had tugged at a single dangling shoot. I know, he thought. I know she's dangerous. It tugged again, more violently this time. It seemed to be pointing straight at Martha who was bent over now and rummaging through a cabinet beneath the sink. As she pushed herself tiredly to her feet, Bloomer leaned to one side for a better look at what she'd found among the boxes and bottles. The plant flapped wildly. Martha drew a set of measuring spoons from a drawer and selected the largest of them. Holding it over the salad, she poured out a quarter cup of bluish liquid, taking care to dispense it evenly over the greens. This being done, she returned the bottle to the cabinet quite openly as if she no longer needed to conceal it. Bloomer felt his mouth go dry. It was a bottle of drain cleanser. He watched in dumb fascination as she carefully rinsed the caustic soda from the spoon before using the same spoon to ladle a cream dressing across the top of the salad. Without a word, she pulled a placemat and napkin from another cabinet and set these before Bloomer with the deadly salad neatly centered.

Once more he saw movement in a single shoot of the Wandering Jew. It floated slowly and deliberately toward the ceiling before slashing violently downward. It repeated that motion three times. Alex? Could that be you? There was something about the rhythm that reminded him of Alex. A chopping motion. Like a blow. It is you, Alex, isn't it? See how stupid it is that Halloran can see you and I can't? You're trying to help me, aren't you?

"Alex?" he called softly.

Martha turned, her eyes flat. The muscles in Bloomer's right thigh began to quiver. He almost flinched as she stepped forward but he forced himself not to back away. Martha picked up his fork and dug it into the salad. She held it silently before his mouth as if she were feeding an infant. Carefully, Bloomer took the fork in his own hand, relieved that she relinquished it, and forced himself to nod and smile. Martha turned back to her silver.

What would Alex do? Bloomer knew damned well what Alex would do but Mordicai was not Alex. But you have to be, don't you, Mordicai. Bloomer cast his eyes about the room in search of a weapon. A rack of carving knives hung on the wall near a butcher block table. Out of the question. No knives, no garrotes, no poison. Maybe a club. Bloomer looked around again but saw nothing that would serve that purpose except maybe the stool he was using. The plant made its chopping motion once more. Judo chops! You're kidding, Alex. Surreptitiously, he stiffened his right hand and tapped its edge against the counter. Maybe. Oh, damn, but maybe. Now, though, before you think too much about it. He rose to his feet and slid back the stool, aware that he was breathing heavily, aware that she would hear it and she would . . . She was turning! Bloomer leaped across the room and aimed a wild blow at Martha's nape. Martha moved. As the blow was descending, he knew it was wrong. That it was missing. That she would duck or ward it off. But she didn't. There were only those eyes. No alarm in them, no surprise. His chop smashed against Martha's collar bone and drove her upper body backward into the array of silver and flatware, scattering it across the kitchen floor. A plastic bottle of polish sprayed its contents over the tile as it bounced crazily toward the dining room door. Alex? Alex? She's not going down!

Martha's right hand reached for his throat. Her shoulder made a sickening crunching sound as she lifted her arm but she showed no sign of feeling it. She had him. Both hands were on his throat. He smashed his fist down across her cheek. Blood erupted from a ragged tear below her eye but her grip did not weaken. Her face seemed to be floating. First growing larger, then smaller, then larger again. He couldn't breathe. The room turned white and her face was gone but he could feel her hands. Don't do that, he heard. Don't do that. That's not me. Who's that? Alex? Help me, Alex, he called from a great distance away. Then he was on the floor and she was on top of him and there was a clanging sound and she was letting go. She was letting go.

"Mordicai?" the voice was stern. His mother, he thought at first, the way she'd sound. "Mordicai? Get up now, Mordicai."

"Okay . . . Wha . . . Barbara?" She settled into focus. The

white mass lying on the floor behind her must be Martha. He could hear her labored breathing.

"You cannot behave in such an indecorous manner, Mordicai," she scolded, although her voice was even and flat as if saying the words by rote.

"You . . . You followed me?" he managed. "Why?" Her expression went blank. It was clear that she didn't know the answer. Lictor. "She hurt Leticia. Poisoned her. Tried to hurt me the same way. What did you . . . How did you stop her?"

"I struck her with a teapot. I'm also going to see that she's discharged."

Bloomer struggled to his feet. He was still light-headed. He had to support himself on the stool that had somehow become bent and broken. Thank God for Barbara. Or whoever. But Barbara was a new problem. He had to clear his head.

"She hurt Leticia, Barbara." He was still gasping. "Leticia can't write your book if she's hurt any more."

A bit of the dimness lifted from Barbara's eyes. "She has to write the book."

"She will, Barbara," he nodded. "We're going to tie Martha up and put her in my car. Then she can't bother Leticia while Leticia's trying to write." Bloomer felt sure that calling the police would not occur to Barbara. If he was right about these people, she was not capable of abstract reasoning to even that extent. Cause, effect. Stimulus, response. If he suggested that crushing Martha's skull was the way to ensure the writing of the book, Barbara almost certainly would have done that. She would have done it never quite understanding that Martha was dead; only that she would not interfere anymore. Calling the police, however, had already occurred to the doctor at Greenwich Hospital. They'd be coming soon to ask questions of Mrs. Browning's brother.

"We should tie her up," Barbara repeated. "We should tie her up and put her in your car where she can't bother Leticia and then we can finish our discussion."

"Yes, Barbara," he nodded. "That's a good idea."

He found a fresh length of clothesline in the broom closet. Rolling Martha onto her stomach, he tied her hands tightly and then bound them to her feet which he drew up behind her. Bloomer piled knot upon knot, trusting that the tension from her arched legs would compensate for the gaps in his memory of Boy Scout training. He needed a gag. In Leticia's desk, as he expected, he quickly found a roll of reinforced packaging tape which Leticia used for mailing manuscripts. Martha was beginning to stir. Quickly, he rushed to Leticia's bedroom where he rummaged through the medicine cabinet in search of any barbiturate or antihistamine that might keep Martha quiet through the night. There were three Librium tablets. Not enough. He took them anyway, along with a full bottle of Nyquil, and returned to the kitchen. Bloomer gritted his teeth and knelt astride Martha, twisting her face upward and pinning it motionless between his thighs. The slits that were Martha's eyes opened fully. He could feel her tugging on the lines. She did not actually struggle, nor did her expression show either fear or surprise. There was only the steady pressure against the bonds and the empty stare. Bloomer tore away a strip of tape and pressed it over her eyes. They remained open and moving underneath. Knowing that made Bloomer sick. He was considering how to get Martha to open her mouth when it opened wide and twisted, teeth bared, against his thigh. He squeezed harder, opening the green Nyquil bottle and jamming its neck deep between her jaws. She chewed at the glass but could not force it away.

Bloomer fished the Libriums from his pocket and dropped them into the space wedged open by the bottle, and then cupped his fingers around the bottle neck and pressed down. Nyquil and saliva oozed beneath his hands. The effort dizzied him. He looked away and shook his head to clear it until at last Martha swallowed. Bloomer threw the empty bottle to one side and tore a second strip of tape which he wrapped across her still opened mouth. Two more pieces covered the first at crossed angles and a third wrapped fully around her head. That done, Bloomer backed away, almost falling to a sitting position on the floor, disgust and loathing on his face. Martha rolled on her stomach. She lifted her blinded face off the floor as if sniffing for his presence. Her head weaved from side to side, listening, and froze at the sound of his shoe brushing against a fallen fork. He watched in horror as Martha arched her body and tried to propel herself toward him like a slug moving across a dampened leaf. He backed away, sickened again, forcing himself to recall that there was a person somewhere inside that revolting thing on the floor.

Barbara! He'd almost forgotten her. He turned to her now, as much to look away from Martha as to see what effect this sight was having upon her. But Barbara wasn't watching. She had found the rack of carving knives and was blankly examining the largest of them.

"Barbara," he said carefully, edging closer to the broken stool,

"I want you to know that I'm going to spend my life being worthy of you." Bloomer didn't know whether that was the right thing to say or not. The stool was in reach as insurance.

"I know, Mordicai," she responded absently. Barbara stepped slowly to the sink. She stopped there. With her left hand, she placed her palm beneath the nearest strand of Wandering Jew, examining the pointed purplish leaves. Her hand closed over several of them, making a fist, crushing them, and the knife followed. She sawed at the stem rather than cutting it, as a torturer might rip at flesh. Barbara hacked lightly at the next stem, taking care not to sever it in a single stroke. She did this with each until the plant was shorn and the sink was covered with a tangle of shoots. Finally, she reached higher and slashed through the braided hemp from which it hung. The ceramic pot shattered in the basin. Barbara stepped back, and laid the butcher knife across her purse. Then she went limp again.

That he had just been warned was clear to Bloomer. Just as clearly, he knew that the warning did not come from Barbara. Why, you vicious old turd, came the thought from inside him. He was not sure whether the voice of that thought was his own or, as he almost imagined, Alex's voice. A part of Bloomer hoped it was his own.

"Barbara?"

"Yes."

"Do you think you can help me now? I must get Martha into my car. Do you think you could open my trunk for me?"

"Your trunk?"

"Yes. Where she can't hurt Leticia."

"Yes." Barbara furrowed her brow. "Martha mustn't interfere. Peter mustn't interfere."

"Are you going home to wait for Peter?"

"Yes."

"Will I see you in the morning?"

"Yes, Mordicai. We'll make love in the morning. And we'll talk."

"Barbara," he said softly, "in the morning, I must be at the railroad station. Very early."

"No," she said quietly. Bloomer saw her hand make the barest movement toward the knife handle. She waited, staring at him. Her clouded eyes not quite in focus and not quite meeting his. And in the silence, there was Martha, her heavy breathing punctuated by muffled grunts. She was inching forward through the scattered flatware and the smears of silver polish. He wanted desperately to run away, screaming.

"As you say, Barbara," he answered, struggling to keep his voice from breaking. "I will come to you tomorrow. If I didn't come, and I went to the station instead when daylight came, I would deserve the same as Peter. I should be punished if I went to the station in the early morning. So I won't. I'll come to you. We'll talk, and make plans. And make love."

Zalman saw him first. Weinberg. Striding purposefully along the Post Road toward the Mianus River Bridge. Turkus had been right. There was no other way to get to Riverside on foot from Greenwich. Other policemen would know that too and might be waiting at the bridge as well as at Weinberg's home now that the alarm was out. Still, waiting at a darkened Gulf station a quarter mile from the Mianus had been a risk. It seemed unlikely that Weinberg could help himself to someone's car unless the keys were left, but what if he'd taken the train? Zalman presumed that Weinberg had no money but he also guessed that the lack of money would not stop him. In the two short stops from Greenwich to Riverside, the conductor might never get around to Weinberg's seat. And what if he did? What if he pressed Weinberg and demanded payment for the ride? Might there be another killing that, this time, might have been prevented? Turkus had dismissed that argument. The walk from the hospital to the station, he pointed out, was a long one and in the wrong direction. In any case, the police were likely to be watching Greenwich Station too. They have to gamble on the bridge, Turkus insisted. Zalman brooded over the word, remembering the effect it had on Jennifer. Now, however, the question was moot. Weinberg had drawn within two hundred yards.

"Let me try talking to him," he said.

"What's to talk about?" Turkus shrugged. "We have to take him."

"Chances are he'll accept a ride home. We may not have to use force." Almost any form of violence offended Zalman.

Turkus shook his head. "I'll have to cuff him between here and wherever we're taking him anyway, Doctor. Let's do it quick and clean where I have room to move." Turkus stepped from the car and backed into the shadow of a billboard.

Weinberg was very close. Zalman could see his head jerking

slightly in the manner of a man talking to himself. The doctor flipped on his lights and started the engine.

"Paul?" he called, leaning his head and arm out the window. Weinberg heard and looked but did not slow his pace.

"Paul?" he tried again. "It's still a long walk. The car is faster." That seemed to do it. What had Bloomer said? Stimulus and response.

Weinberg altered his route and strode directly toward Zalman. His expression showed recognition but neither surprise nor gratitude at finding him here.

"I'm going home," he said. Zalman's smile froze as Weinberg opened the car door. Zalman's door. He stood waiting for Zalman to get out or move over.

"No, Paul. I meant I'd drive you."

Weinberg appeared to consider that option which he quickly rejected as unnecessary. His hand reached for the knot of Zalman's necktie and twisted powerfully. Zalman's cheeks bulged with a rush of blood. There was a dull thudding sound and Weinberg's hand went rigid, twitching in the air before Zalman's face as if a charge of electricity had shot through it. His body crashed against the roof of the car and the arm was yanked away. More sounds. Clinking sounds of metal. Through his stunned surprise, Zalman knew that Weinberg was being handcuffed. The man's mouth was open and gasping. Zalman saw a hand on the back of his neck forcing Weinberg down and into the seat behind him. Recovering quickly, Zalman leaned out of the way and levered his seat-back forward.

"Let's get moving, Doc. Head north before you cross the river." Turkus' voice was calm and professional. Zalman's pulse was pounding as if he'd run a mile. "Doctor, maybe I should drive."

"No," he managed. "I'm just . . . I'm fine. Why are we going north?"

"There won't be any policemen at the upper crossings," Turkus answered, his voice almost casual.

Zalman found himself envying Turkus. It was not the physical courage that he envied so much as the main detachment. A violent encounter like that left him feeling neither good nor bad, neither elated nor sickened. He picked a northbound street and pointed the car in that direction. Weinberg grunted in pain behind him.

"Is Paul hurt?"

"He'll be okay. Kidney punch. It just took the steam out of

him for a few minutes." Turkus drew a card from his wallet and proceeded to read Weinberg his rights.

"What good will that do?" Zalman asked. "I doubt if he either understands or cares."

"It makes this a legal arrest instead of a kidnapping in case anything goes wrong. Unless you'd like to do about ten years."

Zalman almost drove off the road.

"Three years," muttered Weinberg.

"What did he say?" Zalman asked.

"I don't think he knows himself."

"I do know," Weinberg argued. "Super Swissberries. At a six percent share goal, the marketing investment will pay out in three years. It can be two and a half if we coupon twice in the first six months."

Zalman understood what he meant. Ira's younger brother ran a small venture-capital firm in Hartford. He decided to try something.

"Paul, what kind of trial and repurchase rate are you assuming?"

"Eighteen percent trial. Sixty-five percent initial repurchase declining to forty at the fifth turn and an average repeat of eleven a year."

"Isn't thirty months plenty of time for a competitive knock-off to show up?"

"I factored that in. I figure we have eighteen months clean. That's when we have to establish our user base and that's why we should coupon twice. Particularly if we run into any extraordinary counter-spending."

Weinberg droned on, fully absorbed in the esoterica of new product marketing. The doctor in Zalman was more than interested, not in Super Swissberries but in the extent to which Paul Weinberg's world had shrunk. His present circumstances, his battered wife, his murdered nurse, were insignificant to him. On a one-to-ten scale of single-mindedness, Weinberg was at least a nine and a half. The mist had pushed him there, of course, but where had he ranked before it grew? A seven or eight, perhaps? Like fully a quarter of the men and women who shared his train. Men whose children were managed rather than reared. Men whose wives were dealt with and used more than felt and loved. Men who would one day leave legacies of breakfast foods and stock portfolios instead of smiles. Forgettable men who left behind not after-images of their humanity but the fruits of values which their survivors never even shared. Bitter monuments that would serve only to remind grown children and widows of the hours stolen from them. Or, more tragically, that children who knew no other way would see such lives as the standard by which their own would be measured.

Weinberg was still going. Something about allocating a part of his advertising and promotion budget to a three-level spending test. Extraordinary, thought Zalman. His throught process was perfectly linear and his capacity for abstract reasoning gave all appearances of being nil. Guile, therefore, was not to be expected. The doctor wondered if his original intention of binding and gagging Weinberg would be necessary after all. It was enough to keep him talking. All night, if he had to. He'd never have a better opportunity to observe the effect of the Amersham phenomenon.

"What the hell's he talking about?" asked Sgt. Turkus.

"His existence."

Jennifer sat on the edge of Bloomer's second bed and listened to the sounds of his second shower of the evening. She lifted the watch that hung from a finely braided leather chain around her neck, the one Alex had made for her. It was already half past ten. The shower had been running for more than twenty minutes. Long enough that she would have worried had she not been able to hear the changing pitch of the water's flow that told of his body changing position under it. She wondered what it was that he was trying to wash away.

Poor Mordicai, she thought. Poor civilized Mordicai. Rolling around a kitchen floor while pummeling an old woman who was stronger than he. Saying words of submission and conciliation to another woman he despised so that she'd permit him to drag the trussed-up housekeeper to his car. Perhaps that's what he's trying to rub off. The affront to his . . . his what? His manhood? Maybe. His dignity? Probably that too. She giggled and had to bite her lip to stop. It really wasn't funny. More than that was bothering him. Perhaps he'd tell her later.

Jennifer had a feeling, an ordinary human intuition, that it had to do with Peter. Mordicai must have seen the camper when he parked his car with Martha in it. She wondered if he tried to look inside before the long walk back. Afraid to talk to Peter. Afraid of another scene. It would have been alright, though. Peter was calmer now since she gave him some of her peace.

The sound of the shower stopped and the glass door slid open. She checked her watch. It would be eleven o'clock in twenty minutes. There was a tingling of anticipation in her stomach. The overhead light dimmed for a moment followed by the soft roar of Mordicai's blow dryer. He'd spend another five minutes trying to cover the little spot on his crown where scalp was showing through. Peter had very thick hair that he wore just over his collar. He'd never worry about being bald. And he had a nice soft wave that probably curled when it rained. Just like David had except David's was closer to black than brown. She wondered if she and Peter would ever sit in a tub together and sip wine the way she did with David. They shouldn't. They shouldn't try to do the same things. They should build memories of their own and still hold on to the best of what each of them had before. New memories, new dreams. Anyway, there are those big wooden hot tubs now that they didn't have then. That wouldn't be the same. With those tubs, you can even have good friends come visit and sit with you.

The blower stopped and the door clicked open. Bloomer, his expression thoughtful, stepped out wearing a knee-length travel robe and went directly to the ice bucket atop the bureau. He held up two glasses toward Jennifer questioningly. She shook her head. Bloomer poured himself an inch of Scotch, hesitated, then poured another inch and a half. He noticed the yellow legal pad which Jennifer had already laid out on the small table near the window. Bloomer took a breath and guided her to a chair with a sweep of his arm.

"I gather it's to be my nickel," he said, standing as he waited for Jennifer to take the seat across from him. She stared at the pad from her position on the bed as if it had a life of its own, her manner one of reluctance rather than fear. After a short moment, she unfolded her long legs and slipped into the chair that Mordicai indicated. It seemed to Mordicai that she was sniffing the air like a nervous fawn.

"Why Nigel?" he asked. "Why not go to the source?"

"I'd just rather."

"You're afraid, I take it, that Lictor and I will have a con-spiratorial chat if you're not here to witness it." Bloomer did not look into her eyes as he said this. Nor did Jennifer answer. It wasn't strictly true but she was not inclined to debate the point no matter how badly Mordicai wanted to hear that her trust in him was not irrevocably shattered. Jennifer's mistrust was centered on Lictor.

Bloomer made a face and scrawled the word "Nigel" across the first line of the tablet. He dropped his hand to the line below it and poised the pen, expecting it to take off with a rush the instant it touched paper. There was nothing. Not even the normal thrill he would feel running through his fingers. He waited.

"Do you think he's being stubborn?" Jennifer asked. She was prepared to wait out any recalcitrance aimed at forcing her to give her being to Lictor.

"Peevishness, more likely," Bloomer shrugged. "We've pretty much kept them in the dark." He wrote the name again. "Still nothing. There's no chance of a path being anywhere near us, is there?"

"No," she lied. "I'd feel it." It was so faint, she almost missed it. Like a single strand of spider's web in a soft summer breeze. But it would grow. And Bloomer, if he knew it had found him, would surely panic. The thing was only licking at him, probing, not yet embracing him. He would know that and he would run. He could escape the path but he would not outrun the knowledge that he was among those in whom some part was dead. Or missing. Of all men, Mordicai Bloomer would be devastated. If only it was still so weak that Nigel would come. If only Nigel would know to say nothing of the path.

Bloomer's fingers hitched. A word was forming under the ball of his pen. *"yes"* it said. He flashed a wink at Jennifer.

"Plan is to cut power," he wrote. "One hour after sunrise tomorrow morning."

"talkthroughjennifer"

"No need. No need to talk to Lictor."

"talktomethroughjenniferlictorgone"

Bloomer's eyebrows went up. This was Nigel's first indication that he could do any such thing. Was he talking to Nigel? The handwriting was certainly Nigel's archaic script. Except . . . except different. Maybe not different. Slower. That's what it was. The letters were written slowly and were being carefully formed.

"Nigel. Finish this line. There is no such thing as death, in nature nothing dies . . ." It was the Charles Mackay verse that had been Nigel's first message to him some twenty-five years earlier.

"notimeforgames" the hand wrote after a pause. *"talktome-throughjennifer lictorgoneimyourfriendiwillhelpyou."*

Jennifer reached for Mordicai's Scotch and pretended to sip it before putting it down in front of her. Bloomer did not appear to notice.

"It's Lictor, isn't it?" she asked. Nor did Bloomer notice that her voice had become weak and distant. His eyes were riveted to the tablet, his mind a whirlwind as he tried to grasp what was happening and scramble his thoughts at the same time.

"I . . . I don't think so," he said. He wasn't sure. How could he be sure? The poem wouldn't necessarily prove anything. Maybe really it was Nigel.

"Jennifer, maybe we should try it."

"Ask him why," she murmured. "Ask for reasons."

Bloomer heard the curious faraway sound this time and looked up at her. Her eyes were closed and her head was tilted to one side. What's she doing, he wondered? She's concentrating, but on what? She can't tune in to Nigel or whoever it is. On me? Jennifer, listen to me, Jennifer. I want this to end and I want all of us to come out of it in one piece and maybe start over especially if Halloran . . . no . . . Halloran will be fine too, there's no reason why Halloran shouldn't be okay because you can trust me I know I lost my head but it was only because I care so much about you that I almost . . .

"whereisjennifer"

"Jennifer's right here," he scribbled. "She wants reasons. Thinks you are Lictor."

"idiotmakesurejenniferisthere"

Bloomer reddened. It was Lictor all right, the officious bastard. How could he not know whether she was there or not? If she went off to that place of hers, he'd slip into her body like a hand into a glove just as he'd done at least fifty times before. "Jennifer?" Her mouth twitched at the sound of the name but her eyes remained closed. Holy shit! She's going to try it. No, Jennifer, you dope! Don't do it. "Jennifer!" he shouted, and drew back his hand to slap her out of it. But he held the blow, his arm poised and trembling, because he knew that it was useless, that the slap would land and she'd open her eyes and they'd be Lictor's eyes. "No!" he screamed and brought his palm slashing forward against eyes that were open and staring at him by the time it crashed against her cheek.

"Oh God, Jennifer," he cried. "Lictor, you miserable shit!" He drew back a fist this time.

"It's alright, Mordicai," came the voice calmly. "I'm not Lictor."

The skin of her cheek streaked angrily but she showed no sign of feeling pain. The voice was gentle, even kindly. It was not in Lictor's tone. He remembered the pen in his hand.

"Lictor?" he wrote.

"musttalkthroughjennifermusttalkthroughjennifermustta . . ."
Bloomer slammed down the pen. That might have been Lictor.
If it wasn't, why would Lictor bother faking it? Especially if the
son of a bitch had her.

"Jennifer?" he asked. "What am I thinking about right now?"

"That I'm Lictor," she answered. "Be assured that I'm
not . . ."

Too obvious. He shook the thought from his head and tried
another.

"How about now?"

"You're wondering how I'd be in the sack," she smiled. "Eat
your heart out."

Bloomer felt a surge of relief that all but wiped out the tiny
persisting hum he heard. She was right, and she wasn't Lictor
because Lictor couldn't do that. None of them could. Still, there
was something. Was it in her voice? The words? Be assured that
I'm not? One wouldn't expect that phrasing from Jennifer. There
was a little pause at the end, too. There's something about the
pause. And what was that "eat your heart out" business. She
promised she'd . . . At least, Jennifer promised.

"Jennifer? You made me a promise today. What was it?"

In answer, she leaned forward across the table and touched her
lips lightly to his, lingering there. Her soft warm hands brushed
over his ears and ran through the curls at his temples. There was
a melting in Bloomer's stomach. He'd had no idea that any touch
could be so sweet.

"I'll keep my promise," she said to him tenderly.

Bloomer was overcome. It was almost enough to bury any
thought of Lictor except for the spasms that were tugging at his
right hand. To hell with him. Lictor had been told when it would
happen and that was enough. He balled his fist tightly, his nails
dug into his palm as he tried to squeeze out Lictor's frantic tugging
until his forearm ached under the strain.

She took the throbbing hand in both of hers and brought his
fingers to her lips. The grip softened at her touch and he felt a
sweet relaxation that coursed across his shoulder blades and down
his back. She lowered his hand as the fingers opened and let it
come to rest across the smooth bare skin of her arm. The feel of
her skin warmed him and brought a tickling to the hairs of his
neck.

"It's time, Mordicai," she said. "It's time to rest." He almost flinched as her free hand reached its fingers to his chest and brushed lightly over the skin beneath the loose fold of his robe. Parts of him melted or grew rigid as he struggled to accept that the moment was happening. But the hand, too, was stiffening again. Annoyed, he looked down at it.

"Oh, my God!" he cried, tearing it from her arm.

"It's alright, Mordicai," she said, her hand still lightly against his chest. "It doesn't hurt at all." She drew back the hand and laid it over the ugly bleeding furrows that his nails had gouged into her flesh.

"Oh, Jennifer!" he choked. "Oh, God, I'm sorry." It shocked him deeply to realize that his own hand, unnoticed, had done such damage. Not his hand, but Lictor's hand in his. Knowing that caused his jaw to tighten in anger. Lictor made him hurt her again. She knows that. That's why she's pretending that it doesn't hurt. And yet there was no sign from her. Not the suggestion of a wince and not a drop of moisture welling in an eye. How could she have such control that she could . . . ? The thought slipped away as he watched the hand clawing at nothing like a jellyfish sucking through water. For a fleeting instant he wished he had an ax in his other hand. He snatched up the pen.

"Lictor!!!" he wrote, but the pen then fought against him and tried to form words that were not his. Bloomer jerked his hand from the pad and then raked the pen point down in slashing motions across Lictor's words.

"Lictor," he wrote again. "You bloody pig. They'll build a special hell for you, you bastard, if you hurt her again." He waited, inviting Lictor to answer so that he could reject any request or ridicule any order.

"yourchoicebornagainorthirdlevel" came the words in a scribble that abandoned the attempt to duplicate Nigel's script. *"decidenow"*

Bloomer blinked, stunned by what the words might mean. Born again? Why should he be born again? And did Lictor have the power to offer him that kind of a choice? It was a choice not unlike one between starting nursery school afresh or being appointed to the President's Cabinet. The mailroom or the executive committee.

"Don't understand," he wrote. "Why should I be born again?"

She rose from her chair and stepped to a place behind him, her hands resting upon his shoulders, her eyes fixed on the blank line below Mordicai's question.

"punishment" was the word that appeared there. She allowed

herself to breathe. Lictor could have enlightened or he could have threatened. He chose to threaten. Bloomer might still not learn about the path.

"Punishment for what?" he wrote deliberately.

"insolencestupiditydisobedience" came the reply. *"redeem-yourselfandyoumaycometothirdlevelwhenready eventomorrow ifyou desire"*

Tomorrow! Bloomer didn't know whether to be frightened or excited. Lictor was promising him the moon and he didn't even have to live out a natural life. But why? Jennifer must be wondering too, and just as frightened. What if Lictor can really do this? He felt the tension in her hands.

"He's the one who's scared, Mordicai," she said, as calmly as she could manage. "He's losing control and I don't think he can deal with that." Her hands moved to his temples and caressed them soothingly. "You see, Mordicai, it's Lictor who must redeem himself. He needs a success tomorrow and it must be his success, not ours. You and I and this Halloran and Zalman have made the decisions and have assigned no more than a part to Lictor. He can't accept that. He may let those people be lost again before he will accept that."

Bloomer could not believe that. Not of any of them. Especially not of Lictor. He wrote again: "Will you allow the spirits at the station to be lost if I do not comply?"

"comply"

"What do you want?"

"verylittlestartatsunrisenotlater"

"Why?"

"reasonsmine"

He cocked his head toward Jennifer questioningly. Her face was hard. "There's only one reason," she said quietly. "He wants the decision to be his."

Bloomer shook his head. "You've got to be wrong, Jennifer. This isn't some megalomaniacal politician we're dealing with. Have you heard of a developed spirit going off the deep end?"

"Lictor has."

"Let's see."

"Agreed," he wrote. "Anything else?"

"youstoptrainnothalloran halloranunreliable halloraninsolent-hallorantobepunished"

Bloomer hesitated. "He's better suited to it."

"complyornolictornothirdlevelnospiritsfreedfromstation" Lic-

tor answered. *allonyourheadbloomerdonotbeconcernedabouthalloranorabouthatwoman".*

Halloran, he thought? That woman? Jennifer Wilde is now "that woman" as far as Lictor is concerned? And what did Jennifer say a minute ago? That she and I and this Halloran and Zalman have made the decisions. Suddenly Halloran is "this Halloran" as far as Jennifer is concerned? He could almost feel her eyes boring into the back of his head.

"Agreed if no punishment of Halloran," he wrote, phrasing it clearly in his mind because she could no longer see what was written at the bottom of the pad.

"agreednowyouagreeonethingmore nobornagain thirdlevelisyours"

"What is it?"

"tonightnowdestroythatwoman"

Horrified, Bloomer slammed his palm across the words before Jennifer could lean across to read them. He felt her fingers leave his temples and he felt the distance as her body backed away from him, as if she had chosen to allow him room to think. Bloomer needed no room. For the last time in his life, he took the pen between his fingers and wrote a message that would be heard in a world that was not his. The words, black and bold, filled the three remaining lines.

"FUCK OFF, LICTOR!!!"

Halloran rubbed his eyes and blinked through the darkness. It took him several seconds to remember where he was. The Winnebago. The foam rubber mattress with its rough Herculon cover scratched at his bare back. That was a funny dream, he thought dimly. Nice in some parts. Very nice. She . . . it looked like Jennifer except . . . Of course it was Jennifer. Nice. The way she reached over to him with that soft look of hers and brushed her fingers across his chest until he thought he'd . . . What happened to her arm? The other arm. It looked like some animal had . . . Then what happened. Oh yeah! She got up and walked around behind him and stood there rubbing his shoulders and then his temples and it felt good while he was trying to make up his mind about something. About what? Some kind of a job, he thought. He was offered some kind of a job that was a big one but to get it he'd have to do things he didn't want . . . I don't know, he thought. Some job. Anyway I didn't take it and was churlish enough to tell the guy to fuck off but at least that seemed to make her happy. . . . Except the weird part is that she backed away while I was deciding and I had the feeling that if I said yes and meant it I was about to get the edge of her foot against the back of my neck and except I'm not even sure I was the guy. The rest of it was nice, though. Oh, Jennifer, Jennifer. What I wouldn't give to have met you someplace else and for it to have been just plain you and just plain me. Who're you kidding, Peter? Girls like that don't fall for guys like you unless you're really something special. Unless there's more substance to you than having been whacked on the head while waiting for your dumb train to take you to your dumb job. Bloomer's right. You're an accident. Maybe Barbara's even right. Strike that. Don't start thinking about her. Think about Jennifer. Go back to sleep. Maybe she'll come back again and rub your neck and . . .

Bloomer lay on his back, two pillows propped beneath his head, and watched her contentedly, seeing more and more of her as his eyes became accustomed to the darkness. The only light came through the curtain from a streetlamp outside and from the occasional soft strobing of a passing car or truck. So gracefully, she raised her arms for balance as she kicked off her shoes and then reached beneath her jeans to peel off the half stockings that she wore. Standing now, she pinched the pins that held her earrings and laid these down, after a brief search for the safest place, atop the television set. Her hands pulled her blouse free of her belt and she moved closer to Bloomer's side, pulling away her scarf as she did so and letting it fall. Her fingers moved slowly, enchantingly, to the buttons below her throat.

Peter reached a hand toward her and she took it, allowing herself to be drawn to the edge of his cot. She sat lightly on its edge, one hand resting on Peter's thigh, the other held away, allowing him to trace his fingers across her chest and shoulders, then slowly down her arms, discovering her, and across the sideways swell of her breasts. She leaned forward against his hand and kissed him gently, her own fingers drifting across the muscles of his abdomen. His lips searched out her neck and kissed her there through a veil of scented hair. His left hand floated to the buttons of her blouse that remained undone and, in Peter's dream, they seemed to fall open at a touch.

* * *

The last buttons fell away with practiced ease. Bloomer slipped his hand beneath one side of her open blouse and slid it up and across the smooth ball of her shoulder until the blouse fell away from it. She shuddered, her breath coming faster, and the other half of her blouse slid free and down her arms. In the darkness, the scant white bra seemed almost fluorescent against the bronze of her skin. He reached behind her. She leaned forward once more against his chest as his fingers slid the hooks apart. They danced slowly up her back until they eased away the straps that crossed her shoulders.

The bra fell away and came to rest in a tangle across her wrists. Peter took it from her and put it aside. She shuddered again and took in a small breath that seemed almost a sob. Peter heard it, but in his dream he did not seek the cause. Instead, he touched each breast, admiring the fullness and warmth of one and then the other and finding pleasure as the nipples hardened at his touch. She dropped a hand to the braided belt she wore and opened first its clasp and then the top brass button of her jeans. She touched his cheek, bidding him to wait, and then rose slowly to her feet and guided the tight denim over her thighs, peeling away each leg in turn. Next, she hooked her thumbs inside the band of the bikini panties that remained but then stopped and waited, watching Peter. Taking care to move as slowly, Peter leaned over the edge of his cot and slipped his fingers inside of hers, easing the cool and wispy fabric over her thighs and allowing them to fall free. She wore nothing now. And she was lovely.

"Jennifer?" he whispered.

"Yes?" The word came more as a gasp that told of emotions held barely in control.

"Say my name?"

"Peter," she said, through tears that he felt rather than saw. "Peter Halloran. My beautiful Peter Halloran. Oh, please love me, Peter Halloran."

"Your name is Mordicai," she answered distantly.

"And what's your name?"

". . . Jennifer."

"If you say so."

"Hush, Mordicai."

"Suits me," he hissed. "Then let's get down to the screwing." He seized her roughly by the upper arms and pulled her across his body, onto her back at the far side of his bed. His left arm hooked under her right knee and yanked it upward, spreading her thighs and he entered her at once. She grunted in surprise but not in pain. His thrust was cruelly violent. It drove her body upward in a series of rapid jerks until her head was banging solidly against the headboard and she had to brace both hands against it. His final arching thrust came quickly and with an angry heave that bent her head sideways. He fell heavily across her body, his face buried in his pillow, and he lay that way for several moments until his breathing eased.

"Mordicai, dear," she said at last. "I'm afraid you're getting heavy."

He took another breath, then rolled away and lay staring silently at the play of lights upon the ceiling. She slipped from the bed and felt through the darkness to where her clothing was left strewn upon the floor. She gathered all of it and turned toward the bathroom, pausing at the bureau to snatch a small bottle of club soda that stood near Bloomer's Scotch. Behind her, Bloomer lit a cigarette. She shut the door and locked it from the inside.

He was grinding out his second butt when she emerged, still nude but for her white bikini panties. She paused near the bathroom door to steady herself against the burning throb in her groin and she cried out softly when her torn forearm brushed against the doorframe. For the second time in minutes, she considered dressing and returning to her room where she might treat the injured parts of her body but again she put aside the thought. It would not be fair to Mordicai. If he should want her . . . again . . . perhaps this time he'd be more gentle. If he did ask, or demand, she was not sure she could refuse. She approached his bed and stood beside it, looking down at Mordicai. He ignored her. His body sprawled diagonally across the bed and he gave no sign that he would make room for her.

"Mordicai?" she whispered. "Could I . . . perhaps it's time we got some sleep."

"There's another bed," he muttered.

The dismissal hurt rather than relieved her. But she knew that she deserved it. She stood in silence for several moments until she could no longer bear the cramping in her abdomen. Then she turned down the second bed and entered it gingerly.

"Who are you?" he asked, when she was quiet.

"It's Jennifer, Mordicai," she whispered. "It truly is."

It seemed a long time before he spoke.

"How long have you been back?"

"Not long," she answered. "I'm sorry, Mordicai. I hoped you wouldn't know."

"Will you tell me the truth if I ask where you've been?"

"I was asking for help. I couldn't let Lictor know I was gone. Not for sure. And I couldn't leave my body here alone." And that's the truth, Mordicai, she thought. I can't tell you all the truth because it would hurt you and you're going to be hurt enough. And because what else I did would hurt you too.

"What's going to happen with Lictor?"

"They don't know."

"What's not to know? Are they going to stop him or not?"

"They'll stop him. Somehow. At least they'll come to the station. It's difficult for them, Mordicai. This doesn't happen often but it has happened before. Spirits like Lictor are still partially people and sometimes they're just as capable of . . ." She let her voice trail off. Mordicai knew this. He knew it as well as she did. And now that she was back, she knew other things. She knew what Lictor asked of Mordicai and she knew that he rejected Lictor. That he defied Lictor. A terribly brave act for a man like Mordicai and knowing that made her feel all the more deceitful.

"Just one more question, Jennifer."

"Yes?"

"Who was I fucking?"

He asked it brutally and did not wait for her answer. Bloomer rolled over with his back to her and pulled his pillow over his head. He knew damned well who it was. "Be assured that I'm not he" is what she almost said before. "Mordicai, dear, I'm afraid you're getting heavy." Old Lady Edith Pierce had just been laid, such as it was, for the first time in forty years. And Jennifer. She might not have been here but she wasn't there all that time either. She was projecting from here, with a little help from Lady Edith right up until I caught on and asked her to say my name. Who's the lucky guy who had the real Jennifer while I only had the body? As if I don't know. See how you like him tomorrow, Jennifer, if Barbara catches up to him with that pig sticker she's carrying around. It won't be my fault if . . . if she . . . Oh, shit.

"Jennifer?"

"Yes, Mordicai?"

"Is Halloran staying in the camper or is he going home? Because if he goes home, Barbara means to cut his nuts off."

"He's spending the night in the camper," she answered.

"Goodnight, Jennifer."

"Mordicai?"

"Yes?" he asked irritably.

"Thank you, Mordicai."

"Go to sleep," he said.

The rapping sound startled Peter out of a deep and languorous sleep that was charging his strength and spirit even more profoundly than the healing sleep he'd had the night before, the century before. He woke up loving Jennifer, filled by her to all the corners of his being. Accepting it now. He didn't want to wake up fully. He didn't want to think any thought that was not of her or see any face that was not hers or hear any name.

"Dad?"

"What?" He lifted his head.

"It's Jeff and Sgt. Turkus."

"Wha . . . Wait a minute." He struggled into his pants and threw his jacket over his bare chest before groping his way to the door. He opened it upon Jeffrey who shrugged self-consciously toward Turkus.

"I wasn't going to bother you," he said, "but Sgt. Turkus said we had to."

Halloran tilted his watch so he could read the dial in the light of the station lamps. "It's two in the morning. What are you doing awake?"

"Pete, I came to talk to you," said Turkus. "I saw Jeff sitting under that tree watching the camper."

"What for?" he asked his son.

"In case you needed me."

"You haven't seen anything, have you?" Like Jennifer, for instance.

"Like what?"

"Nothing, I guess. Listen," he said, straightening, "you can't stay here, Jeff. You're not in a position to help and I want you home where you belong."

"How about if I stay with you in the Winnebago?"

"Home!" Halloran answered sharply. Oh hell, he thought. He'd be better off here than home considering the state Barbara was likely to be in. Still, what if Jennifer really did come? She probably wouldn't, not before half past five anyway. But when she came he'd like to have some time alone with her, and some time to think alone about her until she came. "Look. After tomorrow, we'll take off together for a couple of days. Right now, you can help the most by being where I won't worry about you."

"A couple of days where?"

"Home, I said."

Jeff jammed his hands into his pockets and turned away. "Jeffrey!" his father called after him, "what about chartering a boat for a couple of days out at Montauk? We'll see if we can catch a shark."

Jeff punched his arm happily. "You got it," he grinned, and took off at a lope toward the overpass.

"What's happening with you?" Turkus asked Peter.

"I don't think you want to know. Come on in, Mike. I'll heat up some coffee."

"No, I better not stay," he said, looking around him. "I came to tell you we have Weinberg. Zalman's got him."

"Ira? Can he handle him?"

"I think so. He has him cuffed in a garage up the street. The owners left word with the department that they'd be out of town. He's like a kid with a new toy. That leaves your wife who's been home with the house dark since midnight, and Ezra Cohen who's home with his basement lights on. I'll try to keep an eye on both houses until morning. Who else is a problem?"

"That's it as far as I know." There was no point in mentioning McShane. Even Sarah might not know he's dead yet.

"Then I'm here to collect. I believe you have two bodies for me."

"Do you have a flashlight?" Halloran asked.

"Does a bear shit in the woods?" Turkus produced a three-battery spotlight from a sleeve on his belt and handed it to Peter, who stepped from the doorway and braced it against the front end of the camper.

"Watch where the beam hits. I'm not going to leave it on very long." The narrow beam quickly picked out the single clump of sumac that hung over the tracks from the rock wall fifteen feet above the bed.

"That bush?" Turkus asked.

"So I'm told. The fat man is buried at its base along with his suitcase. The second body, Alex, may or may not be there yet. What's keeping you from arresting Cohen now and holding him at home until morning?"

"Because I don't know how I'd explain doing that and I need a clean bust. I'll have enough trouble figuring out a way to stumble across the body. Actually, I have an idea if you'll go for it."

"Try me."

"Jeff could be walking along that path up there tomorrow and see a rabbit going into a hole. All he has to do is walk up to me and say he smelled something dead. Then I'd find Charles, suddenly make a connection with Cohen and the missing persons case, and make a very dramatic pinch. I'd never ask you this except your boy's already into the Cohen homicide and he knows how to keep his mouth shut."

"Sorry, Mike," Halloran answered. "You're right about him, but he's still a kid and I'd like him to stay a kid a while longer. He stays out of it."

"Then I'll invent a kid," said Turkus. "If you want the truth, I'm glad you said that. Are you going to be alright otherwise?"

"I'll try to be."

"Tell you what. I'm going to watch Cohen's house until around four in the morning. Then I'll suit up and relieve the man on night duty. I've done it before when I couldn't sleep. Until that shift goes off, I'll handle any calls that come up around here and I'll try to steer any other cops away."

"That'll help," Halloran nodded. "I was going to ask you not to be within five blocks of the station between sun-up and seven. Especially, don't go near Drinkwater Place."

"The overpass?"

"Yeah."

"You're sure you can handle whatever happens?"

"I can handle hit-and-run vandalism. That's my contribution. After that, I have another life to start."

Jeff Halloran was across the Riverside Avenue overpass and had begun climbing the hill when he saw the beam come to rest on a spot up the track toward Drinkwater. He had no idea what it meant. But it had to mean something to his father. It was also not a bad place to sit and watch. For just a while. Dad said go home, but he didn't say right now I don't think. He also said he wanted him where he belonged. Where he belonged was near his father. For just a little while.

Jeffrey leaned into a trot. He crossed the shadows of the eastbound parking lot toward the dirt trail worn by commuters as a shortcut running parallel to the tracks.

* * *

If the light had shone a few seconds later, Ezra Cohen would have seen it. Or if more leaves had fallen or if the underbrush were not as thick or if he had been able to move faster under the weight of the double refuse bag that contained the lower half of Alex Makepeace.

He eased it to the ground near the hole he'd begun to dig and groped in the darkness for his trenching tool. With this, he raked away more rotting grass clippings and discarded branch cuttings dumped over the years by the homeowners nearby. The pointed blade tugged against something soft and yielding. He probed it with his fingertips. Terrycloth. Sorry, Charles. Didn't mean to wake you. I brought you a present. Of course you'll have to assemble it yourself but you have all the time in the world, don't you.

Ezra patted Charles and rose to make his way back to his basement and to the other plastic bag that waited there.

Jeff found the sumac bush. He turned his head back toward the station. The view was perfect. He could see Sgt. Turkus walking in his direction. Coming here? No, it was only to his car.

Sharks! Man, wouldn't that be cool. He wondered how much it would cost to stuff one. A lot, probably. That's assuming he caught one but he bet he would. They'd have two days. And it doesn't have to be a big one. Just so it could go on his wall. If his dad would pay to have it stuffed he wouldn't have to buy him anything else for Christmas this year. Except new skis, maybe. Olin Mark III's. Blue ones.

He heard the branches rustling. Damn! It is the cop after all. That's what the flashlight was all about. My dad showing the sergeant where he goes to stake out the station. Oh well! Maybe he'll let me sit here with him for a little while. He can see all I'm doing is watching. Jeff turned his eyes back toward the Winnebago.

When he turned again it was to say "It's only me, Sgt. Turkus." But it was too late. He saw only the shiny black plastic mass as it crashed down against his face and chest. It felt like being tackled, he thought dimly. But at least it doesn't hurt. Except this guy's punching me in the head in the pile-up where the ref can't see. Next play, you bastard. Next play you get yours.

*   *   *

Halloran touched his arm where Jeff had punched him. When he touched the spot earlier, he could see Jeff crossing the Riverside Avenue bridge and then starting to jog. Now he felt nothing. Jeff must be out of range like the night watchman had been out of range. He smiled, then squeezed the spot as he might squeeze Jeff when he said good night. Halloran went back to bed.

14

Hell

Even Mike Turkus could feel that this morning was different. It was a lot of little things. There was an iciness that went beyond the lonely cold of predawn hours. It came in little flickering breezes that could not have been there because the windows of his radio car were rolled up tight. And there was Barbara's house, which had a ghostly look through the condensation of his side window. He wiped the glass clean and scanned the darkened house one more time. There were no lights at all and yet he sensed movement inside. He imagined Barbara in the darkness, staring at the closed front door.

The red glow of his digital watch showed that it was not quite five o'clock. A shadow passed his car and it startled him. It was only a commuter, on foot and carrying a briefcase. Too early, thought Turkus. There won't be any train at all for forty-five minutes and even that will be a local. The man wore no topcoat but gave no sign of feeling the bite of the early morning air. And his hair was mussed, as if he'd forgotten to comb it. As if he'd forgotten to shower. Turkus shook the thought away as having no probable significance. It was only the policeman's mind and eye picking out the unusual, the out-of-place.

Even so, there were a number of things that didn't feel quite right. More houses seemed to be stirring than there should have been at this hour. And then there were his own feelings. A part of Turkus wanted to go home and shut his bedroom door and press close against his wife until the fear went away. What was he afraid of? It was not a physical fear; Turkus had long since learned to deal with that. Nor was it Halloran's dead friends at the station because, oddly enough, he felt perfectly comfortable about them. In fact, there were moments when he felt they might be the only normal people in Riverside. It was the station. The station and these people frightened him. Guys like Weinberg and some of the others. Sonny Liston used to say he wasn't afraid of anyone in the world except a crazy man because you never knew what he was going to do. Turkus wondered if Liston would have been scared of that character with the messy hair who was now turning onto Summit Road, toward the station.

It still all came down to the station. Turkus had a feeling that he couldn't shake, that he would feel better if he went there. He knew the feeling was there and he knew the feeling was wrong. Perhaps if he thought of something else. Cohen, for example. Time to coast by and see what old Ezra is up to. Except Ezra's house was closer to the station and Turkus felt that if he went that far he might not want to stop. What the hell is happening to me, he wondered?

Turkus put the car in gear and let it roll forward, forcing himself to think about his wife's body laying under an electric blanket that was turned all the way up to nine. Get this over with. He stepped too heavily on the gas pedal and the car whipped, tires squealing, onto Summit Road. His headlights picked up another commuter, then two more farther ahead. Cohen's house was on his left and it was dark. Everything was dark, but not the station. The station was lit and warm and it looked good and even felt good. Warm and inviting. He told himself aloud that his bed was warmer. In his mind he removed the yellow nightgown that Lisa Turkus would be wearing and he made her body hard and full like it was in the beginning when he would have crawled a mile to lie with it. Stay away, Turkus. Stay away from the goddamned station.

He threw the patrol car into a violent left turn and saw too late the woman who appeared in his headlights. His brakes screamed and locked as the car skidded past her but his spinning rear end swiped at her like a fish's tail and sent her splayed backward into a privet hedge. Oh, Jesus! Turkus clawed the lever into park and scrambled out of the car where it had come to rest. He should call in first even before he . . . but the woman was silently pushing to her feet. One shoe was gone and her leg looked twisted. Her purse hung open, half its contents scattered in the road, and her eyeglasses hung at an angle across her face. And she was walking. Turkus was almost in her path but she never looked at him. Her eyes were shiny and dead like a run-over dog and she was limping hideously but she was going to the station. He watched her go.

Standing in the road, a calm came over Turkus. What had happened to him was incomprehensible but perhaps he needed to have it happen. Some event that would wash away the conflict between his actions and his training. Some personal demonstration that the duty to which he had sworn had no application here. Some shock that might break the station's hold on him before it was beyond breaking. He had hurt the woman and he was letting her go and it was right to let her go. He was leaving the scene of an accident and it was right to leave the scene. It was right to let Zalman and Halloran handle it. Halloran wanted five blocks. He could have ten. Twenty, if that's how many it would take to feel warm again and not feel the pull of that station. No, I don't mean that, he thought. I'll stick around. I'll stay as close as I can, Peter. But not as close as you'll be. And God help you.

The luckier housewives were those whose habit it was to sleep as their husbands rose to shower and dress. Luckiest of all were the wives of men who drove to work or who had no job at all. Among the rest, there were wives who saw and questioned the strangeness of the husband's behavior but who dropped the matter when they were ignored or brushed aside. Even these were fortunate, suffering only sadness and hurt and confusion. The greatest peril fell to those wives who forced confrontations and demanded explanations where none could be given. Their motives mattered not at all. A loving wife who expressed her love was no less likely to be thrown aside than the bad-tempered harridan who wagged a finger in his face and said, I'm talking to you, Buster, and I want an answer. Still others would not be touched at all. When one day all the pieces would be put together and all the speculation had been exhausted, still no pattern would emerge that would show why one woman would be left with a hug and a squeeze by a husband who would kill within the hour, while her neighbor had her head held inside an unflushed toilet until she drowned. Kitty Scofield, a notorious harpy, had died that way. Some blocks away, Midge Fuller, a gentle woman who lived for her babies and her greenhouse would be discovered at the foot of her stairs with her neck broken. Neither husband could tell what happened. Neither remembered. No husband did. They only knew that they awoke that morning with the certain knowledge that they would feel better at the station. Few bothered to shower or to take breakfast. Not even coffee. There was coffee at the station. Everything was at the station.

Bloomer knew what would be happening. He lay there wide awake and he could almost feel it. There was a time when he even knew why it was happening. He'd written about Lake Forest, about Amersham, although he couldn't tell the truth about it. Maybe now he could. Except it was getting hard to remember. Didn't he just explain it to Ira Zalman? Then why was it all getting fuzzy? There was a lot of stuff he told Zalman about the acquisitive ethic but that might not have been the biggest part. It was dreaming. It was the loss of the capacity to dream that made those people vulnerable. It's the spirit that dreams. It's the spirit that enriches and enlarges itself through the pursuit of those dreams. You cut the heart out when you stop dreaming. If you can't dream you can't love either, can you? The spirit becomes too crippled to love. No, that's not exactly right. It's not just dreaming that keeps love alive and lets it grow. It's the sharing of dreams. Maybe that's what love is. Maybe it's even what happiness is.

"How the hell would I know?" he mumbled aloud in his misery. The telephone rang with the night clerk's wake-up call.

Jennifer had been awake. She swung her legs to the floor and acknowledged the call. "Are you alright, Mordicai?" she asked, stifling a yawn. She made no attempt to cover her nakedness.

"The station's pulling at me," he said.

She didn't answer.

"You knew that, didn't you?" he half sighed. "You knew it was after me."

She considered lying to him again. She also considered the truth, the partial truth, that the station would be pulling at almost everyone who was close. But Mordicai wasn't close.

"It'll be over soon." She reached across and touched his arm. It was the best she could offer.

"Can I ask you something?"

"Yes."

"This touching thing of yours," he said. "If you can make Zalman want to help us just by touching him, and if you can make

246

Peter Halloran love you by touching him, which I know damned
well you did, why can't your touch make me stop loving you?"

Jennifer felt an impulse to cross to the edge of his bed, the
better to comfort him, but she held back knowing that bringing
her body so close might not be the kindness she intended. Instead,
she answered, "Mordicai, I didn't do either of those things. Not
to Ira and not to Peter. I'm not able to do what you think I can."

"Excuse me, Jennifer, but bullshit."

"And," she continued, "if I could stop you from loving me,
I wouldn't. You ought to love, Mordicai. No matter what else,
you ought to love."

"What's Peter going to do," he asked, ignoring this last, "when
and if he figures out that you hexed him?"

"I'll tell him I didn't. Perhaps he'll listen."

"Jennifer, this is hardly the normal bewitching effect of romantic infatuations. You did go to him last night, didn't you?"

"Only in his dreams." Then, as if she'd shared Mordicai's
waking thoughts, "Dreams matter more to Peter."

"I guess I understand that," he said, "but I still don't believe
you about the touching."

"We've had talks like this before, Mordicai. And I've said
before that you of all people should know better. There's hardly
anything I can do that other people couldn't do if they didn't block
themselves. I'm luckier than most, if lucky is the word, because
I've had the blocks removed. That touch you've seen doesn't make
anyone feel a way that they wouldn't have felt before. One thing
that the touch does is take away fear and pain by sharing it so that
there's not too much for one person to bear. The other thing it
does is it helps the other person to know what's in my heart. And
sometimes, not always, when they feel right about what's there,
they want to share that, too."

"And you think Peter will buy that?"

"He'll understand it."

"I don't much like the man, Jennifer, but he's no dummy."

"Oh, for God's sake, Mordicai." Her voice was still gentle but
firmer. "Don't you recognize what I just described to you?"

"Your touching talent, you mean?"

"I was describing love. Anyone's love."

She crossed to the bathroom and turned on the shower.

Bloomer was dressed when she emerged. He stood behind her
at the bathroom door, watching her image in the wall mirror as

she brushed out her hair. Jennifer had slipped into her jeans and her bra. Her blouse and turtleneck hung from the doorknob.

"I want the station this time," he said.

"No, Mordicai. It's too dangerous."

"I have to be there. I'm Barbara Halloran's bait."

"She'll look for you whether you're there or not. Stay away, Mordicai. You don't know how much longer you'll be in control."

"Jennifer, I have to do this. I want the platform and I want you away from it."

Jennifer lowered her brush and turned to face him directly. She saw a faraway sadness in his eyes, and also a strength she had not seen before.

"Was I to die there, Mordicai?"

"Probably."

"Did Lictor tell you that?"

"No. It's still not much more than a hunch. I never even let myself think about it until last night. I remembered Angela Marcos."

The coincidence startled Jennifer. Peter and Ira had just been asking why Angela was attacked and she was . . . "I gather you know why Angela died?"

"She wasn't set up, if that's what you're wondering. My belief is that it was an accident. Think back about how you were dressed that day. Jennifer, the tailored young businesswoman, was left pretty much alone and Angela the hippie dancer who looked like one was attacked and killed. Here, like Lake Forest, commuters who are different are intimidated and chased away. Commuters who look like the rest are left alone unless they open their mouths. What I think is that Lictor learned something in Lake Forest. What I also think is that your Levi's were going to get you killed today."

"That's hard to believe, Mordicai," she said, for many reasons wanting not to believe it. "Lictor's deceitful and ambitious. Learning that was enough of a shock. But it's hard to believe that he'd actually do . . ."

"Do what?" Bloomer interrupted. "He didn't have to do a damned thing. All he had to do was forget to suggest a suitable wardrobe. And all I had to do was not think about it."

"But you did think about it."

"For what it's worth."

"It's worth a lot to me," she said.

"Watch out for Lictor, Jennifer. You blew the whistle on him last night and you don't even know if it took. Don't expect him to roll over and play dead. He has too much to lose."

"All of us do. But thank you, Mordicai."

He handed Jennifer her shirt and blouse and turned to pull her fleece-lined jacket from its hanger. "Come on," he said. "I'll take you to your dream sharer."

They went in Zalman's car. It started reluctantly, stalling out for the second time as it paused at the curb cut on the Post Road while waiting for some trucks to pass. Bloomer found himself envying the drivers who were probably chatting away on their CB radios and looking forward to nothing more eventful than the morning's first delivery. Bloomer envied almost everyone at that moment and Peter didn't even head the list. True enough that Peter has Jennifer. That's if Peter can accept her and if Peter can hold her, which he doubted. But first Peter had to survive the morning with his body intact, to say nothing of his mind. How can he? What's so special about Peter Halloran? For all the tricks he's able to do lately, he's still a suburban commuter who lives in a box in this insular little town and takes the train to a job that has only the barest significance to any other life. In fairness, he's a bit different from the general run of that pack but so are fingerprints different. Different but the same.

"You're thinking about Peter?" Jennifer asked.

"I suppose." Bloomer let a milk truck pass and then turned behind it toward Riverside Avenue.

"He is special," she said. "He's special to me."

"You mean he's special like you," Bloomer countered. "That's why side-show freaks and the mildly retarded are attracted to each other. I'm sorry, Jennifer. I just think you should be shooting higher."

She sighed, not sure whether there would be any point in answering.

"He's a good man," she said simply. Bloomer waited for more but nothing came.

"That's it?" he asked.

"What would you like, Mordicai?" she asked, irritated. "A formal defense? A list of reasons for loving a man when I didn't know he existed two days ago? He's a good man today and I love him today. I don't have to ask myself why that's so or why he's special. But Peter is a man, now that you ask, who's strong enough to do what he ought to do and to be what he ought to be. Look at the other people here. They live in a tiny little world that has too little substance and they do work that's no more personally enriching than what Peter did. And what's more, they know it. They fight against knowing it because it's a safe world and they're afraid to risk it. And the price they pay is that they'll reach the end of their lives feeling that most of their years have been wasted. And it will be a waste because many of them are going to find out that they have to start all over. Peter won't be like that. He'll never have a big house in the suburbs or a steady job again but he won't feel like that."

"And what about you? What if his new life doesn't include you?"

"It will. Sooner or later."

"But what if it doesn't?"

"Then, Mordicai Bloomer, I'll at least know that I've loved somebody and been loved back at the same time. Most people are lucky if that happens to them once in their lives. It's happened to me twice. That's a great and wonderful thing, Mordicai. If I could wish anything for you, I'd wish that you could know that."

Bloomer heard the words but his attention was elsewhere. He pointed a finger at the road ahead where his headlights picked up two figures who were trudging toward the station.

"That's six I've counted. Isn't it awfully early?"

"What time is the first train?"

"Five-forty. That's in twelve minutes. They won't get on it. It's a local. Anyway, it's the station they want, not the train."

"We have to be sure," she said.

"I'll handle it."

"How, Mordicai?"

"By being what I ought to be and doing what I ought to do."

Bloomer turned the Buick into the station road, passing two more men and a woman, and brought it to a stop some yards away from the Winnebago. The inside lights were on and Jennifer could see at least two shadows moving behind the curtains. Peter and who else? It must be Ira Zalman.

She took Mordicai's hand and squeezed it. Then, hesitating with her own hand on the door latch, she reached both arms around his neck and held him, her lips against his cheek. Bloomer felt a wetness between his face and hers but could not tell whose tear it was.

"I talk too much," he said.

"I know," she whispered.

"But there are two more things. Ten seconds?"

"Yes, Mordicai?"

"He is a good man and I know it. I knew that when I saw how he accepted what happened to him. He's impressed by what he can do but he's not impressed with himself. He'll keep his balance. Another good man is Alex. I guess I didn't know that until I learned what it was like to deal with people like Martha and Barbara. Alex saved my tail. Whatever else he was, I respect him now. I respect both of them."

"Good luck, Mordicai." She kissed his mouth and ran to the camper.

Weinberg had talked himself to sleep by three in the morning. His account of the probable success of Super Swissberries led, in sequential steps, to his ultimate ascendancy to the presidency of his company. He seemed much less clear on what would happen when he reached that office and would appear to go blank whenever Zalman questioned him about his human motives. Zalman had no real idea where the notes he was taking were leading him. Certainly, he was witnessing the extraordinary single-mindedness that Bloomer had described, but how much of it was the effect of the station and how much of it was in Weinberg's make-up to start with? Was Weinberg feeding on the station or was the station feeding on Weinberg? Probably both, he concluded. Bloomer was probably right about that, too.

What would Weinberg be like when the mist was lifted? Would the man still be there underneath? What sort of man? And if there were more Paul Weinbergs either clustered or scattered at random in other places, what would happen if their private mists lifted spontaneously? Weinberg might at least have the comfort of knowing that he was the victim of a collective phenomenon and that his actions were doubtlessly beyond his control. The others, however, would conclude that they were individually going nuts and conceal that suspicion from all save possibly the local shrink who was sure to add to the confusion. What radical personality changes would occur when the human spirit is abruptly freed from the mist? Obviously, the change would be for the better but that's not to say the man's friends of the time would agree. Look at old Joe, they'd say. Tossed all that away one night and took up organic gardening in Vermont. Joe's wife is as batty as he is. Went right along. Tossed her Cuisinart in the garbage and never looked back. Zalman found himself wondering how many middle-aged drop-outs were actually Paul Weinbergs who had somehow been jerked free of another mist before it became too late. Steady, Ira. One mist at a time.

Zalman laid his note pad on the dashboard, yawned, and brought his coat collar up around his neck. Weinberg's rhythmic breathing lulled him to sleep in minutes.

The first metallic crashing sounds were not enough to wake him. They were only enough to call up dreams and to mingle with them. He was in an unfamiliar shack and it was being torn apart. Things, lethal things, were falling all around him and against the glass box in which he sat. A whole wall to his left seemed to fall away with a screeching bang and yet the wall remained standing. He threw up his arms in front of his face, and doing so, raked one hand across the rearview mirror hard enough to break it from its anchor. The pain shocked him into a bewildered consciousness that was not yet sufficient to let him distinguish between nightmare and waking. There was next a great thumping roar and a part of the roof slid away. A tornado? In Connecticut? There wasn't any wind. No, he's in a garage. Zalman's bleeding hand groped for the unfamiliar headlight switch and yanked on it. In the flood of the twin beams, he saw a rusted snow shovel leap from its peg and clatter to the concrete floor of the garage. Next, an oil can toppled from a shelf and hit with a thick wet sound like a sodden towel. The roof shook and Zalman saw that it was lower than before. The door. It was the garage door and Zalman remembered Paul Weinberg. Fully awake now, he clambered through the car door and fell amid a jumble of garden tools. He pushed to his feet and peered into the darkness outside. Weinberg's dim form was pacing toward the station, his briefcase held behind him in hands still manacled. Zalman ran after him.

"No, Paul. Wait," he called as softly as he could manage and still be heard. Weinberg ignored him. Zalman cursed himself for not imagining that a handcuffed man could twist to open a door. Two doors. Now he had to stop a man who was dangerous enough to . . . Oddly, Zalman felt more excited than afraid. Odder still, he did not feel alone. Of course, he thought. All that clamor was a warning. From the station spirits? Halloran's dead neighbors? That would have to mean that the mist has grown in the night if . . . He had to fight an urge that was within his nature to stop and reflect upon the experience. No time for that. He knew that reasoning with Paul was out of the question and that physical force was . . . impossible. A John Wayne crunch to Weinberg's jaw would accomplish a splintered metacarpal bone in his hand and little else. A well-aimed rock or club would leave him, at best, with a comatose Weinberg to drag. He caught up to Weinberg and slowed, matching his stride. A new simulus, Bloomer said. How about telling him the trains aren't running? No good. They could both see the other commuters gathering on the platform. Quite a few for so early.

"Sorry to hear about your new cereal, Paul," he said.

"What about it?" Weinberg turned his head to Zalman but didn't slow his pace.

"It's being recalled by the government. Too bad, because there's nothing wrong with it."

Weinberg stopped. "There's nothing wrong with it," he repeated.

"Nothing. And such a lovely P & L too. It's a shame that a man like Peter Halloran should have such authority." Zalman hoped he wasn't being too subtle for Weinberg but he was feeling his way into Weinberg's mind.

"Halloran?" There was a wildness in Weinberg's eyes that frightened Zalman more than the deadness to which he'd become accustomed.

"It's his new job with the Food and Drug Administration. He wants to stop your cereal. He wants to stop you." Zalman extended his arm and pointed to the lighted camper. "He's in there right now," he said, "probably putting rat hairs in your Super Swissberries. You should stop him." Let Halloran be John Wayne, he decided. He has more of the equipment.

Weinberg set his jaw and homed in on the Winnebago. Zalman jogged alongside of him and agreeably opened the door.

"Oh!" Peter greeted them. "Hello, Paul. Good morning, Doctor. Nice of you to drop in." Whatever Zalman expected, it was not a casual greeting from a relaxed and contented Peter Halloran. He also thought he saw a flicker of disappointment on Peter's face.

"There weren't any rat hairs." Weinberg's tone was low and fierce.

"I never really thought so," Peter smiled. "What do you suppose they were?" Peter didn't even bother looking at Zalman who was furiously making hand and body signals.

"Possibly bran fibers." Weinberg softened.

Then Peter called a meeting while the bemused Ira Zalman shook his head. He should have guessed. After fifteen years of

Madison Avenue diplomacy, Peter would certainly have learned to be fast on his feet. Five minutes later, Paul Weinberg was trussed to a toilet seat, ignoring the knotted ropes as he had ignored his handcuffs, and reciting the results of the Super Swissberries in vitro toxicity tests to no one in particular. Weinberg was exactly where he wanted to be and doing what he wanted to be doing.

Weinberg droned on and Peter stopped listening. Zalman saw that a sudden nervousness had overcome Halloran. More of a fidgeting. Peter checked the button on his jacket, slipped it loose, and then fastened it again. He ran a hand over his freshly shaven cheek and touched the hair at his temple. Now what, Zalman wondered? The man is practically blushing.

"Jennifer's here," said Peter. He touched his button again and turned toward the door and waited. Seconds later she entered, her eyes bright and locked onto Peter's. It seemed to Zalman that the two sets of eyes had held each other even before Jennifer came through the door.

"Hello, Peter," she smiled.

"Good morning, Jennifer." Her hand came forward and he took it.

"Ahem!" said Zalman.

Grinning broadly, she leaned her face into the hollow of Peter's shoulder. "Good morning, Doctor," her muffled happy voice returned his greeting. Peter shyly put his hands around her waist and ran them up her back, his fingers brushing lightly over the small flat mole that he knew would be there.

"Paul Weinberg says hello, too," said Ira. "Now, if you two don't mind too terribly much, I'm going to excuse myself and start observing."

Zalman stopped with his hand on the door knob and listened to the bored voice that came through the static of the station's public address system. ". . . train will be a local to Portchester only. It does not go to Grand Central. The six-forty train is the first train to Grand Central. This train only goes to Portchester and you don't want to go to Portchester. . . ." There was, he thought, a scuffling sound that came over the speaker and then the message was repeated, a bit more breathlessly the second time. Jennifer and Peter did not appear to be listening. Only Weinberg, who cocked his head, nodded, and then resumed his presentation.

"Didn't that sound like Mordicai?" Zalman asked.

"It's Bloomer," Peter confirmed. "He's conning the commuters into passing up the next train."

"Is that going to work?"

"It'll work," Jennifer answered, drawing back from Peter's embrace. "Except for a few confused passengers who aren't affected, the rest will stay. They're happy to stay."

Peter noticed that although she was making an effort to keep her tone light, there was concern on her face. She glanced through the camper wall toward the station.

"Are you worried about Bloomer?" Peter asked. "It sounded like he handled the station manager or whoever that was without much trouble."

"I'm afraid," she answered, "that Mordicai's not going to want to leave the station either before long."

Zalman reacted as if he'd been struck. If anyone, any man, was immune, he'd have thought it would be Mordicai Bloomer. If he wasn't safe, how could any of them be safe? How could Ira Zalman be safe? The question, once formed in his mind, shamed him. But he was not a coward, he argued. A coward and a prudent man are not the same.

Peter heard him. But there was no time for comforting.

"Let's get to work," he said calmly. "Do you have a key to Weinberg's handcuffs? Someone will have to come back here later."

Zalman produced a key with a leather tab and laid it on the galley counter. The knuckles of his hand shone white.

"Is there a woman named Martha," Peter asked, "locked in the trunk of a car?"

"Leticia's housekeeper," Jennifer answered. "Mordicai left her there."

"Good for him. What about those keys?"

"Mordicai must have them."

"Then they'll keep." He reached for the keys to Zalman's car which Jennifer had held in her hand since she entered the camper. "Doctor, you wanted a safe spot where you can watch whatever happens. You've done more than enough. I'm going to drop you off at the far side of the overpass and I suggest you stay there. Jennifer, how far would you guess this has spread?"

"At least ten blocks in either direction. It's probing perhaps a mile beyond that."

"Okay. Weinberg will be fine here. There's a friend of mine watching Barbara and Cohen so no one has to hurt them. McShane's already in there with Alex. Who else do we have to worry about?"

"That's all of them as far as we know."

"Then let's take a look around and then get down to the Drink-water overpass. I think I can check in with Alex or Kornhauser while we're out if it's that wide."

The early train hissed into the station as they stepped to the parking lot surface. Peter checked his watch. Six o'clock. The train was twenty minutes late. Bloomer's voice cut again through the darkness. A bit duller this time, Peter thought. More hesitant. The train doors squealed open, streaming broad paths of light at intervals along the platform. On any other morning, the light would seem warm and inviting. Now the doors seemed more like jaws. There was something obscene about them.

"The five-forty to hell," Zalman muttered.

Peter could see a single conductor at the end of the second car. He spoke animatedly to a group of men and they were backing away from him. A woman pushed through and then a young man of college age. They entered the doors, then turned and shrugged to each other before choosing seats in the nearly empty train. The confused conductor threw up his hands and waved the engineer forward as he stepped into the car.

Peter watched it go until the last car curved out of sight and the only sounds were a distant rumbling echo and the static of Bloomer's open microphone. On the platform, the commuters stood almost motionless, their faces tilted back and their arms held out slightly from their sides as if they were standing still in a warm shower. Like they were when Peter had first seen them on Saturday night; the way Jack Gormley and Paul Weinberg and those others had looked. Before the station started to kill. Zalman was wrong about that train. That was a train to salvation. This was hell.

Someone was calling him. Who . . . was someone crying? A woman. *—Peter? —Yes, I hear you.* Is that Peggy? Halloran heard more voices. A jumble of them. One was shouting. Arguing. He couldn't hear. *—It's alright, Peter. Problem's solved. —Who's that? Marty? —It's Marty, Pete. Go ahead and finish up. —Yeah, we are. Who was that yelling? —Peggy got a bit upset. She's fine now. —No, someone was yelling. —That was Alex and Mr. Hicks. Check in with Alex or me when you're ready. No one else. There won't be time. —Alright, Marty. You people stay in close and together. —What about Weinberg? Are you going to kill him? —Am I what? —I know the question rocks you, Pete. But I'm telling you it's a different horse race than any of us figured. Weinberg's going to wish you did it . . .*

256

*—Then Paul Weinberg can kill Paul Weinberg. Where the hell
would it stop? Am I supposed to kill Barbara and Cohen and that
maid too?   —Not Cohen. Whatever you do, don't help Cohen.
He was a lifelong shit anyway. So long, Pete. We owe you. We
owe you big.   —Take care, Marty.*

"Let's get the hell out of here," he said, and climbed behind
the wheel of Zalman's Buick.

On the overpass, Zalman shook Peter's hand without speaking
and clasped Jennifer's before stepping out onto the vantage point
he chose. Two commuters passed. One with bewilderment and
concern on his face, talking to the other who ignored him. The
second man's jaw was slack and his eyes seemed dull even in the
half light that was working its way down from the tops of the
trees. Halloran pointed the car north, away from the glowing
eastern sky, and began his wide circle.

"There's not much point to this," said Jennifer after the first
few streets were passed. "It's just too big."

"I know," he answered. "At least it gives us a few minutes to
ourselves."

"We've never been alone."

"Sure we . . ." He stopped himself.

"Beg pardon?" Jennifer lightly touched his hand as if to get his
attention.

"Nothing. Just a dream I had last night."

"I had one too."

"Mine was better."

"I don't think so," she smiled coyly. "In mine, the most beautiful man I ever knew made love to me."

"What do you know!"

"Well?"

"Well, what?"

"What about your dream?"

"I caught this fish you wouldn't believe. It was a blue and it
must have reached from . . . ouch!" Jennifer twisted the fingers
which Peter held out to show its length.

"What did you really dream?"

He placed the hand less shyly than before along her thigh. "I
think you know what I dreamed, Jennifer. I'm not sure I want to
know how, but I think you know. Just like I know you have a
scar right there." He traced a line over the inside of her knee.

"Football injury. Lots of girls have them."

"Seriously," he relaxed. "Was it skiing?"

"Sailing. The boom swung in a blow on Lake Michigan and I was snagged in the mainsheet."

What do you know, he said to himself this time! A sailor lady. Somehow he'd known it all along.

"This was before?" he asked. "Before you knew when things like that would happen?"

Her face darkened. "Please don't say that, Peter. I'm not a curiosity. I'm a person just like you."

Just like me, he repeated to himself. "What about causing things to happen? Can you do that?"

"No." Her expression soured. "Dammit, Peter."

"What's wrong with that? A man gets interested in a woman and he asks questions. Does she play tennis, sew, like pizza, fly through the air . . ."

"You're not funny."

"You know I'm in love with you, don't you, Jennifer?"

"I hope you are."

"There's a part of me that can't quite believe you wanted to hear that. And another part that knew you did. I don't have them sorted out yet."

"Why don't you just not try?"

"I don't know why."

"I love you, Peter. If you need to hear reasons for it, I'll try to give them to you. But if none of the reasons make sense to you and you tear them all into pieces, when that's done I'll still be in love with you."

"Bottom line?"

"Bottom line."

Turkus parked his patrol car on the far corner where Spruce Street ended on Summit Road. He could see part of the Halloran house from there and Cohen's house down the hill as well. He could not see the station from where he sat and he wanted it that way. If he saw it he was afraid he'd go there. He had to keep his mind off it. Concentrate on Cohen's house. Try to see right through the wall to whatever the nasty old bastard is up to. Enjoy it, Mr. Cohen, whatever you're doing. You're going to be in your permanent new home in about one hour.

A splash of moving color caught his eye and jerked his head around. Barbara Halloran. Holy Christ! It was Barbara Halloran wearing a long satin nightgown and a frilly pink peignoir over it, arms folded in front of her. She has to be freezing, he thought.

His eyes followed her past him on her way down Summit Road. To the station. It had to be to the station. Good. Then she'd be Halloran's problem. One down, one to go. He watched her turn into the parking lot of the eastbound side, standing out like a flashing light among the blue and gray topcoats that converged with her and then branched off. She's going to the wrong side, he realized, but close enough. Closer than he was going to get. But he could at least get closer to Cohen's house. Just another fifty yards.

Barbara stopped at the four-foot cyclone fence that lined the track bed up to the ends of the raised concrete platform. She glared at it as if it were a living thing.

"Mordicai!" she cried, in a voice that was barely a decibel over her normal speaking voice. He could not have heard. She unfolded her arms, revealing the knife that she'd held through the night.

"Mordicai!" she called again while raking the knife blade murderously against the offending wires of the fence in a quiet mindless fury.

Her stroke slowed and ended as she saw him. He was on the platform across the tracks just where he promised he would not be. He said he'd come and he didn't come. He said he should be punished if he didn't come and he will be punished.

Zalman could scarcely believe the scene before him. He looked down upon the New York-bound side of the platform with perhaps a hundred men and women on it and more were coming. But otherwise, there was so little movement. They stood in clusters at those points where the doors of the train would open when it came. Here and there a man would leave the cluster shouting angrily or else would be rebuffed approaching it. Just moments ago, one man broke and ran. He just ran off. Several more were leaving, going to their cars. A few stood in the parking lot and watched uncomprehendingly. Behind the Winnebago, a group of three men and women were gesturing among themselves and pointing at something that was happening on the platform. What is it! It's that woman who fell down but she's . . . Why is no one helping her? Zalman could see from where he was that there was something terribly wrong with her leg. Her purse was open and her eyeglasses hung broken across her face. Help her, Ira. He moved toward the stairs. No, wait! The other woman from the parking lot is coming to help her. The three men are trying to call her back but she's coming anyway. Good girl. She's got her.

"Look out!" a voice shouted. Zalman wasn't sure if it was his.

Another man, thickly built, wearing a tan raincoat, abruptly seized the parking lot Samaritan by her hair and, before Zalman could grasp what was happening, slammed her into the platform railing. Her legs buckled at the impact. The tan raincoat tore at hands that feebly gripped the aluminum railing and then, failing to loose both of them, he bent to lift up one of her legs and with it pitched her shrieking body over the railing. The scream turned to a gagging sound as she hit the top of a twin parking meter, snapping it under her weight. The three men rushed forward. Two ran to the writhing woman as the third leaped onto the platform at the tan raincoat. The raincoat staggered backward under a blow, straight on and overhand by a running fist, that must certainly have flattened the man's nose and knocked loose his incisors. It also blinded him. The tan raincoat half turned and stepped out into the space above the tracks, landing hard with a crunch that made Zalman wince. The man who struck the blow stared down at what he'd done and then at the faces around him. Few looked at him. None spoke. The tan raincoat rose steadily to his feet and stumbled to the platform edge. Its height baffled him. His attacker was at the pay phone now, the receiver in his hand, the other hand fishing for a coin. The tan raincoat turned, his back resting against the platform, his arms hanging freely at his sides, and he stood there. My God, thought Zalman, he's going to wait for the train right where he is. Zalman scanned the length of the station. The other groups were quiet. None seemed to notice what had happened. Very few moved, except for the man at the telephone and he was leaving now. No, he's being pushed. Another man was shoving him. Zalman saw him draw back the damaged fist that he'd been rubbing but he held the punch. John Wayne backed away. Zalman couldn't tell if he managed to complete his call. Was it to the police?

There's Mordicai now. He's moving for sure. Bloomer had a sweater that he'd picked up somewhere. Probably lost and found. And he was fanning at the air around him and moving in queer jerks as he traversed the platform. He looked like alcoholics Zalman had observed trying to shake away the demons and crawling insects of delirium tremens. Zalman understood what Bloomer was doing and it seemed to be working. Hang on, Mordicai. It's twenty minutes after six.

Barbara was over the cyclone fence before he noticed her. The end of the eastbound platform had obscured her from his view. But now there was no missing her: a blaze of pink with several ragged flapping strands thanks to the barbs atop the fence. To Zalman, the thought of Barbara Wentworth Halloran climbing a fence with or without a negligee was no less astonishing than the behavior of the tan-raincoated lunatic standing on the tracks below him.

He saw men pointing at her. Men who'd just arrived. What were they shouting? Sounds like wife. Peter's wife? No, it's knife. Dear God Almighty, she's carrying a butcher knife.

I know you're hiding, Mordicai, but I'm going to find you. I saw you, all twisting and ducking, from the other side. But it's harder now, so close to these people. Harder to see behind them. It's nice here, though. It feels good here.

"Mordicai!" she called.

She moved slowly down the track bed, looking up at each face that she could see from there. Many faces stared back, some blankly, others with interest, some disturbed, but only a few who seemed shocked or even surprised. These last backed away and so discovered each other, forming new small groups that attracted the attention of the larger groups. The smaller groups wilted back farther away toward the steps, a few of their members blustering as they did so, others attempting to reason with familiar faces in the larger groups that were advancing on them.

Barbara stopped before a tall thin man who was reading a book at the platform's edge.

"I'm having a book written about me," she said, looking up at him. "Leticia Browning's writing it." The man ignored her.

"It's about the Greenwich Wentworths. I'm Barbara Wentworth, you know."

He raised his eyes slowly from his open book and looked down at her, his gaze resting on the breasts that showed clearly from above the loose fitting nightgown. He reached out a hand to her.

"How do you do?" she acknowledged, taking it.

With one arm, he lifted her to the platform where she stood erect, her hand still within his grip. He studied her, saying nothing. Another man's hand reached out and examined the breast that hung loosely under the chemise. He touched her curiously, almost absentmindedly, as he might touch an item in a store that caught his eye. She gave no sign that she noticed. Barbara began to push through the crowd.

"Mordicai," she called.

The tall thin man released her hand and reached now for the bare skin of her back and shoulders where the ruined peignoir fell away several inches below her neck. His fingers closed over the fabric, slowing her. A middle-aged woman, severely dressed, approached from the direction in which she was moving. Her eyes too were on Barbara's chest and on the flatness of her stomach. Her face showed no expression as her hands caressed Barbara, running down to her sides and around to her buttocks. The tall man's lips then pressed against her neck, his hands searching for Barbara's bosom underneath the press of the older woman.

"What the hell are you people doing?" shouted a young man from the top of the stairs. His hair was long and full and he wore a thin uneven beard.

"Mordicai!!" roared Zalman. Bloomer stood not ten feet from the milling group, idly scuffing a shoe against the platform, a dreamy smile on his face.

"Are you people crazy?" The young man pushed through the crowd, stripping off his shearling coat as he moved and shoving the tall man backward. He draped the coat across Barbara's now bare shoulders and began pushing back through the mob of commuters that had closed around him. The middle-aged woman seized his hair in one hand and his beard in the other. His head twisted backward and the forearm of the tall man slid against his throat.

"Mordicai!"

Barbara did not react to the choking, thrashing noises behind her. More hands reached for her body and for her gown. She brushed one man aside with the point of the knife that she still held tightly in her hand. It cut through the tendons of his fingers and sliced deeply across his chest. Soundlessly, he doubled over, his shoulder slamming into her hip and knocking her to the concrete. The tall man knelt astride her. Barbara saw Mordicai, loitering almost within reach, but then her view was blocked by the woman who took Barbara's head in both her hands and kissed her hard upon the mouth. Barbara could feel the tall man entering her. She pushed blindly with the knife and felt it bite into flesh but neither the woman nor the tall man broke their rhythm. She probed again and found new flesh and this time the woman faltered. Her face drew back from Barbara's and grunted softly before her eyes rolled back and she fell over. The knife was pinned beneath her body. The thin man surged and withdrew, still holding his book, and another man took his place. Then another came and others waited soundlessly.

"Mordicai," she called. There was only the faintest tremor in her voice as if some grasp of what was happening to her was somehow beginning to penetrate.

It was hurting. Why are they hurting me? I know this one. He asked me to dance with him last Christmas. Mordicai, he's hurting me. Please make them stop. Please, Mordicai. Peter? Peter, please? Is that you, Peter?

She twisted her head under the silently heaving chest of the man from the Christmas dance, straining to see this new man whose face and upper torso seemed to be growing out of the concrete platform. He wasn't like the others. There was blood on him. But there was light in his eyes and he was smiling. Why is he smiling? Why is he smiling at what they're doing to me?

The man in the tan raincoat turned away from her and walked up the tracks, away from the mounting terror in Barbara's voice as she called Mordicai's name and Peter's name. He stopped, only for a moment, to look up at Mordicai. And he smiled again. Horribly.

Bloomer felt a peace such as he could not remember in his lifetime. It was hard to believe, he thought, that this railroad station had troubled him once. Whatever happened here, it could not have been so terrible or else he'd remember it. It wasn't terrible now. It was beautiful. A warm summer afternoon, a quiet train ride with his newspaper, and then in an hour he'd be with Jennifer and the children in the city. Perhaps they'd have time to shop before dinner. They'd make time. First F.A.O. Schwarz for the kids and then across Fifth Avenue to Van Cleef & Arpels for Jennifer, although she never lets him buy her anything. At least I got her out of those jeans. Only as far as corduroy suits and leather skirts but then one has to crawl before one can walk. Odd that there's no one on the platform at this hour. But that's good. No crowds. The train might even be on time. For dinner, how about the Palm Court of the Plaza? Then maybe a buggy ride through Central Park. Jennifer would like that as much as the kids.

There's someone now. And he's running this way. Why, for heaven's sake! It's Ira Zalman. He must have been driving by and saw me standing here. Ira Zalman! My gosh, how long has it been?

Halloran offered a hand to Jennifer as they scaled the rock wall that lined the road bed under the Drinkwater overpass. There was a small clearing there that was shielded from all views save the track's by a tangle of low conifers. Scattered beer cans, some with lipstick, gave evidence that the place was sufficiently free of casual traffic.

"If it's on time, we have five minutes." Halloran pulled at a thick branch revealing four braided lines that led to an I-beam ledge on the outer edge of the overpass bridge. Twin sets of chains and grappling hooks were laid out neatly on the steel lip of the beam. A wall of corrugated metal blanketed their view from the bridge itself.

"We pull the first two lines when the first car passes. They're rigged so the chain has to fall over the power line. At least one hook will grab the pantograph or a piece of the train itself. One's as good as the other. Either way, the power line gets torn down by the momentum of the train and the pantograph will be wrecked at the same time. The second set of hooks is for insurance, but once either set of hooks grabs, we'll have to get out of the way fast. There'll be one hell of a hot wire dancing around."

"A hot wire? That means there'll still be power."

"Sure, but the only juice will be east of this point until they shut it off. There won't be any at all between here and the Mianus Railway Bridge. The bridge is dead. These trains coast across that bridge and pick up third rail power on the other side. Anyway, no power, no mist."

Jennifer was pleased. Peter wasn't strictly right about the mist. It would take several minutes to disperse. But that shouldn't matter as long as Alex keeps everybody close to the station. No need to burden Peter with details. Better to keep him relaxed, though, and at peace. There's a lovely soft blue light around him.

"It's really very clever," she nodded approvingly. "Looks like you ripped off the local yacht club."

"A night withdrawal," he grinned. "I'll bring them back if they're not fused into a lump. What do you think Alex would have done, by the way?"

"Alex is more into the big bang concept than Rube Goldberg devices. He'd have used dynamite again or else he'd have found a way to drive a truck into the train. Speaking of Alex, are you going to check in one more time?"

"Almost forgot," he said, "I'm dialing now."

—*Alex . . . Alex, can you hear me? . . . Marty, how about you? . . . Anyone? . . . Mr. Hicks? . . .*

"I'm not getting a thing. Could we be out of range?"

"No, we couldn't. Try again, Peter."

"Something has Zalman in a panic. He's running along the platform."

"How do you know that?" Jennifer was becoming frightened.

"From when I touched his hand. I can still . . . I'll tell you later. Who's this coming up the tracks?"

He was a stocky man of about fifty. And he wore a tan raincoat whose front was streaked with watery drippings of the blood that was clotting on his face over swollen lips. He stopped and balanced on a tie below Peter, ignoring Jennifer.

"Your son is dead, Peter Halloran." The voice, too large for the man, boomed out. His eyes pointed toward Peter but they did not focus on him. They drifted like those of a man asleep.

Peter's mouth moved but no sound came out. "Wha . . . What son?" was what he finally managed.

"Young Jeffrey Halloran. The boy is dead. Gone from you. The boy is here. He'll soon be with me."

"Lictor!" Jennifer screamed.

"The boy is dead. The wife is now the wife of many. Reckoning is at hand for the foolish professor. But you, Mr. Halloran, may yet escape. If you please me, you may say your farewells to the boy. Please me greatly and he may linger with you awhile."

"Lictor, you bastard!" she cried. "Peter, please. The train is coming." She reached for the first set of lines.

"No!" he shouted, his eyes wild. "Don't touch that. Where is he?" he hissed at the tan raincoat. "Where is my son?"

—Peter, it's Alex. Peter barely heard. Too much noise. Peggy sobbing again. There was the fat man. Charles. He flickered and went away but the glimpse was enough to show the rage in him. And Marty and Hicks and McShane. All shouting and angry. All popping on like fireflies. Now Alex was shouting. *—Get back! Don't come here! Take him back!*

"Alex!!!" Peter screamed. "Marty!!!"

—We'll top off that dude, Mr. Halloran. We top him off good. *—Hicks. Where is my son?* *—No, boy. Get on back.* *—Dad!!!* The train was in sight.

"Oh, Jesus! Jeffrey?"

—It's okay, Dad. I'm okay. Don't listen to him. Alex thinks he's been shit-canned . . .

"No! Jeff, where are you?"

—Peter, it's Marty. We can't send him back. But we'll take care of him. Peter, trust us. You have to trust us. We're way out here just to tell you this. We're out too far . . .

"Jeffrey!!!!"

"Those who dance must pay the piper, Mr. Halloran."

—Dad, tell him to fuck off. Pull the ropes . . .

"No!!!"

Jennifer snatched all four lines from the grass. Her face was a mask of anguish.

"Don't!" Peter shrieked, lunging at her. "I'll kill you if you do that."

Her body spun away from his grasp as her leg swung wide and crashed in an arc against his temple. Through flashes of light he could see the lines straightening. He saw his hands clawing toward her again and he heard his own voice screaming from far away.

She kicked again and there was blackness.

Turkus was at his radio, intercepting the weird complaints his dispatcher passed on, brushing most aside, when he saw the flash that lit up the morning sky. Through the trees, he could see the white hot snake that snapped and hissed and welded what it touched. He could smell flesh cooking. He tore from his car and turned toward the tracks but spun around at the new crashing sound behind him. Cohen's house! What remained of his front windows was still flying through the air. From inside came the sound of more things being smashed, of metal and glass and wood and of Ezra Cohen screaming. The door flew open and Ezra Cohen burst through it, diving, searing his elbows on the flagstone walk. Hooting in terror, he staggered to his feet and ran, ripping through his hedge and onto Summit Road toward Turkus. The sergeant's pistol flew into his hand.

"Right there, Cohen. Hold it," he called. Cohen froze. He made mewing sounds and his eyes darted around him.

"Down on your face," Turkus snarled. "Down, Cohen, or I'll kill you."

The wind came. And the rocks. And the gravel of driveways. The debris bounced along the road like an army of grasshoppers, each striking Cohen, stinging him. Howling again, Cohen turned and ran, this time toward the track line. Turkus crouched with his gun in both hands and steadied the sights on Cohen's back.

"Last time, Cohen. Halt."

Leaves hit his hands. Leaves and twigs and a wind that gently pushed against the gun, spoiling his aim. It struck him that these bits of vegetation were pricking at no part of him but his outstretched hands. He let the gun fall and the wind withdrew as if in answer and the leaves settled to the road. Not sure, he raised his gun once more and this time rocks began to stutter and roll along the pavement toward him. Turkus slowly holstered his revolver, then watched in disbelief as the rocks swung away and closed on Ezra Cohen.

They pursued him and buffeted him. They drove him onto the track bed and turned him like a lead bull toward the thrashing wire. Cohen saw the hot snake licking out at him. He screamed with new terror and threw himself to the ballast, one hand gripping the silver rail and the other flailing at the stinging rocks. The crushed basalt beneath him came to life, lifting him, rolling and tumbling him toward the wire. Turkus saw it, but still could not believe.

—There's no hell deep enough, Ezra . . . No fire hot enough . . . But we did our best for you . . . Good-bye, Ezra . . . Bon voyage, Ezra . . .

"Charles!!!" Ezra Cohen screeched. "Charles, I'll get you. I'll get y . . ."

His body exploded.

Jennifer lay dazed and sickened in the brush through which she'd crawled. She pushed to her feet calling Peter's name but the sound came out a whisper. So in shock was she that as she walked in search of him, she picked away bits of blackened flesh from her clothing without revulsion. Peter? Where are you, Peter. Oh, please God, don't be dead. Don't be one of those smoking things near the train.

And then she saw him. Stumbling from the brush below her. A plastic bag was in his hand.

"Peter," she cried, the sound a mix of relief and misery. He glanced back at her but did not stop.

"Peter, wait," she called. "He's not gone yet, Peter. You can talk to him."

She ran to him. He had reached the parking lot, the bag tucked under his arm and a bottle in his hand. He shoved his way onto the station platform past milling commuters who bumped stupidly into each other like people half awake. Jennifer saw the yellow flame that topped the bottle's neck.

"Peter," she called. "Don't do that now. Talk to Jeff. He's only got minutes. Maybe seconds. Peter . . ." Jennifer's agony choked off the words as the bottle flew through the air. From across the tracks, Mike Turkus saw the bottle sail and then the burst of orange fire that enveloped the station wall with a roar, rolling upward and curling under the eaves. The sergeant watched as thick red paint blistered and ignited and as the shingles of the roof began to curl. Then Turkus turned and walked away.

Halloran fumbled at his pockets and then, nearly frantic, he searched the platform surface around him. His matches. He dropped his matches. Shaking off Jennifer's hand, he vaulted the station railing and ran toward the Winnebago. Inside, the pantry door came off its hinges, spilling cups and kitchen tools to the floor. The wooden matches fell among them. He scooped up several and kicked toward the open door.

"Who's there?" came the weak voice from the tiny bathroom. Halloran hesitated, then turned and threw open the latch.

"Halloran?" Weinberg squinted at him. "You're Peter Halloran? Right? I'm Weinberg, Paul Weinberg. We played cards the other day."

"I remember," he rasped.

"Peter, why am I like this?" His eyes were alive with fear and confusion as he gestured with his head toward the ropes and manacles that held him.

Halloran picked up the key that lay where Zalman left it. There was a steak knife at his feet. He picked it up. He bent over Weinberg's shoulder and unlocked the handcuffs, then, pausing for one long moment, sliced through the ropes around Weinberg's waist and neck.

"I don't know, Paul," he answered. "I don't know why you're like that."

He placed a knife in Weinberg's hand. Weinberg looked at it, then shook his head to show that he did not understand. Peter walked away, striking a match on the Winnebago's door as he passed through it.

I'm Paul Weinberg, Peter. Remember? We played cards the other day. I remember, Paul, Halloran thought wearily as he lit the second wick, except the other day was six years ago.

15

Redemption

It was summer again. The kind of steamy Chicago day when a cloudless sky seems closer to white than blue.

Jennifer pressed the lobby button reluctantly. She knew what it would be like outside. She checked her watch. Almost noon, she saw, and she'd only thought about him twice so far. Three times counting now.

The elevator door slid open. The lobby felt cold. They shouldn't do it that way, she thought. They should let you ease into the heat. Off to one side she heard the metallic slam that told her the mail had been delivered. She felt her pulse rate climb. Stop it, Jennifer. There won't be anything there.

The blood at her temples began to pound against a dam. Jennifer, there's nothing th . . . Oh, shit. She turned and ran toward the box, nearly bending her key as she twisted it open. Five envelopes. She slowed to stop her breathing. I feel him. I feel him here.

The first four were bills. Her heart died within her. She almost didn't have to look at the fifth. Dear Jennifer Wilde, you may have already won . . . She threw the mail back into the box and flipped it shut. I felt it. I did feel it.

"Hello, Chicago," came the soft voice behind her.

She spun around, her hand against her mouth.

"Where . . . ? When did you . . . ? Oh, Peter." The tears came. Dammit. She promised she wouldn't cry if she ever . . . But his eyes were wet, too.

"Just now," he said. "I took a cab from O'Hare. You look good, Jennifer."

"Oh, so do . . ." She brushed a hand over his cheek near his eye. "Peter, you have a scar. And you're thinner." The touch was as far as she'd go. Damned if she was going to leap at him before he leaped at her.

"Do you think we could talk, Jennifer?"

"Upstairs." She nodded and took his arm.

He let himself down easily onto the soft cushioned sofa like a man who was hurting. Jennifer placed an iced tea on the table before him and insisted upon pulling off his shoes although the act seemed to embarrass him.

"I kept track of you as long as I could," she said. "I know you went to London and I know your insurance check was sent to you there. You're lucky the railroad didn't deduct for a new station." She looked away, not sure what to say next. "And you saw Lady Edith."

"Yes. That's some woman, by the way. Seemed to know a lot about me. About you and me." Jennifer let that pass.

"And you went to Amersham?"

"Yes."

"Why, Peter?"

"I'm not sure I know. To find my way, I guess. Did you know that whole story is locked up under the Official Secrets Act?"

"Riverside hasn't exactly been on the front pages either. A suburban station caught fire. That was most of it."

"What was the final count?"

"Eight dead, if that's how you want to measure it. But Leticia's partially recovered. Martha's back working for her. No one we wanted to save was lost. Ira calls now and then and always asks about you. He saved Barbara, he and Mordicai. And he's treating Paul Weinberg."

"Barbara and Mordicai . . ."

". . . are together. You knew that?"

"I knew it. She's divorcing me and not asking for a thing. I don't understand any part of that."

"Mordicai's being given another chance but he's being punished. Barbara is part of the punishment. 'Til death," she couldn't help but grin, "with no fooling around until then."

"What's the other part?"

"He's finished as a medium. He can call but no one will answer. I might as well be finished. I went away once right after the burial, but not since then."

Peter dropped his eyes. "Did you see anybody there?"

"No, Peter. I . . ."

"I know. You can't do that."

She reached out for his cheek again and turned his face to hers.

"Peter, why did you go?"

"Jeffrey . . . You . . . All of it. Like the kids say, I was trying to find myself."

"You were trying to find Lictor. And Ezra Cohen."

"I suppose."

"Why, Peter?"

"You can ask me that?"

"Peter, they've been hurt just as badly as they can be hurt. Mr. Hicks and his rocks got Ezra Cohen killed where no spirit could meet him. They might have tried, even for him, but they stayed away because they were going to let the man who was Lictor die under that power line, too."

"What about Lictor?"

"No one will look for him."

"I'll find him someday."

"What for? To hear him beg you to speak for him?"

"It would be something."

"And Cohen. I know how you must hate him but try to remember that wherever his spirit is, he's sane now. He's not the same man who killed Jeffrey. And he's paying a terrible price. He and Lictor are in the worst hell there is."

"What makes him sane? Being dead?"

"Yes."

"Then Lictor was sane."

She let her fingers drift to the scar tissue near his eye. "I guess we'll have to wait for some of the answers. But Peter, you have to admit that they solved their problem very neatly." She didn't wait for a rebuttal. "How did you get hurt, Peter?"

"It's nothing."

"It's a hurt."

"I poked into some things and upset some people. Jennifer, there are some men over there looking for me."

"Mordicai was afraid of that. Are they looking for you here?"

"I don't think so."

"Is that why you came back?"

"Not entirely." He looked into her. "Not at all."

"If I'm part of the reason, I'd like to hear that."

"You're almost all of it," he said. "That's never stopped, Jennifer. Not even for a minute."

She put her arms around his neck and drew his head down upon her lap. Jennifer stroked and kneaded the muscles in his shoulders until the steel softened into flesh. She felt a shudder that might have been a sob.

"Where are your bags?" she asked.

"Just one. In a locker at the airport. I didn't know if you'd . . ."

"We'll get it tomorrow."

She poured the ginger ale over the ice and watched the wave of foam first swell and then recede.

"Who do you think you'll get?" he asked nervously.

"I don't know. Maybe no one. I'm not sure where I stand since Riverside."

"Nigel, maybe. It wasn't his fault that . . ."

"Hush, Peter."

"What if Jeff isn't even there? Didn't you say that sometimes they've gone on and you can't . . ."

"Peter!"

"Sorry."

She folded her arms across the table and rested her chin on top of them. For several minutes she sat unmoving, her eyes becoming dreamy, the natural smile of her mouth softening as her lips fell apart. Just when he thought she might be almost there, right on the edge of stepping over, the same muscles of her mouth tightened into a grimace. She straightened in her chair, shaking her head from side to side while looking curiously across the table at Peter.

"It's alright, sweetheart," he said. "We have lots of time."

—*Where did you get that dreadful haircut? Bulgaria?*
It was Alex.

THE OCCULT:

events sometimes real, sometimes imagined. Always haunting. Psychological thrillers guaranteed to keep readers in the grip of fear. Chilling books—

 available now from POCKET BOOKS

_____	42240	JULIA, Peter Straub $2.95
_____	82215	DEVIL'S GAMBLE, Frank G. Slaughter $2.50
_____	82222	SEA CLIFF, Michael T. Hinkemeyer $1.95
_____	43381	EDUCATION OF OVERSOUL #7, Jane Roberts $2.75
_____	81948	DEMON SUMMER, Elaine Booth Selig $1.95
_____	82803	DARK SUMMER, Mark Upton $2.25
_____	81769	THE HELL CANDIDATE, Thomas Luke $2.75
_____	44198	GHOST STORY, Peter Straub $3.95